Echoes

Echoes

Echoes

P.J. ROSCOE

First published in 2012
Third and current edition Published by
Doce Blant Publishing, Dana Point, CA 92629
www.doceblant.com

Cover by Fiona Jayde Media
Interior Design by The Deliberate Page
Editing by Mary Harris

Paperback ISBN: 978-0-9984294-9-6
eBook ISBN: 978-0-9984294-8-9

Library of Congress Control Number: 2017944832
Printed in the United States of America

www.doceblant.com

To Martin, my husband,
whom I have loved in many lifetimes…

PROLOGUE

H IS GUT TOLD HIM SOMETHING was wrong. Eleven years of experience screamed at him to call for back-up, the ambulance service and the coroner, but something stopped him and he looked again at the small house, trying to find the reason for his hesitation.

The terraced home reeked of death; everything from the closed curtains of the front room to the hint of a light he could see through the thin fabric said something was wrong. He suspected that light wouldn't still be on if everything were okay inside. He glanced across at his waiting partner and could see that Darren sensed it too. Their insistent knocking on the front door had elicited no response from the occupants he knew were inside.

He shook himself slightly and turned back to the woman who stood next to him. She was watching him closely, waiting. Clearing his throat, he continued asking for details: 'So, when was the last time you saw Mr Gillespie and his daughter?'

She didn't answer him because her attention had shifted to the house. He saw her shudder and draw her coat closer around her neck; he knew it wasn't because of the cool March breeze that ruffled her skirt. She sensed it too—something bad had happened.

'Mrs Williams?' He spoke a little more harshly than he intended, but it got her attention.

1

'Oh yes...I told the officer on the phone, the walls are very thin and I know I should have telephoned sooner, but didn't, you know how it is...'

Sadly, he did, but kept his expression as passive as possible and waited.

'Anyway, I haven't seen the girl for the last few days. She usually leaves the house at the same time as my son for school. D'ya know it was her thirteenth birthday last Sunday? No party and no friends called round...poor girl. Not since her mother died a few years back, terrible that.' She slowly shook her head and her eyes glazed over as she stared into space. He tried to wait patiently, as he could see how this was affecting her and felt a stab of remorse for the woman, but time was ticking away.

'She's a strange girl,' she continued. 'Quiet, never speaks to anyone, and always keeps herself to herself. I asked my son Robert—he's in the year above her—if he'd seen her, but no-one has seen or heard anything since early Sunday morning. Oh dear, I'm rambling...well, I heard a lot of shouting, not unusual with teenagers I know, but this was...was different.'

'Different?' He glanced toward the silent house. Darren was knocking loudly on the front window. He began to lose his patience as she tried to find the right words.

'Yes. I can't explain it, it just...was. I heard a lot of banging and a loud crash, like something breaking. I heard a scream and then I'm positive I heard her begging, you know, "please don't" and all that. Turned my stomach, I can tell you. Then a strange noise, like whimpering. I thought I heard moaning and Bronwen crying...and then silence. At first, I thought nothing of it, just another argument between them. I hear a lot of shouting, from him anyway. But I began to think about it and I couldn't sleep thinking about it. Perhaps she'd had an accident or...something. I don't like to gossip but there has been talk. And then it went quiet but I'm sure they're in the house but it's too quiet. Ya know?'

He looked across at Darren, who had walked into the small garden. Their eyes met and he nodded; it was time to investigate and find what they both knew they'd find. He turned to thank the neighbour; he was anxious to leave, to get it over with, but he could see her urge to tell him more as she licked her lips and stepped closer to him.

Seeing she had his attention again, she quickly continued. 'My son and others have sometimes mentioned bruising on her arms and legs. She was in the park a few weeks ago, on her own as usual. Some boys started teasing her and lifted her skirt, in a playful way you understand, but you hear so many bad things these days, I just…'

'Yes, yes I see. So no-one has seen or heard Mr Gillespie or his daughter, Bronwen, since Sunday?' He put his notebook away and nodded to his partner, who walked toward the back of the house. He turned back to the waiting neighbour.

'Right, thanks, we'll check it out. I may speak with you later.' Taking a deep breath to calm his growing nerves, he followed his friend. He didn't want to finish the sentence by saying that he would probably need to take a statement after they found what he suspected. She was a witness. Possibly the only witness to a death.

He steadied himself as he peered through the window and the letterbox. The letters delivered that morning were strewn on the floor. He noticed the general neglect of the house: peeled paint, dirty windows and rubbish piled in the front garden that was overgrown with weeds. He was focusing on anything to get his mind ready; a child involved in crime was always a heartbreaker. If it was true, it sounded as if this one had been abused for a while and he felt a surge of fury toward the neighbours. Why did they always wait?

Hearing a shout, he ran around to the back where he found Darren pushing up a window that was unlocked. Another bad sign. The smell hit them immediately and they turned away gagging and tried to breathe fresh air into their lungs. They stopped abruptly as the sounds of a child's whimpering reached them and they turned as one toward the open window.

CHAPTER ONE

BRONWEN FIDGETED IN HER SEAT. Her legs felt hot and itchy; she managed to reach her thigh and scratched nervously. Desperate to stretch her cramped legs, she tried to manoeuvre them over her large bags but gave up as it became too much of an effort. The last thing she wanted was to get the attention of the driver.

She recalled the two hours on the train where she had been crammed into a window seat; she was aware of the people standing along the aisle. Some were openly glaring at her and she'd quickly looked away, knowing they resented her and her three large bags that took up precious space in the overhead and on the table; her shoulder bag rested on her knees.

The train journey had been stressful. Her nerves running at full pelt, she'd sweated profusely and was desperately trying to ignore the need to retch as the acid in her stomach erupted. Her breath stank and when she thought no-one was looking, she slipped a mint into her mouth, hoping it would help; it did. Soon afterward, the crowded carriage began to thin out and more people were able to sit down.

She felt the atmosphere change as people relaxed into their seats.

She'd been determined whilst standing at the station to try very hard to enjoy the journey, to unwind with a magazine or have a go and do a crossword, even if she could never finish them. In fact, anything to distract her from the increasingly nervous bubbles that made her stomach flip over.

The magazine and crosswords remained untouched as the passing scenery got her full attention. Green, miles of it, and hills and distant mountains; her chest felt heavy with emotion.

Now here she was in the back of a taxi, her luggage taking up the small space. She was beginning to wish she hadn't been so finicky when the driver had suggested he put her bags in the boot. She sighed deeply; she just couldn't help herself. Her desire to be Miss Independent didn't always help her to make the right decisions.

Shrewsbury bustled with midday shoppers as the taxi slowly edged its way through the town. Bronwen shuffled her bottom to ease her cramp, but now her nerves had reached a breaking point and her excitement made every muscle in her body ache to hurry up and arrive at her destination.

She opened the window slightly, looked down at her cheap watch and grinned; only three hours ago she had been standing on a cold, damp station in Liverpool or Hell—both meant the same to her. Now she was in Heaven, also known as Shropshire, and soon she could be completely free. She had made it! She was really here.

She closed her eyes and tried to stem her growing anticipation. The smell in the air was different already and she breathed it in. This air was fresh compared to the city. Even here, with all the other cars and buses, it still smelt cleaner. 'Now that's amazing!' she muttered to herself.

Opening her eyes, she realised they were heading out of the town, and green fields swept for miles. She felt as giddy as a schoolgirl on a day trip. One of her favourites had been a trip to Chester, a beautiful Roman city on the North Wales border. It had taken only an hour on the bus, which had, as always, been a nightmare. Children were jumping around, and some were fighting, while others drew rude pictures on the backs of the seats.

She had sat quietly looking out at the beauty, needing to take it all in so that she could take the memory home and use it. She hadn't wanted to miss a thing, even when Rachel Lockwood had started pulling her hair every few minutes for a joke urged on by her gang of five, the bullies of her class. She'd remained silent as always, detaching herself from the mayhem.

As they'd walked along the river, she'd marvelled at its swans and ducks, the greedy pigeons that came close, expectantly waiting for food before being chased away by the shouting boys trying to get attention. Not from her, of course. No-one ever tried to get her attention, but some of the other girls would allow a kiss or even a grope if given the right incentive. Her eyes had briefly glanced at the foolishness but had quickly turned back to the water. It was spanned by two bridges, one for cars and the other for pedestrians. The water was brown, fast in places, powerful and deep. She'd yearned to go out on a boat, to row as far as she could, away from everyone, but the teachers wouldn't allow it and she'd slowly followed the class toward the city.

She'd felt like skipping along the old Roman wall. The very idea that she was walking where Romans had walked was mind-blowing. What had they been thinking and doing? She'd made the mistake of voicing these questions. Mr Rawlings had looked surprised at first that she had asked. She could hardly have blamed him, really, as she never asked questions.

His hesitation, though, allowed the boys in the group to give their own versions of what the Romans had been doing. She'd turned away from the lewd suggestions and demonstrations on the nearest girls who giggled and playfully pushed them away. Any explanation he had been about to give was lost, as Mr Rawlings had had to go and find two boys who had sidled off to sneak a cigarette. She hadn't cared too much; her own imagination as to what life had been like over the years was sufficient, for now.

The museum she had found fascinating and the archaeology dotted everywhere had mesmerised her; digging for things people had perhaps so casually discarded or lost, and then to find them again after hundreds of years, was something she could actually see doing and enjoying. She had decided on that day that she would be an archaeologist. She would dig for all those things long forgotten, and for those poor people sacrificed and dumped in bogs or buried in those stone bumpy things. After all, she had always loved history, other people's history anyway.

The memory of that day had never left her. She'd fought back tears when it had been time to leave Chester and return to the bus. For a fleeting moment she had considered hiding, running away so she wouldn't have to return home. But, she had returned home and Chester had become nothing more than a good memory. Archaeology had remained a good dream.

Today it was different. Today, she never had to leave, and who knew what her future held? Maybe archaeology would be in the cards again? Why not? Perhaps now was the right time to take chances? Maybe she could explore Shrewsbury. She had chosen the area for its history; perhaps there were history classes or…

Taking a deep breath, she stopped herself and smiled. *One thing at a time, Bronwen*, she scolded herself.

The cottage was hers for at least a year, paid in full. She had a year to decide whether to stay, get a job, go to college; she had time, and then, who knew? One thing she knew for sure: She would never go back to live in a city again, ever.

Her butterflies grew worse and she gently rubbed her tummy. Nothing remained in her stomach for long lately with her nerves so on edge; she looked forward to a feast of whatever she fancied, because she could now.

The car picked up speed as they headed out onto a dual carriage-way. It wasn't long before the small turning for the village of Derwen appeared, and they left the busy roads behind. The hedges on either side of the narrow lane were too high to catch any more than a fleeting glance at what lay on the other side, but it didn't bother her too much. She had all the time in the world to explore her new surroundings, and she could hardly wait.

Reaching for her old battered shoulder bag, she fumbled around for the keys and a worn piece of paper that had the directions to her new home. She had memorised every word, saying the address over and over, forming the words slowly and liking the sounds, but now she couldn't remember a single word. Her mind had gone blank with excitement and nerves. Gripping the keys tightly, she asked too loudly. 'Are we near the village yet?'

Without turning, the driver nodded. 'Just coming to it now, love.'

She cringed. There was nothing worse than being called 'love'; it had annoyed her for as long as she could remember, but the moment was forgotten as they rounded a sharp bend and entered the village. As the car passed two small cottages, she stared at them, fascinated; she hadn't seen thatched roofs so close up before. She turned to look at them through the back window and thought they looked like old dolls houses and wondered if they were as snug and warm as they looked. They were the first houses she had seen since leaving the main road.

The taxi stopped to allow another car going the opposite way to pass. She found herself staring at the driver as though she had never seen another person before. This was the first sign of traffic since the dual carriageway; perfect. The elderly driver stared back with obvious interest, and then was gone.

The lane opened up and joined a junction. The village of Derwen stood within a clearing. She wondered if 'village' was the right word. A small shop, a few small cottages, a couple of detached houses, a tiny pub and a run-down old chapel hardly felt like a village…or did it? How the hell would she know anyway?

The taxi slowly drove around a large circular patch of green grass that looked as if it was the centre of the 'village'. She had heard of village carnivals and fairs and wondered if they had them here. She could picture the brightly coloured stalls heaving with homemade jams, cakes, and whatever else they might be selling. She hoped they did have one.

On one side of the green was a basic playground with two swings, a slide, a roundabout, and three benches, all in immaculate condition. There was not a sign of vandalism anywhere. Around the edges of the green, brightly coloured flowers filled the narrow trenches of soil. Oranges, reds, blues, and purples moved gently in the wind, but beyond that there was no sign of life.

The taxi stopped at another T-junction. To the right stood a line of ten little, whitewashed cottages with slate roofs and quirky gardens filled to bursting with plants, flowers, and cute statues of various characters. Each cottage had a quaint front door reached by two steps, and each door was a different colour with a matching gate that let out onto the narrow road. Adjoining these was the pub. She could tell that at one time it had been an eleventh cottage, but had been converted with a small extension at the side. Even so, it still looked small and cosy; she hoped it was friendly too. The old sign swinging slightly over the entrance was too faded and far away for her to make out the picture but it looked like a building of some sort.

Farther along the lane stood five old red brick terraces and two detached houses that were much more modern-looking than any of the others, but at least whoever had built them had used grey stone, which helped a little. Anything too modern would have looked terrible.

On the opposite side to these stood a dilapidated chapel whose walls appeared from a distance to be badly in need of a lick of paint. Beyond the chapel, an incline blocked further scrutiny. In the distance, though, she could see fields and hedges for miles, and the tops of a few large trees were also visible above the tall hedge that ran along both sides of the road leading out of the village; she wondered what lay beyond and where it would lead.

***

The driver watched her through his rearview mirror. *A pretty girl*, he thought, *very nervous and odd, possessive about her belongings.*

However, watching her now, he thought, *She looks a fragile thing*.

Her actions toward her bags and general body language made him wonder if she had escaped from somewhere, or been set free, perhaps? She didn't look like a bad girl so he didn't think it was prison; not like his cousin Sheila. A bad marriage, perhaps?

Good-looking face, but her body was hidden under layers of clothes and a black fleece; shame, really. He wondered how long her lovely hair was because she had it tied back in a tight bun; old women had buns, she should show it off. Lovely colour, not blonde, or brown, a bit of both. Golden. Yes, a nice girl, but a strange one definitely. Clearing his throat to get her attention, he called out, 'Which way, miss?'

***

Bronwen jumped. Flustered, she dropped her paper on the floor; blushing crimson, she reached for it quickly. 'Right…I mean…okay, there's the shop, so we go left…yes, left.'

The driver gave her a smile but she had already turned away to stare out the window. Tears pricked the back of her eyes and she quickly blinked them away. Winding down the window farther, she felt the cool breeze flow over her burning cheeks. Damn her! Why did she get so worked up over stupid things? Archaeologist! Village fair! Ha! She got nervous just being in a damned taxi, so who was she kidding?

Would she ever have the guts to be herself? Did she even know what that meant? Her heartbeat slowed down but her stomach continued churning as huge flying monsters flapped against her insides.

As the car turned left into the lane, she quickly glanced at the small corner shop that for the most part would be her only lifeline, at least for the time being. She could see some lights were on inside but there was no sign of anyone, though something told her she was being watched from within. It was to be expected, she supposed, being a stranger in such a small place. Besides, they would be wondering about the woman who made a rather large order a week before; she hoped it had arrived as promised.

At first glance it certainly didn't look like the 'gold mine' she had been assured it was by that awful estate agent.

'It's an amazing shop!' he had promised. 'Sells absolutely everything and if she hasn't got it, she'll get it for you, apparently. The locals swear by her.' Edging closer, he'd whispered knowingly. 'If you like, I could let her know you're coming and put in an order for you. She would deliver it to the cottage ready for your arrival.'

She'd moved away from his hot breath, shook her head, and fought the urge to leave the office completely.

'Shops don't really do things like that, do they?'

He'd laughed and casually leant on his desk. 'Of course. Things are different in the country. Apparently, this woman'—he shook his head—'has forgotten her name, strange sounding…Welsh, I think. Anyway, she sends deliveries to farmers and people who live up in the hills. A few years ago they had a bad winter and a lot of them were stranded in their homes. This woman was a godsend and managed to get food and other necessities to them until the cavalry arrived with a snow plough.'

He'd looked her up and down in a way that made her insides curl and she took another step backward. 'So, Miss Mortimer, how about it? I could phone ahead for you and let them know to send you basics, perhaps even a surprise house-warming gift? I could take your number and give you a call, celebrate your new move? We have an office in Shrewsbury, as you know. I usually work there, but I'm checking staff today.'

She shuddered, remembering the way he'd looked at her. He hadn't bothered to hide the fact that he was undressing her with his eyes; he was enjoying himself. Every muscle in her cringing body had wanted to hit him and run out of that office but somehow she'd kept her control, focusing on what really mattered. 'Thanks but no, I'll take the number and the address of the shop myself.'

12

He'd grinned and reached for the lease, which she'd signed. Grabbed her coat and the information, muttered a goodbye, and fled, leaving his proffered hand untouched.

She let out her breath, which until that moment she hadn't realised she had been holding. That encounter had happened over three weeks ago. Since then, the sale of her aunt's house had been completed without any setbacks and she had been selling off all of her junk. By the end of the second week she had almost given things away; she wanted none of it. Charity shops all over Liverpool had praised her generosity as box after box was carried in, all overflowing with dresses, suits, kitchenware, books, cheap prints, and tacky porcelain figurines; all of it had to go; nothing had any value to her.

Looking down at her three large bags, she now wished she had taken that little bit of extra time to sort out her own mess. By the time the house was cleared and there was only her room to sort out, the days had passed in a blur, leaving her to scrub the empty rooms for something to pass the time. She'd plucked up the courage to telephone the small shop and had left her order on the answering machine. The machine surprised her; it felt wrong somehow, and she found it a little disappointing.

She'd sent a large cheque, which she knew would cover the bill and any change she would collect at a later date when she had settled in. Just doing that action made it all very real. Six days later, her impatience to leave was spurring her on; she was almost there, cramped, tired but extremely happy. Her thoughts returned to her luggage. *Once I'm settled, most of this junk can go*, she decided. *I'll buy new stuff for my new life.*

The taxi slowed to almost a crawl and she eagerly looked ahead as the lane became nothing more than a track with passing places. The large entrance to the Kenward Estate loomed up on her right. The imposing black gates stood open; the high brick wall on either side swept in an arch, following the curve of a large, passing place before a very high hedge carried on along the road. A cattle grid at the entrance gave way to a tarmac road that ran straight until it disappeared over a slight ridge; fields on either side were dotted with horses of various colours and size. *Well, let them keep themselves to themselves*, she decided hopefully. They had her year's money, there wasn't any need for them to contact each other, and that suited her just fine.

Realising where she was, she reached inside her shoulder bag and brought out her old, tattered purse. She decided on two twenty-pound notes but knew the fare would be less; she wasn't going to wait for change now that they were here. The lane turned sharply to the left and there, snuggled in the opposite corner, sat Oak Cottage. Her new home.

Before the driver had put the handbrake on and undone his seat belt, she was opening the door and yanking out her bags. Throwing them on the ground, she grabbed her shoulder bag and slammed the door shut. Bronwen thrust the money into the driver's hand, thanked him, and turned away.

***

He stared at the money, then the girl, and shrugged, but seeing he wasn't needed he quickly put the car in reverse. He needed to do a four-point turn before he could head back the same way, and all the time she didn't move. For a second he wondered if he should stop and ask if everything was all right, but just as quickly decided against it. Driving slowly away, he glanced up into the darkening sky and then checked his rearview mirror; he hoped she was okay. Spatters of light rain began to obstruct his vision. Why was she just standing there like that? If she didn't move soon, she'd get wet. He turned a corner and she was gone from sight.

The slight drizzle suddenly became a downpour as he emerged into the village. He was glad to be going back to town, his shift finished soon. He shuddered as he passed the shop. This place gave him the willies! The place looked dead. Switching on his radio, he hummed loudly to the tune and drove as fast as he dared back to civilisation.

***

Bronwen didn't move. Her eyes travelled upward over every grey and white stone to the slate roof and small chimney. Ivy covered almost half of the left side of the small, two-storey cottage. Two wide windows peeped out from among the green leaves. One she knew was in the kitchen; the one above might be in her bedroom. Her gaze took in the four trees that stood within the overgrown grass. 'Mature apple trees stand amidst a well-developed garden with plenty of opportunities', she had read at the estate agents' office. *A small, well established garden with apple trees, all right.*

She took a step forward. 'And where, may I ask, are the established blackberry bushes?' The small, brown bird that had landed briefly on the branch of the farthest tree hopped along for a moment as if listening and then abruptly left as a large drop of water shook the delicate branch. She smiled at the sight. She couldn't see the blackberries, but didn't they grow later on? Autumn, perhaps? It was late April and if that was the case, she'd have plenty of time to clear away, cut back and let's be honest, actually find one. She felt so stupid sometimes. Everyone knew what a blackberry bush looked like, didn't they? She would learn. Positive attitude was all it took!

She was only fretting now because she'd never had a garden of her own before. Pots. That was as far as her green thumb went: a couple of basic kitchen herbs like rosemary, coriander, sage, and of course, parsley. Her aunt would grow a large pot of daffodils every year as they were her aunt's favourite, and she'd occasionally be allowed to attempt to grow tomatoes in the old, run-down greenhouse, but that enterprise had never been successful; perhaps here it would be different. She'd always longed for a garden of her own. Okay, she hadn't quite expected her first garden to be so overgrown and neglected, but she would manage. It was all a learning curve starting today.

'I can do this.' She spoke to no-one in particular, but hearing it out loud made her feel a little calmer.

The silence suddenly hit her like a punch. She whirled around to look at her new surroundings, fields, wherever she could see. Hedges on either side of the lane blocked a lot of her view, but she got the general idea: She was alone. The hedges enclosed the garden, followed the lane, down the lane, everywhere. She felt entombed by them, cut off from the rest of the world. Glancing toward the Kenward Estate, she was glad she couldn't see the hall through the network of hedges and trees; it meant they couldn't spy on her, either, so that was another worry off her mind.

She refused to acknowledge the sudden rainstorm. She stood in the middle of the road and listened but there was nothing except the rain, the breeze moving the branches of nearby trees, and one or two birds giving a quick whistle. Were they warning each other about the rain or of an intruder in their peaceful world? 'Well, don't worry, little ones, I won't hurt you.' The sound of her voice breaking nature's peace sounded weird, intrusive. She stood silent for a long time, just listening to her new world.

She took in the cow parsley that littered the side of the lane and a small clump of yellow primroses nearby. She'd begun reading about wildflowers and was proud that some information had crept in. May was only days away, summer not long behind, and then this lane would be filled with colour.

By now the rain had soaked her coat and her hair was plastered against her scalp. A large drop ran down her nose and she gently wiped it away where it mixed with a tear that silently rolled down her cheek. She was truly happy at that moment and she couldn't believe it was happening.

Taking a deep breath, she turned back to her luggage. She picked up the two heaviest bags and walked awkwardly, pushing her way through the waist-high gate, which needed mending; it hung from one hinge. The narrow stone path that led directly to the front porch could hardly be seen as the knee-high grass brushed against her, wetting her jeans even more. Bronwen threw the luggage down inside the dry porch, and jogged back to the other one and her large, black shoulder bag. Almost running now, she dived under cover and fumbled around in her pocket for the key.

It was easy to find, the large, heavy thing, and now looking at the front door she could see why. Although the information had said it was a nineteenth-century original, she hadn't been able to see the door clearly in the picture. Stepping backward, she wiped the raindrops from her eyes as she glanced up at the beautiful porch. The advert had said that this was original too, and it certainly looked it.

It was of the same dark wood as the door. Only this wood had been bent and shaped to make an arch above her head. On either side she could see where different planks of the wood had been fitted together to form the small, cosy space. She wondered how many trees had been used to make it.

Reaching up, she could just touch the top, where carved into the wood was the date '1875'. She ran her hand along the sturdy frame; it felt strong and solid. *They certainly knew how to make things that lasted*, she thought.

She slowly ran her fingers over the door as she stepped back under the porch. The old, dark wood felt rough. Pushing the key into the lock, she could feel the strength of the wood. She heard the click and then a soft groan as she pushed opened the door; the thickness of it made her feel safe already. It was heavy, not like a twenty-first-century door, this one was solid and strong. This one kept out unwanted visitors.

She stood dripping in the narrow hallway and the tears welled up again. She found herself recalling all those years of tangible dreams where she had woken in tears, hating the moment of waking, of hoping for an escape. She yearned for something she wasn't sure of, but knew she would know it when it happened. The dream had finally happened.

The photograph in the Liverpool estate agents didn't do the cottage justice now that she was here; it was much more perfect. How long had she stood mesmerised by the picture in the window before some horrid brute had pushed past her, literally knocking her back to reality? She'd watched his departure through the throng of people, waiting for an apology but none came; none ever came.

Her legs had turned to jelly and she blinked back the hot, angry tears that burned behind her eyes. Leaning against the shop window, she had felt dizzy and disorientated for a moment. She'd watched the mass of pushing, shoving people, each one oblivious to the other while they fought to shop for Christmas. A few looked the worse for wear as their celebrations had already begun in earnest; they obviously used any excuse for a drink.

They never asked her at the large office where she had been given a job. Working as a temp always meant moving around, never settling anywhere, never making friends, but that never bothered her, until now. She had never felt so alone as in that moment.

Her dream was looking back at her from that window and it was out of reach. She memorised her perfect home to the last detail. The seclusion of the house was paramount: A place where no-one would ever bother her or expect anything from her, where she could begin to live again. She'd been told often enough that she was allowed to do this, but no-one had actually showed her how. Her aunt blankly refused to tolerate the absurd idea, so how was she ever to learn?

Abruptly, she had pushed herself away from the window and flinging her bag over her shoulder had stormed away from it. Her shoulder ached where the stranger had knocked her, and her heart was heavy with the knowledge that her life was shit and nothing would ever change.

'Get a grip, dearie,' she said to herself and grinned at her melancholy, brushed her tears and the rain away from her face. All that had changed, and she was here. Her dream was now a reality; this was her life and now came the hard part. The gods had decided to hear her prayers at last and she was standing in her home. A new beginning. She turned to grab the first of her bags and noticed the covered box in the corner.

'My order!' Bending down, she tried to lift it. 'No way could a granny carry this!'

Instead, she slowly dragged it inside the hallway and the newspaper covering the contents fell off to reveal tins, fresh bread, jam, margarine, tea, coffee, biscuits, pasta, juice, and much more, including two bottles of wine, one red, one white. Her stomach growled at the sight of food; perhaps now she would be able to keep something in.

She was about to close the door when out of the corner of her eye, she saw movement. Stepping over her luggage, she stood within the porch and looked closely past the apple trees toward the hedge. It was shoulder high and unruly. It would be easy for someone to hide. She laughed out loud and scolded herself. What the hell was she doing? Why on earth would anyone be hiding in this weather out here? Smiling to herself, she stepped back into her new home and gently closed the front door.

CHAPTER TWO

ADAM SLOWLY EASED THE VAN into the lay-by, then switched off the engine. Stretching his arms above his head, he heard the satisfying clicks from his aching bones and the pull of tension in his muscles. He yawned loudly, rubbed his eyes hard, as they felt gritty and he could feel the pull of sleep. His body was giving up, ready to lie down and lose all thoughts and worries in that dark, black sleep; he couldn't allow that yet. Judging from the traffic, the weather, and the distance still to go, he wouldn't be surrendering his body to the Sandman for quite a while.

A headache threatened to take hold at the back of his head; he knew it was from the tension of driving his old heap. 'God!' He wished he were home. At least back at the stables. He considered staying at Geoff's bungalow instead of going back to the house, since a stable would be preferable to another confrontation with his father over the cottage. 'My cottage!' he corrected himself out loud. And now, its new inhabitant. 'Bloody woman!'

He lit a cigarette, inhaled deeply, and closed his eyes. He really didn't want to think about that woman now but every time he had a moment to think about anything, she always crept into his head. 'Damn the bitch!'

He took another long drag of his cigarette and the images of that day filled his head when his anger had erupted after he'd found out that his damned father had gone behind his back and placed an

21

advert with estate agents around the country showing *his* cottage for
rent. It was *his* home, for Christ's sake, not his father's. Not for the
first time, he'd wished he'd demanded something in writing when his
father had given him the run-down cottage to renovate. He'd been
stupid enough to believe he could trust him. 'A Kenward's word is
his bond,' his father had preached many times. Rubbish!

Three months earlier, they'd had that damned argument and he
made it perfectly clear then that Oak Cottage was not for sale or
rent. As far as he'd been concerned, the matter was finished. His
father hadn't even had the decency to tell him that he'd continued to
advertise; that awful estate agent, James Hawthorn, informed him
that the cottage had been rented out.

A year earlier, James had offered to buy the cottage and the land
that surrounded it, saying he'd be doing the Kenwards a favour. How
James had found out about the family's money problems was anyone's
guess, but Adam had managed to keep his cool on the phone and not
tell James exactly where he could stick his money. He'd never mentioned the conversation to his father. Inwardly, he'd boiled with fury.

He uncurled his fist and tried to relax, but it wasn't working.
After everything he'd said, his father had betrayed him and rented
his cottage to some bitch from Liverpool for a whole year! A whole
fucking year to some stranger, for God's sake. He still couldn't believe
his father could do that behind his back. Okay, they hadn't been
getting on for a long time, but he'd never expected this from his father.

Had he not been clear enough about his cottage? He guessed that
money would have played a huge part in his father's decision, but
still…was it revenge? Did his father hate him for all the trouble he'd
caused? He'd demanded to know before leaving on this trip and his
father had denied everything; Adam knew he was lying.

He opened the window, blew the smoke outside and watched it
disappear into the darkening sky. To disappear like the untouched
equipment he'd left in boxes, stacked in his newly refurbished
lounge. Not to mention the couch, the brand new fitted kitchen,

and the king-size bed he'd bought…for her. He'd probably never see them again.

He inhaled deeply and watched again as the smoke disappeared into the dark. Just like his dreams. Perhaps he should go round and demand his stuff? His father had said that it had all been done above-board and properly, but still, it didn't help him to feel better, and he shied away from remembering how he'd behaved; a bloody tantrum had not helped his cause.

Perhaps he should meet the woman? He dismissed the idea as quickly as he thought it; he had no interest in her beyond her being in his home. 'Could put your mind at rest.' He spoke out loud to himself and sighed deeply. It could, but he doubted it. She'd paid a year's rent in full and fair play to his father; he hadn't rented it cheaply, either. Maybe this woman was rich? Maybe she'd have connections that might be of benefit to him? He shook his head at the thoughts, but it didn't help.

The rain was coming down harder and he slowly wound his window back up. April had been a wet one, and he yearned for summer. The noise of the passing traffic was increasing too; it was rush hour. He'd wait another hour before continuing the long journey home; besides, he had nothing to go home to. A loud horn caused him to glance over just in time to see some idiot overtake a lorry and barely make it back into his lane before an oncoming van would have hit him. The car sped on regardless of the horn abuse directed toward him.

That clinched it. He snuggled closer into his jacket, finishing his cigarette. He sat for a moment, listening to the rain as it pelted down on the roof, making quite a din. He had to check her. He used one hand to hold the jacket tightly around his neck and quickly stepped outside into the weather.

It would be dark soon and he sighed loudly; he was annoyed at him-self for leaving so late. Pushing his wet hair out of his eyes, he walked around to the side of the large van and gently opened a small door. He climbed inside and was struck by how warm and cosy it felt back here. He groped for the light switch, flicked it on, and instantly the van was lit by a warming glow that showed him his new love, Scarlet.

'Good evening, Scarlet.' He spoke gently as he eased his way toward her, not wanting to frighten her. He talked softly about how awful the weather was, and the long journey. How beautiful and strong she was, and anything he could think of to help her feel safe and get used to his voice. He liked to talk to his horses because they listened and never answered back. It was his way of getting to know them and vice versa.

He checked each leg and along her back. He moved cautiously to stand in front of her and gently rubbed her soft nose and the tiny white mark on her forehead. 'You're all right, aren't you, girl?'

Scarlet whinnied with the attention and nudged his shoulder. Adam reached into his pocket and brought out a soggy packet of mints. Giving one to the horse, he popped one into his own mouth, grimacing as he felt the mint turn to mush; it was gone in seconds. He leant against the side of the horse van for a moment, enjoying the heady smell of the horse and the straw. Scarlet gently sniffed his arm, his shoulder, and nibbled his hair; he grinned and gently pushed her back, stroking her soft neck. He could stay that way all night, cocooned in the warmth.

He quickly pushed that idea away because he needed to get home to his own bed. The horse needed her stable and besides, he'd have to see his father sometime. It was inevitable; after all, they shared Kenward Hall and it wasn't that big. He gave the horse one last pat, flicked off the light, climbed out of the warmth, and back into the cold rain. He slammed the door shut and walked quickly toward the hedge as his bladder had decided it would be a good idea to empty. Muttering curses about the damned weather, he finally climbed back into the driver's seat, peeled off his sodden jacket, and threw it on the passenger side.

He used an old rag to wipe the excess water off his face and hair, aware that he probably now wore oil and dirt streaks too. He lit another cigarette and sat back. He was cold, tired, and bloody hungry. Looking across at the busy road and angry sky, he reckoned it would be at least another hour or two before he reached Shrewsbury. If he rushed, he could easily make it by seven but he knew there wasn't a chance in hell that he would rush. Besides, if anything happened to Scarlet, Joseph would tear off his arms!

Feeling around under the passenger seat, he finally found the large flask of strong coffee Brenda had given him for the journey. 'You can't drink café muck. You need good, strong stuff inside you for such a long journey.'

He smiled at his memory of Brenda. What a woman! Tall as he was and twice as wide, she seemed to glow with motherly love. It emanated off her in waves. Her bright blue eyes sparkled as she'd ushered him into the large, cheery kitchen and set about making tea, whilst organising two children to help with scones and napkins. He warmed to her immediately, but tried very hard not to show it; his reserve lasted about two minutes. 'Those cigarettes will kill you, Adam!' she'd scolded as he pulled them out of his pocket. 'Smoke a good pipe instead, like Jo. Here, have a scone.'

Adam had laughed when he'd asked her what the difference was.

'Well, a pipe won't stunt your growth and your stamina in the bedroom won't be quashed!' Brenda had grinned wickedly, seeing how she'd made him blush.

'Well, darling Brenda, I don't have a sex life, I'm five foot eleven, and I know I'll die one day anyway, so I'll stick with these for now.' He giggled to himself, remembering how he'd flirted with her, a stranger, then.

Joseph had smoked a pipe. Every night before checking the stables one last time he would sit beside the fireplace and lose himself for a while or he would talk about anything to whoever would listen. For the last three nights it had been Adam's honour to be his fireside friend. Bellies full, muscles relaxing in the heat, a large whiskey in their hands, the pair of them had sat and discussed topics ranging from sports to charities, food to places abroad. Of course, their favourite topic had been horses. They had talked well into the night. Joseph certainly knew his business and Adam had to admit that it had been a welcome distraction.

What a man Joseph was! At least two men in one body, he was as broad as a tree trunk, six foot five, and not an ounce of fat. His arms were huge and his hands were enormous. Years as a blacksmith had moulded his frame, yet to see him with a horse, this giant of a man became as gentle as a lamb. He bred and trained each horse and could tame the most vicious animal in hours. Adam had stood transfixed the first time he had watched it happen. A horse whisperer if ever he saw one.

He found himself growing very fond of this odd couple. For him, business had always been done cold and ruthlessly. He saw the animal, bartered a price, and left. Arriving at Brenda and Joseph's stables had completely thrown him, as it was impossible to be callous and professional while children ran around the place.

Clean-shaven and ready for the deal, he'd arrived promptly, stepping out of the van to be greeted by three young girls who almost knocked him over as they ran pell-mell at him. The oldest-looking girl bombarded him with questions as the other two stared up at him open-mouthed.

'Who are you, mister? Why are you here? Are you the one who wants Scarlet? Can you ride? I can trot.' Pointing at one of her companions, she continued without pausing for breath, 'She's still learning but Michelle can jump on Blackberry. Look at my doll, mister, do you like her? We're cleaning some tack in there; do you want to help us?'

He had looked down at the three upturned faces, and their pink cheeks and innocent eyes had flustered him; this was not how he did business. For a second he wondered if this was a ploy, a way to knock him off his guard, but he quickly pushed that idea aside and cleared his throat. 'I'm here to see Mr Atkins. Do you know where he is?'

The girls giggled and looked at each other before screaming in unison, '*Joseph!*'

Almost immediately a giant appeared in the nearest stable doorway wiping his hands. The girls, who were still giggling, ran off toward him and disappeared behind his massive frame. He in turn made a loud growling noise, and chased the girls back outside onto the cobbled courtyard, catching one and swinging her up into the air, causing her to squeal with delight. He let her go and watched as they fled back toward the tack room, then turned to face Adam who hadn't moved from the safety of his van.

For a moment, Adam said nothing, feeling the giant scrutinise him very carefully before a huge grin spread across his face and he strode toward him, arm extended, offering a very large hand that covered his completely.

'Adam, welcome to my stables.

'Mr Atkins—'

'No, no, you must call me Joseph; none of this formal stuff if you want one of my mares, okay? So now that's sorted, come and meet the wife.'

And that had been that. Within an hour he had been made to feel like one of the family; his cold, practiced manner had dissolved faster than he would ever have admitted. Their kindness and warmth overwhelmed him. He'd felt fragile after his fight with his father, but he hadn't realised just how much it had affected him until he entered the warm bosom of Joseph and Brenda's home. She had insisted he should stay at the large farmhouse and no hadn't been an option. He hadn't put up much of an argument anyway, especially after sampling her cooking!

He sipped the now lukewarm coffee and already missed the friendly atmosphere. He had happily allowed himself to become wrapped up in their warm lives. A night had become two and then a third; in fact, he might have stayed longer but the pull of home and business always lurked in the back of his head.

Today he had woken from another deep sleep with a small feeling of regret that he had to get home and settle Scarlet. Unfortunately, Joseph had promised the children he would take them on a day's ride. Adam had been invited but he reluctantly refused, deciding to leave as soon after breakfast as possible. He had helped saddle the horses for the children of various ages; nine in total and none of them Joseph's or Brenda's. Unable to have children of their own, they had opened their stables and home to the local children.

The parents were happy for their children to be with them but Joseph insisted on good reports from home and school; in return, he would teach them to ride and to look after the horses. Brenda mothered everyone and everyone was happy; he understood why.

Before leaving with the children, Joseph had checked Scarlet in her stable before hugging Adam with a squeeze that pushed the breath out of him. 'I'll phone you later on tonight to make sure you arrived home safely, okay?'

'Don't worry, I'll take good care of her, she'll breed well with my Dulas.'

He had watched them ride away with a feeling of regret. The morning was fresh with a warm sun when it broke from behind the cloud; a good day for riding. Deciding on the spur of the moment, he had quickly saddled a decent mare called Tara and had cantered off over the open fields that surrounded the farm. Half an hour later he was contented, sweating, exhilarated, and feeling guilty about leaving Scarlet. He had a quick shower and prepared to leave. Yet, when it came time, he found he was reluctant. He didn't argue when Brenda made him a coffee and plied him with homemade fruitcake. He didn't rush when he found himself telling her everything that awaited him back home. It felt the most natural thing in the world.

He hadn't missed his own mother so much since childhood when she had been cruelly taken from them. He'd pushed himself away from the table with an effort, tears in his eyes, fighting the urge to stay. He'd quickly walked Scarlet into the horsebox, checking the horse again before closing the door. He'd returned the huge hug from Brenda and waved good-bye.

Within forty minutes, he wished he hadn't been so reckless, confirming his inner voice that told him he was stupid and should have left hours before. Reaching the outskirts of York, he hit his first traffic jam. Then the drizzle started, and although he was genuinely sorry for the children who would be coming home soaking wet, more important to him was the fact that he would have to slow down as the weather turned wet and nasty; that had been over five hours ago.

His coffee finished, he stretched again. The traffic had eased slightly, so he started the engine and let it warm up before he slowly edged toward the main road. Rubbing his cold hands together, he waited impatiently for a large enough gap for his van. Finally, he pulled out onto the road and settled himself for another long and tense drive home.

***

Her new clock chimed six as she fell back exhausted onto the couch. She looked around her clean and tidy lounge and grinned like the Cheshire cat. The large, open fireplace faced her but she hadn't lit it yet; the room felt warm anyway with the radiators on. Listening to the rain and growing winds, she decided she would light it shortly. There was nothing better than curling up in front of a log fire feeling cosy and warm and safe, with a loved one, perhaps, a bottle of wine, chocolates, music drifting around the room, a lovely romantic picture… not that she'd know anything about things like that.

Empty boxes stood stacked in the corner, the top one stuffed with newspapers, and her three empty bags lay next to them. She had been surprised to find the boxes held a television, a video and a hi-fi system, all expensive looking. In another she had found two beautiful pictures depicting The *Lady of Shalott* and *The Tempest*. She loved the pre-Raphaelite pictures. They were hauntingly beautiful. She'd borrowed a book from the library last year that showed an array of pictures painted by various artists of that period. She'd found them fascinating.

She had pondered about what to do with the pictures. She considered telephoning the Kenward Estate to ask about them, but realised the telephone hadn't been connected yet. It had never occurred to her to buy herself a mobile phone; she didn't know anyone to ring anyway. Perhaps tomorrow she should walk up to the Hall and ask? There wasn't any note, only an inventory of what was already in the cottage; the electrical goods had been written as '*Can be found boxed up*'.

So she'd decided to use them. If they complained, she would give them back. So the pictures now hung on either side of the fireplace, giving the cream walls much-needed colour. The television and hi-fi stood in opposite corners of the room, her miserable DVD and CD collections in a small pile beside each one.

Throughout the afternoon she had been surprised at how new everything looked; the kitchen was definitely brand new. No dust, no marks on the walls, no stains; someone had been keeping it clean, but it didn't look as though anyone had lived in it. What she did know was that it had been renovated by the Kenwards over eight years ago, but it looked like no-one had moved in since then. Perhaps the rent had been too high? Thankfully, that hadn't been an issue, because her aunt had left everything to her, much to her great surprise, but it meant she could have her dream.

It suddenly occurred to her that the Kenwards had another set of keys to the cottage. The porch could be locked, but when she had arrived, it hadn't been. Who had brought her order? Who could get in? She sat intently listening to the wind and rain outside and remembered the movement by the hedge. Could someone really have been watching her? Was she safe here? She'd watched films about country people going mad with an axe or turning into werewolves… she pushed the anxiety-induced thoughts away.

The intense silence inside the cottage was penetrating; she needed to hear noise. That was it, it was too quiet. Jumping off the couch, she turned the knob on the stereo and flinched as loud music blared from the two speakers. Turning it down, she chose a favourite CD and sighed loudly as the music filled the room. 'I need a drink.' She was surprised how shaky her voice sounded. God! She had to get a grip!

In the small, warm kitchen she reached up and took down a large glass tumbler. Opening a cupboard she had earmarked for alcohol, she brought out a bottle of eighteen-year-old malt. She had become a whiskey drinker a while ago when she'd been allowed to go to a party with her aunt. Of course there had been a snag; she had to serve the guests and clean up afterward.

During the evening, she slipped outside unnoticed, taking a few bottles of alcoholic drinks with her to try, and one had been a fifteen-year-old single malt whiskey she'd found hidden at the back of the man's drinks cabinet; it became a favourite.

Over time, she'd experimented with various malts from Scotland and Ireland. She'd concluded after years of secretly testing that she only liked the expensive whiskies because they made the warmth in her chest and stomach last longer and the amber coloured ones were a slightly thicker consistency. The cheaper ones made her feel too tipsy too quickly and she had to be so careful.

One of the first things she bought once the lease had been signed was this lovely malt. She'd been waiting patiently for the right time to open it; now was that time. She checked to see if her cheese on toast was ready, placed it all on a tray and happily carried it through. Coming back to switch off the kitchen light, she wondered why anyone would go to so much trouble to build such a lovely home and then abandon it.

A horrible thought suddenly occurred to her: What if they had died? That would be awful and no doubt hard for the Kenwards, having a stranger in the cottage, but if that was the case, there was nothing she could do about it. She switched off the light and firmly turned her back on the darkness; she wouldn't think about that now.

She threw herself down on the couch, poured a generous measure of single malt, and swallowed, enjoying the warming, honey taste. Bringing the tray closer, she tucked into her meal; wrapping a terracotta throw around her shoulders, she lost herself in her first evening of happiness.

**

Outside, the rain had finally stopped. The large grey clouds raced across the pitch-black sky and the wind blew strong, bending the branches on the trees. For a moment, the quarter-moon shone down and cast shadows. Silently, one shadow moved. It stayed close to the hedge and stood for a while by the broken gate, watching…waiting. The clouds blew across the moon and the shadow was gone; it was dark again.

CHAPTER THREE

ADAM SLOWLY OPENED HIS EYES but lay very still. His head felt fuzzy and he was confused for a second as to where he was. His back ached terribly and his left leg was missing. This realisation made him ease his head up and look down. Moving up onto his elbows, he saw that in fact, thankfully, his leg was still there but a fat spaniel had decided to use it as a pillow and was now looking back at him and wagging its tail. 'Barnaby! Get off!'

His throat felt dry so his voice sounded more like a croak, but the dog did as he was told and flopped heavily onto the floor with a loud thud; the bed jolted. '*Fuckyabloodyhell!*' Adam yelped and hissed through his teeth as the blood rushed back into his leg, bringing with it a billion jabs of pins and needles. He bit the pillow, not daring to move until eventually his leg began to feel normal; carefully he wriggled his foot and sighed with relief.

He gently eased himself into a sitting position, rubbed his eyes, then frowned as he looked around his room. Something was different. It was clean. That bloody Judith! His dirty jeans lay where he had thrown them last night, or had it been this morning? He looked around at the general lack of dog hairs, rubbish, and general muck that usually littered his floor. The carpet had probably never looked that spotless.

His jacket lay across the end of the double bed on top of crisp, clean sheets, which he had rumpled and stained with mud. His bedside

33

table was polished, his windows gleaming, the ashtray gone, and his books and magazines were now neatly stacked on his window seat. Empty beer bottles, stained coffee cups, and old plates had vanished. Damn the woman! But he had to admit it looked great, so for now he would forgive her, as she knew he would—scheming old witch!

They had argued just last week about her cleaning his room. He'd caught her when he'd returned early from the stables to get changed since he was covered in mud after that evil horse, Dulas, had thrown him. She had been standing outside his room with a Hoover. Sneaking up the stairs, he'd stood behind her. 'What's going on, woman?'

Startled, she had dropped the Hoover and turned on him. '*Adam!* You little—' Playfully smacking his arm, she turned and picked up the nozzle to hide her blushing face.

Adam had grinned wickedly, knowing she felt uncomfortable at being caught. 'You won't find any pornography today, Judith.'

Smacking him with the end of the nozzle, she tutted, 'You foul boy, don't be so disgusting. I'm only going to Hoover quickly and—'

'No you're not.' He'd moved himself around her and stood in front of his doorway. 'This is my room, Judith, I've told you before. When I want it clean I'll do the bloody thing myself, okay?'

Adam grinned; he had watched her fighting her impulse to reply and remembered thinking she'd given up too easily. Now he knew why, the crafty old goat. She knew about his coming trip to York and had bided her time. He should have known she'd never give up without a fight. He shook his head and chuckled to himself, Darling Judith; he loved her dearly. Sneaky old bag!

She had become something of a surrogate mum after his mother had passed away. In his heart he knew she would always interfere whether he liked it or not, which he didn't. Not for the first time, he wondered whether he should move out again and then remembered why he couldn't: that new inhabitant in his cottage!

Easing himself back he lay looking up at the ceiling and smiled; at least she hadn't cleaned that! Or had she? He certainly wouldn't put it past the old fox. He rubbed his eyes as they still felt gritty, and it was tempting to turn over and go back to sleep, but judging from the glare coming in through the windows, it was getting late and he had a new horse to deal with. But, perhaps just a few more minutes wouldn't hurt.

He called the dog back onto the bed and stroked its floppy ears and listened to the muffled sounds from downstairs. It had been silent when he'd dragged himself up the stairs to bed. On his way, he'd raided the biscuit tin as he'd crept through the cold kitchen. He could never resist Lucy's homemade biscuits; they were decadence itself!

He touched his crumpled shirt, which had still been damp when he'd crawled into bed. The pleasurable darkness had drawn him deeper. He'd had no dreams; his mind was too exhausted to have any. How many times had he stopped on the way home? Three, four? No, it had been more than that. Any excuse had made him pull over into the nearest lay-by. At one point the rain had lashed down so hard he could hardly see to the end of his van, never mind the road. That had been quite frightening and he had pulled over to wait it out, which had delayed him longer. By then, Scarlet had become restless and he had stayed with her for a while to calm her down before she tried to kick her way out.

Almost three hours later than expected, he had driven through the village. Soaked to the skin, chilled, tired, and starving. He'd pulled up outside the shop and wasn't too surprised to see a light on. As always, whenever he went away, Eira would be waiting for his return; as if by magic, she always knew. She really shouldn't have been waiting up for him at her age. She had to be getting on now and lately she looked older, more haggard, fragile, and not for the first time he wondered how old she really was.

He knew he'd have to check on her regardless of his exhaustion. She always took delight in his trips away and questioned him about every little detail; he hoped she wouldn't want a full account tonight. He'd often joked that she'd never leave the village; he'd have to drag her out. Eira would laugh with him and smack him playfully on the arm for being so cheeky, but now thinking about it, when *had* she ever left the village?

Surely she went to Shrewsbury on the weekly bus? He couldn't recall any time that he had seen her on the bus, or in fact anywhere other than the village. Why was that? Didn't all old ladies like to take the 'gossip bus', as he called it? He yawned loudly. No time for gossip and details tonight though, as this would be a quick visit; he was worried about the horse. He switched off the engine and wearily climbed out.

The surrounding fields smelled sweet; the dark, rich soil was fertile. The air was washed clean and fresh by the rain and the wind that blew his hair was chilled. More rain was coming so he'd have to be quick. He opened the wooden door that led into a beautifully scented herb garden behind the shop and, as his legs brushed past bushes of rosemary and blackcurrant sage, they filled the air and his nostrils with their glorious scent. It was early in the year for these herbs but everything grew under Eira's fingers. He breathed deeply before gently tapping on the back door. Not waiting for a reply, he stepped inside, leaving the door ajar. The warmth that hit his tired body made his eyes droop and his muscles instantly relax.

'Eira, are you up?' He called softly, knowing the answer already. His legs felt like jelly as he walked along the dim hallway toward the small sitting room where he could see through the open door a faint light, which he presumed was only the fire.

He gently pushed the door wider and stepped inside and saw the old woman sitting in her usual armchair staring unblinking into the dying flames. 'Eira?'

Nothing. She remained perfectly still, watching the flames. Stepping farther into the room, he bent over her, his concern for her foremost in his thoughts. 'Eira? Are you okay?' Tentatively he reached out and lightly touched her shoulder, which was wrapped in her usual cream shawl.

'*Adam!*' Eira turned and looked up at him.

'Christ, Eira!' Grabbing his heart in a mock gesture of pain, he laughed in relief. 'You scared the shit out of me, you mean old woman!' He bent down to give her a kiss and she let him have her cheek but her eyes had returned to the fire. 'So, how is my favourite lady tonight? Just stayed up to give me a heart attack, did you?'

***

Eira shifted her gaze from the fireplace and smiled warmly up at him. 'Sit down, you foolish boy, before you fall down.' She had known he was coming. He was late, of course, as she knew he would be with the weather and such, but what had happened?

She could remember thinking about making a pot of hot, sweet tea for him and then something had stopped her. She had seen… felt…something she hadn't sensed for such a long time, something old and forgotten.

'Eira, are you all right?'

She looked up to find Adam watching her closely and managed a weak smile. 'Yes, of course, my dear, tired and old, you know. I know what you're going to say so don't bother, but you know I like to make sure you're home safe. The weather's been bad all day, all over the country. I'm sure the roads were treacherous?'

He sat back with his hands resting gently in his lap. His eyes drooped heavily and he mumbled an answer. Another minute and he'd be fast asleep. She watched him for a moment and felt a surge of love, fear, and regret all at the same time. He was the grandchild she would never have, the grandchild she would lose one day and the regret that the natural order of things might go wrong again.

'Up!'

He jumped.

'Come on, time for you to go, you're exhausted. You're done in, boy. Go and sort out that beautiful mare and come back when you're energised. Go on, off with you!'

***

For a second, the thought of moving had been impossible and his bed seemed so far away, but with her words came a surge of energy and he pulled himself up onto his feet and groaned with fatigue. Shaking himself awake, he bent and kissed her gently on the forehead. 'Are you sure you're okay, Eira?'

'I'm fine, Adam, get off to bed, I'll see you again soon.'

After he shuffled out with heavy legs and an aching back, he had closed the door.

'You can owe me for the tobacco.' Her muffled voice reached him in his exhausted haze and he looked down on the small table next to the back door. Two pouches lay on it. He pushed them into his pocket and grinned; strange how she knew the little things. Little insignificant things, but over the years they had added up. Like the time when he was ten years old and he had stolen Mr Gregory's apple pie from his kitchen table while he'd gone to the toilet. He'd been sure no-one had seen him. Or that time, at nineteen, when he'd slept with Molly Turner and had crept home afterward without saying good-bye or leaving his phone number. As usual, he'd noticed Eira's light on and had checked in on her only to be greeted with a barrage of insults and reprimands for treating a woman so terribly!

He wondered what she'd been thinking about when he'd arrived. For just a fleeting moment, he could have sworn she'd looked frightened. Was he imagining it? That look on her face worried him; Eira never looked like that. He'd stood undecided as to whether or not he should return or go home. The lure of his bed and settling Scarlet won, but he'd come back tomorrow.

Dragging himself back into the van, he wound down his window in the hopes that the cool air would help him stay awake. The warmth in Eira's house had made him feel very sleepy. Scarlet remained quiet as he carefully drove along the narrow lane. He tried not to think about his cottage that was only a mile away. Would she be in by now?

He turned into the driveway and slowed right down as the pot-holed road jolted him about. That was another job he had planned to fix once the business was settled. He could see the Hall to his left, lit up by the four yellow lights strategically placed around the outside that made the ancient building look beautiful, not that it needed them. He reached the fork in the road, veered right, and headed for the stables that were nestled in a slight dip a quarter of a mile from the Hall, which meant it was lost from sight.

He hoped his father had gone to bed. He glanced up at his father's bedroom window but no lights could be seen. Either he was asleep or he'd broken a lifetime habit and closed his curtains for once. He doubted that, as his father preferred to have them open to watch the stars. He liked that too, but he'd never admitted it. His favourite night was when the moon was full. He'd lie in bed and watch it move across the sky. It was too cloudy to see the moon tonight, though he could see roughly where it was.

He heard them long before he saw them as he finally stopped the van in the middle of the large, square courtyard. Switching off the engine, he stretched quickly before stepping out to be almost knocked over by the four dogs: his two yellow Labradors, Roger and Henry, Barnaby, the fat spaniel, and his mongrel Tobias. The courtyard lights gave off a welcoming blaze and he had an overwhelming rush of plea-sure; this was his—all his years of hard work--and now he had brought home another golden mare that he knew would turn his fortune around completely. For a minute, his excitement at wanting to get started over-rode his exhausted state as he ruffled and patted his delirious hounds.

He fought to keep his feet as each dog jumped at him, licking every part they could reach. Tobias gave up on the ground and jumped up onto the bonnet of the van and licked his ears from there. 'All right, boys! Yes, lovely to see you too. Come on, down boys! *Down!*'

'At least someone's pleased to see you.'

Adam looked across the courtyard and grinned sheepishly. 'Hello, Geoff. Stable ready?'

'Well, of course it's ready. It's been ready for the past two days. Where the hell have you been? And while we're about it, what did you think just storming off like that?'

Adam took a deep breath to calm himself. 'Okay, thanks, Geoff, you've made your point. I'm a miserable bastard and I was wrong to just go without leaving instructions, but you knew I was going and besides, I knew I could trust you to do what was needed.'

'Aye, you told us you were leaving on Monday, not Sunday. I came back from the pub to find you gone and no-one telling me a bloody thing.' The old man stepped closer. 'You look exhausted.' He sounded concerned. 'Never mind, you get off to bed. I'll sort her out.'

Adam shook his head; as tired as he was, Scarlet was his new baby. 'No thanks, I'll deal with her.' He tried to keep his tone light but he bristled for being chastised. Geoff was an employee, regardless of the fact that he'd been with the family since before Adam was born, and ignoring the fact that Geoff had taken him under his wing and taught him to ride. He was still an employee and, damn the man, he wasn't the boss!

***

Geoff realised he'd overstepped his mark and backed off. It was hard for him to hold his tongue sometimes and besides, why should he? He considered Adam his own foster son, after watching him grow up and reprimanding his backside when he'd done something naughty, which was quite frequently, as he remembered. He had been a part of everything in his life from his coming birth to his first day at school, catching him with his first cigarette to becoming his confidante regarding girls.

He had been the one who comforted him throughout the inquest into his mother's death and the one who had sat up throughout the night, waiting for the sobbing to subside, listening for the steady rhythm of his breathing once he had cried himself to sleep. He was the one who sat on the stairs, quiet, unmoving, listening, waiting, a loaded gun ready at hand. A crucifix hanging around his neck, the circle of salt in which he sat had been invisible in the darkness. For weeks he had let himself into the Hall, silently guarding the family. It only seemed natural that he would help at the stables when Adam had announced his intentions, and to be close, just in case.

He watched Adam slowly lower the ramp and listened to his soft-spoken words as he gently guided the mare backward. He let out a wolf whistle as Adam walked the mare slowly around the yard. 'What a beauty!' When Adam stopped beside him, he carefully inspected the legs and ran his hand along her smooth back. 'Good stock?'

***

Adam led her round the yard before he nodded and patted her neck. Handing the reins to Geoff, he stepped back and admired her himself. She was worth every penny. The moment he'd seen her he knew there was no point in haggling; he'd have paid almost anything. 'Her last foal looked very much like her. Dulas will make a lovely father. Let's get her into her warm stable before it pelts down again.'

He laughed as Dulas gave a loud whinny and Scarlet returned the call. 'Okay, you two, there'll be plenty of time for all that. Let the poor girl get some rest, ya filthy beast!'

Geoff laughed with him. 'I don't think this one will take any nonsense off him. She'll use him and dump him. I reckon this mare knows what she wants and gets her own way. How old is she?'

Adam stroked her long neck. He felt very pleased with himself. He'd done it. His stock would grow and all he'd had to endure was a journey from hell. 'She's nearly eight. She's had two foals; her last one was not for sale and the other had already been sold on.'

As he took off her bridle, he watched her walk into the stable now covered with straw; it felt warm and cosy with a nice 'horsy' smell. He could have lain down with her, he felt so exhausted. Instead, he lit a cigarette and leant over the stable door to watch her for any signs of limping.

Geoff remained with him, rolling his own tobacco before joining him on the door. He seemed to sense Adam was itching to ask him something and knew exactly what it would be, but he waited. 'So, what's her name?'

'Scarlet.' Adam kept his eyes fixed on the horse. 'The stallion they bred was called Rhett. Brenda had this whole *Gone with the Wind* thing going on a few years ago so…'

'A good name, suits her. What is she, fourteen hands?'

Adam nodded. 'Fifteen hands, actually.'

Pulling his collar up around his neck, Geoff shivered. 'The wind's picking up again. I've just felt more spots of rain. So, what took you so long? I had to lie to Mr Atkins, Joseph, wasn't it? I told him you'd already arrived exhausted and was busy settling her in. I told him you'd phone first thing.'

Adam nodded. 'Okay, good, thanks.' He coughed to clear his throat. 'Is he still up?'

Geoff watched him for a moment. Adam was aware that he was choosing his words carefully and wondered if he knew how much it cost him to ask. 'No, he went to bed about an hour ago. Whether he's awake or not is another matter. He hasn't slept properly since you… well, you know, since you left.'

Adam met his gaze. 'And is she here yet?' He managed to keep his voice calm, portraying none of his inner feelings.

Geoff nodded and squashed his cigarette butt out under his boot before picking it up and throwing it into a sand bucket hanging next to the stable door. 'Arrived today. I was out riding Fred over the back; his hoof has healed, you know. Anyway, I saw her arrive and she only had a few bags with her. I heard that Eira sent down a large box the girl had ordered. She's quite a looker if you ask me…which I know you're not, but…' He shrugged in a noncommittal way.

Seeing the expression on Adam's face, Geoff sighed loudly with exasperation. 'Adam, it's been eight years and not all women are bitches, you know! Yes, you hoped to live happily ever after with Catherine and she screwed you! Let it go! I'll see you in the morning.' Lightly thumping him on the shoulder, he turned away and walked fast in the direction of his own small bungalow that stood behind the stables. The two Labradors followed him.

Adam watched him go. He knew Geoff was right. He should be out there enjoying himself, meeting women, getting married, having kids, but he didn't have any enthusiasm for it. Catherine hadn't just taken his money; she'd taken his hopes, his dreams, his trust, everything. And yes, everyone knew about it, but how could they understand it when he didn't understand it himself?

During those moments when he had time to really dwell on what she had done, the pain in his heart felt just as raw. The very idea of allowing himself to get close to a woman again appalled him and he couldn't see that changing in the near future.

If he behaved badly, it meant he couldn't get hurt. After weeks of heart-wrenching grief, pleading, disbelief, and anger, it had hit him just how pathetic he had been not to have seen what she was.

'I want a real man, not some whimpering boy!' she'd screamed at him when he'd finally found her and begged her to come home. Well, now he was ruthless, in business and with the women who flocked to him. He played the games on his terms and dropped them once they'd become tiresome. He ignored the disapproving looks and comments of his father and the rest of the household. He knew their thoughts on his behaviour and ignored the fleeting moments of shame he felt. He'd never tell them they were right. So, he firmly pushed away any sense of remorse for these people. To feel remorse was to be trampled on, and he would never be trampled on again.

He sighed. Hadn't he let his guard down over Scarlet? Being a bastard wasn't as easy as he'd thought. But then, Joseph and Brenda were different. They weren't some scheming little whores after his money and his family name; better to be alone than some poor fool. He allowed a small number of people into his life and the rare dalliance with a willing woman if he ever felt frisky. That was enough. Lonely sometimes, but safe.

The sudden downpour broke into his thoughts and he quickly shut and bolted the stable door. He ordered Tobias and Barnaby to their beds and rushed across the cobbled yard to switch off the lights, leaving the two night-lights on. One last look around and he darted up the path that led to the Hall. A minute's run brought him breathless and saturated to the back door, which was lit overhead. Trying the door, he frowned when it opened easily; it should have been locked. Diving inside, he jumped as Barnaby ran in behind him. 'What the hell…?' The dog ignored this and shook himself, sending rainwater and mud splatters in every direction.

'You'll be sorry in the morning when Lucy sees her nice clean kitchen ruined!' Closing the door firmly, he locked and bolted it. 'You'll get into trouble with Judith as well, you bad dog!' he said gravely.

He flung his wet boots into the corner, and tiptoed through the large kitchen, shivering as droplets slithered down his neck. Grabbing a tea towel, he quickly rubbed his head, and then draped it round his neck. He pinched a handful of Lucy's biscuits and walked through the dark house to his bed.

***

A loud knock at the bedroom door made Barnaby jump, then leap off the bed. 'Yes, Judith, I'm up.' Adam rolled out of bed and went into his bathroom. Sparkling!

'What's that filthy little animal doing in here? Look at the bed? *Out!*'

Adam chuckled as he heard poor Barnaby being chased from the room. He listened as the dog pelted down the stairs and barked with excitement when his father greeted him. Judith was still muttering curses about its fat belly when he peeped round the doorframe. He watched her making the bed and was about to chastise her for it, but abruptly changed his mind. Let her do it, let her feel needed; he had other, more important things to think of today. Slinking back into the bathroom, he eased the bolt across quietly so that she'd not know he'd seen her. He could hear her constant mumbling about the state of the room already. He shook his head as he stepped under the hot shower. She must be touching sixty by now but she certainly still had some fire left in her!

The hot water forced his aching muscles to unwind. He stood under the jet and thought about how to go about the next few days. Scarlet couldn't be ridden for a while, at least a day or two. He'd put her out into the paddock with the other mares, and Dulas could meet her in due time; she wasn't in season just yet. This was the mare that would turn things around, he was sure of it. Besides, it had to be; his account was getting rather low on funds.

He flung open his bathroom door regardless of whether Judith was hanging around or not; she wasn't. He threw on a clean jumper and some old jeans. Finding another pair of black riding boots, he pulled them on and dived out of his room, almost colliding with Judith carrying a tray.

'Adam!'

'Sorry, Judith, must dash.'

'But your breakfast!'

'No time.'

'Adam, you look, well, actually, you look really well but…' Silently, her eyes pleaded with him; she knew she'd win as she pushed the loaded tray in his direction expectantly.

'Okay. Fine!' He grabbed a sausage and a piece of bacon, stuffed it into his mouth, and pinched a piece of toast and grinned. 'Thanks, darlin',' he said and fled back downstairs, shouting over his shoulder, 'My new girl won't wait. 'Bye!'

***

Judith shook her head, appalled at his manners, and listened to his route through the kitchen, greeting Lucy as he passed and then slamming the door. Slowly she followed; the boy was damned irritating sometimes. Silly woman! He wasn't a boy anymore. He was a grown man with his own responsibilities, his own worries; she shouldn't mother him anymore, she knew that, but she just couldn't help it. Perhaps it was because she had never had children of her own, or was it because she had been here since the beginning? She saw all his faults and ignored them for the man she knew he really was.

She tried to be the same with his sister, Rosalyn, but it seemed harder to ignore her faults since she'd moved out suddenly, declaring she 'hated the bloody country and wanted to be surrounded by people who still had a pulse!' That had hurt. She had tried hard not to take that last dig personally, but she hadn't succeeded. Too many other insults had preceded it.

She sighed loudly at the plate of freshly cooked food. He didn't eat properly, that was for sure, but she had to admit he looked fit just now. Obviously, the sale had been successful and it looked like he had been eating well. She wondered where he'd stayed to look so much more fit and healthy in just a few days.

He had grown into a very handsome man, but lately his face was looking gaunt, and he had dark circles beneath his green eyes. His dark, wavy hair looked lank and he hadn't had it cut for some time; it almost reached his shoulders. Given that he always had a tan from working outside all day, he sometimes looked foreign. His broad shoulders, strong arms, and large hands were useful having to control that devil horse of his, but she watched him with frightened horses and he could be gentle when he wanted to be.

Most people took him at face value, seeing and hearing only the bad-tempered man who gave nothing away and never let anyone get close to him. This latest argument with Sir Richard had hurt them both; she understood both sides and hated the reason more than ever.

But, he was still beautiful. He would always be beautiful to her. Lucy teased him that he had emeralds for eyes, the skin of an angel, and a smile like a wicked imp! As a boy, he had the look of an innocent kitten whenever he was caught doing boy's mischief. So angelic, so pure that it couldn't possibly be his fault!

But she had seen the other side of him many times, more than she'd cared to remember. His fury could be so sudden and his eyes seemed to flash with rage. She likened it to the sun catching a stormy sea, and you did not want to be within his sights when he allowed his anger to erupt. She defied anyone to hurt the ones he loved. He'd always had a quick temper, but the girls would congregate around him nonetheless. Whether it was for his physique, his money, or his bad boy attitude, she didn't know. Girls could be so strange! Except Catherine; she had known exactly what she was doing.

For a while it had seemed all Judith's nightmares were coming true. He drank excessively with Catherine. He spent his money without care or regard on the hussy. When asked why he was behaving like an idiot, he'd reply, 'Life is for living and you old dears are always saying you can't take it with you! So, I'm enjoying mine while I'm alive!'

It was a shame that everyone else could see who exactly was spending his inheritance and why, but after a few quiet words it became obvious that he wasn't listening to anyone, not even to his sister, which came as a huge shock to Rosalyn. They had always been close, watching out for each other, but not this time. This time, he was listening only to Catherine. So everyone had made the mistake of backing off a little to see what devastation would occur. When it did happen, everyone felt sick with guilt that they hadn't done enough.

Rosalyn refused to talk to Adam for months afterward. His phone calls and his texts were never returned and when he'd turned up in Chester needing a place to stay, to reconnect, Rosalyn hadn't been available. Adam had disappeared elsewhere; to this day, no-one knew where he had gone for six days but he finally surfaced to face the damage done.

Still, Judith was very proud of him. He had picked himself up these past eight years and had worked hard—sometimes too hard; a day off wouldn't hurt him. Even she had those occasionally, but not Adam, not since that bloody woman! She had tried hard not to allow Catherine into her thoughts, she wasn't worthy, but now that she was remembering, it was hard to get rid of her. Just as in life! The irony!

Did Catherine ever care about the damage she had done? What would she do if she came knocking at the door? She looked down at the enormous nineteenth-century wood doors and grinned; God, how she'd love to slam those in her face!

She reached the last step and stood in the Great Hall and looked around her at the three suits of armour that stood proudly against the dark wood panels. High above her head, shields of some of the old Welsh families hung proudly, spaced evenly apart with two swords crossed between each one. Nine shields in all. Each one lovingly cleaned each week. She loved her heritage, even if it wasn't connected to royalty; Sir Richard had his too and she would lovingly clean all that he loved and held dear until the end of time.

She vividly remembered the small boy who would run and play, teasing her about sliding along the polished wooden floors, sliding down the banisters and attempting to reach the shields by pulling chairs into the Hall. Once she had caught the children sword fighting! With ancient swords! How many times had she chased him? How happy and uncomplicated his young life had been then, when his mother had been alive…quickly she forced that thought away, no point in dwelling on those things.

Seeing the closed study door, she took a step toward it, and stopped. Should she tell Sir Richard that Adam had returned? Then she turned and headed toward the kitchen, chastising herself for interfering; of course he knew Adam was home. She must stop meddling because they would have to sort it out for themselves. She hoped it would be soon, for both their sakes.

The kitchen was warm and smelled of delicious pasties; it was Lucy's baking day. Lucy nodded her acknowledgement of Judith's entry into her sacred domain and carried on kneading the dough for another steak and ale pie; three others sat waiting on top of the oven. Next to these were four apple pies, two apple crumbles, a tin of shortbread biscuits, and two large vegetable and cheese pastries that were all cooling. Various quiches and a large cake of some kind were scheduled for the afternoon. Once finished, everything would be frozen for the weeks ahead except the cake, of course—that would be consumed in no time. The kitchen always felt warm and comforting and of course, on baking days it made everyone feel hungry!

Setting the tray down on the sideboard, she was about to make a cup of tea for everyone, knowing that at any moment the baking scents would entice them, hoping for a biscuit, a slice, or two. She heard a faint knocking at the back door. Smiling with knowledge, she opened it. 'Hello, Mathew, what can I do for you today?'

The small, thin boy stood awkwardly in the doorway, shuffling his feet one to the other as his big eyes remained staring at the floor. Judith liked him; in fact, everyone did. It never stopped surprising her how young he looked whenever she saw him . At sixteen, he could easily be mistaken for a twelve-year-old.

On many occasions, Mathew had been mentioned by various members of the household as to how 'ill and pale' he looked. Only the other day, Lucy had noticed the high winds and lashing rain and had declared that 'Mathew would have to be tied down to something heavy or he would be lifted into the air and carried off!'

He was a nice lad, always polite and courteous. In the five months since Geoff had employed him to help at the stables, he never spoke out of line, and in fact, if he spoke at all it was a surprise; the trouble was, the poor lad was incredibly shy. Adam had been a little cautious because of this, but left it up to Geoff and there was no doubt the boy was a hard and willing worker.

However nervous the boy was with people, he transformed whenever they saw him riding—at those times his face shone. The horses loved him. His quiet way soothed them, and even Dulas, who was notorious for being a nasty piece of work, would tolerate Mathew, to a point anyway. Geoff had told her that watching little Mathew at work was like the sunshine moving from stable to stable. He always had a smile for the animals and unbeknownst to him, Geoff and the other stable lad had often listened to Mathew singing or reciting poems to the horses when he thought no-one was about.

Poor boy. He had to come out of his shell if he was going to make it in that business; he wanted desperately to be a jockey and he could be too. Geoff had told her the boy had potential if only he didn't grow anymore, which was highly unlikely. These past few months, whenever Adam was away on business, they had set out an impromptu racecourse and had raced some of the fitter horses. Watching Mathew sitting atop like a scrawny fly, a huge smile lighting him up from inside, was amazing and often brought tears to her and Lucy's eyes.

The other main problem was Adam. Everyone else either ignored his insults, gave as good as they got, or were able to shrug it off; Adam apologised eventually. Mathew seemed to shrink farther into his body, skinny as he was, whenever Adam shouted, even if it wasn't directed at him. He reminded Sir Richard of a frightened rabbit.

Geoff shielded him as best as he could and both Judith and Lucy had spoken up for the boy; God help them! Sometimes, Adam got in such a temper they thought he might swing for someone. Judith knew that Adam, as bad as he could get, would never hit the boy. She knew he liked him in his own way, though to an outsider, and almost certainly to poor Mathew, it was very hard to see it.

Mathew was sometimes sent up to the kitchen by Geoff to give Adam a cooling off period, but it would also give Geoff time to argue back without belittling Adam in front of the lad. Judith and Lucy had become his allies. At least they could protect and comfort the boy who got the brunt of Adam's moods the only way they knew how, which was by mothering.

'Bad morning, love? Come in, I was just putting the kettle on. Here,' she said as she pushed the half-eaten plate of breakfast toward him. 'I think it should still be hot if you fancy it?'

They both watched him tuck in before going about their business. Tea was duly made and hot pasties and another apple pie came out of the large oven. Lucy quickly placed her newly made steak and ale pies in, and washed her hands. Pulling up a chair on either side of him, they glanced at each other and sipped the tea while they waited for him to finish.

Mathew wiped his mouth with his sleeve and slurped his tea down before giving the two waiting ladies a generous smile. 'Thanks, I, erm, didn't have time…' They watched as his cheeks turned a hot pink. 'Mr Kenward…I mean, Adam sent me for a…a…I mean, could he have a cup…'

'His lordship wants a cup of coffee, now does he?' Judith finished for him angrily. 'Well, he can come up here and make it himself. I made him breakfast in bed thinking he would want a lie-in, but oh no, he pushes past me and off he goes.' Seeing Mathew's look of horror she added soothingly, 'Don't you worry, my dear. I'll deal with him. You finish your tea.'

She watched him from the corner of her eye as he curled his slim hands around the mug; she sipped her lemon tea from a cup and saucer. Lucy stood up with a loud sigh and carried on with her baking, humming a tune as she rolled out her pastry that had been chilling in the fridge. She set down a plate of her shortbread biscuits beside Mathew and Judith poured him another cup. He wolfed down two biscuits before dipping his third in his tea.

'Have you always been thin?'

Mathew stopped his dipping and looked up at Lucy who now looked embarrassed at having asked the question, and Judith who smiled encouragingly. They were presented with one of his beautiful smiles that lit up his bony face. 'Yeah, I've always been small. I want to be a jockey. I think I've told you that.' Seeing her nod, he quickly continued. 'Well, you see, Geoff told me I'd be perfect. You should see my cousins, they're huge! It's weird, I can eat anything, and I don't put on weight. My mum hates me!'

His face was a deep crimson, but as he spoke proudly, Judith and Lucy wanted to applaud him for managing a sentence. It wasn't often they heard him speak more than a few words at a time.

The chair squeaked as he pushed it back, and he nodded his thanks, darted for the door, then sprinted down the path toward the stables, leaving the kitchen door swinging wide open. Lucy chuckled to herself as she watched him before closing the door. She caught Judith's eye and they laughed together; he was such a strange lad. Lucy poured another cup and turned their attention to other, more important matters and soon Mathew was forgotten.

CHAPTER FOUR

THE DARKNESS WHIRLED AROUND HER. The eyes, so many eyes, watched her from the surrounding shadows. She knew they were screaming at her but their words made no sense. She froze, too afraid to move. Voices grew louder, retreated, and then drew close again. Whispering inside her head, jumbled and confused, and the noise became louder and louder as her legs gave way beneath her, kicking violently, trying to find anything solid, but she was falling deeper and deeper into the swirling blackness and the voices followed her—always pushing, always watching. Down, down into the never-ending blackness…

'*Get off me please! Please help me…please it wasn't me! I am innocent!*' Her scream died away; no-one heard her.

Bronwen groaned with pain. Clutching her throbbing head, she turned away from the blinding light, cursing herself for leaving the curtains open. The movement made her feel nauseated, and she swallowed hard. The acid rose and lurched in her stomach. Her headache suddenly became irrelevant as she dived out of bed and staggered to the bathroom opposite. Minutes later, she returned to the warmth and comfort of her new bed and blissfully returned to oblivion. No more dreams.

***

The midday sun glared through the window and warmed the sheets that finally roused her again. She sat up slowly, holding her head, which still felt fuzzy. Bronwen listened intently. Had that been a noise? A car? Strange that a sound she had become so accustomed to hearing every day should wake her.

She sat for a while, straining her ears to hear anything else. Every muscle in her fragile body was tensed. Who had been driving it? Someone local or perhaps one of the Kenward family? She had been waiting for someone to turn up unexpectedly just to check her out. Easing her legs out of bed, she sat on the edge, flinching slightly when her head reminded her of the excess alcohol consumed last night; she did feel fragile. Had they parked up outside looking for any signs of life? She had a weird feeling that they had, but why, except to see her? It was the last thing she wanted. She held her breath and waited. No-one knocked. No-one came up the front path; she would have heard the squeal of the broken gate. She must have been wrong.

She let out her breath loudly and felt her body relax. Whatever else, she definitely didn't want to meet his lordship looking and feeling like some haggard, old lush with breath that could kill anyone within fifty feet! No, she was happy not to have to meet any of them, but in reality she was here for at least a year; a meeting was bound to happen and when it did, she would prefer to be prepared and in control.

Rubbing her eyes and temples, she considered going back to bed but with the sunshine warming her body she suddenly had an urge to get out and explore. Yesterday had been a day of sorting out, followed by eating and drinking in excess. What she needed was a shower, lunch, pain killers, and a walk somewhere near her new home, not too far.

She set about her first task, and began to feel alive again as the hot water pounded her skin. Regardless of the headache and the queasy feeling in her stomach, she had to admit she felt really good, a little bit more settled and ready. For what? She wasn't entirely sure, but it just felt good to have energy, an enthusiasm for life.

The sun was bright whenever the fast moving clouds allowed it to shine. She had no doubt that it would rain again at some point, but her eagerness to explore where the lane went was new to her; she began to rush. She would head away from the village and see where it took her. She wasn't ready to meet her fellow villagers, either. 'And that's okay!' she said to herself. 'One step at a time!'

***

The white car slowed to a crawl as it neared the cottage. This was the third time he had driven past, hoping for a sign that Bronwen was in, but now he stopped right outside the little gate and wound his window down, letting the cool breeze dry the sweat that threatened to stain his shirt.

After a few minutes he moved on, rounding the sharp bend and stopping again, but kept the engine ticking over. In the rearview mirror, he could just see the chimney, but the windows were lost thanks to these damned high hedges. He really hoped to get a glimpse of her bedroom window; he'd have to get out. Glancing at his watch, he hissed with frustration; he couldn't get out. There wasn't time. Gordon had a lunch meeting with his new girlfriend, and he was already late getting back to the office. He smiled wickedly; poor Sarah would just have to wait, forego the foreplay and go straight onto the main course. Gordon always was a fast worker anyway; he'd have to bang her twice as fast.

For a second he considered really annoying Gordon and knocking on her door, which would make him incredibly late, especially with what he had in mind. Would she be in? There hadn't been any sign of life all morning but perhaps she'd been in the back garden or the lounge? The bedroom curtains were open, so perhaps she was about?

He wanted her. He wanted to feel that beautiful golden brown hair. Even though she'd had it up in a plaited ponytail when she'd come into the office, he was sure it reached that curvy arse of hers. And those eyes! Deepest colour blue he'd ever seen…and those tits!

He opened the door, looked toward the cottage, and closed it again; he didn't have time for this, he had to get to that appointment in an hour. Business first or Gordon was going to kill him. Stupid bugger! He should have made his move an hour ago. She deserved more time. With another woman he would never have hesitated. So why this time with this woman? She made him feel horny just thinking about her, but, something else? She intrigued him. There was something different about her that he couldn't quite place. A mystery for sure, but one he would uncover.

Frustrated, he fumbled with his trousers and made himself more comfortable. Edging the car slowly forward, he waited until he was around another bend in the lane; he could tell that it was barely used—weeds grew everywhere and brambles scratched his car. Once he knew he was well away from the cottage, he put his foot down, wound up and annoyed for not making a move, he drove as fast as he could back to Shrewsbury.

***

The smell of stale air and alcohol hit her as she descended the wooden stairs and stepped into the lounge. She grimaced with revulsion as she glanced around. Dirty plates lay on the carpet, a wine glass with remnants of the red wine on top of one of them, the whiskey tumbler next to it. Two dirty mugs which had contained coffee sat on the small table, surrounded by crumbs from the fruit loaf she had found as a welcoming gift from the shop owner; she'd devoured the lot.

At some point in the early hours, and fairly drunk, she'd decided to try smoking and could now see why her mouth tasted so disgusting; three half-smoked cigarettes and ash covered a small metal ashtray which now sat precariously on the end of the settee.

Ashamed, she quickly edged her way around it all and threw back the French door curtains and opened the doors wide. The fresh, clean, chilly April air came rushing in. She breathed a deep lungful and turned back to the beautiful lounge she had made into her own personal squalor.

Was this really how she wanted to live now that she was free? Freedom had gone to her head last night, which was perhaps understandable, but not an excuse; she was better than this. Tears pricked the back of her eyes and she angrily wiped them away. No! This was excessive behaviour and she had now got it all out of her system. She could hardly believe that she had bought a packet of cigarettes, an impulse buy, to see if she would like them; she hadn't.

Collecting all the plates and mugs, she threw open the kitchen window, and then she set about scrubbing everything clean. She left them to dry naturally while she polished and straightened the coffee table and settee, even plumping up the pillows before contemplating the vacuum. After a lot of consideration, she decided to leave it until she came back from her walk. For two good reasons: Firstly, she didn't think her head could take the noise just yet, and secondly, she needed something to eat as her stomach gave a loud, complaining growl.

Half an hour later, fed, watered, paracetamol working its way through her body, she felt much better and raring to go. Checking everywhere was locked up, she decided to take the small, full bin bag outside to the main bin. She hoped the bin men came this far, though it looked doubtful the large lorry would be able to manage the lane. If nothing came in a day or two, she'd have to carry it to the village. She sighed loudly at the prospect; something else to get used to, but it was also another reason to make her go into the village.

As she bent down to tie the black bin ends together, she noticed the small, white business card she had found the other day in her purse. Not realising it had fallen into her bag, she'd thrown it into the bin, hardly wanting to touch it, knowing who it belonged to. With everything that had happened over the past few weeks, she'd completely forgotten about it until it had occurred to her yesterday that she had better check how much money she had left in her purse.

Rummaging in her bag, she'd found the card; now she stared down at it with renewed revulsion.

What on earth made that awful estate agent think that she would ever want to see him again? It was the most preposterous idea she'd ever heard, but no doubt, he wasn't used to rejection. Well, tough. Hell would freeze over before she'd see him again.

She would have signed anything to have left that office; his excitement had been undisguised; she'd been only too aware of him watching her. She grimaced, remembering how his hand kept moving to his trousers and the way he'd lick his lips. The very idea of him was sickening, and very frightening. Yes, he was revolting in every sense of the word, but something else made her flesh crawl. He knew she felt uncomfortable and he knew that there was no way that she would want him and that didn't matter. He would take her anyway if the chance was there, and it excited him even more.

When she'd arrived home from signing the lease, she'd stripped off and scrubbed herself, feeling dirty just being in the same room as him. And he'd wanted to take her for a drink! Perhaps she should have made a complaint; it had crossed her mind, but then, who would have listened to her and taken her seriously? At least he was out of her life now. Grabbing the bin bag, she hurried outside to put it where it belonged.

***

Adam was busy grooming Scarlet. Dulas was in the end stable making an awful racket because Adam hadn't been in to see him yet and he could smell Scarlet. Adam shouted that he'd be in soon and laughed when Dulas answered. He had every intention of riding today; he'd decided to ride near his cottage and see if he could catch sight of that woman.

Instead, for now, he was lovingly brushing Scarlet who had gained his attention by whinnying pitifully from her stable. On investigating, he hadn't the heart to leave her; she looked at him with such sorrowful eyes. 'Homesick, love? You'll soon settle in, I promise.'

He'd heard a noise behind him and quickly sent Mathew away to fetch him a cup of coffee before he saw him blush. He hadn't realised Matthew was there; that damned boy was too quiet. His embarrassment at being caught had made him sharper than he'd intended as he watched the skinny lad run off toward the Hall.

Five minutes later, he was lost in his job; coffee forgotten, the ride on Dulas that he had been so full of enthusiasm for forgotten. She was beautiful. Her gleaming, soft brown coat caught the glare of the sun through the doorway, making it look golden. With the brush gliding over her strong back and smooth neck, he was soon lost in his own thoughts until Geoff came storming over. 'What the hell has Mathew done now? Why is he running off? What did you say this time?'

Geoff saw Mathew come running out of the stable, which wasn't unusual, but then Adam had stepped into the doorway watching him go before disappearing back inside. Geoff waited a moment wondering how to handle it. He had had every intention of talking to Adam about Mathew training to be a jockey, but seeing the smug-looking smile on Adam's face threw away all ideas of a gentle approach.

Adam rounded on him, his quiet moment gone; he wasn't tolerating that from Geoff; his defences immediately went up. 'None of your Goddamn business! Saddle Dulas. I'll ride him once I've finished Scarlet. Then go and sort Fred and Cleo.'

Turning his back, he carried on brushing her mane vigorously, much harder than was necessary. He'd arrived at his stables in a good mood. Okay, a little guilty about lying in, leaving the cleaning out to Geoff and the stable lads, but wasn't that what he paid them for? He'd seen David, the older stable boy, sorting out the far stable. He was never any problem, kept himself to himself and did the job, went home. Adam liked him, no problems.

He'd noticed on arriving this morning that Mathew and Geoff had been laughing about something but he hadn't said anything, knowing he was late, but now, his guilt and their apparent laziness was too near the surface for him to have Geoff start with him.

'What the hell is wrong with you, Adam? Had such a nice lie-in that you have the energy to pick on someone? Well pick on me, not Mathew, the lad's done nothing wrong, he's—'

'Go away, Geoff, I'm in no mood.'

'I don't care if you are or not. I saw the look on your face when you arrived this morning when you saw us having a chat. It pissed you off, didn't it? Well, I'm the one who stopped Mathew. I'm the one who dared to ask him if his grandmother was feeling any better. Then I dared to tell him what had happened to my grandfather once, pretending to be ill, so go ahead, shout at me, not an innocent boy.'

Adam swung round to face him. The sarcasm in Geoff's voice was heavy. He could feel his blood pumping; he saw red. 'Fuck off! The day I need a lecture from an employee is the day hell freezes over. I'm sick and tired of lectures from you and Father. I know what I'm doing, this is my business, and you're my employee, so get on with your job.'

Geoff didn't move. Adam turned away first and busied himself with cleaning the brushes. He'd regretted the words even as he'd spoken them; he must say something to make amends. God! What was wrong with him?

Geoff felt more like an uncle than an employee, but he was paying him a salary, wasn't he? Did he really need a lecture from him? He took a deep breath and turned round. Geoff was gone. He stared at the empty doorway and felt miserable. Scarlet, sensing his emotion wandered over to him and nuzzled his shoulder before giving it a quick nip. 'Ow! Damn it! I'll sort you out first and then I've got to ride.' Putting away the brushes, he muttered to himself, 'I need to get out of here and calm down.'

***

Sir Richard stood on the brow of the hill looking across at the stable yard. Sound sometimes carried in the direction of the Hall, as well as smells; this time he had plainly heard two voices, both shouting, both angry. He had been about to turn away and go home when he saw Geoff slowly walking away from one of the stables and entering another. Something about his movement worried him; what had they argued about this time?

He had known Geoff for thirty-odd years now, probably closer to forty? He loved him like a brother, and worried about him; he must be sixty by now. He should have been slowing down, taking things easier, but whenever he had tried to bring up the issue of retirement, Geoff wouldn't even consider it.

It had become their custom to get together about twice a month, on a Friday. They'd play chess and chat about life, their worries, the Hall, and of course the fear they both shared and hid from the others. A cigar would be enjoyed and one or more brandies consumed. He looked forward to their evenings, but lately he'd noticed a change in Geoff; he seemed preoccupied and it concerned him deeply.

Geoff was his only connection to the past. If he left because of Adam, or worse, he died, there would be nobody to keep his memories alive, or help him cope with all his dark fears; no-one to share his pain. Geoff could handle Adam, he was sure of it. He remained standing, watching for a sign of anything else that might give him a clue as to the fight. The sunshine warmed his shoulders and he felt them gently relax under the hot rays. It was good to feel the sun again; it had begun to feel like it would rain forever.

With his hands thrust deeply into his trouser pockets, he remained motionless just enjoying the warmth. He heard little Mathew scuttle past a while later. He acknowledged the boy and watched as he ran back toward the stables, but his eyes and thoughts returned to the stable Geoff had walked away from. The stable he knew his son was in.

Yes, Adam had problems. Mostly with the business, money problems possibly, Adam never shared information. He hadn't asked where the money had come from when Adam had completely renovated the old stables seven years before. He'd managed to keep the feel of the place. The original features of the nineteenth-century stables were plain to see; even the parts that had needed complete renovation had been done perfectly. It was easy to imagine his great-grandfather looking down at his stables as they looked now. All he could do was what he always had done: wait and watch…and cross his fingers.

***

Adam eventually left the sanctuary of Scarlet's stable and went in to see Dulas. Within a minute, he could be heard chastising the beast for trying to bite him. A while later, he walked him out holding tightly onto the reins. He blinked as the sunshine blinded him; the sudden glare was intense, and he searched his jacket for sunglasses. If the wind dropped, it would be a glorious warm day, but he could tell rain was coming again so he'd have to make the ride a quick one, an hour, perhaps.

Movement caught his attention and he stopped hitching himself up into the saddle. He turned and faced his father; he removed his glasses. His mouth and throat suddenly felt parched and he remembered the coffee Mathew had been sent for; he really was a nasty bastard. No doubt his father had come to put his ten pence's worth in. Tying Dulas to a nearby post, he waited for the onslaught.

'Adam, morning.' His father's voice quivered slightly, was it nerves?

He nodded and waited, watching the man look around at the stables. He stood outside Scarlet's doorway and looked inside. 'She is a fine mare. Worth every penny, I should think? What is she, a thoroughbred?' Walking inside, he waited for Adam to follow him; Adam remained unmoving. 'A bad journey home, was it?'

Adam watched his father stroke Scarlet for a moment before answering. 'It took longer than expected. I had no reason to rush home anyway.' He wondered what his father was up to. But, seeing his hurt expression, he added, 'The traffic and that awful rain made it impossible to rush; the cargo was much too precious. You should know by now how much I hate driving my horses in bad conditions, and Scarlet is definitely precious, and yes, she's a thoroughbred. The stallion was amazing.'

'Scarlet, eh? A nice name. Suits her.' Richard stroked her neck. Adam waited impatiently for his real reason for the visit. After a few minutes, Dulas gave a snort of dissatisfaction at being tied up for so long. Hearing it, Adam shrugged his apology. 'Gotta go, Dad, see ya.'

'Adam! Is everything, all right, you know…between us?'

Finally he gets to the point. 'I suppose it will have to be, won't it.' Heaving himself up into the saddle, he looked down at his father who leaned against the stable doorway. He couldn't be bothered talking about any of it now. 'I'll see you later, Dad, and maybe you'll explain the real reason you rented my home to some stranger, eh?' He clicked the huge, black horse into a trot, rode out of the yard, and headed for the open fields. For a very long time he was aware of his father watching as he rode away.

***

She stood rooted to the spot by the gate as an unexpected pang of fear intruded on her jovial mood. Would she be safe? With no-one around, attackers could have their way with her without ever being caught. What if someone was lurking about now? She glanced around to be sure; not a soul. Except for that car she was sure that she'd heard, but that had been over an hour ago; surely it was long gone? Who had it been? Where had it gone? She hated herself for being so ridiculous, damn it, why was she so over-cautious? She knew the answer, of course, and hated it even more.

She looked both ways before stepping out into the lane. She breathed in deeply the freshly laundered air and smiled; clean air, fresh flowers, birds flying and singing nearby. Standing up straight, she tried to ignore her fears; any problems, she'd just come straight back. Small steps. No pressure.

She frowned as she looked up into the sky. Rain would come soon anyway, judging from the growing grey clouds; she wouldn't be long. Hands in her jacket pocket, she quickly walked away from the comfort of her home. Determination, excitement, and a feeling of defiance spread through her; her exploring had begun, and it felt very good.

***

Richard stood for a long time watching his son ride away, getting smaller and smaller with each passing second, eventually disappearing. Moving slowly, he wandered around the yard, picking up a forgotten hat, a bridle left hanging over a stable door. It was quiet. The horses had been let out into the fields; only Scarlet remained, and Jess, an older mare who had sprained her front leg. Both horses watched him. He felt deflated, stupid; he'd accomplished nothing by coming to the stables looking for him. Adam was still angry, his feelings obviously still raw but he hated leaving things to fester and these past few days had been too awful for him to allow it to carry on.

The night Adam had stormed off, he had paced the floor in his study for most of the evening convinced he had gone too far and had pushed Adam away for good. Yes, he knew he was in the wrong, well, technically, anyway. Yes, he had given Oak Cottage to Adam to renovate and to live in, but, after eight years of being left to rot, it had been ridiculous not to do something with it. Eight years of standing empty after such hard work, making it look beautiful was a farce. He'd made a choice, sell or rent it out.

He'd decided on renting, half-expecting it to remain empty as it was such a lonely spot and he was asking quite a lot of rent for it; perhaps too much. He'd been as surprised as anyone when the estate agent had phoned to say he had a tenant. A lady. Even more surprised when he had been told she had paid a full year's rent instead of the usual monthly payments. Was that okay?

Of course it was okay! It was better than okay, he desperately needed the money. Strange how it had happened just as Eira had told him it would. 'Stop worrying, Richard dear,' she'd said. 'When you really need it, the money will turn up, perhaps better than you expected!'

He was curious to meet the woman; young, the estate agent had told him. With one thing or another, he hadn't had the time or the inclination to go and meet her, and on second thought, it was best to give her time to move in. There would be plenty of opportunities if she planned on staying for a year.

A year. A long time, but at least this way, Adam could have a year to make his decision as to what he wanted to do. Of course, he hadn't seen it that way.

'Is this your way of getting back at me for marrying her behind your back?'

Hurt by the accusation, he'd answered more harshly than intended. 'That cottage has stood empty for far too long, Adam; it's ridiculous! It's stupid to think I'd do this because of that, I can understand why—'

'You don't understand anything. You only gave it to me to keep her away from you and your precious Hall. Too damned common to live up at the mansion you said, it's what drove her away.'

Furious, Richard had turned on him. 'Are you really that dumb or are you still in denial? That whore left you because she'd drained you of your money and then found another idiot who would pay her bills. She used you like she'd used many others that we found out about; you weren't the first lapdog to be seduced by her. I was given a very long list.' Deflated, he'd sat down heavily in his armchair, hoping the warmth from the fire would thaw his chilled hands; he saw how they trembled when he reached for his half-finished brandy. He drained the rest in one mouthful and, for a moment, closed his eyes.

'I have to admit, Adam, she was convincing. For a while she had me fooled, but I knew we would see the real Catherine when she found out she wasn't going to get to play Lady of Kenward Hall with my money. It's about time you let her go.'

Adam had stared at his face; the shock of everything showed as he fought to control his emotions. Richard had suddenly realised that Adam hadn't known about his friend in the police force who had supplied him with every gory detail of that woman's history. The list had gone on and on, her conquests left sad and embarrassed and poorer. Two had died by their own hand, the reason his friend had her file; she had been the last to see them alive.

Adam had stormed out, slamming the study door behind him, cutting off his plea to come back and sort it out. Richard had started after him but gave up, knowing he was wasting his time. An hour later, Geoff had arrived asking where Adam was going. Richard knew. The York trip wasn't due for another day or so, but he guessed that's where he'd headed.

Now, glancing once more in the direction Adam had gone, he shrugged; there wasn't any point in wishing their relationship was better. Since his mother had died, their father and son bond had quickly deteriorated, but since Catherine had entered their lives, it had become much worse. Who was to blame for that?

David walked out from the nearest stable and waved a hello. They made small talk for a while before Richard walked quickly back toward the Hall. He couldn't quite work out whether he liked David. He was good at his job, there wasn't any doubt about that, but there was something sly about him. He'd heard that he gave as good as he got verbally, so perhaps that was why he and Adam got on quite well?

Adam was a stubborn idiot, nothing he could do about it, and he'd just have to wait it out. If only Adam knew the problems they faced, the rising bills, the building work that was desperately needed, the rising taxes, the wages—keeping a Hall wasn't cheap.

He hadn't had a choice but to bring money into the estate. The cottage was a liability standing empty; at least now it was paying for itself and he'd had a year's money up front off the girl, which hadn't gone far, but it had helped keep the wolves from his door...for now.

Ironic, really; if only Catherine had known; he might be 'Sir' Richard, titled, deserved, but in name only. The Kenward fortune had long since gone. One day he would have to tell Adam, and he dreaded it.

CHAPTER FIVE

THE DARKNESS WAS INTENSE, ALMOST solid. For a moment, Eira wasn't sure if her eyes were even open. She felt confused, disorientated. It took her a long time before she could find the strength to sit up; her arms shook with the strain as she heaved her aching body into a comfortable position. Her fragile lungs gasped for air, the movement making her feel breathless and in pain. Her stomach felt as though someone had pummelled her; she felt bruised. She winced as her legs suddenly cramped and she quickly rubbed them as best as she could, though the movement hurt her.

Finally, the moment of pain passed and she leant slowly back onto her pillow and tried to slow her breathing. Her head whirled with so many images, it was hard to focus on any one thing. The voices, so many voices screaming, shouting, chanting, the noise pounded her head, the words jumbled, incoherent. Squeezing her eyelids tight, she tried to banish the noise all from her mind, her nightmare, but knew it was a waste of time, they were there, always. Although, could it be…

She frowned deeply trying to remember how it had felt…yes, it had felt different…hadn't it? Could it possibly be what she'd hoped for all these years? Was it time?

The pain was hard to ignore as she edged herself out of bed, walked to her window, and flung it wide open, gasping as the chilly night air rushed in, sending a shiver through her body. Taking deep breaths, she shivered as her hot, sweat-drenched body quickly cooled, taking the swellings down, the pain in her joints easing slightly.

Gradually, her body relaxed and she gently placed her elbows onto the windowsill and leant out. How free it felt after her claustrophobic bedroom; she savoured the feeling. Closing her eyes, she leant farther until her long grey hair was caught by the wind and flew around her face. It almost felt like flying.

The movement she heard below didn't bother her; she knew it was the fox visiting her garden. She frowned, she hadn't put anything out for her this evening and she mouthed the word 'sorry'. A bat swooped down nearby, but she didn't flinch, she was concentrating on something. Something she hadn't felt for a long time, but had never forgotten. Every cell in her body began to vibrate and tingle, until it felt like her body burned from within. She gasped, frightened as its intensity grew and spread. Her cooled skin fevered to the touch. Her hand shook violently as it wiped the sweat from her brow. Pushing back her flowing hair, she gazed out into the night and tried to focus, to search, and finally she smiled. She had never really dared to hope, to believe that the time would come when it would end. She was here. Her prayers had finally been answered.

***

'My lady?' The voice sounded familiar, hesitant, soft and frightened.

'My lady…please, come away from the window, I beg you…you are not decent, my lady… Lady Anne?' She heard the movement as the maid gave up calling and took the heavy blanket off the bed and came up behind her, throwing it around her chilled shoulders; she didn't move or acknowledge the kindness. 'My lady, you will catch a chill, please, come away.'

She allowed herself to be tempted into walking back to the arm-chair by the roaring fire where she was pushed gently into a sitting position. Her eyes focused on nothing but her senses told her there were many others in the room. Whispers, always whispers. A cup of mulled wine was pressed to her lips, but she refused to drink it. And the whispers carried on and on and on…

***

Eira stood for a long time, the windowsill holding her up as the sobs racked through her old body; how quickly the memories came flooding back to haunt her. The voices, oh how well she knew them. All long gone, but never forgotten. She should be gone too. Was it too late? Her heart-broken cries for those once loved were lost on the night wind, but the ghosts took no notice, yet. Time had no meaning for them, but to her, she knew time meant everything; they'd made it that way.

***

Bronwen sat huddled by the side of her bed, the duvet wrapped around her, covering her shivering body. Her backside was numb, but she wouldn't move, not just yet. The large kitchen knife lay across her knees, where she'd placed it after gripping it so tightly, her hands had sweat so much, but she grasped it from time to time to make sure she could get it quickly enough if…

Her eyes remained fixed on her closed bedroom door. Had it followed her? Could it follow her? Would it?

Her eyes darted toward the window. It was pitch black outside. Surely it would have come by now? She eased her legs out straight and waited for the pins and needles to subside. Taking deep breaths, she finally managed to stop shaking from overwhelming fear, and began to think logically about what had happened. She started to feel daft. She'd overreacted, perhaps?

Bronwen got to her knees and flicked on her bedside lamp. The warm, yellow glow proved that no-one and nothing was in the room with her, as far as she could see anyway. Holding the knife firmly, she crawled on all fours to the window and quickly closed the curtains. She felt calmer as she stood, rubbing her back and her cramped legs.

Tiptoeing to the door, she listened for any sounds. None came; the cottage was silent. Was it listening to her? Waiting quietly downstairs? Her thoughts raced with all the different scenarios, Christ! Had she closed and bolted the front door? She couldn't remember. In her panic, perhaps she had left it standing wide open? Then again, surely it could get in anyway? There was nothing she could do to defend herself. Strangely, this revelation helped her accept it. If she couldn't fight it, if there really wasn't any way to get away from it, then perhaps she could find another way to…survive it? Did she need to survive it?

She threw open her door, and ran into the bathroom to finally relieve herself. Moments later, she began to giggle, from nerves most likely. What must she look like, some mad woman skulking around her own home, carrying a knife to defend herself against what? A ghost? She could feel the anger rising again and took another deep breath. Why her? Why now after everything? Just when her life was getting good, and she was feeling brave, crazy and excited, and now this shit?

Should she even be frightened? She had read a few books and stories about people who had lived with these things. Were they frightened? Some people even helped move them into the light or something like that. Could she do that? Did she have the nerve? Who could she ask?

She started to shake again, then began to cry. What exactly had she been a witness to? An act so horrendous that it'd left an imprint or something? Or had she slipped back in time like she'd read in a newspaper. An article about a woman in Liverpool who'd been walking along a street and noticed it had changed, to another time, the Victorian age, and she had somehow walked into it. Could that really happen? She could remember wishing while reading the article that it would happen to her and she'd made an effort to find the street, but nothing happened. She'd felt disappointed as the urge to leave her life had been desperate. Her old life, she quickly reminded herself. Not this one. Please not this one.

She believed strange things did happen, not necessarily UFO's or silly ideas like that, but she had seen pictures of stigmata, supposed photographs of ghosts, programmes on the TV. Was it all bullshit? She'd often wondered how she'd react to seeing a ghost and hoped she'd be all right. *After all, they're dead, they can't hurt me.* But, now, she wasn't so sure.

She splashed cold water on her hot face to revive herself as exhaustion began to take hold of her aching muscles. Disgusted with herself for being so pathetic, she noticed that it was almost two o' clock in the morning. She must have sat for hours. Stupid! Bloody stupid!

She opened the bathroom door and stepped out onto the landing. A quick check in the spare room and she descended the stairs slowly. The hall light blazed, showing her that no-one was waiting to lunge at her. She was thankful that at least the front door was closed; quickly, she walked over and bolted it.

In the kitchen, she made herself a large mug of tea and found a cigarette, her resolve that it was horrible forgotten, at least for now. She stood for a long time leaning against the cupboard, staring into space. Occasionally she'd sip her tea, smoking the cigarette slowly, barely noticing the smell or taste, desperately trying to make sense of her ordeal.

She had walked for nearly an hour, stopping every once in a while to look over gates and low hedges at the scenery beyond. She started to hear the noise of traffic and quickly turned around; the last thing she wanted was noise after such a peaceful afternoon. Heading back, she meandered along, feeling pleased with herself and very happy at that moment.

She watched the cows, fearful of their size, but finding them fascinating as they stared back at her. Birds whooshing past would then whistle from a tree or from within a hedge. Their singing was so beautiful, she stayed listening longer than she'd intended. Walking on, she'd watched some horses neighing to each other and then run around the large field.

Time rolled on, but she wasn't worried. Every so often, she'd feel a spot of rain, but she didn't care. Slowly she wandered toward home, picking dandelions and blades of long grass, tearing them gently as she walked, enjoying the smells and feeling of freedom.

As she reached the top of a slight incline, she stopped to rest. She knew her cottage was only another five-minute walk but she wasn't quite ready to go inside just yet. Noticing an old stile, she climbed up the bank toward it, fighting her way through brambles and high weeds. It was very old and forgotten by the looks of it. The wood appeared rotten; it certainly wouldn't hold her weight. Pushing her way closer, she stared into the field beyond and noticed that in the centre stood an enormous mound that appeared to be circular in shape, judging from the way the sides disappeared from view. On top and surrounding it, a large clump of trees almost hid it from view. The grass was long and full of weeds but she could still make out a path trodden by someone fairly recently. Unsure, she glanced around; no-one could be seen, of course, and it did look interesting. She decided a quick peek wouldn't hurt, and she'd eased herself over the stile; it held its lopsided position.

Walking quickly, she noticed there weren't any animals in the field. She couldn't see any buildings. Turning to face the direction of the cottage and the village, she stood on tiptoe: nothing. High hedges dominated everything; all she could see were a few fields and large trees; perhaps the village was in a dip? The field was certainly not as flat as it had first appeared, and by the time she reached the first trees her calf muscles were aching and she was out of breath.

She stopped and looked beyond the trees and saw the remains of a castle and the enormous trees circling it. The large mound circled these but the gap she was walking through showed where perhaps the old gatehouse might have stood.

On either side, the earth reached her shoulders, and from where she stood, she could see the ground on the outside had at some point been dug into to make a ditch. Now it contained nettles, rocks, and clumps of earth. Stepping through the entrance, she gazed up at the enormous trees that stood guard on either side; she thought they looked like huge spears of broccoli! Oak trees. She surprised herself. She knew nothing about trees; she must have read it somewhere.

She walked on, occasionally stumbling on hidden rocks. She got closer to the castle. One tower still stood intact, rising perhaps eighty feet or more. She headed toward the main entrance, which was now a large hole; only the remains of an arch, seven or eight feet high, showed her how high and strong the door would have been. Did it greet friends, and enemies? The door was long gone, of course. Had it been burnt in a raid or a war? Or just chopped up for firewood? Either way seemed sad somehow.

She tried to remember any wars and battles that had happened around Shrewsbury, but nothing sprang to mind. She walked carefully into what would have been the Grand Hall, looked up at the surrounding walls, and tried to imagine what it would have looked like. Ivy covered every inch of the shell, but it must have belonged to someone of importance; even years of neglect couldn't wipe out how impressive it was. A lord, perhaps, or a knight? Maybe they were related to the Kenwards. He was a sir.

When had peace reigned in Britain? Beyond the mounds and the ditches, the castle didn't look like it had had any other defences. So what had it been? Had it been built during a quiet time? It was easy to imagine the lords and their ladies walking around, coming down the sweeping steps of which very little remained, to dine and sing, perhaps dance and watch entertainment. When the evening was finished, the lord would retire to his bedchamber and no doubt ravish some poor woman.

She had lost all track of time as she roamed every inch of the ruins, at least the ground floor anyway. Some steps remained, but only went halfway up the walls before nothing but crumbling stone took hold. As she wandered from room to room, she tried to guess what each one could have been and had a weird sensation of déjà vu, which was daft; she'd never been here before.

A sense of panic sent her stumbling out of the ruins, which had suddenly become claustrophobic; its crumbling walls felt too high, too enclosed. She found herself back near the front entrance and breathed a sigh of relief and felt stupid. Looking around one last time, meaning to head for home, her eyes were drawn toward the tower. At its base, the dark doorway, now covered in mould and ivy, held her interest. There were only a few feet between her and the doorway and she quickly took a few steps backward, needing more space between her and it. She had the strongest feeling of dread; she wasn't alone. Slowly, she backed away farther.

Every nerve in her body sprang to attention. She felt her adrenaline pumping through her veins, ready to run or fight because someone was definitely there, just beyond the doorway, watching from the dark. A shiver ran through her. Her head screamed *Run!* But she couldn't. Her eyes remained fixed; she knew her gaze was locked with another's, but whose?

Stepping slowly backward, knowing if she turned and fled as she wanted to that whatever it was, was faster. Her feet stumbled on hidden rocks and rabbit holes, her breathing became heavier, and her body began to shake with the effort. It occurred to her as she moved from beneath the cover of the trees that it had become darker, that dusk was rapidly approaching. Her panic intensified; she couldn't be here, not with that, not at night!

The shadows lengthened, the beautiful ruins became menacing, a threat. The old stones that only an hour before had looked interesting now dripped with malice; she knew she had to get away from this hostile place, but her body refused to cooperate. The air changed; it became cold, an intense, unnatural coldness that pierced her bones and made her shiver all the more. Her heart beat faster and her mouth became so dry she knew she would not be able to scream when it came, for she knew now without any doubt that something was coming.

Her glance darted toward the stile somewhere behind her, and back to the darkening doorway. She tried to focus on it. How far away was it? A five-minute walk, or had it been ten? Could she make it?

Before she could react, it was there. Her head screamed in terror as it rushed to engulf her. She tried to swallow, to scream out for help, knowing it was pointless. No-one was around. She felt the air around her change, becoming almost solid as it wrapped itself around her rigid body, its icy breath freezing her blood. This was death. She knew for sure. For what seemed like forever, she couldn't take a breath. It questioned her presence. Death invaded every pore; it filled her soul... and then blackness.

It had been dark when she'd woken from oblivion. Confused, cold, and wet, she'd slowly sat up. The grass beneath her was soaking, as the rain that had threatened all day was now hammering down very hard. A stone dug into her hip, and she tried to move but her body felt like rubber, all void of energy or strength. She sat for a while, huddled into herself, trying to find remnants of warmth and crying with relief that she was still alive. Eventually, she had heaved herself onto all fours before getting to her unsteady feet. Her head spun and ached with the cold and effort but she managed to stay upright.

She looked around her, trying to guess how long she had been unconscious. Fear crept back into her bones. Where was it? Looking into the semidarkness toward the ruins, she could vaguely make out its bulk, but of the other, nothing. She had turned and fled, stumbling her way through the fort's gatehouse and out into the open field. Her sense of direction had vanished, so she headed toward the high hedge, which she could just make out against the darkening sky. Twice she'd tripped over a rock or slipped on wet grass, crying with frustration and fear; she quickly picked herself up and carried on.

It'd felt like forever. Her legs like lead, her body shivered with cold and shock. She tried to jog but only managed a few feet before collapsing. The hedge was only an arm's width away, but no stile. She cried out wildly, scrambling along the thorny brambles, searching for the opening, not caring that her skin was being torn to shreds as she pushed herself along, until, with a cry of triumph, she found it. Throwing herself over it, she tumbled down the embankment as the wood gave way, falling with her as she rolled head over heels before finally landing on the tarmac lane.

For a moment, she gasped for breath, her chest heaving with the effort, and then carefully she checked her body for any bad injuries. Her head hurt, her arms were scratched raw, and she could feel a couple of bruises on her legs and shoulder, but otherwise, she had survived. She stood up slowly and took some deep breaths. Movement stopped her. Her eyes travelled toward where the stile had been and she felt nausea well up. A dark figure stood watching her. For a second, her breath caught in her throat but this time she was able to move. Backing away, her eyes fixed on the unmoving figure, she walked fast until she felt able to turn and run.

Picking up speed, she didn't look to see if she was being chased; all she knew was she had to get home. She had to run, get space between it and her. Finally, she saw the bend, the cottage. Panic consumed her as she pushed open the gate, fumbling in her jacket for her keys. She thrust the large key into the lock, and she dived through, slamming the door behind her.

Without thought or planning, she ran into the kitchen, grabbing the first knife she could find and then ran upstairs, slamming her bedroom door shut and diving toward the far corner, behind her bed. After a while, she had pulled the duvet around herself and waited.

She'd wept bitterly until too exhausted to weep anymore. Her body had also stopped shivering and clenching with fear; the knife she held rigidly before her slowly sank down to knee level, where it remained for the next few hours. She considered, at that point, how it was strange how bodies work. When fear takes hold and the danger seems to have passed, the body turns toward resting, perhaps for the next fight or flight scenario, but soon she drifted off into a fitful sleep.

Her dreams were images of what she had been a witness to. She had stood silently amongst them; they didn't know she was there. Everyone was busy doing their work, going about their day; no-one had taken any notice of her even when she'd attempted to touch them. They became wisps of smoke, fading away, till becoming solid looking once more beyond her reach.

She'd stood outside the castle and marvelled at its beauty. It had been everything she'd imagined. Its solid grey walls, proud and strong now, held men, women and children. A child. Couldn't anyone else hear that shouting? Looking up toward the tower, she watched as two people came into view. They were arguing, shouting, and then someone was pleading. She looked around trying to get someone's attention, because in that moment, she knew what was going to happen. '*Oh God!*'

She'd woken with a start and curled herself into a tight ball, the knife again clenched against her bosom, and she'd gently rocked herself, the tears soaking her face and arms unnoticed. The look of horror on the child's face would haunt her forever.

She hadn't seen the child hit the ground, but she'd heard it and the screams from those nearby. Her eyes had travelled back to the top. Her eyes searched the ramparts for the person responsible. She knew her. Their eyes locked for a second before the figure disappeared. The figure dressed in purple. A woman.

***

The tea had gone cold. The cottage felt chilled, but she remained, staring at nothing. A tear quickly fell onto her hand, which still held her cigarette, now nothing more than a stub, and then another fell. She remembered everything now; it flooded her mind, and it hurt. She dropped the stub and clutched her stomach as it clenched with fear and outrage at what she had witnessed.

That poor child. Murdered. Pushed to her death. *But why show me?* She wished more than anything it had been some weird episode, a dream, perhaps. A fit, or hallucination, anything except what she knew to be right. What she witnessed was too incredible, too insane, and too horrific. She slammed her fist down hard on the kitchen surface, smashing the mug. 'Damn it to hell!'

The sobs came loud and heavy with anger and grief. It felt personal, but why? Looking down at her stinging arms, she gently touched one of the many cuts that zigzagged its way down her skin. The bleeding had stopped a while ago and she picked at a dried clot of blood. As it welled up again, she grabbed her tea towel and wrapped it over her arm before moving to the lounge and slumping in the settee. No use fighting it, she knew that; it would haunt her dreams. Let it come now while she was wide awake.

***

The small, pathetic figure watched, unmoving, as the broken gate gently swung backward and forward with the wind. She smiled; it had begun.

CHAPTER SIX

LUCY STOOD WITHIN THE DOORWAY, her shopping bag heavy with supplies, but it was obvious she felt reluctant to leave. Eira waited for the inevitable. She sighed loudly, resigned to the fact that the woman was bursting with gossip about something. She could guess what.

On and on she talked about things Eira had heard before. The grandson, new and bonny, but oh how the birth had been dreadful; thankfully, both had pulled through. Eira nodded in the right places and smiled warmly when she was shown another photograph. Lucy certainly knew how to exaggerate; mother and baby had both been fine. All that had happened was she'd gone into labour four weeks earlier than expected, so Sandra, Lucy's daughter, had been caught out at a garage getting petrol! Dramatic, yes, but the owner had driven her the few miles to the hospital and everything turned out okay. Lucy had forgotten that she'd already told her, so the story changed slightly; no doubt it would be different next week.

Eira continued to nod and grin while she patiently waited for the real reason for Lucy's visit; it certainly wasn't for more supplies. She'd bought almost exactly the same things four days ago; it had to do with the new tenant. Almost half the village had wandered in for one thing or another in the past week, hoping to hear something about this mysterious woman who had moved into Oak Cottage.

'Oh, by the way, have you seen her yet?' *Finally!* Eira pretended to be puzzled, so she continued. 'You know, the new woman up at Oak Cottage?'

Eira tried not to laugh. Looking at Lucy's expectant face. 'No, I'm afraid I haven't.' She lowered her voice conspicuously; Lucy edged forward and shut the shop door. 'But you know, those supplies she ordered won't last too long, at least the basics like bread and milk.'

'Maybe she's one of these anorexic girls. You've seen them, model types who don't eat. Was she like that?'

'I'm sure she isn't one of those, besides, Geoff said he saw her moving in and he described her as "a healthy looking lass". He'd never call some skinny, pale girl healthy, would he?'

Lucy grunted and swapped her heavy basket to the other arm.

Eira sighed again, hoping she'd get the message and go; she'd had a terrible headache since last night and she ached from lack of sleep.

Lucy didn't notice. 'Well, I think it's very strange we haven't seen this girl. What on earth could she be doing up there by herself? That is, of course, if she is alone.'

Eira frowned and rubbed her forehead. 'What on earth do you think she's doing, running a brothel? She's only been there three days. Give her some time to settle in. And maybe she enjoys her own company. I should think she wants some peace and quiet, why else would anyone move into Oak Cottage? It's a good mile from here, and here is six miles from the outskirts of Shrewsbury, so it's very quiet. When she's ready, I'm sure she'll introduce herself…if she's left alone,' Eira quickly added; she could sense what Lucy was thinking. The last thing that poor girl needed was some busybody gossip invading her space.

For a moment, Lucy looked doubtful, but then nodded. 'Perhaps so, but I do think it's strange. Anyway, if she is a nice, decent girl, perhaps she might be good for…you know?'

'If you mean Adam, then I'm very sure he doesn't need your interfering to find a decent young lady. Now you stop thinking what I know you're thinking! He's had a lot on his mind these past few years, as you well know, Lucy, it would go against you if…' Eira stopped and frowned; she knew Lucy's tongue got carried away causing trouble. 'You haven't said anything, have you?'

Lucy looked hurt. 'Of course I haven't. But he needs someone, quick. His temper is dreadful lately; he's so unhappy and no doubt lonely. Do you know he shouted at Geoff when he got back with his new horse? Called him an employee and that he should know his place! I mean, isn't that terrible? He can be a real bugger sometimes but never so cruel, and to Geoff?'

Eira nodded sadly. It had been an awful thing to say and she knew Adam would be feeling bad. Given time, he'd make it up to Geoff, if allowed to do so in his own way. Of course, that was doubtful if people like Lucy had the chance to give their own opinions.

'And another thing, he fired Mathew today.'

'No, he wouldn't do that!' Eira exclaimed. But she already knew it to be true.

Lucy positively glowed, seeing her shock. 'Oh yes he would. Mathew lost something. Swore he'd put a new bridle bought for the new horse in its stable, they searched high and low for it, gone. Adam called him a thief amongst other things and sacked him. Geoff stormed off to speak to Sir Richard about it and hasn't spoken to Adam since. The atmosphere at those stables is icy.' Leaning forward, she whispered, 'Geoff told me he'd leave if Adam didn't apologise to the boy and give him his job back.'

She watched Lucy's cheeks burn pink with delight at having passed on such new and delicious gossip. Eira felt nothing but utter misery for the family. She could do nothing to help them…as always. Everything had to run its course. So many times she watched as they fell apart, only to come crawling back from the brink. It was a curse all right for the Kenwards. But, maybe, just maybe, her instincts were right this time. Perhaps this was the beginning? Perhaps this woman would change everything? For Adam? For her?

She closed her eyes and said a little prayer of hope. Was anyone listening anymore?

The clink of the old bell brought her swiftly back to the present. She managed a weak smile as Lucy, glowing with delight, swept out of the shop and headed straight across the road where another 'gossiper' opened her door long before Lucy knocked; she must have been watching and waiting.

With both hands on the counter to support her, she heaved a sigh of relief, then gently rubbed her fingers and flexed them. Everything felt swollen and sore now; her arthritis was hurting more and more these days, but maybe not for much longer?

Turning the sign on the door to Closed, she shuffled slowly out toward her kitchen and out into her garden. Feverfew, that's what she needed for the headache. That and a cold compress soaked in lavender. Herbs and an hour's rest, perhaps then she'd feel better, more focused. But even as she poured herself a glass of water, she knew she was convincing no-one.

***

Richard stood within the small, walled garden and breathed slowly and deeply, trying to regain his composure. Geoff had left ten minutes ago; his words echoed in his head. Adam had to apologise within the week or he was definitely leaving. Richard had begged Geoff to change his mind, telling him everything the man already knew regarding his son's behaviour. Geoff had agreed on all points, except his latest actions toward Mathew, and rightfully so. Damn that son of his!

He hoped more than anything that after a day or two, Geoff might reconsider his threat. In his heart, he knew he wouldn't; Adam had gone too far this time.

And what of little Mathew? The poor lad was never a thief. If only they could find that damned bridle, then, perhaps…he shuddered. Had something else taken the bridle, just because it could, for its own evil gain? It would certainly make sense; it had worked. Mathew was gone, Geoff was threatening to leave, his son was in danger of losing everybody who had helped him, the business would suffer, and that was its end, that the family should suffer.

He would try again. Tell Geoff his theory. He knew only too well the evil that stalked the family; perhaps he might change his mind and stay. Richard rubbed his forehead. Was this what he was reduced to? Emotional blackmail of a friend? But what if it was the truth? What if that little devil had taken it knowing it would cause all this? He was convinced that it had intelligence. The long debates with Geoff had perhaps convinced him too; after all, how long could their family disasters be called coincidences? When he looked through the archives on his family, bad luck, death, and ruin had plagued them all.

He closed his eyes and turned to face the warm sun. He felt his cheeks become hot and his head and shoulders gently relax. It felt lovely; if only he could stay like this forever. But the sun reminded him of his son's temper, and he felt his shoulders tense once again. What was going to happen to them? It felt like they were falling apart as a family. Was history really repeating itself?

He hadn't seen Adam since yesterday though he wasn't consciously avoiding him. He just didn't want any more confrontations because it might completely sever their father/son relationship. Geoff thought he was an idiot walking on eggshells in his own house just because Adam had a temper. He was right. It was pathetic, but he didn't want to lose his son.

And what of his daughter, Roslyn? He hadn't heard from her in months. He'd left lots of messages on that stupid machine of hers, and on her mobile; he'd even spoken with her secretary, but from his darling daughter, nothing. At this rate, he was beginning to think she didn't exist, God forbid! Was he losing her too? No, he lost her years ago when she moved out to live in Chester, declaring that the country and everyone in it were dead.

He should have been harder on her, and Adam. After their mother was killed, he didn't have the heart to chastise them, deciding they had suffered enough. Discipline went out of the door; he could only shower them with love, and in Rosalyn's case, gifts, any gifts as long as she was happy. They all said he spoilt them; they were right. Now, he had lost them too.

Melancholia was never far away. He wandered slowly around the garden, touching flowers, breathing in their scent, losing himself in memory with each fragrance. Pinching off a sprig of lemon balm, he rubbed it gently. His eyes wandered over the almost bare cherry blossoms that had bloomed early and had now become the victims of the terrible weather. The blooms of pink and white now swished around his feet, caught by the slight breeze; it saddened him that he couldn't have enjoyed them for longer.

He bent to sniff the pungent smell of chives and wondered what Lucy would use them for this year? Every herb he knew grew within this garden. Lucy wouldn't dream of buying; she preferred fresh. He was grateful to her for finishing the garden. If she had listened to him all those years ago, it would be nothing but a cobbled yard with weeds sprouting where now parsley, sage, and many other culinary delights sprang. Geoff had had a hand in it as well of course. The pair of them had enjoyed planning what would go where.

He'd left them to it. This had been his wife's pride and joy. When he'd become Lord Kenward and given full responsibility of the Hall by his father, the first thing Helen had done was clear out all the overgrown weeds and bushes and make it her mission to turn the old walled garden into a haven. Her haven. When she died, he couldn't bring himself to come within its walls for a long time. Years later, after a lot of nagging, he'd been persuaded to allow Lucy to use it. He was very glad he had.

Now he had given her full responsibility of it and it thrived. The transformation over the years had been both brilliant and heartbreaking for him; he wondered if Adam felt the same. He never ventured into his mother's old garden.

He bent to pick a sprig of parsley and suddenly became aware of the figure standing quietly, watching him from the arched doorway. His stomach lurched with panic. Had he somehow summoned it by thinking about it? The sun in his eyes obscured his vision. He quickly straightened up and took a step backward, then grinned. 'Eira!' Walking toward her, he hugged her tightly. 'My dear, how are you?'

Holding her at arm's length, his smile dropped as he saw the lines of tension, the pale skin; she'd changed considerably since he'd last seen her. She looked so tired and fragile, and if it were possible, she seemed to have aged dramatically. Just how old was she?

Taking her cold hand, he slowly walked to the bench and sat, gently pulling her down too. The sunshine was warm on his shoulders, but she looked cold. He took off his jacket and wrapped it around her, noticing how her bones protruded through her blouse. Ignoring her argument that she was all right, he wrapped the jacket tighter around her before changing his mind and insisting she put it on instead, chastising her for not wearing her own. She obliged him, and he knew she was grateful for it. Once settled, she sighed and leant back. For a moment, she closed her eyes and he could tell she was enjoying the comforting warmth; he left her alone, sitting quietly beside her, enjoying the moment of peace himself.

'What's worrying you, Richard?'

Her soft voice broke into his thoughts, surprising him. He turned to see her watching him closely with those piercing green eyes of hers. He shrugged. 'Adam, I suppose.'

He looked away from her knowing stare and focused on the purple basil that sprang up beside the bench.

'I've always known his temper was out of control, but this time he's gone too far. I'm at a loss what to do, Eira. Geoff is right. Mathew should never have been sacked, especially without proof. I'm appalled at this. Should I interfere and risk a further gulf between my son and me? Should I wait to see if he will do the right thing? I know he will eventually, but the longer he leaves it...'

Eira reached for his hand and gently squeezed it. 'You've always known Adam flies off the rails and feels wretched later. I'm sure you're right that he's regretting his action already. This behaviour is all part and parcel of his loyalty to this family. You know he is frightened of letting you down. He's lonely and scared of his new venture, of letting the name Kenward become nothing, mean nothing. He's poured all his hopes, his love, and his energy into those stables, but he is blinded by his fear. He has made all the right decisions and the stables will work, eventually, it's such a shame he can't see the other decisions he's made for himself are a complete mess. Especially ones he's made over his love life. He feels he has so much to make up for...'

'But that's not true, Eira, I forgave him years ago.'

'Yes, I know, but did he forgive himself? His pride, his love, his trust took a huge fall. He can't stop hurting himself and those around him.'

'Damn that bloody woman. She took more than just his money, my money. Ruthless bitch! How can I blame him for falling for such a deceitful woman? She fooled all of us, for a while, except you.'

Eira drew the jacket tighter as a wisp of cool air touched the back of her neck. 'Yes, I knew she was a viper. I should have spoken sooner. Should I blame myself? I do, but blame and guilt can tear a person apart. If you could turn the clock back, if you could change the past, get rid of the burdens you carry, would you? If it meant risking everyone you held dear, innocent lives in your hands, would you do it for the sake of peace?'

He didn't answer her. She was now staring off into space, her eyes glazed over, and he wondered if that question had really been for him. She sounded frightened; it unnerved him. Eira had never been afraid of anything, ever. She was the rock everyone turned to, always had been. For a fleeting moment, a memory entered his head, something about his father. Hadn't he talked about someone called Eira? No, but surely not. That would make her...

No, it had to have been someone else, though she never talked about her own family and he never pushed. Yet, the memory nagged at him; it felt like a black cloud hiding something. He knew it was important, and yet…

Eira squeezed his hand. 'Where were you?'

'I'm sorry I…I can't remember now. I think it had something to do with my father…but I can't remember. Oh well. Couldn't have been important, I suppose. Shall we go inside? Lucy's been baking, as you probably know already. I heard she'd gone down to the village this morning, gossiping no doubt. What was it this week, Adam? Mathew?'

'Actually, it was a bit of both, and this new tenant of yours. Have you seen this mysterious lady whose occupation ranges from anorexic prostitute to hiding murderers and stolen goods according to our local gossips, Hilary and Lucy?'

Richard laughed out loud. He pulled Eira up and putting his arm through hers, he grinned sheepishly. 'I'm sorry, nothing so exciting I'm afraid. Wanted to move away from a city, Liverpool, I believe. Wanted a year off, not sure what she did for a living. Paid a year up front though, which suited both of us, and no, I'm afraid even I haven't had the privilege of her company. Thought I'd give her a week or so before calling on her By the way, are you skiving? It's only four–thirty.'

'Yes, I suppose I am. Headache that wouldn't go away, so I thought a walk would clear it better than a stifling shop.'

Richard grunted and nodded his approval. 'I thought you looked pale. Come on then, tea, scones, and a good old chin-wag should do the trick. If not, I have good old-fashioned painkillers!'

***

Heading toward the kitchen, they fell silent. Eira gripped Richard's arm, hoping he wouldn't notice how much she needed the support. Was it a sign that Richard was remembering? The curse had to be breaking, surely? It would certainly make sense if it were. Her mixed emotions, mostly fear and joy, were hard to contain, but she managed.

She had to meet this new tenant, and meet her soon. Only then would she know for sure if she were the one.

As they stepped into the warm kitchen, she smiled warmly at Lucy and Judith who looked up as they entered. She loved these people and had known them for so long. Longer than she'd liked to remember. All these years of lying and pretending to be someone they could trust. Playing the same game over and over was tiring. Tired of keeping her lonely secrets, wanting so badly to cry out, to tell them everything, but knowing no-one would ever believe her. No-one knew her. If they did, nobody would want to know her; she would be cast out and rightly so. She deserved hell, and hell she'd got.

Richard's voice got her attention and she made an effort to join in. 'So, ladies, what, or who can we talk about?' Richard grinned mischievously and placed a plate of Lucy's biscuits in the centre of the table. Lucy and Judith exchanged glances and immediately stopped doing their jobs and came to sit around the table; they could sense an hour's worth of speculation and gossip, and she tried to join in and ignore the growing anxiety of the new tenant. She caught their glances and the exchanged looks. They knew something was amiss.

***

Adam walked away quickly before he was noticed. He'd watched Eira arrive and had dropped everything and tried to catch her, but for an elderly woman she certainly could move fast. He was surprised to see her walk around to the back of the Hall and head toward his mother's garden. He went there sometimes when he knew no-one was around. He loved to walk around it and touch the flowers, rub the herbs and remember; it was the only place he felt close to her.

He watched as Eira slowed down before stopping at the open doorway. She seemed to be watching someone; he guessed who. From where he stood he couldn't see her face properly, but there seemed to be something about the way she stood that worried him. He edged closer when she walked through the doorway and into the garden.

The only clear memories he had of his mother were in that walled garden. Together they had planted seeds and weeded. He'd ridden his trucks around the cobbled pathways, enjoying the bumping sensation. She had sat, heavily pregnant with Roslyn, laughing at his noises, chasing him between the trees when she could. They planted yellow daffodils in abundance; their vibrant yellow splashed every corner, every border, giving the various greens of the herbs a more interesting look. He would go every March and take one and keep it in his pocket; no-one knew that. March, the month of her death. It often felt like the flowers were mocking her passing, as each year they grew anew. He tried to think of it as their remembrance to her, but it was hard.

He knew Lucy and Geoff had made it a working herb garden, but he wasn't sure if anyone else ever went in there. As he drew closer to the wall, he was surprised to hear his father's voice greeting Eira.

He had avoided him since their awkward meeting and hated himself for it. In fact, right at that moment he hated himself for a lot of things. Mathew. What a bloody mess! He'd give him his job back and apologise, that was the obvious thing to do and the right thing, but his pride had stopped him so far. The new bridle was still missing and he'd noticed other things had gone too. Brushes, a new bucket, one of his new riding whips, all silly things, but it was all adding up.

Mathew had good potential as a jockey. He was great with the horses, though a bit of a daydreamer. Adam tried in his own way to help Mathew get a bit of backbone, wanted him to answer back, like David did from time to time. Show a bit of spark, prove that he could look after himself and then…who knew? Now, it had all gone wrong. Geoff was threatening to leave, and to be honest, he couldn't blame him. He felt like a complete bastard.

He was about to turn back when he heard his name being spoken and it stopped him. Edging closer toward the doorway, he listened and felt much worse from what he heard. The distress he was causing his father was tearing him apart and every muscle in his body wanted to run into the garden and tell him he would make it right. He didn't. Instead, he slowly walked back to the stables, back to his sanctuary where he could try to forget the mess he'd created, for a while at least. His head remained a whirl though, a constant niggling, emotional turmoil of memories. Memories that refused to go away.

***

It was time to live. That was her first thought as she sat bolt upright after another broken sleep filled with nightmares. She felt like a trapped rabbit, but she had the keys to get out. Two days she had sat and listened to every tiny noise, ready to bolt. Two days she had kept the curtains closed, a knife nearby, which was of course absurd, ghosts had nothing physical, only…well, she wasn't sure what ghosts were made up of but whatever it was, she was sure she wouldn't be able to knife it.

For hours, she had sat reliving it over and over again and asking the questions: *Why her? Who was it? Who was the murderer? When had it happened? Why did horrible things happen to her?*

Flinging back the covers, she stormed across the hallway into the bathroom and turned on the shower. She had done this. She had survived and she was a strong woman; her past had proved that. Okay, she had run, a normal reaction for self-preservation; others might have done the same.

An acquaintance once told her, 'Bronwen, to be alive, you have to live, not merely exist.' Sitting here, clutching a knife, frightened of every shadow was not why she'd come to this beautiful cottage. This was not a place just to exist. Was she still a frightened wimp who was so weak that the slightest, okay, actually, rather nasty frightening experience was going to ruin her plans?

'*No!*' She shouted it loudly and smiled; that felt better.

The hot shower helped immensely and she sang loudly, the tension in her shoulders easing slightly now that she'd made a decision. Clad in a large towel, she strode downstairs and unbolted the front door and yanked it open. The clean, fresh air wafted into the hall and she breathed deeply. The sun was out; it looked like a beautiful morning, clean and inviting. The sounds of a bird singing nearby seemed to entice her out and she stood on her porch step listening, enjoying the moment. It felt good to be alive. Now she would live.

Today was the day she would put the villagers out of their misery. She would visit that shop; today she would meet her new neighbours and to hell with what they thought about her. Running back inside, she felt a mixture of nerves and excitement at the prospect. She quickly toasted the last of the loaf which was stale and grimaced as she tried to drink black tea; she definitely needed milk!

Dressed in her jeans, black long-sleeve top, and her black jacket, she put on her black Doc Martens, threw her hair into a quick ponytail, grabbed her purse, and quickly walked out, locking the door behind her. Without thinking too much about it, she headed out into the lane. A quick check proved to her that no-one was lurking about. She glanced once in the direction of the ruins, then firmly turned away and walked with purpose toward the village of Derwen.

CHAPTER SEVEN

ROSE RUBBED THE WOODEN BANISTER idly; her mind wandered to thoughts of Adam, her master, and what she would let him do to her, if only he would. Hearing voices coming from the kitchen, she quickly rubbed harder but gave up after a while when she realised no-one was coming into the hallway. Straining to hear, she recognised Lucy and Judith's voices immediately and heard them mention her mum's friend, Eira.

It was Eira who'd got her this boring job. She'd hated it at first, but decided she could tolerate it most days, as long as Adam was around. Problem was, he stayed down at those stables of his for most of the day so she hardly saw him. She'd have to think about changing that somehow.

As she moved farther up the staircase, she stared at the one closed door she wished was open: Adam's bedroom. The hope that he'd notice her was what got her up in the mornings. That, and the anticipation that he'd actually speak to her, or better still, declare his undying love and ravish her!

The duster moved lazily over the solid dark oak as her mind drifted toward scenes of a lustful nature; all involved Adam. She imagined the solid, dark wood was him as she ran her hand over it. Closing her eyes, she pictured his firm, muscular body quivering as her hands moved slowly, teasingly. She was confident that she could make him hard; he was a man, after all, and the boys in the village told her she was good.

Her fingers caressed the banister while her other hand dropped the duster and her fingers gently teased her hardened nipples through her cotton uniform. Moving lower, she pressed firmly between her legs, enjoying the sudden rush of excitement, and gently began to move them rhythmically.

'*Rose!*'

Her eyes snapped open and she grabbed the discarded duster just in time before Judith appeared at the bottom of the stairs.

'Haven't you finished that yet? Hurry up, please. I'd like you to start on the silver next.'

Rose smiled weakly and nodded. She felt dizzy and her heart was beating so fast she felt sick. She didn't trust herself to say anything so she turned her back on Judith who hovered in the hallway and began to rub the banisters vigorously whilst holding tightly to stop herself from falling. At last she heard Judith walk away, back into the kitchen, and she collapsed onto the stairs.

That was too close. What had come over her? If she had been caught doing that, it didn't bear thinking about. She knew Judith didn't think much of her, which was fine. Rose thought she was an old hag anyway who was in desperate need of sex herself. Yuk! She grimaced at the thought of Judith spread-eagled on a bed with some poor bugger grunting away on top of her. She glanced over at Adam's door and sighed; at least they didn't know that she had been inside his bedroom once and imagined their lovemaking on his bed.

***

Bronwen's heart banged against her chest as she walked toward the shop. From the corner of her eye, she was aware of two old men watching her approach. They stood outside the small pub but they stopped their conversation and openly stared. Their observations unnerved her, and she felt the heat rise in her neck and up into her cheeks, but she kept her eyes fixed firmly on the ground, swallowed hard, and as she reached the shop, she shot them a glance and a weak smile. They in turn nodded and resumed their conversation; she had no doubt that she was now their topic.

On climbing the one step, she reached for the handle of the door and was dismayed to find it closed. Damn it! Frustrated and feeling embarrassed, she could feel the stares burning into her back. She felt such a fool.

She had to do something. She couldn't just stand staring at a closed door forever. Biting her lower lip, she glanced behind her and was thankful to see the two men disappear inside the pub as it opened for business early. In the small cottage next door she noticed a middle-aged woman was loitering in her front garden, pretending to be weeding or something. Her blatant nosiness was so obvious, it made her smile. Was she really that interesting?

Feeling a mixture of emotions--scared, amused, anxious, annoyed at the inconvenience--she decided to grab the bull by the horns. It was what she'd decided to do, wasn't it? Bronwen walked with purpose across the road toward the woman. She noticed that her eyes darted nervously around at having been caught. This small gesture helped her nerves.

'Hello. Could you possibly tell me when the shop opens, please?' She noticed her voice quivered slightly, but she drew herself up straighter and looked the woman in the eye.

The woman frowned and glanced away toward the shop. 'It should be open already…perhaps Eira is round the back…in her garden.' She pointed to a high wooden gate at the side of the hedge.

Looking toward where the woman pointed, Bronwen nodded. 'Okay, thanks.'

'You're the new tenant, then?'

Bronwen turned back to face the woman.

'It's a bit quiet for a single woman on her own up there at Oak Cottage?' The woman's gaze slowly travelled over her before finishing back at her face. She gave her a little smile of encouragement.

Taking a deep breath, she answered as calmly as she could. 'Yes, I am the new tenant, and it's a beautiful cottage, isn't it?' Not waiting for a reply, she quickly continued, 'I don't feel lonely up there all by myself, I like it. Having lived in a busy city for so long, it's nice to have space, you know?'

The woman's eyes widened. 'Oh, erm…yes, I…'

Bronwen turned to go. 'Well, nice to meet you and thanks. I'll go to the shop another time…'bye.'

She turned and walked briskly, needing to get away as heat rose up her neck and into her cheeks. Bronwen headed toward the old chapel. Keeping her head down, she knew that if she turned round the woman would still be staring after her, her mouth open in aston- ishment. Bronwen smiled to herself. Her hands shook, but it felt good, her first confrontation.

She heard the faint mumblings from inside the pub as she passed and glanced up at the stilled sign. It really was as worn and old as she had first thought when she'd arrived. Her heart jumped as she managed to work out the outline of a castle ruin and above it, The Old Castle. Moving swiftly, she picked up pace, almost running away. From that sign, that picture, knowing now what it was. She didn't want those memories of that place to come. She didn't want to remember the tower and what dark forces lingered there.

She reached the chapel and climbed the four steps to its doors. Locked. She leant against them and allowed her heartbeat to slow down. Looking back toward the village she realised it was actually a steeper incline than she had first thought. Something else struck her: Where were all the people? It was so quiet, it unnerved her. Perhaps everyone in the country piled into the pub?

From her vantage point, she cast her gaze over everything. The woman had gone, but she could still feel eyes upon her. Were they watching from behind lace curtains whilst gossiping on the telephone? Nothing would surprise her, especially after what she'd witnessed. Perhaps it was a ghost village? That would just be her luck!

The murdered child entered her thoughts, as she knew she would. Had she lived in the village? Had the village existed then? Some of the cottages looked quite old, but perhaps not quite as old as that castle. As she leant against the chapel doors, it occurred to her that she was okay now about the ghost. She'd freaked out, which was understandable; it was probably the most natural thing to do, surely? She could accept it. She didn't particularly like what had happened to her, but she felt a bit different, now that she had had time to think about it all. In a strange way, she felt honoured to have had the privilege of seeing a ghost. How many people could say that?

And there was something else. Somehow she knew the child was not there to hurt her. And in that instant of realisation, the fear left her and something else took its place: sorrow. A feeling so deep it felt like a knife piercing her heart. That poor child. How could someone do that? What evil would…? But of course, she knew what evil could.

She had survived such evil. Was that why this child had shown herself? It made some sort of sense. Perhaps they had connected on some level of empathy and yet, she had a niggling feeling, almost like déjà vu. Every bone in her body told her she had never been here before, but seeing that old picture above the pub had made her feel something. Like a dream she couldn't quite remember, but knew it was there.

A loud click made her jump and she turned toward the sound; the large chapel door she had been leaning against had clicked open and now stood slightly ajar. Surely it had been locked? Hesitating briefly, she pushed on the iron handle and managed to open it farther, though the door gave a loud creak and was very stiff. Perhaps this chapel wasn't used very often?

Inside it was a typical old chapel with white plaster walls and rows of wooden pews on either side of a short aisle. A few tables with various dead flowers and pamphlets lined the far wall, leading up to a small organ with a stool neatly placed next to it. The altar seemed nothing more than a large chest with a white, faded cloth covering it; a pair of empty candle holders stood on either side of a sad-looking cross. It was wood, with a metal Jesus hanging forlornly from it. Someone had once placed a flower underneath it; it had now long since dried up. The whole place had an empty feel about it, and she shivered. Four large windows on either side of the chapel allowed light into the building, but didn't help the feeling of being completely alone. It strengthened her previous thought that the place wasn't used often, and she wondered why.

She felt like an intruder and left, slamming the door shut. She wasn't a religious person and never went to church, except for a christening a very long time ago. She turned her attention toward the lane leading out of the village. She had to get away from this sad building. She felt sorry for it; regardless of what it was used for, it was neglected, so with a quick glance toward the village, knowing her every move was being monitored judging by the twitching of curtains, she turned her back and headed farther along the road.

The house on her left looked empty; she couldn't see any cars, but it was obviously occupied at some point. What also surprised her was that she could see toys lined up on one windowsill, and a child's bike stood against the house. She hadn't seen any children since she'd arrived. It felt good to know there were some nearby and that the park was used; perhaps it wasn't such a ghost town after all!

She knew what it was that was making her feel this way. It was the silence. Even here, it the middle of the day, in a village not too many miles from a busy town, it was so quiet. She just wasn't used to it yet. She hadn't realised until now just how much she had relied on other people's company and at the same time, hated it. When other people were around, it had made her feel safe, able to hide and blend in. Here, she was alone, nowhere to hide, nowhere to blend in and if someone tried anything, who would help her?

She walked briskly past the last of the houses, and carried on for a few more minutes, then stopped to catch her breath. The narrow lane continued for miles; she could see it winding away over the hills and dips. A couple of small cottages dotted the landscape, a farmhouse, and a few barns, but no other sign of life except fields, cows, and bloody big trees!

She stared up at the gigantic tree that stood proudly in the field next to where she'd stopped. A nearby gate stood ajar, so she wandered over to it and stepped into the field. Up close, the trunk alone had to be at least four times the width of her. She tried to wrap her arms around it; she didn't get close to a third of it. Of course, she knew nothing about trees, but it looked familiar. Wasn't this the same kind that had circled the old castle? An oak tree, but this one was much bigger and older looking.

She hugged it again. The bark felt rough beneath her cheek and strangely warm. 'I'm glad they didn't knock you down when they built the road.' She looked up into the branches and sighed. What had this tree witnessed over the years? If only it could talk, she was sure it would be able to tell her tales of how the village had changed over generations. The invention of cars, the change in fashion, the different houses…

The shift came so quickly she wasn't sure if she'd imagined it at first. Hugging the tree, it had seemed as if everything around her had stopped and become still. She released the trunk and pushed herself away from it but her movements dragged, as if she was in slow motion and the air around her felt thick and hard to breathe. Her head spun and she lost her balance, collapsing onto the damp grass, she gazed up into the branches. She became aware that her hand hurt and she could feel blood, but knew it wasn't a bad cut. She kept her eyes fixed firmly on the branches above her head to try to stop the spinning vertigo that was making her feel queasy.

People. She became aware of voices first, and then she could see them in the distance. It was an effort to move her head toward the images, as if her whole body was heavy, but she managed to turn her head enough to see the women. One of them laughed and another woman playfully pushed her. What was happening?

Their long skirts blew in the breeze, as did their dirty pinafores. Each woman wore a white cap on her head, and there were four of them, all with a basket. Something about them looked odd. She tried calling out, but her mouth wouldn't open. Her throat constricted as a waft of smoke choked her and she gagged, trying to catch her breath as the air became thick with it. She became aware of small buildings nearby, shacks with thatched roofs. People bustled about; all ignored her.

Then she saw them, men on horses, all riding toward her at full gallop. Would they see her in time? If they didn't stop, she would be trampled to death. But all she could do was watch as they approached with growing horror as it dawned on her what was so strange: It was the way they were dressed.

Her limbs would not move. Her eyes remained fixed on the group of horsemen. A noise escaped her lips; she was going to die. No-one was going to save her. No-one cared about her. And then they were gone.

She didn't know how long she sat shivering beneath the tree. Her body refused to move from her sanctuary as her senses tried to understand what she had witnessed. She was in a field, nothing more, a field with a large oak tree. When at last she felt able to stand, she leant against the tree for support and clenched her bloodied hand. Wiping the blood off, using the wet grass, she slowly wiped the rain-sodden hand over her face. The cold water felt good against her burning cheeks. She rummaged in her jacket pocket for a tissue. She blew her nose and began to slowly walk back to the road.

Her legs felt jelly-like but she managed to reach the gate, then stumbled onto the narrow lane. She turned and looked back toward the lone tree, except it wasn't alone. Farther 'round the field she saw another large oak and in the next field there was another. From where she stood, it looked as if they were in a curved line with each other. Turning 'round, she went on her tiptoes and managed to just see over the hedge into the next field and saw two more.

A loud hoot from a car made her jump. She quickly moved to the side of the road to allow the mini to pass. The elderly couple glared at her from within and their small terrier yapped its disapproval as the car passed slowly, the couple watching her openly.

Bronwen viewed its departure toward the village with regret, as the need for human contact was very strong; real human contact and not some dream or whatever her brain was trying to ignore, the possibility that it had happened again: another time-slip; another ghostly encounter? But, she hadn't really been afraid, not of the women anyway. She'd felt a strange sense of belonging. Only the horsemen had frightened her. The power they held was unnerving, yet she couldn't possibly know that. Forcing her legs to move, she slowly headed back toward Derwen, where at last she saw the slate rooftops. At least she was in the right century.

Twice now she had been shown another world, another time. Why her? A fleeting thought of insanity was quickly brushed aside. She wasn't hallucinating, not anymore, she was almost sure of it. Was she being haunted for some reason? Did ghosts pick who they troubled or was she one of these medium people she'd seen on television who could see the dead? She wasn't sure she liked that idea at all.

Clutching her head, she ran her fingers through her hair, pulled the tie out and let her hair fly loose. The tension in her skull eased slightly but the burning questions that filled her head wouldn't go away. Unless... She should do some investigations of her own. Yes, why not? Someone important had once lived in those ruins by the size of it. There would be records. She could piece together the facts. Would that stop the apparitions? Would it help the child? Grabbing her hair, she piled it on top of her head again and began to feel a little more positive as she wandered back into the village.

***

Mathew remained crouched behind the hedge and watched the woman walk slowly back into the village. She staggered a bit and he wondered if she was drunk? Why had she acted so weird around that old oak tree? It was just a bloody tree, but she'd looked terrified. He stood up and, checking she was gone, climbed over the gate and looked at it. Strange really that he'd never climbed it, or any of the others that surrounded the village.

Perhaps it was the stories his Aunt Jenny used to tell them about witches and evil curses. She used to say they had hanged a witch from one of the trees, and by the next morning, other oak trees had sprung up and surrounded the village. The witch's curse. He smiled to himself; how could a tree hurt a village? It was just a tree, wasn't it?

He stood by the gate. It was just a tree, but he suddenly didn't want to walk toward it. Feeling daft, he tried to leave, but he couldn't move. There was something by the tree. Beneath its dark branches, within its shadow, something dark, menacing. Someone was there, watching him. He felt his flesh crawl and his stomach clenched with fear as his senses told him a fraction of a second before his eyes confirmed it. The feet did not touch the ground.

CHAPTER EIGHT

Eira wearily unlocked the shop door and had just managed to walk away from it when Martha, another local gossip who lived in the village, came rushing in, cheeks glowing, high as a kite on adrenaline. 'I've seen her, Eira! I spoke to her. Where were you? She wanted to buy something. Young girl, and pretty too. Lovely hair. I wonder why she has it all tied back in a tight ponytail? Doesn't suit her. So, finally, eh, she comes out from that cottage. What do you think took her so long eh?'

Eira glanced at her beaming face and shrugged. She was much too tired for this banter and looked out of her shop window. Martha noticed her glance and smiled. 'She walked off toward John's farm. That's three miles away, though. Do you think she'll go that far? She went into the old chapel.'

Eira stopped putting on her apron and looked directly at Martha, who was looking very proud of herself. 'Really? Well, there's no harm in that, is there? I thought it'd be locked?'

'No, sometimes he forgets, although she didn't stay in there long. Do you think she's religious?'

Eira grinned. 'How on earth should I know that? If she is, you'll no doubt see her at the next service.'

They all knew she didn't go to chapel and some of the women had their own opinions about that, but she didn't care. Sometimes at night, when she knew no-one was awake, she'd creep along and place a fresh flower on the altar.

Before Martha could reply, the worst gossip of all, Elizabeth, came in all excited. She looked a little deflated when she saw Martha, but they drew together like spies exchanging juicy bits of information.

Eira sighed and wandered behind the counter and began cutting up various cheeses. No doubt Hilary and Lucy would hear of all this soon enough and join the gossip.

'Have you seen her?' Elizabeth began. 'I watched her walk past the park and then she—'

'Well, I spoke to her. Seemed a nice young girl, but of course, you never know these days…girls today?'

'Honestly, for God's sake!'

Martha and Elizabeth both jumped and turned toward Eira who stood glowering at them. 'Anyone would think this poor woman is evil, the way you two go on. You'd have her as some murderess, hung, drawn, and quartered before she's settled. Just leave it.'

The two women huffed a bit. 'Well really, Eira, surely you don't believe we're that bad? I mean…oh, there she is!'

Eira was forgotten. They turned as one and watched Bronwen walk toward the shop. 'I suppose while I'm here I'll have some of your lovely ham.' Martha called over her shoulder.

Eira wasn't listening. She needed to sit down; her legs felt wobbly and butterflies fought to get out of her stomach. She felt the room spin and pretended to reach for something off the floor so that she could put her head between her legs. Her back didn't like the uncomfortable stretch and she eased herself over and sat down in a chair for a second to catch her breath, just as the door opened.

***

Bronwen couldn't ignore the women in the shop because they stood motionless, staring at her as she entered. After her experience in the field, nothing would surprise her if she opened this shop door and a skeleton stood behind the counter! Not that she'd enjoy that experience, either. Hoping her stomach could take the pressure, she licked her lips and opened the shop door wider.

She jerked at the sound of the tinkling bell above it and quickly looked around the shop. It was bigger than she had expected, with three aisles to her left, each of which seemed to have four shelves. The walls were stacked to the brim, and in the far corner she could see two deep freezers. The two women, one she recognised as being the woman in the garden, now watched her with open curiosity. They stood before a long, chilled counter which housed various meats, and farther along, she noticed cheeses. An elderly woman was sitting behind the counter staring at her with an odd expression which she quickly hid and slowly stood up.

'My dear, welcome. You must be the new tenant. I'm Eira.'

'Erm…yes, I'm—' Before she had time to finish, the door burst open behind her and two boys came rushing in, pushing past her rudely, their goal the sweet aisle. She was so surprised she stood gawking at them. Children! Somehow this desperate madness to reach their sweets made her feel so much better.

'You naughty boys! What do you say to this poor woman you've pushed past?'

Eira's tone was playful but firm, and the boys hung their heads in shame. 'Sorry.'

Bronwen felt herself blush. 'Oh, that's fine, I'll just…' Grabbing a basket from the pile next to the door, she hurried away, up the farthest aisle to get away from all the prying eyes. She heard Eira tut at the children and heard the bell tinkle their escape. She knew the two women hadn't left.

She tried to ignore the obvious silence and inspected the shelves of food. That estate agent was right; it did have quite a lot of stuff, for a village shop. She piled her basket with tinned goods, a fresh loaf, butter, eggs, and some naughty goodies, and peeped into the freezers.

Grabbing some frozen meals, she headed back to the counter and the waiting women. Leaving the basket on the top, she went for some orange juice and two bottles of red wine. 'I'll have some of that honey roast ham and I'll try some of that cheese, please.'

Her eyes locked with Eira's for a moment longer than was comfortable. The old woman was looking at her in such a peculiar way, Bronwen found herself about to ask if she was all right, but the moment passed and Bronwen quickly looked away.

'They didn't hurt you too badly, did they?'

Bronwen was fiddling with her purse; her head jerked up when Eira spoke. 'What?'

Eira finished cutting the slices of ham and indicated the boys outside.

'Erm, no, I'm fine, thanks.'

'So, what's your name?' The woman from the garden stepped forward and smiled. 'Do you like Oak Cottage, then?'

Bronwen blushed; she had answered these questions, a little harshly, perhaps, and she could see the woman was enjoying making her feel uncomfortable. *Bitch!* 'My name is Bronwen Mortimer. I believe we met earlier?'

The woman looked away toward her friend and widened her eyes. Bronwen turned back to her basket, but the woman persisted. 'I'm Martha, that's Elizabeth, and Eira, of course. You come from a city? Hated it, did you?'

Bronwen turned and opened her mouth, but it was Eira who spoke. 'Now, now, ladies, leave her alone. You'll scare my customers away with your tittle-tattle. Here's your ham, Martha, I'll see you again soon.' Eira handed over the wrapped meat.

Martha thankfully took the hint, paid, and flounced out of the shop, quickly followed by Elizabeth who slammed the door shut. From the shop they could hear them chattering away as they crossed the street.

Neither of them spoke until the door of Martha's cottage had shut. They both heaved sighs of relief, which made them giggle.

'Oh dear, I hope they haven't scared you.' Stepping closer to the counter, Eira peeped over. 'You look a little pale, dear.'

'Wow! Is everyone like that?' She felt flustered at being noticed.

But Eira smiled warmly and began cutting up more ham. 'Thankfully, no. How many slices, four, five?' Ignoring Bronwen's answer of five, she cut two more pieces. 'On the house as a welcome present! Now for the cheese. This much?'

Bronwen nodded and went over to a small shelf with various jams and marmalades on it. They looked homemade and wondered if Eira made them.

'Yes, I do.'

'What?' Bronwen swung round, bringing a jar with her.

'I said, I do make them.'

'How did you know…?' Placing the jar of blackcurrant jam on the counter, she waited as Eira counted everything up. How was she going to carry all this back to the cottage?

'I have a few boys who help me out; they can bring them to your cottage for you if you like?'

She stared at the elderly woman. How did she know what she was thinking? It should have been freaking her out, but it wasn't. Something about Eira felt comfortably familiar. As if she'd known her, like an old grandma she'd forgotten about, which was weird, but comforting. Besides, after her ordeal, anything else felt lame! 'Yes, sure, I'll take two bags. If someone could bring the other two sometime today, that would be great. Did I have any change left over from my last order, which, by the way, thank you, it was most welcome.'

Eira nodded. 'You did indeed, so no charge today. We'll call it even.'

Eira watched as the young woman placed the things she wanted to carry into the bags. Every cell in her body screamed out to rush around the counter and hug her. It was true. The time had come, a second chance. Here she was, standing less than five feet away. The one who could save her; the one who could save them all. Did Bronwen feel it too? Looking carefully at her face, she looked for signs of recognition, but there was nothing. But when Bronwen looked up, she saw it: her eyes. The eyes never changed. It was the same ocean blue. The same eyes that held so much pain and suffering. The eyes she remembered only too well.

Bronwen began to feel uncomfortable as she quickly put the essentials into two bags. The woman was watching her closely and something started to feel very wrong. She had felt relatively okay a moment ago. The woman, Eira, seemed friendly, but now her skin felt like it was crawling, her throat felt tight, and her skin felt flushed. She had to get out of the shop and away from the old woman.

Finally looking up, she noticed Eira had begun busying herself with her other groceries; she looked uncomfortable too. 'So…erm… I'll see you again. When will these be delivered?' She indicated the remaining two bags.

'Some time later on this afternoon, dear, once they've finished their homework. Don't worry about a thing.'

Thanking her, Bronwen left the shop and almost ran around the corner. The last hour all seemed out of this world. What was it about this place and these people that was extraordinary? She slowed down once the shop was out of sight and almost collapsed as a wave of dizziness swept over her. Dropping the bags, she put her head down and took deep breaths, almost laughing at how absurd she must look.

Minutes passed and she began to feel better. At least no-one had seen her. Yet again, she felt completely alone. If her encounters at the strange shop and its people had all been a dream, she would believe it. The strangest dream she could ever remember having, but the people looked familiar, especially the shop owner; the way she'd behaved had been odd and it made her feel uncomfortable.

Her head a whirl of questions, she picked up her shopping and carried on until she stood opposite the entrance to Kenward Hall. The big, black gates were wide open and she wandered over to them. She placed the bags against the high wall, and slowly eased herself down and sat facing the afternoon sun, enjoying its warmth; she felt completely drained. Were strange forces at work here? Battling over her body and mind? At this moment in time, she didn't care; they could have her mind and body if only someone would explain what the hell was going on.

She tried to think about it all rationally. The people she had seen from the tree had obviously been ghosts or an illusion. The article she'd read about time-slips happening in Liverpool, surely they could happen anywhere? Was that it? Was this area known for time-slips? If that were the case, she had certainly had her fill. She was beginning to think the country was a hazardous place!

Obviously, the logical thing to do would be to do research, but where? Shrewsbury? Ludlow? The thought excited and frightened her. What would she find? Did she feel ready to go that far away, on her own? She'd hated being around people for so long, but since moving, it had become clear just how safe she felt being near people, which was ironic. She would go to Shrewsbury and try her luck, but when?

With her eyes shut, she rubbed her forehead and down her neck. Rotating her shoulders slowly, she felt the tension ease as her muscles clicked and popped. She had to get answers about the village, there was nothing else for it, and whether she felt comfortable or not, this Eira might be able to help. Or she'd find out if they'd met before, someone from her childhood, perhaps; she shuddered at the thought.

'What the bloody hell do you think you're doing? This isn't a fucking squat, move on!'

Her head jerked up and her heart missed a beat seeing a man scowling at her from his car, his window wound down. She didn't move. Her eyes remained locked on his, waiting to see what he'd do. She knew her keys to the cottage were in her pocket. Could she get to them quickly if he made a move? She was sure she could.

'Waiting for something? Perhaps you want me to help you get off your fat arse?' The sarcasm dripped from every word.

She edged herself up, using the wall to keep herself steady. Bending down, she yelped as one of the bags snapped and its contents spilled out onto the road. She ran after a rolling tin of beans and pushed the loaf and the jar of pasta sauce back into the bag, overwhelmingly grateful it hadn't smashed. She heard a grunt and looked up to see the man still watching her with a smirk on his arrogant face. She cracked. 'You arrogant bastard! Instead of sitting on your own fat arse, perhaps it wouldn't be too much trouble to help me?'

She saw his eyes widen and immediately bit her lip. He was angry. She clutched her door key. She was breathing heavily, waiting for a fight.

He remained seated and just grinned. 'Greedy little bitches should learn not to carry too much. Now bugger off! Your sort bring down the tone of the place.'

Before she could reply, he put the car into gear and sped off, skidding over the cattle grid and flattening her cheese in the process. *Bastard!* She'd been looking forward to trying that.

The Land Rover disappeared from view and she turned to survey the damage. Squashed cheese, a few dented tins; not as bad as it could have been, but tears of anger, relief, and shock fell anyway, and she was shaking.

Horrible, horrible man. Hateful, arrogant pig! Had to be a Kenward. Rich, spoilt, arrogant pig! Thank God she hadn't introduced herself when she'd arrived, if that was what was waiting for her. Couldn't be Sir Richard though, could he? She'd expected someone old. Leaving the squashed cheese, she managed to get everything back into the broken bag and carried it in front of her, dangling the other bag from her arm. It was uncomfortable, but nothing would induce her to stay a minute longer; the quicker she got back to the cottage, the better. *Her* cottage, she quickly and defiantly corrected herself and strode purposefully away from Kenward gates.

***

Adam slammed on his brakes and came to a sudden full stop. He knew he was out of sight of the gates, but he looked anyway; he couldn't see them. What the hell was wrong with him? He'd recognişed the shopping bags from Eira's shop and knew instantly who the woman was. When she hadn't moved as he'd driven up to the gates, his first thought had been how beautiful she looked sitting in the sun. The warmth adding a pink tinge to her cheeks with wisps of her golden hair playing around her cheekbones. The rest of her hair was hidden in a loose ponytail and he couldn't help but wish she'd had it loose. He'd wondered if she was asleep and if he'd been honest with himself, he probably could have watched her for a long time.

Then he'd remembered the cottage. *His* cottage! And this woman had taken it for a year. Beautiful she might be, but an annoyance he could do without. It had been no surprise to him when she'd argued back, and that language! Although she hadn't sounded as if she came from Liverpool, she didn't have an accent. What a lovely mouth, small and petite, until she opened it and the fury came out. And those eyes, such a beautiful deep blue. The problem was, although she'd behaved like a cat ready to fight back, he'd frightened her.

He put the car into gear; the guilt wouldn't go away. He'd overreacted with Mathew and everything was turning bad, but he would make amends as soon as he could. He knew he'd frightened Mathew and hated that, although he didn't really know what he could do about that, unless everyone expected him to tiptoe around the boy, and he wouldn't do that; the boy had to toughen up.

This woman, though. He'd no right to behave the way he had. He was coming back from the farm, looking for Mathew to apologise and ask him to return, but his parents hadn't seen him for a while. Their attitude toward him had been cold and hostile, nothing he didn't deserve, but it had hurt. Then, seeing that woman, beautiful as she was, he'd taken his anger and hurt out on her.

He swung the car round, drove back to the gates, and got out; she wasn't there. He wasn't surprised and looked toward the cottage; he knew where she had gone. He saw the squashed cheese. Should he go after her? And say what? Apologise? Explain why he'd behaved like a tyrant? Would she listen or would it frighten her to see him striding up the path toward the cottage? He knew the answer was yes and he hated how it made him feel. Leaving the cheese, he got back into his car and headed back toward the stables, wishing that his horrible life would change for the better. He had to start somewhere; he had to find Mathew.

CHAPTER NINE

'ANNE. MY LADY…ANNE.' THE VOICE was sharp, cold. 'Come on, child, we must hurry, you cannot keep your future husband waiting. Come now, hurry.'

Hitching her long skirt up a little higher, Anne kept her eyes on the stone corridor floor, trying to ignore the butterflies that beat violently against her stomach. She had already vomited once this morning and had gratefully accepted a small glass of mulled wine in the hopes it would help her nerves and freshen her breath.

She saw people stopping to watch her progress and sensed the hostility toward her. She desperately wanted to pause and talk with these people with a desire that they'd not see her as any threat. She quickly glanced at her cousin, but the woman was already walking ahead of her, head held high. She knew what her cousin's answer would be if she asked to stop for a moment to speak with the servants. Margaret tolerated the servants as much as she'd tolerated having her in her household. As long as they remained useful, all was well and good.

Now, Margaret's haste in wishing her gone was undeniable once she had been given the reassurance that William didn't require her lands; only Anne and a small dowry. But she felt no ill will; she was just as excited about the fact that she was leaving, though she managed to hide it better.

Margaret and her husband had become her guardians after her own mother passed away ten years before. She'd never known her father. Over the years she'd often wondered why Margaret had insisted she

115

come and stay in their home. Aged eleven, she hadn't considered any-thing other than love as the motive, but as she'd grown, it had become clear that love was not the reason. Her mother's land, her home, the servants, they had all become the property of Margaret and Philip; the only complication was Anne, and they had never let her forget it.

None of it mattered now. Suitors had been few and far between, as her foster parents knew that to relieve themselves of their ward would be to relieve themselves of their newly acquired land. They hadn't counted on William.

Oh William! How she loved him, but she would never tell. She kept her secret hidden in case it was used against her. She pretended to be submissive, allowing them to believe she was marrying against her own wishes, to continue believing they had full control over her, when in fact, they did not.

William had visited with his wife on many occasions, but when she'd died in childbirth, he had withdrawn into himself. Margaret and Philip had slowly coaxed him out of his shell. Together they had dined, celebrated, ridden, hunted, always believing he was too old for her; or he was indifferent. They had been wrong.

Now, standing outside the small chapel with the woman she loathed, nothing could diminish her happiness. She would be free. Free to love, to have children she could love and spoil. Taking a deep breath, she straightened her skirt and clung onto the small posy of wildflowers. Her heart skipped a beat as Margaret opened the door and walked inside. She followed slowly, her eyes remained fixed firmly on the tall man standing watching her, a smile lighting up his face. Her future husband held the hand of a young girl whose face did not light up as she approached. She only frowned, her eyes full of hate.

***

Eira woke with a start. She tried to hold on to the images in her head, but within minutes, they were fading away. She wasn't sure how she felt about the dream, doubted that she would ever make up her mind, and had to resign herself to that fact. The people she dreamt of would never be far away anyway.

She rubbed her eyes and arched her back, hoping to ease the tension. This constant feeling of unease had plagued her for so long she couldn't remember when her life had been free of care and worries, pain and sorrow. Perhaps when she had been a child? Her mother had loved her completely but hard as she tried, she couldn't bring forth the image of her mother's face or a memory of that time. She only had the sure knowledge of being loved once.

A tear crept down her cheek, remembering that it really was so very long ago since she had played as a child. She craved a memory, to relive something of when she had been innocent. She could not believe that such evil, dark forces had blighted her whole life. But, this had been part of the curse, her ordeal. Never to know a happy thought, never to remember what had once been before that fateful time of her life when it had all gone wrong. When she had made it all go wrong. This was her penance. The villagers were cruel beyond measure.

Pulling the shawl tighter around her shoulders, she silently wept for what she'd lost. No-one heard her cries. No-one but the growing shadows…and the dead.

***

It had been over four hours since she'd rushed through her front door, slamming it shut and bolting it, just in case. She had listened intently for any sign that he would follow her, but all she heard was her breath and her heartbeat. As she'd walked home, she had had visions of him turning round and racing after her. The last few steps, she'd been convinced that at any moment he would come tearing round the bend, but he hadn't. Was that disappointment she felt? Surely not, unless only to tell him exactly what she thought of him, the spoilt pig!

She caught a glimpse of her reflection in the hallway mirror and chuckled to herself. That had been an exciting finish to a terrifying, out-of-this-world day! Where had all that venom come from? She'd never have thought she could answer back with such wanton hatred. It frightened her. She was almost sorry he hadn't tried it on, to see if she could fight as well.

Glancing at the clock, she realised how late it was. It was getting dark outside. Would he come? A horrible thought struck her: Did he have a key? She double-checked the bolts were still in place. For the first time since moving in, she regretted not having a phone. She'd made the decision not to have one reconnected as she didn't have anyone to talk to, but now, perhaps, it was time to think about a mobile one, just in case?

She walked into the kitchen to fix herself some tea and noticed that the gate was hanging open. Hadn't she closed that behind her? She bit her lower lip and tried to remember. Surely, she would have heard someone outside? Creeping to the front door, she eased the two bolts across, turned the key and peeped outside, ready to slam the door if anyone should jump out. On seeing the two bags propped against the porch wall, her shoulders sagged with relief; in all the excitement, she'd completely forgotten that they were bringing the rest of her groceries. When had they come? She hadn't heard anyone knocking.

She carried the frozen goods into the kitchen, selected a chicken curry and put the rest into the small freezer. While it was cooking, she found her lease and checked it again to be sure everything was in order. As for that vile little man, she hoped she'd never see him again.

***

Rose stood motionless outside the study door. The tray she was carrying felt heavy in her hands, but she couldn't move. From inside she could hear Sir Richard and Adam arguing. Her heart skipped a beat and she swallowed hard; bloody hell, she looked a mess.

118

It was nearly seven o'clock. She should have left an hour ago, but with one job after another not being up to Judith's satisfaction, she was late. It was Friday night, party night in Shrewsbury. She should have been meeting her friends by now, slamming back shots and eyeing up the good-looking men; this boring village had none. Only Adam, and he was just behind this door, and she looked dishevelled and smelt of the kitchen and sweat. Damn that bloody woman!

Looking around her, she placed the supper tray carefully on a polished side table and quickly ran her hands through her hair. She pulled out her pink lipstick triumphantly from her apron and applied it expertly without a mirror. Undoing the top button on her white blouse, she picked up the tray and went to knock on the closed door. Something in their tone stopped her.

'What the hell do you think you were doing?' Sir Richard's voice boomed from inside. 'She's my bloody tenant, not yours...oh I do know how much you hate the fact, but there it is.'

'Yes, I know that all right, I think you've made that perfectly clear. I know I was in the wrong, damn it. I'll do something to make amends with the woman, buy her some more cheese or something.'

'What is this to you, a joke? You can't treat people any damned way you please, Adam. As for Mathew—'

'Yes, wondered when he'd be brought up. Well, yes, I hold my hands up to him too. I tried looking for him today, but only got a cold reception off his parents.'

'What the hell do you expect? Your temper has gone too far lately. I hope you can control yourself long enough until the May Ball or nobody will come.'

Rose heard a chair scraped back and heard Sir Richard sigh loudly. She heard someone, possibly Adam, walk away from the door and heard the tinkle of glass as drinks were poured from the decanter. She was desperate to go in but felt torn between seeing Adam and attempting to rub past him while she placed the tray on the table, and wanting to hear more about this tenant and the Ball.

'By the way, those gates could do with a lick of paint if you're going to go ahead with this stupid May thing. I hadn't noticed just how neglected they looked until I stopped next to them.'

'I'll deal with those gates as and when. In the meantime, I think it might be a good idea if you looked on Bronwen's invitation as a kind of—'

'You're not seriously considering inviting her to the Ball? We don't even know who she is and besides, what I heard coming out of her mouth today, she has very low standards.'

'You bloody snob! You said yourself that you behaved wrongly, you admit that, so I can only assume that you gave as good as you got? Besides, she *is* our new tenant and she should be invited. You can get to know her better at the Ball.'

'You smug bastard. If you want to invite that wench then so be it, but don't expect me to take the invitation round to humbly beg her to come. She can rot before I speak to her again!'

'But you said you'd make amends.'

Rose managed to jump back just in time as Adam flung open the door and strode past her without a glance, his face a picture of thunder, a beautiful god. 'Good evening…Adam,' she whispered as he took the stairs two at a time before disappearing from view. With a sigh of regret, she knocked softly and went into the warm study. Moving a forgotten newspaper, she placed the tray of scones and pot of tea, which was probably stewed by now, onto the worn table. 'Will there be anything else, sir?'

Sir Richard sat staring into the fire and didn't answer straight-away; he only glanced quickly at the tray and acknowledged her presence.

She turned and walked back toward the door before jumping as a loud roar from behind her made her turn. Sir Richard was laughing. He was frantically wiping tears from his face as he chuckled loudly.

'Are you all right, sir?' Rose felt uneasy. She'd never been in this situation before.

He attempted to reply, but only managed to nod his head and wave his hand toward the door. She quickly turned and fled, shutting it firmly behind her. His howls of mirth continued to be heard as she rushed away to the kitchen to grab her coat and freedom.

***

Richard got up and wandered over to the French doors. The curtains weren't drawn and he stared out into the growing darkness. He looked at his watch; the outside lights should have come on by now. Perhaps they were broken; just like everything else around here.

His thoughts returned to Adam and he grinned. He wished he could have seen the confrontation between him and Bronwen Mortimer. He liked the sound of this young lady, regardless of Adam's opinion of her manners. Anyone could be forgiven for retaliating against Adam. Besides, Eira had phoned him earlier, wanting him to know before he'd heard it from anyone else and it being exaggerated, namely by Lucy, that she'd met Bronwen Mortimer, and a very nice lady she was too. Not some harlot on the run, but a pleasant, if shy woman who obviously had fire if she could stand up to Adam. He liked that.

Going back to his armchair, he ate a scone and cringed at the lukewarm tea. Reaching for the brandy, he poured himself a generous amount and sat back. His thoughts wandered over what Adam had said about the gates. He had known for months that they needed urgent attention. The black paint had all but peeled off and the gold tips looked pathetic, but what could he do? Geoff was busy, and it would cost too much to get professional painters to do it. He could ask someone in the village if they fancied earning some extra money, but that might get tongues wagging. It had to be Geoff, but they hadn't spoken since he'd threatened to leave.

The National Trust, namely his friend, John Cartwright, had been in touch again yesterday. He and John had grown up together. John's wife had recently passed away from cancer. The last few months had been hard for John and he'd invited him over as often as possible. During one of their many talks, the state of the Hall had come up. Richard finally admitted that he was in serious debt and the Hall needed urgent repairs.

'You could always consider giving it to the Trust, you know,' John had replied tentatively. 'I know how much you love this old place, but as you said, you can't afford it anymore.'

Richard dismissed the idea, but over the last few weeks, it had plagued his thoughts as a possible solution. He didn't want to lose his home, but he found the idea of the Hall being knocked down because of decay even worse. It had stood proudly on this site since 1565, though the foundations were much older. Yes, it had been altered a little and bits knocked down over the years, but the heart of Kenward Hall still stood; he would just have to find a way.

John had shown him a way out. He took a large mouthful of the warming liquid and swirled it around his mouth before swallowing, enjoying the pleasurable warmth. If only life could be as simple as a glass of brandy. Enjoy it, savour every moment, and when it's gone, there is always what's left in the decanter to look forward to.

He'd never dreamt of leaving this place, even when his Helen died. He'd inherited it, always knew he would, being the only son. Would his sisters have wanted it? He'd never really thought of it before, but no, he didn't think they would have wanted this old place. Couldn't ask them now anyway, both were dead.

The tears were unexpected. He'd grieved for them both when they'd passed away. First Alice had died ten years ago, in a car accident, then Violet, from cancer, five years ago. He hadn't kept in touch with their husbands except occasional Christmas cards; he had nothing to say to them. He missed his sisters dearly. He being the youngest, they'd looked after him and teased him in equal measure, but they'd loved him. The choked-up feeling in his throat gave way to sobs; that's what he missed, love. Everyone he had ever loved was gone or felt as if they were leaving; it had always been that way in the Kenward family.

He wiped his eyes with his sleeve and took another mouthful of brandy and tried to calm down. He had to think rationally. He had to think about his home, Adam's home. It could all be solved, the repairs, the bills, the constant worry: One decision was all it took. He gazed at the amber liquid and swirled the last remaining dregs around the crystal. Adam was angry with him now for renting out the cottage, their relationship was on thinner ground than he had ever thought possible. How would he react if he knew he was considering allowing the National Trust to have Kenward Hall?

***

Adam stood motionless; his breathing slowed down as his heart slowed. The sun was on the verge of setting and the sky on this side of the house was full of deep greys and pinks, breathtaking and simple. Why couldn't life be like that? Living day-to-day for the moment, knowing the sun will set and the moon will rise.

The slam of a door behind him brought him quickly out of his melancholy mood. Turning, he was disappointed to see the maid putting on her jacket. What had he expected, his father? He turned away and lit a cigarette.

'Good-night…Sir…erm…Adam'

He inhaled deeply and grunted his acknowledgement, his eyes fixed firmly onto the distance. He sensed her reluctance to leave. He'd always thought she had a crush on him but had never dwelt on the idea. Glancing across at her now, he realised that even in the fading light, he could see a yearning that shocked him so much he felt embarrassed.

'Could I…I mean, I have run out…' She pointed to his cigarette.

He couldn't think of any reason to say no; she looked old enough. Handing her his lit one, he quickly rolled a fresh one. In the flare of the lighter, her eyes met his directly He saw everything. He hadn't been vain. Oh God!

He turned away abruptly, moving swiftly toward the stables. Anywhere away from that girl, who in that moment had shown him that she would do anything for him. The lust that flowed from her was almost tangible; he had to get away from the temptation. He felt weak and in need of comfort to help him forget what a complete bastard he was, even for a moment. It had been too long since a woman had offered herself to him; far too long since a young girl was remotely tempting, and what a bastard he'd be if he took her up on her offer…

***

Rose watched as he walked away. It felt hard to breathe. Her chest heaved with the effort; she was dizzy with lust. He had almost considered her for the briefest moment, she was sure of it. She hadn't hidden her desire; he'd got the message. Her lips tingled with wanting; her crotch throbbed with longing. Someone was going to get lucky tonight. She'd close her eyes and pretend it was Adam.

Snuffing out the half-smoked cigarette, she put it into her jacket pocket. She'd smoke it after sex; at least that way she'd have something of his tonight. She hitched up her skirt and pulled her bike away from the bush where she'd thrown it earlier. Pedalling along the driveway, she wished for the thousandth time it was shorter. Her brother would give her a lift into Shrewsbury if she was quick. Easing the bike over the cattle grid, her only thought was to get home as fast as possible, get to Shrewsbury after a short shower, get drunk, and dance till she fell into bed with someone…good-looking. She did not see the small silent figure standing beside the black gates, watching as she pedalled away.

CHAPTER TEN

MIDNIGHT CHIMED LOUDLY IN THE silent night from the old grandfather clock that stood proudly in the hallway. She had long since given up attempting to sleep and now stared out of her kitchen window, enjoying the warmth that her cup of hot chocolate was giving to her cold hands. She took another sip. God, how she loved chocolate! One of her few remaining pleasures.

Eira turned away from the darkness outside and went in search of some light. The small fire in the sitting room still glowed warmly, and she sat back in her armchair, feeling snug and safe. For just a little while, she felt cocooned from the outside world. For just a few minutes she could make believe that nothing could harm her. There was only her and her mug of hot chocolate…

She sensed the sudden change in temperature and gripped the mug tighter. Every muscle in her body wanted to curl up into a tight ball, squeeze her eyes shut, and keep it all away. She wanted to plead for one night's grace, but nothing could or would give her that and she knew it. She was finding it difficult to breathe, but she forced each breath in a vain attempt to calm herself. *After all*, the voices in her head screamed louder, *you deserved this…* and she did, didn't she?

***

Nia's grey, woollen gown was smeared with blood and mucus. The cloth she was using to wipe her bloodied hands shook with fatigue

125

and fear as she approached her lord. 'My lord, I'm sorry, my lord, the child is dead.' She took a step backward as his eyes met hers. 'It was born too soon, my lord.'

'And my wife?' His voice flat, showing no emotion, but his drawn, tired face showed his grief and worry all too clearly.

'Your wife is resting, my lord. She is alive and still young.' The older woman watched him for a moment, seeing the fleeting emotions on his face. She stepped forward and touched his arm gently. 'My lord… William, she is healthy. Her body will heal quickly. Grieve the child and try again. As I remember, your mother lost two children before giving birth to a healthy baby boy that I helped pull from her belly. Are you not strong and healthy, my lord? As I recall, you screamed and wailed until my hearing left me.'

William attempted a smile. He strode over to the table on which stood goblets and wine, poured himself a full cup, and drained it before pouring himself another. Seeing Nia watching him, he poured her a cup and handed it to her. Glancing toward the large bed where his young wife lay asleep, he raised the goblet. 'I am grateful to you for saving my wife. Let us drink to her recovery and then I shall pray for my dead child.'

***

Anne lay exhausted beneath the warm sheets. Her body ached and her insides felt torn and ruined. She had felt Nia place a damp pad between her legs. It smelt of something strange, but she hadn't the energy to ask about it. In fact, she didn't care what they did to her body. She felt utterly ashamed at having lost the child. She should have listened when they told her not to ride, but the temptation to be with William had been too great and now he would blame her for this. She didn't blame him.

With her eyes closed, pretending to sleep so no-one would vainly profess to care about her, she heard the conversation between her

William and the old hag whom he'd insisted help her during the birth. Even this old woman was part of William's past and had known him since his birth. There was no-one for her. No-one liked her. They had made it plain since her arrival that she would be tolerated, for William's sake. Nearly a year since their wedding; she'd hoped it would have changed by now. This failure would not help her cause.

His first wife had been adored by everyone, and she'd managed to give birth to a healthy little brat. Of course, dying in the process had devastated the household. Oh God, why hadn't she died? Another three months was all she'd had to wait. Her damned impatience had led to this.

William drained his second goblet and stormed out of the bed-chamber. No-one followed him. Before he left, he'd turned back to Nia, the wine untouched in her small hands. 'The child, was it a boy?'

Nia shook her head. 'No, my lord, it was a girl.'

Anne fought back the tears as she heard his sorrow and disap-pointment. The man needed sons. Daughters were only good for making alliances. He had Gwenllian for that. His precious daughter was five years old, and the image of her mother a constant reminder of his lost love.

The brat's life was already decided, at least. William's friend, Sir Rhys ap Thomas, had a son slightly older; their union would strengthen family bonds. It was her duty to provide sons. Maybe then she would be accepted? They would love her for making William happy.

*****

Eira's vision blurred with hot tears before they rolled down her cold cheeks. The hot chocolate slipped from her hands and soaked through her nightgown before landing on the floor. She didn't move. She felt the warmth of the fire—she could see its soft light out of the corner of her eye—but her eyes remained fixed onto the far, dark corner of the room. The warmth seemed to melt away as the chill filled the air, invading every pore until she was numb.

The effort it took to control herself was incredible, but she managed to hold out her arms. 'Come…tto…mmmeee…thenn.' Her voice quavered with the cold, but she lifted her chin defiantly and waited.

The small figure stood in the shadows, watching her before stepping forward into the light of the fire. Their eyes met, united in fear and pain, sadness and anger. Moving slowly, the child climbed onto Eira's lap and curled into her as Eira embraced her tightly.

***

Bronwen was on edge for days following her encounter with that man. She'd convinced herself that he'd been one of the Kenward family, but in hindsight, who the hell was he? She'd half expected some kind of retaliation but none happened. Since that day, she'd sensed a strange feeling of contentment come over her. She really could handle possibly anything the living or the dead threw at her.

For years, she had shied away from everything and everyone, never meeting anyone's eye and never answering for herself. She had convinced herself that she couldn't do it and her aunt had done the rest. Always picking on her and reminding her that she was nothing and would stay nothing. She was unimportant and evil and would remain so forever.

Her terrible job as a temp had been decided for her. '*She was good at typing; therefore, she'd make a good temp, possibly secretary, if she could assert herself better.*' The words of her career advisor to her aunt, not to her, though she'd been in the same room.

Now that she had done something wild and jumped into some horror film, she found that she did have some courage after all! And she liked it. She needed to prove to everyone, but more importantly to herself, that she wasn't a weak little woman and never had been.

She had guts, and damn anyone, including a ghost, who thought she'd be scared away.

The wait for the doorbell to ring had finally driven her mad with frustration and, she had to admit, boredom. The house had been completely spring cleaned, and she'd even attempted to do some gardening when the rain stopped long enough and now, armfuls of brambles, dead twigs, and hedge clippings lay in a pile at the side of the garden. As yet, she hadn't explored the shed, hidden away in a dark corner; the threat of a multitude of spiders had kept her away, for now. She hoped once the grass was dry, she might find a lawn mower.

Her attempts at fixing the garden gate had fallen through; it came away in her hand and she'd admitted defeat and it now leant against the hedge. She decided to draw up a list of all the things she needed and where she would find them. At the moment, a garden centre was her main need, which meant people, which meant going back to that shop and facing the lions again and that strange woman, Eira.

Her thoughts had been occupied for a while, but every now and then that strange old woman had come into them. Once, she was sure she'd dreamt about her. She'd woken shaking with fear, sitting in bed with her knees drawn up, waiting for the images to disappear. By morning, she'd almost forgotten what it had been about. Only that Eira had been in it, and the child, and herself, and she had been running, but from what?

She shoved that thought aside as she wrote a list of what she should do. Seeing it on paper made her feel brave. It meant that she had subconsciously decided to do them, to take charge. So, today was the day she would start on her list: supplies, nearby garden centres, and bus timetables to Shrewsbury. She would go and do some research; perhaps that would help the child in some way. It might hopefully help her work out why this was happening to her.

The walk to the village was very brisk, almost a run, but she slowed down as she neared the corner shop. It was Friday; she hoped that the buses ran regularly during the week because she wasn't prepared to go into Shrewsbury on a Saturday. People were one thing. Crowds of busy shoppers were another.

Reaching the front door of the shop, her guts suddenly felt like jelly. To meet this strange woman again gave her a variety of emotions and a headache. She felt scared of her, irrational, perhaps, but also comforted, like an old familiar blanket. Something about Eira was familiar, she couldn't argue with it anymore, yet she knew she had never met the woman. A mystery, of that there was no mistake, just like this village and those ruins, but the more she tried to make sense of it, the more it hurt her head.

The shop was empty. The shelves, the freezers, the deli counter all looked as they had days before, but of Eira, no sign. The only sound came from the freezers as they buzzed gently. Grabbing a basket, she quickly picked up the essentials she needed, feeling like a thief. She placed the half-full basket on the deli counter and leant over to look through the open doorway that she presumed led into Eira's house. 'Hello?' No answer. 'Hello? Anybody home?'

'Good morning, my dear.'

Bronwen jumped and spun round to find Eira standing at the front door. She looked dreadful, older and frailer than she'd been only days before. 'Jesus! You scared me!'

'Sorry. I saw you walk past.' Seeing Bronwen's puzzled look, she added, 'I was in my garden, takes me a little longer these days to catch people up.' She smiled weakly and her eyes held Bronwen's for a long time. 'So, shall I put those onto Adam's account?'

'What?' She'd suddenly felt dreamy, lost in Eira's gaze. She shook herself and blinked hard to clear her vision. 'What?' she repeated confused.

Eira indicated the basket. 'I'll put those on his account. I believe he owes you after his rudeness the other day.' Without waiting for her reply, she slowly walked behind the counter and began putting the shopping into a bag.

'How did you know? Been in, has he, this Adam?' She heard her tone and tried to calm down. She unclenched her fist and helped pack another bag.

Eira chuckled. 'Not for a while, but as you've probably noticed, gossip is quick!'

'Yes, I had noticed. Do you know him?' She felt herself blush.

Eira watched her for a moment before answering. She quickly glanced away, pretending to be interested in a flyer left on the counter.

'Yes, I know everyone here. The Kenwards are...old friends, you might say.'

Something in her voice made Bronwen look up at her. 'So, he is a Kenward. You've known them a long time then?'

'I have, yes. I've known the Kenwards for a very long time. Too long, it seems sometimes.' She smiled weakly. 'They aren't a bad lot, you know.'

Bronwen made a noncommittal noise. 'Well, I suppose I should pay for these. After all, he hasn't offered and I'll be damned if—'

'He will have been sorry the very moment he did it. I can guarantee you that, Bronwen. He truly isn't a horrible man.'

Hearing the woman speak her name sent a shiver down her spine and she suddenly felt uncomfortable. She coughed nervously. 'Well, erm...I suppose so...you must know him better than I do...but anyway, I'll pay for these. Thanks.'

There was an awkward silence as she paid. She desperately wanted to leave, but something about the old woman worried her. Close up, she did look awful. Was she dying? 'I hope you don't mind me asking... but, are you okay?'

Eira smiled warmly as Bronwen blushed even deeper and shifted feet. The poor child was so nervous. Tears welled up in her eyes. *She cares about me. About* me! *Oh God! She didn't deserve it.* 'I...I'm just a bit tired today...and hungry...would you like a cup of tea and a freshly made scone?'

Before she could protest, Bronwen was ushered behind the counter, her two bags left where they sat. Trying to think of something as an excuse, she quickly blurted out about going to Shrewsbury.

'Oh, no, dear, there's only one bus to Shrewsbury, leaves at nine o'clock every morning and one returns at around four, except on Wednesdays and Saturdays. It's eight-thirty and again at eleven-thirty, returning at three and again at five-thirty. It rambles everywhere, I believe.' Ushering her into the sitting room, Eira quickly left and went into her kitchen where the sounds of tea preparations could be heard.

Shocked at such a turn of events, she looked around the small, cosy sitting room before perching nervously on the couch. The room looked and felt old, as if it was stuck in a time warp. Both the armchair and the settee were made of soft, dark green velvet, and she could see where it had worn in places.

The shelves that lined the walls, the skirting boards, the mantel piece, all of it was dark wood, making the room dim but cosy. Photos galore covered every available space. Patches of flowered wallpaper could be spotted in between the multitude of photographs, mostly black and white ones. The worn, flowery carpet peeped out from beneath a brown, woollen rug.

She bit her nails nervously as she waited for her host. Damn everything! She felt deflated after building herself up to going into the town. Despite her mood though, within a few minutes, she could feel herself relaxing, easing herself backward and allowed her tense body to unwind. How bizarre! She almost felt at home here and wondered if it was the room. She'd read about feng shui and how changing things around in the home could help create different moods and bring good or bad luck into your life. She wasn't sure if she bought all that, but there was definitely something about this room that was making her feel very relaxed.

'Here we are.' Eira carried in a large silver tray on which an old brown teapot, two white china cups and saucers, a white sugar bowl, and a silver milk jug sat. Putting them down onto a small, dark wood table next to the armchair, she disappeared again before returning with a pine-coloured tray on which sat a large plate of scones, a bowl of jam, and a plate of butter with knives and spoons. Bronwen's stomach growled loudly, betraying her outward, calm appearance.

Sitting down in the armchair, Eira began setting out the cups and pouring the milk. 'Come, come, my dear, no need to be on your guard here. I made them myself last night. Some have currants in. Here, help yourself to jam and butter. Sugar?'

Sitting forward, Bronwen began helping herself, trying to ignore the emotions that fought for supremacy. Nervousness, determination, curiosity, fear, disappointment, and hunger. For now, hunger won. 'One small sugar, please.'

They both settled back with their tea and scones. Embarrassed, Bronwen wolfed hers down quickly to get it out of the way; Eira only nibbled on hers. Torn between wanting another and wanting to leave, she reached for her cup instead. Eira laughed, pushing the plate toward her. 'I'm pleased you like my baking. Have another.'

A long silence fell on the room as each woman carefully studied the other while sipping tea and buttering scones. Bronwen couldn't quite put her finger on it, but she couldn't get rid of the nagging feeling that this Eira wasn't a total stranger to her. It was her voice. It was soft, gentle, and motherly. How she imagined her own mother to have been like. Was that it? Her need for a mother figure? Her mother would not have been this old, but her grandmother would have been, if she'd lived.

She swallowed the last of her scone and finished her tea as it stuck in her throat. Her sudden thoughts for her mother overwhelmed her and she blinked hard to fight back the tears that threatened to overflow.

'Are you all right, my dear?'

She glanced up to see Eira leaning forward, holding out a napkin, her concern evident, which only managed to make her feel worse and her lower lip trembled. 'Oh God, I'm so sorry…I'm…oh God!'

Mortified, she dabbed at her cheeks furiously to soak up the tell-tale tears.

Eira watched and waited patiently. Poor child. What hell had she endured in her lifetime? What gods could have given her such a life; she didn't deserve it. She yearned to leave her armchair and cross the few feet to the couch, take her in her arms and beg forgiveness, but she'd never understand why, so for now, she made herself sit still and wait.

Eventually, Bronwen managed to control herself and she lifted her reddened face. The look of panic was quickly replaced with inconceivable embarrassment. Eira poured her another cup of tea, then slowly stood up, biting her lip as the pain shot through her knees. Stepping carefully around the table, she walked over to a small cabinet and brought out a bottle. She waited until she was sitting back in the armchair before opening it. The whiskey fumes wafted toward Bronwen and she sighed. Without asking, Eira poured a generous amount into both teacups and sat back, holding her own, sipping occasionally, savouring the aroma and its warmth. Without hesitation, Bronwen reached for her own cup.

'So, my dear, how are you now?'

Eira's question made her blush again. She felt hot and sleepy. 'I'm okay. Memories, you know. Sometimes they come unbidden and it can take my breath away. I feel so embarrassed. I'm sorry, but you pinched my question, I was about to ask you that.' Taking a large mouthful, she looked at Eira over her cup. 'If you don't mind my saying, you don't look very well.'

Eira shrugged. 'No, I'm not well, dear. It's called old age!' Her attempt at lightening the mood worked and they both smiled. 'So, we'll leave things as they are, as I can see that you feel uncomfortable. So let's talk about other things. How are you enjoying the cottage?'

Glad of the change of subject, Bronwen sat up straighter and tried to relax, feeling the warmth of the whiskey reaching her limbs. 'I love it. It's so quiet. Sometimes I think, perhaps, it's too quiet, but then I remember the city…'

'Liverpool, wasn't it?' Eira bit into her scone.

'Yes, have you been speaking to Sir Richard Kenward?'

'My dear, nothing is private in this village. You'll learn that pretty quickly.'

Bronwen smirked. 'Yes, I've gathered that already.'

'You'll get used to it. You could fart at one end of this small village and they'd know about it the other end within a minute, it's terrible!'

Bronwen burst out laughing, scattering a few scone crumbs over her lap. She picked them up while she struggled to control herself. 'What's Shrewsbury like?'

Eira watched her. So, she could laugh and enjoy herself. Should she mention the Ball now? Sir Richard had told her of his intentions of inviting her and she had encouraged him; Bronwen had to go, of that she was absolutely certain.

'Oh, my dear, I haven't been there for…well, a very long time. I'll bet it's changed since I was there last. I believe it has become quite busy, with lots of shops and cafés. It is a beautiful town.' From the many pictures she had seen over the years, Shrewsbury truly was beautiful; she yearned to walk around it again.

'It's not too far away. Why haven't you been there for a long time?'

'I'm a village woman, also a very busy one. I just never seem to have the time to go…*not* that I'm saying I haven't got time for a neighbour,' she quickly added seeing Bronwen begin to fidget. 'I always have time for a neighbour.'

Bronwen smiled; her head felt fuzzy and she knew she should have said no when Eira poured out more tea and another large measure of whiskey, but her mouth wouldn't work quickly enough. Instead, she carefully reached for her cup and sat back. Her cares felt trivial at that moment as her body became heavier. Vaguely, she became aware that Eira was still talking.

'So, my dear, you'll get used to the way of a village soon enough, and besides, after the Ball, once everyone has met you, you'll find they'll leave you alone and—'

'What did you say?' Her words sounded slurred to her ears, but Eira didn't notice.

'The Ball, dear. It's the second weekend in May, always around the full moon. You'll love it, it's ever so grand.' She hated herself for doing it this way, but now that she'd begun... 'It's an old custom. The Ball has been held at the Hall for centuries, even during both World Wars. The lights had to be blocked out and the rations meant the buffet wasn't as grand as other years, but oh, how we danced and enjoyed ourselves. I don't think I stopped dancing all night.' She quickly added. 'The lord of the Manor has always invited his tenants and the surrounding farms. It's wonderful.'

'But, I don't—'

'Of course you do, my dear,' Eira butted in. 'Everyone will be there. No-one misses it.'

'But...I can't go...I...' Bronwen could feel the panic welling up inside her again and felt sick. She leant forward, and carelessly put her cup and saucer down on the table, slopping some tea. Her head felt heavy and she felt very dizzy. Eira quickly came and sat next to her, patting her arm in a comforting gesture.

'My dear, really, you shouldn't get yourself so wound up about it. It's a lovely evening, truly it is.' Handing her a tissue, Eira waited while she blew her nose. 'I do understand, you know. It's scary meeting new people, but once you get to know the villagers, they'll all leave you alone...except, perhaps, for the occasional cake just to have a good nosey around the cottage!' She kept her tone light, knowing the gossips would have a field day if this woman didn't turn up at the Ball; they'd *never* leave her alone. 'Now then, it's getting late and I have things to do. I'll send one of my boys up later with your bags and your invitation. Now, you go on home and rest.'

Bronwen stood tentatively, feeling wobbly. The abrupt ending of the visit caught her off guard and she followed Eira through to the back of the cottage in a dream-like state. She walked outside into a beautiful garden, but she didn't have time to register its many flowers and herbs as Eira opened the wooden gate and she stepped out onto the lane.

It was like stepping back into reality. She wanted to ask about the garden, but she couldn't form words; her mouth felt numb. She attempted another smile and nodded her head in what she hoped was a gesture of thanks. Eira smiled reassuringly and Bronwen thought she was going to say something, but changed her mind.

Patting her jacket, checking for her key and purse, she turned and walked away, rather unsteadily, knowing that Eira was watching her progress for a long time.

***

He sat, willing the front door to open. After almost an hour, he had to accept the possibility that she really wasn't in. He'd crept round the back and peered in through the French doors. It all looked tidy, hardly looked lived in except for a cardigan thrown over the back of the settee. He wanted that cardigan. He wanted to smell it and breathe in her scent, knowing it had covered her breasts. Had she wrapped it tightly around herself? He walked quickly all around the cottage, but she wasn't there. It had a feel of abandonment, and the frustration bubbled away inside him.

He stood for a while in the front garden looking around at the pile of branches and twigs, the broken gate, and thought how sweet it was that she was making herself at home. He tried to imagine life there with her. He looked toward the apple trees and thought about how pleasant it would be to have her, lying on her back, or against the ivy-covered wall where he would hear her screaming for more as he took her from behind, using the wall to support herself. Or the lounge floor where he would ride her like the bitch she was.

His breathing grew heavier and he smiled with pleasure. She was clever. He had to give her that. Managing to avoid him for this long was amazing. Was teasing him all part of her game? Well, he had been patient, but now his body ached for her beyond anything he'd known before and she was going to pay for making him wait.

He laughed suddenly and turned away, heading for his car. He was still laughing as he climbed in remembering the whore he'd had last night. They all whinged about his treatment of them, bloody bitches! They loved it really. What was he paying them for? They were there for his pleasure, not their own. Too rough? Fuck 'em! He liked that.

He wiped his sweating palms on his trousers and swept back his blonde hair. Looking in the rearview mirror, he thought he'd better have his roots touched up. Checking no-one was around; he unzipped his trousers and eased his erection out. Closing his eyes, he wrapped his hot hand around it and gently moved rhythmically, imagining it her hand, her breasts, her legs wrapped around him, begging for more.

A minute later, he was cleaning his hand on a wet wipe, his flaccid penis now hidden away. He knew giving himself pleasure wouldn't last long, but for now that would have to do. Opening his window, he enjoyed the cool breeze on his face for a few minutes before starting up the car. Looking again toward what he presumed was her bedroom, he knew he would be in there soon, very soon. He would take her in there and it would last a very, long time, he would make sure of that. Grinning to himself, he put the car into gear and sped off down the lane; anticipation was half the excitement.

***

Bronwen stopped and listened. Somewhere within her fuzzy head, she registered a car; the noise of its engine reached her, and instinctively she moved to the side of the road, but it never passed her. The noise quickly vanished and she was once more left in the silence.

She clutched her head and tried to wake up by rubbing her eyes hard and massaging her neck. It worked a little, though she still felt quite tipsy. Had she really had that much to drink?

The gates to Kenward Hall stood open, but she gave them nothing more than a glance. She had to get home to rest, just like Anne had…

She stopped dead. Anne. Who the hell was Anne? She abruptly glanced behind her; visions of Eira floated into her mind, disappearing just as quickly as another face took her place: a woman with the same eyes.

Shaking her head, she tried to dislodge the pictures that invaded it. She covered her eyes to drown out the images that whirled before her eyes. Memories flooded her mind but each one was so fleeting, so unreal, it felt like someone else was trying to get in. Rubbing her forehead hard, she almost stumbled, only knowing that she had to get home. Her head was beginning to hurt. The throbbing which had been nothing more than an annoyance had suddenly become a hard-hitting migraine. She hadn't had one of these for years and never so quickly.

She had to get into her safe bed, knowing that if she didn't soon, she would collapse here, outside Kenward Hall; she knew she would be vulnerable.

CHAPTER ELEVEN

EIRA WATCHED HER GO FOR a long time. She vaguely heard the shop bell, telling her someone had come in, but she didn't want to move. Tears burned the back of her eyes and as she watched and listened. She let them fall down over her cheeks, soaking into the collar of her blouse. The need to run after her was hard to fight, but the reality of the situation was winning. She couldn't run, even if her life depended on it. It would only scare her, which she didn't want to do. She had to have patience for just a little while longer and then, perhaps, she'd tell her everything.

Finally, she slowly walked back into her small, tidy garden, and for a moment, she remembered another garden. With herbs galore and flowers of every colour that ran the length of the walls. The knee-high hedges that swirled and curved, and the green grass beneath her feet. It had been her favourite place to escape the looks and the whispers. William had called her his garden nymph because she was always there, whatever the weather.

There weren't any tall trees in this small garden she now stood in, but in another there had been young oaks, chestnut, cherry blossom, ash, and rowan. She would dance around them, laughing and sheltered beneath them when it rained; once, William had made love to her beneath one and it had become their tree. The garden was her sanctuary; nature was as powerful to her as God. In secret, she'd believed that Mother Nature was all powerful and God was nothing more than her puppet; now it was all gone.

***

James quickly parked his car in his space and walked around the corner to the Shrewsbury offices. Ignoring the receptionist, he walked purposefully toward his own small office behind her. On opening the door, he stopped abruptly. 'What the hell are you doing in here?'

'Now, now, temper, temper!' His visitor smiled cheekily and swung his chubby legs off James's desk where he had been resting them whilst reading a porn magazine he'd found hidden in one of James's files. 'Can't I get a better welcome than that?' Easing himself out of the chair, he quickly walked up to James who hadn't moved from the doorway. He reached past him, closing the door firmly. 'Now, then...' Going back to the desk, he picked up a packet of cigarettes and lit one. 'My dearest friend, have you anything to say to me?'

James stared at his visitor, his face impassive until he glanced at the clock on the wall. 'Oh shit! I missed that bloody appointment!' Walking quickly, he found his diary. Moving the file and the magazine out of the way, he sat down and began to dial frantically. 'Will they still be there, do you think, Gordon?'

Gordon stood by the desk silently smirking as he watched James. Finally after a few minutes, he started to chuckle. 'I'm sorry, couldn't help it. Stop worrying, James, it's all sorted.'

Replacing the receiver, he frowned. 'What the hell do you mean? Stop messing with me, you stupid prick! Tell me.'

'They called this morning and had to move the appointment to Monday.' Gordon stubbed out the half-finished cigarette, moved the ashtray to the farthest corner of the desk, and grinned slyly. 'So, do you want to tell me where you've been? Was she worth it?' Still grinning like the Cheshire cat, Gordon sat opposite James and stretched his legs out in front of him, his hands clasped behind his head. 'Come on, tell me all the gory details.'

James said nothing for a moment as he controlled his overwhelming desire to break this bastard's neck. He tolerated Gordon because girls felt safer in pairs, so when they went out on the pull he was, more often than not, successful. Even though Gordon had a casual girlfriend and was married, it never stopped them trying.

He got up and poured himself a cup of black coffee. Leaning against the table, he ignored the spilled sugar, two used tea bags and a large coffee stain and savoured the strong, hot liquid. He finally met Gordon's eyes and grinned. 'What can I say...?'

Gordon laughed out loud. 'You dirty bugger! Someone I know?'

James shrugged and continued sipping his coffee, his thoughts drifting off, back to that cottage, back to that cardigan. Gordon's voice finally broke into his daydreaming.

'Yeah, okay, keep your secrets, back to business. It looks like we've got a couple for that flat, a Mr and Mrs Thomas. He's the main earner and she could quite easily be a porn model, the tits on it! Bloody hell! It was all I could do not to grab 'em!'

Gordon picked up the packet of cigarettes and rolled it between his palms. He continued, 'He looks a good bit older, bit of a sugar daddy judging from the age gap. Should decide by tomorrow as I told them we had another couple looking at it. So you should get a chance to have a peek at her assets.'

'Gone off Susan then? I thought she was your sex slave? Did anything for you? Damned good at it too, you said.'

Gordon shrugged. 'I didn't say I'd get rid of her. It's just, you know, having the same pussy for so long, gets a bit...boring. At least while the wife was at home, I had a bit more variety. Sometimes, I just fancy something younger, maybe, or exotic.' Seeing James' expression, he smiled. 'Not jail-bait, but something virginal, something tighter, you know, but what are the chances these days, eh?'

James shook his head and quickly poured himself another coffee. He was beginning to feel excited with all this talk about young girls.

Gordon continued. 'So come on, how old is this woman of yours? Come on, you've got to tell me something, I tell you everything!'

Which was true. Gordon had been rubbing his nose in it for the past nine months, since he'd somehow managed to seduce a twenty-four-year-old tart into being his lover. The only good thing as far as James was concerned was that this tart, Susan, had friends. Although, he hadn't had much luck as yet, only a quick blowjob, and the girl had thrown up afterward. Gordon had laughed at that.

He would never tell him, of course, that because of that humiliating experience, he had been the one to tell Gordon's wife of seventeen years about his numerous one-night stands. She'd threatened to leave him. Not that it stopped Gordon. He liked to believe he had a way with women and loved telling James everything in great detail.

James took it all. He listened and congratulated and joined in the lewd jokes, all the time smiling to himself about his own little secret. What would Gordon say about all of his bitches that he took and made his own? And when he couldn't find one, the prostitutes he used and the things he made them do. What would he say?

'Shit, look at the time!' Gordon stood up and straightened his jacket. He had been watching James's face and had seen a look that sent a shiver down his spine. He liked James as a drinking buddy and a partner in business, but there was something about him that sometimes made Gordon wary of him. He knew without a doubt that he'd never leave him alone with his daughter, if he had one.

Susan hated him. Gave her the creeps, she said. Even his wife, Laura, refused to stay in a room alone with him. She would always follow Gordon out into the kitchen making some excuse whenever they'd had parties.

For years, he'd ignored it, making some joke about it, but now and again, he could see what they meant. When they joined forces four years ago and gone into the estate agent business, he hadn't cared at that point if he'd gone into business with Hitler, James had had the money and he was a bloody good estate agent. Within months, they'd had some good houses on their list. Nothing cheap, they had high standards. James had charmed his way into people's homes, before proving how good he was by either selling or renting them very quickly.

James stared at the closed door for a long time after Gordon suddenly rushed off in search of a quickie with Susan. His thoughts were racing with ideas that would satisfy and would accomplish every desire. Finally, he picked up the phone and dialled a number he knew by heart. On the fourth ring, it was answered. 'It's me, James. I'll be there after work, be ready for me.' Replacing the receiver quickly before the woman could argue, he smiled to himself. It felt good being in control and he was determined to be in control for the rest of the evening.

***

The walk home seemed to take a lifetime. By the time she did finally get up to her door, she slumped against the porch for a moment as her eyesight blurred. She pushed herself away from the wooden frame with a grunt, clutching her head as the jolt caused a bolt of lightning pain to rip through her brain and down her neck. As much as she wanted fresh air, she had to get inside where she could collapse in safety.

Unconsciously, she glanced in all directions, checking that she was alone, but she couldn't focus. Clutching her keys, Bronwen staggered inside the porch, thrust the key in the lock, then blindly felt her way into the warm hall and very gently and deliberately closed the heavy door behind her. Carefully, she eased the bolt across and finally allowed herself to cry, from fear and from the pain.

It was the early hours of the morning before anything registered again. She had no recollection how she had got to bed, but she woke with the grey dawn, still dressed and her head feeling mushy. The clock had at some point been knocked off the bedside table, it now lay somewhere on the carpet. She left it there.

The dream that had woken her was fading. She screwed up her eyes to try to bring it back, but it was gone. The sadness that enveloped her was a shock. The dream had been a good dream, a happy dream, and now that was gone.

She turned over and found a cool spot on her pillow. Her head and neck always felt detached after a migraine, and it made her feel woozy for a while. She was just thankful the throbbing had stopped. She drifted off to oblivion. When she'd had them as a teenager, she had more than once attempted to knock herself out with a hammer or a sideboard. Anything to be somewhere else so she didn't feel the excruciating agony; nothing else mattered except oblivion.

If she was lucky and caught it early on, with a couple of strong painkillers everything would be okay. If not, she endured hours of clutching her head, wailing, often screaming with the agony, begging her aunt to kill her.

To kill her. Slowly she sat up and drew her legs up. Wrapping her arms around her knees, she stared into the semi-darkness. Those three words conjured so many memories that should remain buried; they didn't belong in her new life, in her new home. Those memories came flooding back to her now and she stiffened as each one passed before her eyes.

Her father. She cringed away from any memory associated with him. She had managed to block out her early childhood; only vague images remained, like dreams she couldn't quite remember, and she didn't try anymore. Even those precious memories of her mother were sadly lost somewhere inside her head. A kind, loving woman was all she knew for certain, a woman with a Welsh accent and a warm smile, frightened eyes hidden behind sunglasses, hiding the truth from everyone. She'd learnt early that bruises couldn't be hidden well.

Yes, she accepted now that her father deserved to die for the things he'd done to her and her mother. By accident or intention, it was meant to be. What followed, she couldn't decide whether it was a worse part of her life, or not. The care home filled with kids who pulled her hair and called her names and beat her whenever the social workers weren't looking. The staff who whispered and pretended to care.

The constant flow of specialists, therapists, counsellors, all talking kindly, but their so-called concerns never quite convinced her. After years of telling grownups what they wanted to hear, her hell was replaced by another: her aunt. Her cruel taunts and accusations went unheard by the outside world, who believed her to be a kindly woman taking in a lost cause. One less in the system, a success story; a child saved.

Murderer! She heard this word repeatedly for the next ten years as her aunt refused to believe that her stepbrother could be at fault. He didn't deserve it. He had done his best for his daughter after the mother died and nothing would make her change her mind. The facts, the evidence, the reports were nonsense as far as she was concerned. Her brother was a saint. All of it was lies.

Her aunt had believed wholeheartedly that she should be punished, as justice had not, in her eyes, been forthcoming. And so, she'd taken her in once the authorities finished with her. As a good Christian, she would hound her with God's punishment and fill her head with God's words. She would never forgive Bronwen and told her repeatedly that God wouldn't, either.

Bronwen never argued or explained her actions, however many times her aunt had beaten her. She'd known that her aunt would never accept her reason for killing her father because she'd never believe what her father had been capable of. His was a deserved death, a necessity to preserve her innocence.

How many pathetic attempts had she endured to try to save her soul from the Devil? In the ten years she lived with her aunt, her soul, as far as she was concerned, was still her own. No Devil or God could claim it. Her aunt had failed. The cancer had finally taken her before the liver damage could. Hypocrisy at its worst, as far as she was concerned. Her aunt was no better than a drunken lush who berated anyone for sinning. But not anymore.

The woman had died peacefully in a hospice, holding her bible. Bronwen hadn't remained with her body for long, needing to put some distance between herself and the corpse of a cruel and hated woman. She'd expected nothing from her aunt in life and so being left a substantial amount of money, plus the house and all the belongings had been quite a shock. Now, it was over. She was free of it all. Her aunt had tried so hard to destroy every last ounce of life within her whilst alive, just like her stepbrother had. Both had failed.

She was alive and fairly certain she was content, though having never experienced such an emotion, she couldn't be sure. Whatever she was enduring right now, the fact remained: Blood flowed, tears fell, air was expelled, and she was living her own life, not merely existing as she had for so many years. She was feeling and seeing things that fried her brain trying to understand, but she was experiencing them. This was her life, but was it possible to have lived other lives?

The time-slip theory seemed to be the best bet so far concerning the people she had seen, but a past life could also be a possibility. She smirked; getting one good life had been her dream. Finding out she might have lived before would be amazing.

Had she had some kind of fit or a warning of her coming migraine, perhaps? No, she doubted that because it had happened days ago. Was she drunk or high on drugs? Not at that time. Perfectly sober and had never taken drugs. Of course, if she'd had the experience after drinking all that whiskey at Eira's, she could easily persuade herself it had been a drink-induced hallucination.

Her first encounter with the ghosts might have awoken something inside her. It felt like it was all connected somehow. Another way to look at this logically: that since moving in, she had experienced more terrifying and strange events, and maybe this was her brain's way of ruining her newfound freedom. Maybe, on some level, she didn't believe she deserved it?

After everyone she'd known was dead and now here she was living her life, could it be somehow connected? Could it be that hidden somewhere deep inside, she believed that she didn't deserve to live? That could make sense. Ruin her new life to compensate for what happened; it was a possibility. But, if that were true, she'd be very pissed off with herself.

She took a long, calming breath and tried to think. The only ghost who had come across as any kind of threat had been that bitch who'd killed the child. Tears sprang into her eyes and she brushed them away. Thinking of the little girl made her heart break. She knew only too well what kind of person hurt children and it strengthened her belief that somehow the child's ghost had felt a kindred spirit.

Perhaps the child wanted help? Perhaps she had been curious about who had witnessed her death? She felt a rush of affection for the little pretty girl. Why should anybody want to kill her? Who knew? All that she knew was that yesterday's adventure had hardened her idea about going into Shrewsbury. The people she had seen might be some residue of energy from this girl's past. Perhaps she was reaching out? There had to be records.

She climbed out of bed and stretched. The sun was just peeking over the horizon. The thought of catching the bus filled her with dread, being surrounded by strangers staring and questioning her for however long the journey might take, with no escape, but she knew she had to try.

She stopped and stood by the window, gently pulling open the dark, maroon curtains. The fabric felt like velvet and she stroked it absentmindedly as she watched the sun slowly rise, bringing with it some warmth. The rain had dried off, although there were large clouds in the sky. She could see bits of blue peeking out in between the clouds. It was going to be a nice day.

Fabric. Slowly rubbing the soft fabric, something stirred in the back of her head. It exploded forward and she froze. 'Oh God!' Moving slowly back to the bed, she flopped down. 'Oh God! The Ball!' Her conversation with Eira jumped into her mind. The invitation. Needing a new dress. Everyone will be there. Have to go. 'Oh God!'

Curling up into a ball, she tried to ignore the clenching butterflies that invaded her stomach. How could she possibly go? Worse still, to be stuck in a house with that man. What had Eira called him? Adam, was it? 'God, no, no, no, no, *no!*'

CHAPTER TWELVE

S IR RICHARD SLOWLY REPLACED THE receiver on its hook and sat back. Letting out a long, deep breath, he realised that he was shaking. Running his cold fingers through his white hair, he nibbled his lower lip as he tried to focus his thoughts. The conversation he had just had with his friend ran around his head.

'The Trust is interested, Richard,' John assured him. 'It's up to you, of course, but personally, I'd be quick if I were you. They only have so much funding for this type of thing, you know.'

'I can't decide what's for the best, John.' Richard sighed loudly. 'I can't afford living here anymore and besides, my body aches so much these days from the bloody cold. So much needs doing to the old place, I couldn't even begin to tell you where to start. But, it's my family home…'

'That's where the Trust can help. If, and I mean a big *if*, they do decide to bring Kenward Hall into its protection and conservation, then at least the Hall has a chance of surviving. From what you've told me, it is rotting away before your very eyes. Am I right?'

Richard could almost feel his friend's anticipation and frowned. 'I know you're right, John, it's just…this is my home. This is Adam's home. This was Helen's home and I just don't know if I can bear…'

'I know, old friend…I know.'

For a moment, neither one of them spoke, both lost in their thoughts for the woman they had known and loved in their own way. John finally broke the silence. He coughed, clearing his throat, fighting back the sudden emotion he felt. 'Well, I'll leave you with your thoughts, Richard. You know the deal and you know how much time you have. If I don't hear from you before we see you at the Ball—presuming it's still on, old boy?'

'Of course. It has to be, doesn't it, but between you and me, John, I don't have any enthusiasm for it anymore, not since…Helen. It's one tradition I could well do without.'

He heard his friend hesitate. 'What is it, John?'

'It's nothing, really, it's just that…well, I wasn't sure if I should bring it up but…the Trust asked about…you know, your lands and they asked about the old castle.'

Richard felt himself go cold. 'What do you mean, the castle? What could they possibly want to know about that place for?'

'Well, for a start, it was built in the middle of the fifteenth century by your ancestor, Robert Cenwaerde, whose son, Sir William, lived in it for a long time before he began the foundations of Kenward Hall. He became quite well known, didn't he? If his nephew hadn't finished building Kenward Hall, you might still have been living in your ancestral home. The Trust wondered if it might be worth rebuilding—'

'*What?*' Richard shot up from his chair, shaking with emotion. 'There is no way on this Earth I would allow anyone to touch that place. Leave it. Let the place rot.'

He heard John's sharply indrawn breath on hearing his roar of fury. 'Okay, old boy. It's only that it's believed to be the last one of its kind. You know, it's built on an old Iron Age settlement or something.'

'Yes, I know what the place is built on, John, and the answer is still no. Look, I'm sorry, but believe me when I say it's best to forget that place…' He was finding it difficult to keep his voice sounding even as the fear swept through him. 'I'll see you at the Ball, John.'

Reaching for the brandy, he poured himself a tumbler full and wandered over to the French doors, his favourite place to look out at the estate, and almost finished the brandy in one mouthful. His eyes watered as he glanced back at the decanter, tempted to refill it and get absolutely drunk. Forget his worries and his fears, just for one day. He fought the urge. It was still morning, after all. He had to keep a clear head if he was to have discussions with Judith and Lucy over the preparations for the damned Ball.

He laughed suddenly, feeling very naughty drinking so early in the day. The alcohol seemed to work quicker as he felt the warmth rising through his legs and along his chest. He could easily make a habit of this. What the hell Judith and Lucy wanted to talk to him for anyway was beyond him. They had already prepared enough food to feed two villages. Judith had organised a band and a DJ for later on in the evening, which he knew she'd hated doing. 'Terrible racket,' she'd called it.

Finishing the last of his brandy, he walked back to his favourite seat by the fire and unsteadily flopped down. 'Why oh why had my ancestors decided that this May Ball would be a good idea?'

He'd done some small bits of research years ago when the children had been small, when they'd begun to ask questions about their ancestors. He hadn't found any answers as to why they had the yearly Ball, but had come across an old letter dating from 1714. He opened his desk and found the letter easily enough. It was a letter from his many times great-grandfather to an old friend, Sir Thomas, thanking him for attending the May Ball, but enquiring as to why he and his wife had departed so quickly.

12th day of May 1714

My dear friend,
May I enquire as to your wife's health after your abrupt leaving of us last night? I sincerely hope that none of my household insulted you in any way. Have you witnessed something not to your liking? I await your reply with much anticipation.

Your friend,
Sir George Kenward

Had he got the reply? He'd often wondered about that. If it had been something trivial, why would his ancestor write the letter? What had happened on that May Ball in 1714? There were other letters, quite a few, in fact, from Kenwards throughout the centuries, asking why guests had fled the May Ball, or enquiries about their health following yet another absconder. Most resided in the Shrewsbury library; the very old ones, he kept behind glass in his bedroom.

He had his suspicions. He'd found diaries of his great-grand-father that hinted about the curse upon the family and something that walked Kenward Hall's corridors, terrifying servants and family alike. He'd spoken to Geoff about these matters frequently. Geoff was another problem he couldn't think about now. He'd said his piece about leaving and hoped that Adam had found it in his heart to apologise; he hated the idea of losing his old friend, his confidante.

And Helen, darling Helen. How many times had they spoken in whispers about the cold spots, the strange happenings in and around the Hall? She had told him of feeling eyes watching her. How she'd put objects down and find them moved within a few minutes. She'd told him of her growing fear that something evil was lurking in the shadows, waiting. He'd tried to laugh it off. His mistake.

Helen. She'd loved the May Balls. She'd dance and mingle with everyone. No-one was allowed to feel lonely or uncomfortable while Helen had been there with her warm smile. He felt the tears well up and quickly blinked them away. That was another reason he dreaded the Ball; it reminded him so much of Helen. She loved organising it with Judith. Another reminder that she was taken from him by the evil that walked those cursed ruins…his home. Another reminder of his deep guilt that he hadn't taken her seriously regarding her fears. It was a ghost, a wandering, lonely spirit, what harm could it do? If the Trust did take the Hall, would he finally be free?

***

Geoff watched Adam as he slowly led Scarlet into the stable yard. He looked tired but exhilarated after his ride. It pissed him off seeing Adam look so happy, but he hid it, keeping his face blank. 'A good ride, was it?' he asked, already knowing the answer.

Adam grinned sheepishly and patted the horse. 'Yes. This beauty is fast. Jumped her a few times, wow! You should see her fly.' Realising Geoff wasn't really interested, he added quietly, 'Sorry, get a bit carried away with this one…how's things?'

Geoff ground his teeth to stop himself from exploding. For a moment, he glared at Adam before managing to get his feelings under control. 'Where exactly would you like me to start?' He just managed to stop himself from adding, 'You arrogant bastard.'

Adam turned away and began undoing the heavy saddle. 'Well, let's see, you look like you want to punch me, and as it happens, I wouldn't blame you, I behaved terribly and for what it's worth, I'm sorry for what I said to you.' He glanced at the old man who remained leaning against the stable wall, then carried on. 'You know I think of you as an uncle…or something, anyway.' He frowned. 'Come on, Geoff, you know I'm not good at this, what do you want?' He pulled the saddle off the horse, placed it on the ground, and stood waiting for some response. None came.

Geoff met his eye for a while before reaching into his jacket pocket and pulling out his packet of tobacco. Rolling a cigarette, he lit it, all the while watching Adam.

Finally he spoke, his concern evident. 'I'm worried about this place, Adam. I feel it will fall apart if you don't stop this temper of yours. I'm sick of defending you, *No, wait!*' He put up his hand as Adam tried to speak. 'You'll bloody well listen. I said I'd leave today if you didn't apologise to Mathew, but I know you've tried to find him.' Seeing Adam's confused look, he added, 'Yes, his parents phoned me. They're worried about him. Whether or not it has anything to do with your sacking him, I don't know, but they said the boy has changed.'

Adam took hold of Scarlet's bridle. 'What do you mean, changed?'

'They said he was frightened. Something…or…someone has scared him. He isn't sleeping or eating and he loved coming here regardless of the shitty way you treated him. You know he isn't a thief. Can I find him and bring him back?'

Gripping the bridle, Adam slowly led the horse into the warm stable. Geoff followed him. Picking up the brush, he slowly began to groom the glossy coat. He always found this movement therapeutic, calming. He knew Geoff was waiting. 'I never really wanted to believe that Mathew was a thief, but God only knows where the bridle, whip, and everything else have disappeared to. Yes, of course he can come back and…let's see if we can't train that boy into a decent jockey, eh?'

Geoff stepped farther into the stable and inhaled deeply on his cigarette. 'You knew what we were doing, didn't you?'

Grinning, Adam stopped brushing and turned to his friend. 'Of course I bloody did. I'm not blind, you know. Fred is one bloody fast gelding, but not a racing horse; neither is Jess. Besides, she's in season now. Scarlet is a racing horse possibly, but I want her for breeding too. Dulas, possibly, though I'd sooner not allow little Mathew on that bugger. If he wants to practise, fine, but this stable is for breeding and getting the experience of working in stables. What he needs is a stable where they breed racing horses, where he can really get his training. I want the best for him, you know. I've been in touch with an old friend up near Ludlow. He races and he's willing to take him on a trial period.'

Geoff threw the stub onto the cobbled yard and extinguished it with his boot. He couldn't help but smile. He knew in his heart Adam would come right and at that moment he felt proud of him and fought the urge to give him a big bear-hug. Instead, he turned back to Adam who had begun brushing faster, moving to the other side of the horse, so he couldn't see his face. 'You're a good lad, Adam, thanks.'

Adam listened as Geoff walked away. He grinned to himself. It did feel good and he was pleased about finding Mathew something that could benefit him, better than this place anyway. Of course, it would mean he'd have to advertise for another stable boy. Damn it!

***

As it happened, he didn't manage to talk to Mathew until the next morning. Geoff had phoned and managed to track down the boy to invite him back to the stables.

Mathew kept himself to himself for the rest of the day, scuttling away if Adam or Geoff came near him, muttering excuses to be somewhere else. A horse needed fetching, grooming, or feeding. They backed off, letting him settle down, hoping he'd talk to them when he was ready.

Adam finally managed to corner him in Fred's stable as he mucked it out. Even as Adam walked toward him, he could see the boy had changed. If possible, he looked thinner. When he turned at the sound of Adam's boots on the cobbled floor, he quickly lowered his eyes and continued heaping the horse manure onto the wheelbarrow.

Adam tried to hide his shock at seeing a skeleton. His face pale and pinched, with black circles around his deep, brown eyes. God, he looked like he was dying. He felt a wave of fear for the boy. How could he change so dramatically over a few days?

'Mathew? How's things with you?' His voice croaked and he coughed to clear it, embarrassed. This was new territory for him.

Mathew's voice was barely audible, a whisper. 'Okay.'

Adam reached out and put his hand on the skinny shoulder. He could feel the bones beneath his fingers and he abruptly let go. 'Mathew, please stop that, we need to talk.'

Obediently Mathew stopped and leant the fork against the stable door. He kept his head down, refusing to look up, and kept his hands in his pockets. He sniffed loudly and Adam realised with a shock that the boy was crying. Jesus! He'd never dealt with anything like this before! His feelings for the boy ran amok. He wanted to hug him tightly and beg his forgiveness for being such a bastard to him. He wanted to rush him to a hospital to get him checked out, as he looked so damned ill. He wanted to pick him up and carry him up to the Hall and order Lucy and Judith to feed him till he burst. He wanted to tell the boy about his new job and hope for a smile. For a moment, he fought over which one to do first. 'Have you got a tissue, Mathew?' Pathetic!

Mathew shook his head and used his sleeve instead. 'What do you need doing?'

Adam frowned and went to sit down on a bale of hay. Mathew hadn't moved. 'Mathew, we need to talk, as I said. Here's the deal. I've spoken to a friend of mine out past Ludlow and he breeds and races horses. You've probably heard of Snow Queen?' Not waiting for an answer, he cleared his throat and continued. 'Well, he has a place for a trainee jockey and I've told him about you. What do you say?'

Mathew looked up, his eyes wide, face tear-stained and shocked. 'You do want to get rid of me?'

'No. Believe it or not, Mathew, I like you. You worry me to hell, especially at the moment.' He waved his hand in Mathew's direction, taking in his appearance; Mathew blushed and looked down again. 'You can practise on my horses till the cows come home, but frankly, if you really want to be a jockey, you have to be in the right environ-ment, and this isn't it. Look, will you come and sit here before you fall down.' He patted the hay and waited.

Mathew came and sat on the edge, slightly turned away.

The silence spread out, broken only by the occasional shudder that ran through Mathew's scrawny shoulders and occasional sniff. Adam felt completely out of his depth. He hadn't realised it before just how much he really did care for this boy. What was he, sixteen? He looked much younger.

Eventually he couldn't stand it any longer. He touched Mathew's arm gently. 'Come on, lad, can you tell me what's wrong?' No reply. 'I know I'm a horrible man and I'm sorry for it. I'll try to keep my temper under control, and I can tell you, Robin up at Ludlow is a bloody big softy. You won't miss us a bit.' The wretched sound of a stifled sob from the shivering boy next to him almost ripped his heart out. 'Please, Mathew, can't you tell me, please?'

The sobs grew. It was too much for him. He either had to walk away or hold him; the latter one won out. Feeling unsure, expecting Mathew to pull away, he pulled the shaking boy into his arms awkwardly and held him tightly. At first the boy was rigid against him, but eventually he crumpled in his arms and Adam had to hold him up, his arm wrapped around the boy's waist as he wept uncontrollably. Each cry seemed to wrench the strength out of him. The tears came in waves and soon Adam's jacket was soaked with them and, no doubt, mucus. He didn't really care. At one point he noticed movement from the opposite stable. David coming to see what was going on. He expected Geoff too, but he didn't come, or if he did, he hid better than David.

Finally, exhausted, Mathew stopped and lay limp in his arms for a moment before sitting up and frantically wiping his face on his soaked sleeves. Adam rummaged in his own pocket and found a bit of kitchen roll. Clean or not, he handed it to Mathew and rolled a cigarette while he waited for the boy to compose himself.

'Okay, now can you tell me?' He offered Mathew the cigarette, knowing he would refuse. Lighting it himself, he leant back and waited.

'I don't know what to say.' The quiet words were almost lost on the slight wind that had picked up.

Adam frowned and said nothing.

'I mean...' Mathew turned toward him, looking embarrassed. 'I know this will sound...crazy.'

Adam leant forward. 'However it sounds, you need to talk to someone.'

'IthinkI'mbeinghauntedandIthinkI'mgoingtodie.' The words tumbled out so quickly Adam wasn't sure if he'd heard them right.

'Erm...right...what...I mean...what?'

159

'I know you'll think I'm mad. Perhaps I am going mad.' Tears began to spill down his cheeks again and he angrily wiped them away. 'I've seen things, heard things. Horrible things that…oh God! I hear screams, begging for mercy, so loud sometimes I can't block it out so I can't sleep. Even when I sleep, they're there, in my head.'

'Who's there, Mathew?' His hand shook as he inhaled deeply on his cigarette.

For a moment, he wondered if Mathew had heard him as he stared down at the floor. 'People dressed differently to us. Sometimes the smells, they make me want to be sick. I can't eat. Food tastes rotten, like rotting flesh. Water feels like mud sliding down my throat. But the worst bit is seeing her.'

'Her? Who's her?' Adam finished the cigarette, squashing it beneath his boot. He hugged himself to try to stop the fear that ran through his body.

'The woman, she mocks me, taunts me all the time, day and night… the child murderer. But she let another woman die for it and I hear her screams as they torture her. I see and smell the blood, the piss, the shit. I see it all. They show me. And then…I see her hanging. I see her kicking her legs, stained with blood and shit, and I see her eyes…oh God! Her eyes, begging…'

'Jesus-fucking-Christ!'

Adam spun round to find Geoff standing within the doorway of the next stable, brush in one hand while the other clutched the door. He looked pale, his eyes fixed on Mathew, who hadn't heard him as he slowly rocked himself, the tears running freely down his cheeks.

For a moment, Adam stared at him, the shock of seeing him quickly fading. 'Mathew, listen to me. They are just nightmares. Horrible nasty nightmares. You're anxious. I've been a bastard. It's just anxiety about me, your job, your future.'

Mathew shook his head slowly. 'No, you're wrong. I'm not always asleep. I saw them the other day, in the trees. She was there. She saw them too. So they must be real, and now, they've followed me here. She is taking your things, not me...not me.'

Adam and Geoff exchanged looks. What the hell was this? For a moment, Adam thought he saw something shift in Geoff's expression and wondered if he knew anything, but he turned away to replace the brush.

'Come on, lad, what you need is a hot cup of tea, Lucy's biscuits, and then home. I'll take him.' He didn't wait for a nod from Adam, but gently pulled Mathew to his unsteady feet and wrapping his strong arm around his waist, he half carried, half walked him toward the Hall.

Adam watched until they disappeared from view.

He'd stood up to help, but now he flopped back onto the hay, reaching for his tobacco, his hands shaking. It took two tries before he could roll a decent cigarette. He stared at the opposite stable door, not really seeing the forest green colour or the horse that popped its head out and whinnied. He didn't notice David scuttle past pushing a wheelbarrow full of dirty straw. He was remembering stories long forgotten. He'd heard the ghost stories associated with Kenward Hall and stories of a murder and an injustice. And something else nagged away in his memory, a memory he'd forgotten. Something he badly wanted to shy away from. After all, they were only stories. Right?

***

The scream echoed around the walls. The eyes! They watched her... hatred burned on each face. That noise as the child hit the ground beneath and then that fraction of a second of silence before the screaming began...William!

Fumbling for the light beside the bed, Bronwen inhaled deeply as the orange glow gave her some comfort. Wiping her face with the sheet, she wasn't surprised to find it wet with sweat and tears. She sniffed hard and rubbed her face quickly to dispel the images, until finally, they were gone.

Just another nightmare. After all these years, she thought that she'd be used to them by now, but she wasn't. It had been the one question she had ever asked the counsellor during one of her many sessions. She could still remember the badly hidden look of surprise on her face.

'Nightmares? Well yes, that's hardly surprising. You have been through a lot of trauma. It's your brain's way of working it out, understanding it, and, hopefully accepting and finding peace with it…does that help you?'

Bronwen hadn't answered, but taken the response and put it with all the other answers she'd been given or overheard and waited for a time when she'd be alone. When she could think clearly about her life, her thoughts, and her nightmares. What the counsellor said made sense.

Seeing that re-enactment of a child's murder was traumatic and being attacked by that blackness had terrified her more than she'd cared to dwell on, but tonight's nightmare had felt different. She'd been there. It'd felt too real. Looking up at the tower, feeling her heart racing as she'd run toward the steps leading upward, hampered by her long, heavy skirt, her bare feet. The blinding of the sun as she'd reached the top, the feel of the cool breeze and then seeing…

She rubbed her eyes hard. No point in thinking these things, it was just a bloody dream. Who knew why it was slowly changing? Who cared? It had to be anxiety. After all, she was a mess, wasn't she?

Her nightgown was soaked with sweat; she tugged it off and threw it on the floor. Shuffling back under the covers, she tried to think of something nice; nothing came to mind. She'd come here to relax, to start a new life away from the shackles of her prison and be independent, and look at her! Nightmares and visions of a murdered child and ghosts in fields, and now the horror of attending some damned Ball keeping her awake! It was no wonder that she was a wreck, but it had to stop. She had to get a good night's sleep soon.

She flopped onto her back and glanced at the clock: ten past four. She'd been asleep four hours. The weekend had been spent passing the time of day in the cottage; she wasn't tired enough to sleep properly. That was a good reason for a nightmare: a busy head. The last remnant of her migraine had subsided by Saturday dinnertime, but she still hadn't left the cottage. Someone had brought her bags of shopping and left them in the porch. For fresh air, she sat half in and half out of the French doors and watched the sparrows fly in and around her back hedge. Beyond this she could hear horses in the field, but the hedge was too high to see them.

By Sunday, she'd watched a couple of old films, started to read an old book she'd found on the shelf, ate, drank tea, and told herself she was relaxing, but in honesty, she was hiding. She hadn't gone to Shrewsbury because it had been Saturday and far too busy and besides, her head had still felt mushy and Sunday she'd convinced herself the library wouldn't be open and that was her main reason for going. Shops didn't interest her.

Part of her wanted to go for a walk, but she was afraid of meeting anyone in her fragile state, so, instead, she'd sat around, thinking, listening, half-expecting someone to call and invite her to this Ball, and hiding. She was afraid. What could she do? To reject the invite might cause bad feeling and all she wanted was a quiet life, not tension between her and the villagers. Eira had said they'd leave her alone if she went. Once the gossipers saw she was no-one of importance, she could get on with her life. Although she'd paid for a year, she preferred the chance to have options to stay if life was pleasant here.

Could she perhaps stay for an hour, say hello and make an excuse to leave? Could she possibly do that? She smiled to herself and curled up under the warm duvet. Yes, she would do that. She could endure one hour of smiling and gritting her teeth as people watched her every move. Maybe if she was late, they'd all be so drunk, she wouldn't be noticed? It would please everyone that she'd arrived and made the effort. Surely no-one could judge her if she had a migraine or something. Yes, she could do that.

She was woken up hours later by insistent knocking. Her stomach clenched in fear, but she forced herself to get out of bed and creep over to the window. A small crack in the curtains showed her a white car parked in the lane opposite the cottage. Who the hell could that be? Whoever brought her shopping the other day hadn't forgotten anything, so it couldn't be the shop. Besides, she was sure Eira didn't drive.

Another loud knock came from downstairs and she froze, hugging herself for warmth. Who the hell would knock so hard? Only a man would do that. Was it Adam? Edging forward, she peeked through the crack in the curtain and quickly jumped back as the man stormed back down the path. She recognised him immediately and grimaced. That awful estate agent!

Standing in the middle of her bedroom, she wondered what to do. Get dressed; she felt too vulnerable with only a pair of knickers on. Frantically, she grabbed her discarded nightgown and jeans and dressed. She found a large black hair band and pulled her hair into a ponytail.

She edged toward the curtains and froze. He was still there, standing by the hedge, staring up at her bedroom window with a smirk on his face. He knew she was here, so now the question was, what was he going to do? She looked back at the clock: 8.15. How long would he stand there? She felt such anger at this intrusion that she clenched her fists. Damn the lecherous bastard!

She'd overslept, so she'd miss the nine o'clock bus unless he went now. And she didn't want another day cooped up in her cottage. She would take her mind off the Ball and try to get some answers about the child and those ruins. The determination to go to Shrewsbury had surprised her, but it was an urgent need she couldn't ignore it any longer. Now he was here. Why?

Stepping back into the middle of the room, she took off her nightgown and found a clean bra and a jumper. Walking across the landing, she used the bathroom and quickly washed her face. Every movement was carefully done so as not to make any noise. Could he hear the creaks and groans of the old floorboards? Of course not, but she did it anyway. Edging close to her bedroom window again, she held her breath. The car was still there; he wasn't.

Her mind raced. Every door and window was definitely shut and locked downstairs. Did he have any keys? Her heart began to thump madly and she shook. Where was the bastard? Relief flooded through her as she saw him walk from around the side of the cottage and toward his car. Stepping back so he couldn't see her, she watched as he turned and looked up again. *Could* he see her? He stood for a moment longer before checking his watch. Cursing, he opened his door and started the engine. With one more look, he drove off toward the village. In a cloud of dust, he was gone.

She walked slowly down the stairs, checking the empty room, knowing he had driven away but feeling violated somehow. Seeing the French door curtains open, she frowned. He would have looked through and seen everything. She did a quick check: only a plate, a mug of cold tea, and her dirty, black cardigan which hadn't been moved for ages. So, he'd seen nothing that could excite him. She shivered. He had to be the most repulsive insect she had ever met.

But, what did he want? Had Adam sent him round? The thought of the two men talking about her made her feel so angry. Two vile little men plotting her extraction, no doubt, and the thought of seeing him at the Ball repulsed her very core, but nothing was going to get in the way of her trip, nothing and no-one. Adam Kenward could go and die for all she cared, and his estate agent lecher.

Would he return? He'd known she was there, of that she was sure. Heading for the kitchen, she quickly poured herself some orange juice and buttered two slices of bread. If it was a fight he wanted, so be it. She had read and reread her rent documents, which had been drawn up especially because she'd wanted to pay a full year. She was fairly sure it was airtight and he could do nothing to her. Finishing her juice, she grabbed her key, her shoulder bag, and her sandwiches, stuffing one in her mouth while she pulled on her boots. She would go into Shrewsbury and try to find answers. The Kenwards and their estate agent could bloody well wait.

***

Eira was fretting about Bronwen's health and the Ball. Twice she had been about to walk up to the cottage and speak with her again, to check on her migraine which she'd seen coming, but the shop had been busy throughout the weekend and by early evening, her body was too exhausted. Yet the need to see her was overwhelming. The fear in Bronwen's eyes had been so real and painful to see, but hardly surprising in the circumstances, as her first meeting with the Kenwards hadn't been successful.

The tears came quickly; she picked up a dishcloth and wiped her face with it. Now, she had a chance to redeem herself and to make things right, for everyone. Bronwen was the key, the one she needed to save, she was sure of it. How and why remained unknown for now and it was very frustrating. She deserved this chance, surely. They all did and it was a long time coming; she didn't dare mess it up.

An innocent visit couldn't do any harm, surely? Besides, she could do with the walk and the fresh air, and she loved the cottage; all good reasons to go. She knew she was talking herself into it, finding excuses to visit. It was only a mile down the lane, but she knew that each step would be like needles in her feet, especially once she passed the Kenward gates. The cottage sat on the outskirts of the village, but within its boundary, just.

She hadn't walked past the gates for many years and longed to see the cottage that she knew so well. She'd hated the idea of another beautiful old building falling into ruins and been very happy on hearing that Adam was renovating it. No-one knew just how old it was, the foundations anyway.

The last time she'd attempted to walk that far, she'd stood in the lane crying openly, knowing that no-one would hear her. It was very rare that the villagers came this way. The cottage barely stood, the roof completely gone, as had every window, and what was left, nature claimed. The large, ancient door clung on by one rotten hinge. The porch door lay on the grass. The garden, once abundant with vegetables and herbs, had long since given up. No-one even picked the apples anymore; they had lain forgotten, just like everything else. It needed life and it needed love, and she wondered if Adam knew it had been she who'd first put the idea of giving Oak Cottage to him into Richard's head to renovate, to make something his.

Lost in her thoughts, she hadn't heard the bell above the shop door until it sounded again as the door was closed. She looked at the man who walked in and now stared around the shop with an interested look on his face. His eyes alighted on her, standing behind the counter. She suddenly felt very glad for it; evil had just walked into her shop.

He walked purposefully toward her and leant on the counter, his face a foot from hers; he smiled. 'Good morning. I've heard about this place.'

Instinctively, she took a step back. He saw it, and something in his eyes changed. He was enjoying making her uncomfortable. She straightened herself. She knew his face, but couldn't quite place it. 'Can I help you?' Her voice quivered slightly and she coughed to try to cover it up; it didn't.

'I certainly hope so, love. I'm looking for a Bronwen Mortimer.'

She shook her head, pretending not to comprehend. 'I…don't think I know the name.'

'Oh sure you do, love.' She cringed as a wicked smile played at the corners of his mouth. 'She's just moved into Oak Cottage. Apparently, she ordered some goods off you. I'm sure you know who I mean?'

Her mind raced with indecision. 'Oh yes, of course. Miss Mortimer. I believe I did do an order for her.' She kept her eyes fixed on his. 'So, you are…'

He straightened and quickly glanced around the shop as if he was checking for anyone else lurking behind the shelves. She wondered why he should do that. 'Of course, let me introduce myself, James Hawthorn, of Hawthorn and Briggs estates agents.' He produced a small card from his breast pocket and held it out for her. Seeing her hesitate, he placed it on the counter and grinned. 'I helped Sir Richard with the transaction and I was just driving nearby and thought I'd call in, to see if she's settled in.'

Oh yes, she could see only too well just how he'd like to see her and a shiver ran through her. She'd known men like this. Men who wanted to hurt women. If he found Bronwen, she would suffer. 'Yes, I believe I do know you, Mr Hawthorn, but unfortunately, I don't really know Miss Mortimer. She's hardly ever around. In fact, when she came in the other day for supplies, she mentioned going away to see some friends, I think.'

He knew she was lying, she knew it without a doubt, and she kicked herself for trying too hard. Her heart hammered against her ribs as he took a step forward, resting his hands on the counter again.

'I see…a shame. I had hoped to see her again.'

'I'm sure she's fine, Mr Hawthorn. She looked quite all right when I last saw her. Perhaps I can give her a message?'

'A messaging service now, eh?' His sarcasm dripped from every word. 'No, no messages today for gossiping old ladies. I'll catch up with her soon.' He turned to go.

'I'd leave her alone if I were you, Mr Hawthorn. Sir Richard would not take kindly to you hounding Miss Mortimer…would he?' Her voice sounded stronger than she felt and she thrust her hands into her cardigan pockets so he wouldn't see them shaking.

He whirled round to face her, his anger clearly visible. 'I'm not hounding Bron—Miss Mortimer, but I do like to check on my clients as I like to know they are happy with my services. Sir Richard knows this.'

'Strange, I didn't see you care about Mr and Mrs Yates when they rented their house through your offices. In fact, this is the first time I've seen or heard of you since they moved in two years ago, isn't it?'

Her eyes met his and she forced herself not to waver. He grinned and shrugged. 'What can I say? My caring side for my clients is quite new. The new me, you might say.'

'There is nothing new about you, Mr Hawthorn.' She emphasised her words carefully. 'If I ever do see Miss Mortimer, I'll be sure to warn her that you are looking for her. In the meantime, if there's nothing else, I'm closing the shop for a while, so...' She indicated the door. For a moment, he didn't move. She thought he was about to say something else, but he abruptly changed his mind and stormed out, slamming the door behind him.

Eira kept her eyes on the door as she felt underneath the counter for her small stool. Finding it, she slowly eased herself down. Her hands shook violently as adrenalin rushed through her body. Taking deep breaths, she prayed no customers would come in. She looked up as she heard a car skidding away; it was white.

Standing up, she quickly sat down again; her legs felt like jelly. She reached for a hankie and wiped the sweat that had popped out on her forehead. Her face felt very hot, and she fanned herself with a magazine. Eventually, she felt well enough to stand. She slowly made her way through into her cottage and poured herself a large glass of water.

Her mind raced. What would he do if he found Bronwen? Evil dripped off this man like water from the roof after a rainstorm. Should she phone the police? Give a statement, perhaps? Have him arrested? But for what? For coming into her shop and asking for Bronwen? She had to warn her. Nothing and no-one must harm Bronwen Mortimer; there was too much at stake now.

***

He slammed on the brakes; the car skidded to a halt at the T-junction that led onto the A49 to Shrewsbury. He glanced quickly in his rearview mirror but knew there wouldn't be another car coming up behind him. There never was.

James wiped his face with his hand. He was surprised to find it wet with sweat. Winding down the window, he closed his eyes for a moment. The cool breeze played over his hot face and neck. Damn the bitch! It had been going so well; he'd been enjoying himself, seeing how nervous she was. He hadn't got an erection, but torture had crossed his mind; he'd enjoyed that once before on some elderly lady down south. Stupid bitch had dared to answer back, like this one, but then, something had changed.

That woman knew what he was capable of. How could she, though? No-one knew. He was damned good at hiding his true self. No-one guessed what he did, but she definitely had, he'd swear it. He could see it in her eyes. What did he feel? Not fear, he wasn't afraid of anyone, especially a woman, an old woman! What could he do? Kill her? That would be easy.

Putting the car into gear, he edged it forward and waited for a space in the traffic. He headed toward Shrewsbury and the office. He'd deal with the old bitch another time, her and his beautiful Bronwen. Smiling now, he tried to ignore the knot in his stomach; it wasn't fear…it couldn't be.

CHAPTER THIRTEEN

HER INITIAL BRAVERY HAD DIMINISHED by the time she reached the entrance to the Kenward Estate. Turning the corner, she almost dived into the hedge as a car came out of the driveway. The male driver glanced at her longer than was necessary, then sped off toward the village. She stood stock still, unsure, feeling stupid and slightly shaken. She looked up at the sky as a large drop of rain fell onto her head. That decided it. She turned, hating herself for being so weak, and marched quickly back to the cottage, cursing herself, the bloody weather, and men.

***

Adam sat staring out into space. His office door stood open and he could hear various noises coming from the stable yard. Usually they were noises that comforted him. Their familiarity felt like his comfort blanket. Years of hard work, sweat, and tears had made those noises real. Years of sacrifices that he knew in his heart were worth it, but sometimes he had creeping doubts, which he firmly pushed away when he could hear his horses and his employees. The stables would be a success, he had to believe that. He should have been happy, especially now he had Scarlet, but he wasn't.

He felt like a shit. Geoff was right; he was bad tempered, rude, and arrogant. He'd treated little Mathew appallingly and he would make amends with the Ludlow transfer. What else could he do?

He couldn't get the boy's face out of his head. Had he been responsible for that? He glanced down at his stained jacket and felt his chest tighten; it was a disturbing thought. He'd given Mathew the rest of the weekend off, but so far, he hadn't seen him this morning.

Who was the woman Mathew said had seen them too? Of course, that was the question to ask if he went down the road of believing that Mathew was seeing murders and hangings. Mathew was obviously having some kind of hallucination induced by stress, perhaps, or drugs or alcohol. He quickly dismissed the last two; Mathew was not that kind of lad. So stress seemed a logical explanation, but he wasn't completely convinced. He'd seen the fear in the boy's eyes, and something stirred in his own memory; it felt important but he couldn't remember. Geoff knew something, he was sure of it.

Lighting a cigarette, he inhaled deeply as images of his mother flooded his head. He felt the sting of tears and quickly blinked them away. His heart hammered against his chest and his hand shook as he lifted the cigarette to his lips again.

He suddenly felt afraid, but couldn't understand why that should be. His mother had been a good woman; he knew that for certain, yet whenever he tried to remember her death, it felt like a blanket came down over his thoughts, and however hard he tried, he just couldn't think about it. One day, he'd have to have to ask his father, but not yet. Any conversations they'd had lately turned into slanging matches and he wouldn't do that to his mother.

***

It rained on and off for the rest of the day. It didn't matter, though; she had to admit defeat, for now at least. Seeing that man, a stranger, looking at her, had filled her with such fear and anxiety, she would have rushed back anyway. She felt utterly deflated and disgusted with herself.

By early evening, the wind picked up. She listened as it howled around the cottage. Lighting the fire, she sat on the floor, her legs drawn up, a large whisky clutched in her hand. She'd been drinking all afternoon trying to forget how pathetic she was. Her eyes felt heavy, her body warm and fuzzy with the heat and alcohol.

This was not how she had seen herself behaving when she'd dreamt of living here. She would be Miss Independent who was brave and strong and did her own planting and sowing and general gardening and stuff. Perhaps made her own wine from the fruits of her labour, knitted her own jumpers and socks, baked and experimented with new foods, and got knowledge from reading loads of books and things! She'd wanted to live 'The Good Life' alone.

Instead, she was allowing outside factors to dictate her life, and why? Because of her damned fear, that was why. Fear of people. Fear of what they'd do and say. Okay, granted, some of these people were, um, dead, but still. Any activity would bring with it some level of anxiety, be it in Shrewsbury playing detective, or clearing out her garden, so it was either, get off her backside and face her fears, or she might as well go back to the city. That thought alone made her stand up and go to the French doors.

She finished the last bit of whiskey and belched softly. She was so sick of feeling sorry for herself. She remembered all the advice she'd been given. All the telephone numbers she could ring for support. She'd never rung any of them in all the years since, and had no idea where those telephone numbers were now.

She huffed loudly. Tomorrow she would make a start. Bored. That was what she was. Well, boredom wasn't on her to-do list. Enough was enough, damn it! Making herself a cup of tea, she carefully walked back into the lounge and rummaged around until she found a scrap of paper. The voice of her counsellor echoed around her head. 'If in doubt, write things down. It can feel different once you see it on paper.'

Okay, she'd do what she suggested. On the top of the paper she wrote, 'Raining: go by bus to Shrewsbury', and on the other side she wrote, 'Fine: go and begin on the garden'. Taking the paper and her tea upstairs, she had to admit to feeling quite optimistic.

***

The next morning, she woke after another fitful sleep, but the optimism hadn't evaporated overnight. Jumping out of bed, she quickly went to the window and peeped out from behind the curtain. It was fine. Clouds gathered and it looked unsettled, but fine it was; the garden won. She felt a small pang of regret for Shrewsbury, but fair's fair, the garden it would be today.

She rushed through breakfast, then quickly dressed in some old jeans and a fleece. Yanking on her old boots, she opened the front door and was blinded by the sudden rays of the sun that chose that moment to come out from behind a huge cloud. She stood for a moment in the porch, her eyes closed, enjoying the warmth on her skin.

She stepped out and took in a lungful of fresh, clean air. She looked around wondering what to do and where to start. She had worked a little on the front hedge a few days before, and the grass was too wet to mow, but perhaps she could make a start on the back hedge which was threatening to overpower the entire garden.

With a plan in mind, she headed round the side of the cottage. The small shed half hidden beneath the dense shrubbery looked as menacing as ever. The sun hadn't reached this part of the garden. She shivered; it didn't feel as nice. She sighed loudly and scolded herself for being a wimp. The wooden shed, which had all but disappeared beneath the thorny brush, looked far worse than she remembered and she wondered how she could get at the door.

Pulling the arm of her fleece over her hand, she reached out at the nearest bit of bramble and yanked. She squealed as large droplets of water soaked her arm and the material got caught; a quick pull and she was free. Racing back into the cottage, she found the large pair of scissors from the kitchen and purposefully walked back to the shed. They wouldn't be ideal, but she hoped large garden tools would be found in the shed. Slowly but surely, it worked. The small shed door became more and more visible and the way to it became easier.

***

'My lord, I must speak with you. I beg you to hear me, my lord! It is your daughter. She runs too wild. She will not listen to me or to anyone…except you, my lord. If she is to become the lady you want, then this behaviour must end…now.'

William sighed heavily. He knew what she said was true, but still, his heart ached that Anne and Gwenllian had not bonded as he had hoped. 'Very well, my love, I will speak with her, but she is only a child still. Can we not allow her to enjoy her childhood a little longer, for all too soon, it is over.'

He watched as she fought to control her facial expressions. Married six years now, he finally admitted defeat where his wife and daughter were concerned, but it saddened him deeply.

Gwenllian's hatred had been undisguised from the start, but he tried to be patient with her being she was only five when he'd taken Anne as his wife. After all, she'd had him all to herself all those years, and they had formed a special bond, but his daughter could not take away his longing for a son, or keep him company at night.

Sadly, after Anne's four miscarriages, he was beginning to lose hope of ever having the son he desired. Gwenllian was a constant reminder that another woman had managed to provide him with a child, a live one, even if she died doing it. Could he dare to believe that Anne would conceive again? Her courses were late. Could this time be the miracle he dreamed of?

Holding out his arms, he held her close as Anne snuggled into his chest; he could smell lavender in her hair. They had placed bunches of lavender with his children; the memory hurt him deeply and he tightened his embrace, trying to drive it away. Three daughters, and lastly, his son and heir, had all died before the eighth month. He held his son, willing him to breath, to live, but instead, his son died in his arms.

Anne had wept for weeks. Too distraught to eat or sleep, she wandered around the castle at night, wailing that God betrayed her.

The monks at the nearby monastery had been called to come and pray for her soul.

He took comfort in another woman's arms for a while. Gwenllian also gave him comfort in the knowledge that he could father children; it was possible. Could he take another woman and raise bastards? His friend Rhys had done so on many occasions and accepted them all, but he loved Anne greatly, so, for now, they would try again. Surely if he bedded her enough times, he would succeed?

The thought of his daughter as always brought a smile to his face and warmth to his heart. From the moment she was laid in his arms, he loved her, but it was a bittersweet moment as minutes later he was told his wife had perished; Gwenllian reminded him of her so much, it hurt.

Four months after his wife's death, his grief had not diminished as others told him it would. It grew worse. He was drinking heavily, long into the night; the servants would hear him sobbing for his Lady Jane. No-one could help him, and after a while, they gave up.

He'd been drinking one evening when he heard a commotion outside his Hall. On opening it, he caught a servant girl carrying a large bowl of cold water. After many threats, she told him that Gwenllian had a bad fever. Dropping his goblet, he'd taken the stairs two at a time and burst into the room, the servant girl quickly following, the water sloshing out of the basin. The nurse, shocked at his entrance, quickly directed him to bathe his daughter using the cold water. It had saved her life. All that night he'd stayed with her, rocking her gently by the fire until she'd slept soundly, the fever gone. He promised her there and then that he would love her all her days.

Now, nearing her eleventh birthday, she had grown into a beautiful young girl. She was an accomplished rider on her small pony. He watched over her education and was amazed at her ability to write in Latin and French. She kept friends and guests amused with her wit and her conversation and would sit, curled up on his knees, listening to the talks of politics for hours among him and his guests.

This last one caused him concern, but he hadn't, as yet, the heart to change it. A girl should not be so interested in such matters, but he had long since given up ordering her to finish her embroidery. She would flatly refuse. Instead, she would disappear for hours, returning eventually, muddied, sometimes wet, and a huge grin on her face, her long, golden hair flying about, untied and dirty.

It made him unhappy to dwell on the matter of her proposed engagement to Sir Rhys' son. Having spoken with his friend, they agreed to wait until Gwenllian was older before announcing it; that time was coming. Every moment he managed to spend with Gwenllian felt precious. War was coming. Plans had to be made. Time was running short. He could feel it.

'I'll speak with her now, my love.' Kissing Anne on the forehead, he squeezed her hands before quickly walking out of the bedroom. Heading downstairs, he knew exactly where to find his daughter: the courtyard. A new foal had been born yesterday. Gwenllian had been promised a look if she helped with caring for it; she had, of course, jumped at the chance. He grinned warmly as he heard her shriek of joy and excited babble.

**

Left standing alone in her bedchamber, Anne closed her eyes and clenched her hands. Now that he had left, she could let out the rage that she managed to keep hidden from him. The jealousy she felt for that spoilt little monster boiled within her so much that she could almost feel the air thicken with it. Damn his first wife and all that had come out of her!

Her hands gently caressed her flat stomach and she grinned wickedly. She was pregnant; she was sure. Soon, that damned brat would be gone. She would see to it that she was married off as quickly as possible to that Welsh boy, whether William considered it the right time or not, and her child would take its place in his heart. Soon, Gwenllian would be forgotten; of that, she would make sure.

***

Eira groaned loudly. Her body ached with old age and arthritis. She was getting weaker by the day. Surely she would be freed soon. Death. She welcomed it with open arms now. It seemed an age ago that she'd have done anything to live; it was a different life then.

She looked up at the hot sun, shielding her eyes against the glare. Its warmth was soothing on her skin, but its rays didn't seem to penetrate and thaw her completely anymore. Her head throbbed from yet another restless night of dreams she'd rather forget. Sitting up long before dawn, refusing to allow her eyes to close, not wanting to return to those nightmares.

Instead, she had tried to fill her mind with images of the many May Balls she had been to and tried to remember the fun times she experienced in her long life. The dancing, laughing, loving? Tears welled up and she let them fall. Oh, how she had loved, but they were all gone. Everyone she'd ever known now lay as bones or dust. She was the last of her generation and she yearned to be free. One last ball and then…maybe…

The walk to the cottage took much longer than she'd expected. Pain shot up her legs and the air became thicker, harder to breathe, and each movement was an effort. She sweated profusely, but this journey had to be made, for all their sakes. Knowing she needed to see Bronwen, she'd waited for a lull in customers and turned the sign to Closed before walking quickly into the back to retrieve her coat and be out through her gate before anyone else came to buy their wares.

Bronwen. Her mind reeled with what she was going to say. Try to explain. Should she explain? Perhaps it was better to see how things went? Perhaps after the Ball, once she'd been to the Hall and met Sir Richard. Would that be the right thing to do? All these years she hoped, prayed, but never really believed that it would happen. Prayed that the gods would give her another chance, a chance to redeem herself, make things right. Now that they had, she felt unprepared and flustered, never knowing if she should act, wait, or tell everything and…be believed?

As the cottage came into view, she had to shield her eyes from the glare of the sun as it reflected off a huge puddle in the middle of the lane. She stopped and stared at it. The air around it seemed to shimmer; it changed colour as it rose from the ground. Wasn't there supposed to be a pot of gold at the end of rainbows? *Perhaps this is a good sign*, she thought.

Her breath caught in her throat as her eyes travelled farther down the lane. Near the hedge, the child stood motionless, watching her arrival. Eira froze. Their eyes met and she took a step backward. Hatred burned in the child's eyes. No words were needed to convey her meaning: *You are not welcome here.* Shutting her eyes tightly, Eira willed her feet to move forward, taking deep breaths. She opened her eyes; she was alone.

CHAPTER FOURTEEN

BRONWEN STARED AT THE SMALL, wooden door. It had a keyhole. She hoped it wasn't locked. Tentatively reaching out, she pulled at the small, metal handle. Nothing moved. She edged closer, aware of the many thorns around her; she tried again, yanking harder. She felt the door give way slightly. Feeling brave and more determined, she used both hands and tugged. With the sound of a very loud fart, the door gave way and opened.

Unfortunately, the handle, not used to such force after who knew how many years of neglect, came away in her hands. She staggered backward and fell. Her jeans, already wet up to her knees from the rain-soaked grass, were now wet through to her backside too. Bronwen jumped up, rubbing her sore bum. She knew there would be a decent-size bruise there tomorrow.

She stopped rubbing and stared at the shed. The door stood open a couple of inches. She edged backward, until her rear came up against the side of the cottage. The shed was ten feet away. She shivered violently and hugged herself. Something changed; she couldn't see what it was but every nerve was on alert. She realised just how lonely and quiet it was on this side of the garden; even the birds became silent.

Her stare darted between the front of the cottage where the sun warmed the grass and back to the shaded nook, where the old shed could be seen peeking out from beneath the hedge. Wooden debris littered the grass. Every inch of her wanted to turn and walk away.

Find something to do in the front garden. Enjoy the warmth on her skin and forget about this neglected area and pretend she hadn't opened the shed door. Pretend it didn't exist and let nature reclaim it.

Her legs refused to move. A slight movement from within the shed made her glance sharply toward the door. A rat? A cat? She knew instinctively it wasn't an animal. Whatever it was, it was watching her. 'I'm losing it here.' Her voice sounded strange, which broke the tension a little. 'Erm...okay. I'm feeling...a bit...scared of you...is that...all right with you?'

She thought she heard a giggle coming from within the shed. She took a deep breath and pushed herself away from the cottage wall. It was the child. *What the hell do you say to a ghost?* 'Hello? I...erm, oh God, I don't really know...what to, say to you, but I...' Cautiously, she edged closer and stiffened as freezing cold air wrapped itself around her body, making her shiver and catch her breath. The door squeaked as its hinges reluctantly gave way. The door opened wider.

'Hello, my dear...'

Her stomach clenched in fear and her scream pierced the air. Swinging round, she fell back against the wall, trying to keep herself upright as her legs turned to jelly beneath her. She tried to speak, but nothing would come out. Her heart hammered against her ribs and she found it difficult to breathe.

'Oh, my dear. You poor lamb. I'm so sorry, I did call, but, obviously, you hadn't heard me.' Stepping forward, Eira patted her shoulder reassuringly. 'Gave you quite a start, didn't I?'

All Bronwen could manage was a slight nod. She glanced toward the shed door; it stood slightly open as before. Eira followed her glance and stepped in front of her, blocking her view. 'Come along, I think you need a cup of tea more than I do.'

Letting Bronwen go inside first, Eira hesitated a moment and glanced back toward the garden; she was sure the child had gone. The child was angry at her for coming this far from the village, but especially to this place. Eira had to ignore all of that now. Bronwen was her main concern. Eira sensed the courage in her, but she was so frightened of pushing Bronwen too far, too quickly, that was why she'd interfered just now; she wasn't ready to be shown the truth…not yet, surely? She couldn't bear another life on her conscience, not this one. Yet, time was running out. The indecision was hurting her head.

There was another decision to make: James Hawthorn. Evil emanated off that man, and he had set his sights on Bronwen. Her life was at risk from him, but she couldn't shake the feeling that he was somehow involved, as horrific as that felt. She was stumbling around in the dark. Should she be still and do nothing? Allow the threads of life to unfold as they will? Or was she supposed to help it along? Grasp the threads and manipulate them to her will? No-one had given her instructions as to her fate.

***

Geoff slouched in the saddle and let go of the horse's reins, confident in the knowledge Fred wasn't going anywhere. Sure enough, the ten-year-old gelding shook his mane and bent his head to the grass. He smiled to himself, reached into his pocket, and slowly rolled his own cigarette. Finished, he lit it and relaxed back in the saddle, allowing the horse to wander where it pleased, slowly and calmly.

He'd ridden around the many paddocks for the past hour, checking the fencing and the fourteen other horses that littered Kenward land. Deciding he needed to get away for a while, he'd cantered up the farthest field to a high ridge where he could see for miles; it was his favourite place. He'd once heard that Romany gypsies believed that if you had a problem, you climbed high to look down on it and see it for what it really was. From this vantage point, he could see all his troubles.

Below him to the left stood Kenward Hall. From where he sat, he could make out a large rectangular shape and a round shape under the grass: the remains of the first Kenward Hall built around the middle of the fifteenth century by William Cynwearde and finished by his nephew years later. The new hall used part of it, when sometime in the sixteenth century, the Kenward at the time had remodelled the Hall to impress some woman or other, probably Queen Elizabeth. The foundations had been incorporated into the gardens now, but dig down a few feet, the stone was there.

He didn't ride farther up the field to where he would have seen the old castle, built on an Iron Age fort, where the Kenwards began. No one went there anymore.

Beyond those, slightly to the right, were the stables, the yard and the two barns, now looking bigger and more splendid than when he last stood on this spot. Adam did a fine job rebuilding and expanding. He admired him for that.

Eight years ago, they'd bought four horses: two mares, a filly, and Fred. Adam bought Dulas to impress his new wife before the idea of stables became real. No-one else wanted the stallion, despite its breeding potential; he was such a vicious beast. Catherine hadn't been impressed and she'd laughed at him when he'd first begun to train the stallion, which was no easy thing to do. She'd never shown any concern or interest in either Adam or the potential project and for a while, Adam was led away like a puppy on a string; Geoff struggled to keep the horses.

His gaze travelled over the area of land between the Hall and the stables, over the slight rising on which the Hall stood. He could see the pot-holed driveway all the way to the black gates that stood wide open in the distance. He'd caught a few comments about the state of the drive at last year's Ball; God help them this year! He'd already told Richard he doubted he could find the time to paint them.

Clicking the horse into a walk, he headed for the farthest corner, allowing the horse to go at its own pace. From here he could see the small village and some of the surrounding farms. His gaze travelled along the narrow lane, past the old chapel and onward to Mathew's parents' farm. His heart felt heavy thinking about the poor lad. He felt so helpless.

He'd had to half carry the skinny wretch up to the kitchen. Lucy immediately made a large pot of sweet tea and brought out her home-made Victoria sponge, knowing this was one of Mathew's favourites. The lad wouldn't touch a thing. All the coaxing did nothing but make them fret. At last, they gave up and Geoff drove the lad home. He'd heard nothing over the following days and Mathew hadn't shown up for work this morning.

He shivered suddenly in the warm sunshine and quickly glanced around him. Fred felt the change and his head sprang up. 'All right, lad, steady now. It's just me.'

Geoff's soothing voice did the trick and Fred resumed his grazing, the bridle tinkling with each movement. The smell of leather and horse reached Geoff's nostrils and he breathed deeply. He loved the smell; it was a comforting scent to him. That's what that lad needed. Comfort and reassurance, but he had no idea how to provide that.

What he'd heard Mathew talking about had haunted his own dreams and waking hours for many years. The look on Mathew's pale face, Geoff knew only too well. He'd seen that look of horror on Richard's face a number of times over the years, Judith's on one occasion, and again on Lucy. People in the village whispered about it. Even as a boy, he'd heard rumours, and his father had come home one night with that same look of fear.

They all spoke of a child. Nothing more, only that evil surrounded it. He'd heard many stories concerning it, but they were all spoken in drink and never outside the comfort of the pub except, of course, with Richard. They had spoken of it many times over the years, again always with a glass of something in their trembling hands. Perhaps that was the curse people spoke of. If you see her, you're going to die a drink-related death?

He grimaced and began making himself another cigarette. No, jokes couldn't lighten his mood, or Mathew's. Why Mathew? He'd never heard of it showing itself to a child before. Then again, Mathew was sixteen, a child no longer, perhaps, in its eyes? He was such an innocent boy, but then, weren't they all? Helen had been an innocent, kind, and loving mother and wife, her only downfall being married to a Kenward.

He turned and looked back toward Kenward Hall. He could just see the tops of the roof and the chimneys. Quickly, he looked away. It was hard to look and not remember that terrible day. He swallowed hard and quickly lit his roll. For years afterward he'd relived that day, hearing the scream, the thud, frantically searching the garden for the children to protect them. He'd found them eventually, but he'd been too late. Adam had seen everything.

Before Adam and Rosalyn were born, the Hall had been home to a wonderful maze built in 1820. It was constructed of waist-high hedges and covered about half an acre at the back of the Hall. This had become the children's favourite place to play. Geoff helped the gardener in those days and he'd listen to their playing. Adam would pretend for hours that he couldn't find Rosalyn as her stifled squeals of mirth could clearly be heard.

That morning, there was a frost; snow was expected. The children still had three days left of the Christmas break before going back to school. Helen decided that it was time for the decorations to come down, but the children had wanted to go outside to play; she hadn't argued and off they'd run. It was the last time they'd seen her alive.

An hour or so later, Geoff was busy taking the lights down off the cherry trees in the walled garden. From where he stood, he could vaguely hear Adam calling to Rosalyn. He heard a strange kind of grating noise from above and he'd turned to look. The small attic window that as far as anyone knew couldn't be opened now stood wide open. He could remember thinking, *Well done, Helen, but why open it now when it's freezing?*

Watching, he noticed movement from within, but the glare of the January sun prevented him from seeing who it was. The person was getting closer to the open window. He recognised Helen's green jumper. He opened his mouth to shout a warning. Too late, she plunged backward to her death. Her scream pierced the air.

For a moment, he'd remained paralysed, unable to move, knowing she was dead. From where he stood on the ladder, he could see her staring eyes and the pool of blood oozing outward from her head. Suddenly, his limbs went into action. He shot down the ladder, ran to Helen's body, checked for a pulse, and then he went to find the children; that was all that filled his head.

He'd run to the garden, heading for the maze. Silence. No laughter. No giggling or shrieks of joy. For a moment, fear clutched his heart, and then he'd seen him. Adam peered over a bush; Rosalyn, too young to see over, sat beside him on the grassy path. Adam stared toward the Hall, his eyes wide, but a vacant stare; he was six years old.

Kicking the horse into a trot, he turned away from the Hall and its memories and headed down to the lower paddock. To the left he could see the roofs of the cottages and the pub; he'd have a pint later, though he had no time for the gossiping regulars at Ye Olde Castle. He'd occasionally chat with the local farmers, maybe have a game of dominoes or poker, if it was quiet. But usually he'd sit by the huge log fire, a pint in his hand, and they'd leave him be with his thoughts if he was lucky.

Sometimes though, someone would have too much to drink and the gossip would start, usually because of a woman. Bloody hypocrites, the lot of them. He couldn't stand the wives and refused to be drawn into their tittle-tattle. They liked to think of themselves as God-fearing, good people, Hah! Most of them were good for nothing, gossiping grannies with evil tongues. In the old days they knew how to deal with hags like them--gag 'em! That was what he'd do with them.

He could just see the small chapel on the hill. That was something that was left to rot. They went on religious occasions like Easter and Christmas, but it was only for fuel to ignite another round of gossip. See who was wearing what? Why hadn't so and so turned up? See if any new people turned up, if not why not? If they did, God help 'em.

He cantered up to the higher fields, past the Hall, and up to the outskirts of the Kenwards' land. From here he could see the small squared-off land a Kenward had given years ago to a family who'd wanted to build their own home in some long-ago century. The cottage being left to rot, Adam renovated it to live in with Catherine. The high conifer hedges now hid the cottage from view. A shame really; it was a lovely, traditional-looking cottage with ivy and maple trees growing over one side, which only added to its charm. Perhaps he should offer his help to the young woman who was renting it.

None of the villagers would help her. He'd already heard the various stories about the poor woman: whore seemed to be the juiciest. He didn't believe that and said so one evening down at the pub. He'd told them he'd seen her when she'd arrived, granted it was from a distance, but still, she looked a very nice, decent young woman and his thinking had been confirmed again when he saw her yesterday from the car. He also added that she had the best idea staying away from this gossiping village! The men agreed; no doubt their wives would not.

He hoped that she would come to the Ball, and then the 'ifs and whys' might calm down. When she'd seen him in the car yesterday, she'd looked terrified. Poor woman almost dived into the nearest bush, which was odd, but endeared her to him. He hoped that she'd be accepted, and she'd stay, for Adam's sake as much as her own. A nice young lady in the village might do him some good.

He thought about riding over to the cottage and introducing himself, but decided against it. He'd been gone too long, there was work to be done. Perhaps another time and if not, the May Ball was only two weeks away; he could ask her then if she needed help with the garden. He'd seen the state of it a week or so before she'd moved in.

Guiding the horse round, he clicked him into a trot. What a farce the Ball was. Sir Richard hated it. Adam despised it and often either got so drunk he'd pass out upstairs or he wouldn't show up at all. Rosalyn always made excuses not to come.

The only people who looked forward to it were the villagers, and Lucy of course, who planned the buffet for weeks beforehand and then sat back and enjoyed the compliments that came from all sides. She'd sit like a Queen holding court, attempting to be modest about her fine cooking. Her cheeks would beam and her eyes would sparkle, and you'd know she was enjoying every last moment. Then of course, there was Judith, who he suspected loved to organise anything that involved Sir Richard.

***

The initial shock of Eira's sudden appearance was slowly beginning to wear off. Her heart returned to its normal rhythm and her legs felt as if they could hold her up, but her stomach remained in a knot and Bronwen fought down the bile. Needing to be away from Eira's concerned expression, she mumbled something about the kettle and headed as fast as she dared away from the lounge. Once inside the small room, she closed the door and allowed herself to shake all over again.

She leant against the kitchen sink and tried to focus on what happened. The ghost of the child had been there, she was sure of it. Although it felt strange, she didn't think that she'd been too afraid; something told her the girl wouldn't harm her. Maybe she had some kind of rapport with the girl now? People had those, didn't they? They'd shared something terrifying at the ruins, well, she'd experienced it, the ghost had just, been there…oh Christ! She was rambling!

She slowly went about preparing a pot of tea. She poured the boiling water and was about to take the tray in when she stopped, remembering how the atmosphere changed seconds before Eira appeared. The atmosphere became hostile and she knew that hostility and anger well, from the castle. What was it that surrounded that child? How could a child generate such anger and evil intent?

'Are you all right, dear?'

Eira's voice broke her chain of thought. She hurried through with the tray. The expression on Eira's face was of obvious concern, but something else lurked behind her composure, and she wondered if Eira had seen the girl?

Placing the tray on the table, she busied herself with pouring and offering milk, sugar, until there was nothing else to occupy the awkward moments. Bronwen sat back, her cup resting on her knee; she waited. Eira looked uncomfortable, and although sorry for it, Bronwen kept her mouth shut and continued to wait.

***

'The place looks just as I remember it.' Eira's voice shook slightly and she quickly had a sip of tea to hide her discomfort. Bronwen said nothing but looked at her expectantly. 'I mean, it hasn't changed since Adam renovated it, about eight years ago now.'

Bronwen looked surprised. 'You mean, this is his place?'

'No. Well, sort of, yes, actually, I suppose it is…I mean…was.'

They both fell into silence that stretched on into another awkward moment. Bronwen broke it first. 'More tea?'

Eira offered her half-empty cup and smiled as warmly as she could. She knew the woman was feeling confused, frightened, and no doubt curious as to her own arrival. She glanced up and also saw impatience and expectation in Bronwen's eyes. Impatience! That had been her, many years ago, but she'd learnt to be patient. She'd had no choice.

Now to be patient for just a little longer, and trust in this woman, the woman she once betrayed. Eira glanced toward the wall that separated them from the outside, from the small shed hidden beneath years of neglect. She felt the stirrings of energy and knew that time was running out. Purposefully, she put down her cup on the small table and took a deep breath.

CHAPTER FIFTEEN

JUDITH EASED HERSELF DOWN ONTO the stair and quickly fanned herself with the magazine. The hot flush seemed to burn from within and heat every last cell of her body. Sweat instantly coated her skin, and she pulled her white blouse away from her steaming chest, fanning the exposed skin violently. The cool breeze didn't seem to touch the burning heat, but she persevered. Her armpits felt soggy, as did her knickers beneath her tights, and she cursed womanhood for the thousandth time that month.

She quickly mopped her face and neck with a clean handkerchief, moving into her hairline and down the back of her neck; it was soaked through in seconds. Ten minutes later, she began to feel normal again.

She thanked the gods that no-one came and saw her in that manner as she slowly made her way back to her room on the second floor. Locking the door behind her, she gratefully peeled off the cotton blouse and black skirt, her light brown tights, followed by her Marks and Spencer knickers. Her camisole and bra were quickly discarded, and for a moment, she stood completely naked, the cool air playing lovingly on her damp skin. *Lovely*, she thought and then caught a glimpse of herself in the full-length mirror standing in the corner of the large room and blushed. 'Silly woman!' She scolded her reflection. 'You've no time to be enjoying yourself. You have a Ball to organise!'

Gathering up her sweat-drenched clothes, she hastily walked into her en suite bathroom and threw them all into the washing basket.

Within minutes she had showered again and got out another set of clean clothes, a white blouse and black skirt. She opened a new packet of light brown tights and a clean set of bra and knickers, but decided against another camisole. Moments later she was dressed and putting on her black shoes.

Judith checked her image in the mirror, and felt a pang of misery at her wardrobe. She was fifty-nine. Where had her life gone when all she ever wore day after day were the same clothes? No husband. No children. Thirty years of running Kenward Hall and never one offer. Every year she'd daydream about the May Ball and wonder if her Prince Charming would finally arrive, in the shape of Sir Richard, of course. He'd realise he was in love with her and take her in his arms.

She let her hand wander over her 'evening' dresses. Separate from her working clothes, these were beautiful and made her feel attractive. Every year he told her how lovely she looked, and he would dance at least one waltz with her before being snatched away by his other guests. She'd savour the feel of him as they waltzed around the room and dream about it over and over again in the privacy of her bedroom.

She gave herself one last look in the mirror, then quickly left and closed her door. Walking down the stairs, she picked up the discarded magazine. Footsteps along the corridor made her check her hair and touch her face for any signs of her hot flush, but there were none.

Rose appeared at the bottom of the stairs.

'Where have you been? You're late—again'. Placing the magazine under her arm, she frowned down at Rose who hadn't answered, merely shrugged as she took off her jacket. 'This isn't good, you know. There's so much to do'.

She took in Rose's face, pale beneath the over-use of makeup, her crumpled shirt with the top two buttons undone to show an ample bosom. No tights under her short skirt and worn, heeled black shoes. She sighed and, shaking her head, walked toward the kitchen to get her list of jobs needing to be finished. Without turning, she gently called back. 'By the way, take off some of that makeup, we don't want you looking like a cheap tart, and fasten your buttons. You seem to have forgotten the top two.'

***

Rose watched her leave before pulling a face at the closed kitchen door. 'Bad tempered old hag. Just because she can't get away with dressing seductively anymore, why should I look old?'

Rose took out her compact, and looked at herself in the small, round mirror. Possibly get rid of the red lipstick and change it to a nice, soft pink. Tone down the blusher. It did look too heavy now that she was standing in natural light. But her eyes, no way. The black eyeliner and mascara emphasised her brown eyes nicely, and the old HRT dependant could go and jump.

Fixing her face, she caught a glimpse of her breasts. 'Well, maybe just one button. I have to give Adam something to look at and admire.'

***

Richard stood against his study door and waited. He'd been about to leave when he heard the exchange between Judith and young Rose. Slowly he'd closed the door over, but opened it slightly again to see if the coast was clear, only to see Rose pulling faces at what he presumed was the back of Judith. Rose then proceeded to mess about with her hair and face. He shut the door again.

Poor Judith. Every year he listened to her seemingly endless lists of cleaning and restoration work that needed doing. If it couldn't be done in time, or afforded, she'd re-organise the Hall so old paintings, heirlooms and such, disappeared upstairs and others took their place or she'd rearrange the furniture to cover up the space; a miracle woman indeed.

Not that it ever really mattered. By the night of the Ball, the lighting was dimmed to help make the Hall look more authentic and hide any dampness or dry rot and besides, the villagers were only interested in the free buffet and bar. The gossip never changed. The attitudes never changed. Only the music had changed over the years. Fifteen years ago, they'd insisted on a 'disco'. Judith, appalled at the idea, had argued against it, but he'd compromised and said old dancing till ten, then they could have their disco until the end. For a few years, he'd actually enjoyed himself giving it a go! Too old these days, perhaps?

The May Ball was his spring nightmare, but he couldn't stop it without dealing with the villagers who had the right to 'party' on his land each May Day. The old document written by the nephew of Sir William Cynwearde clearly stated that he offer the villagers and tenants within a four-mile radius of the Hall a night of pleasure every year on the May full moon.

The original document now rested in some local archive some- where, not that it did much good to anyone Most of it was damaged and the bottom half was gone. A copy sat in his desk, which he would bring out every year for anyone interested to read it; no-one did anymore.

Rosalyn was the only Kenward who showed any interest during her teenage years in the history of the promise made by her ancestor, but that had been brief. He glanced at the telephone, where only minutes before he'd been speaking with her, trying to convince her to come and stay for a while. She'd moaned about work and it not being a good time and sadly, he'd used his old card. 'But, Rosalyn, I haven't seen you for months. You don't phone when you say you will and I am getting on, you know. It would be nice to remind myself what my daughter looks like.' He cringed as he said it and heard the exasperated sigh the other end of the line. She'd finally agreed to come to the Ball and stay overnight. Judith would be thrilled.

Grabbing his coat from the closet, he quietly got himself ready to go out. He felt very silly behaving in such a manner, but the last thing he wanted right now was somebody asking him where he was going. His meeting with John was one he was already dreading, he didn't need the hassle of lying about it too.

He firmly put on his old flat cap, picked up his keys and sneaked out of the front door, gently closing it behind him. He was in his car and away before anyone noticed; he was glad of that.

***

Rose hung up her jacket and slowly wandered over to the large cupboard next to the pantry where the cleaning equipment was kept. Two vacuums, every type of duster, rag, and mop made by man. Cleaning solutions by the gallon for every surface and everything kept in perfect order, nothing out of place. Sometimes she'd move a bottle and swap things around. Judith said nothing, knowing she was doing it to annoy her, but she'd come in the next day and it would all be spotless and intact again. Sad bitch!

Opening a packet of mints, she popped two in her mouth before grabbing a duster, a cloth, window solution, and polish. The upper bedrooms were on the list next, but not the beds. Those would be made up the day before. Everything listed and ticked off. It was pathetic really; didn't the old bat have a life?

She grimaced at the horrible thought that Judith might have some kind of love life away from the Hall. Shaking her head, she slowly wandered up the stairs trying not to picture Judith lying on her back. *I'll bet she's still a virgin.*

Rose stopped at the top of the stairs, looked out of the small window, and watched Sir Richard drive away. 'Where is he going?' She liked Sir Richard and hoped that he liked her enough to give his blessing if Adam declared his love. That sister of his would definitely be a problem. She was a bitch! Just because she had a couple of shops dotted around the country, she thought she was the Queen.

A few years ago she had visited Chester on a girls' weekend. She'd gone into Rosalyn's clothes shop and the women told her to leave.

Okay, so she was pissed off her head, but still, when she'd told them she knew Rosalyn they should have been nicer. Instead, they'd threatened to call the police. One of her friends threw up outside the shop and then they'd staggered away laughing.

Perhaps she should try to be nice to Judith; after all, Adam loved the woman and it might be in her favour? Her mum was going through the menopause; maybe she could give her a few pointers to tell Judith. If she could be nice, maybe on the night of the ball, Judith might encourage Adam to dance with her. What if she gave Judith some sob story about her life? Would she take pity on her?

A noise from behind her made her jump round. Was it Judith? The corridor was empty yet she was sure she could hear footsteps at the far end. Stepping away from the small window, she walked to the top of the stairs and glanced down. She could hear Judith in one of the main bedrooms with a vacuum. There it was again—footsteps. Now they sounded as if they were coming from the far bedroom.

She walked toward the door; it stood ajar. 'Hello.' No-one answered, but the sound stopped. She felt very alone up here. She glanced back down the dark, narrow corridor and realised just how dark it had become. The old oak panelling didn't help, and with only a small window at each end, hardly any light was allowed into the old place.

Tentatively, she reached out and pushed open the door. It creaked loudly as it slowly swung wider to reveal the small bedroom. The single bed, unmade and covered with a dust-sheet, stood in the centre of the room. The small, pine wardrobe and matching dressing table were empty. The rose coloured walls and curtains looked the same, as did the white carpet, yet something about the room made her back away.

She couldn't see behind the door, and every cell in her body knew no-one could be in there, but something in her head screamed that someone stood within. They didn't like her very much. The hairs on the back of her neck sprang up and she shivered as a sudden blast of cold air hit her before quickly disappearing. She licked her dry lips and tasted the mints.

Marching into the room, she checked behind the door. Satisfied and feeling a bit foolish, she began sorting the cloths and the polish. She decided the room needed a good airing. She went over to the window and yanked the handle upward; it was so stiff from lack of use. Pushing hard, she managed to open the small window wide enough to stick her head out and breathe deeply. The sky was clearer, the air was fresh. She could see a rider heading back toward the stables and wondered for a moment if it was Adam; it wasn't. Disappointed, she stood daydreaming; the cleaning could wait a minute or two.

***

Behind her, the small figure stood still and watched. The young woman was pretty. Her effort to open the window made her smile, but then she remembered how she had once enjoyed breathing the fresh air, the smell of hay and horses. The smell of the flowers, bread, even manure, they were all smells she yearned for. Smells she couldn't have anymore. She stood watching and remembering, and her piercing blue eyes turned cold.

***

'Come away, child!' The old nurse hobbled as quickly as she could into the large chamber and made a grab for the small thin child who stood on tiptoe at the narrow window. Wriggling free, the child giggled as she skipped around the room, staying just out of reach. The nurse grew tired first and collapsed into a chair beside the warm fire. 'You'll be the death of me, girl!'

Still giggling, ignoring her nurse's protests, the child climbed back onto the ledge and peered down into the courtyard. It was busy with men and boys running around trying to saddle the horses as quickly as possible.

'You come away now, Gwenllian. If you fall…'

She wondered if the child heard her. She'd noticed the sparkling eyes, the rosy cheeks; the child was as excited as a kitten with a piece of string. 'What are you looking at?' Easing herself out of the chair, she peered over Gwenllian's head and sighed loudly; so it had begun. Many men had come and gone over the past few months. She could sense the change, and the uncertainty frightened her. Glancing down at her charge, she wasn't sure who she was more frightened for, herself or this beautiful child.

Gwenllian might be safer than she was, although, being the child's nurse might save her if the war did come. If the English King won, what would happen to Sir William and his family? If, and it was a big if, this Welshman did manage to cross the channel and invade the country, where would Sir William's loyalty lie? Everything was just too uncertain.

Stepping away from the cold, stone ledge, she hobbled back to the dying fire and threw some logs onto it. Once they caught, she poked them with a long stick before easing herself back into the comfortable chair. Feeling the warming embers on her cold legs, she closed her eyes.

'Nia?' The child sounded concerned, so she opened one eye and saw she had climbed down and was watching her.

'Yes, my dear. Do not fret. I am well, only cold with that window wide open.'

The child heard the teasing note in the voice and smiled. Coming forward, she sat with her knees drawn up, staring into the growing flames. 'When can I go out again, Nia? I'm bored with this room, and it is such a lovely, warm day. Spring is here, isn't it?'

Nia gently stroked Gwenllian's long, golden hair. 'You are much better, child, that much I will give you, but your body is still weak from lack of sustenance, and you haven't been able to keep any food inside you yet. A few more days, perhaps.'

'A few days? Oh no, Nia, please! I'll eat anything you say. I'll try that watery broth.

'But you're so thin, child, you might catch a chill.'

'I'll wear anything you say. I'll wear those horrible, itchy stockings and not take them off. I'll even wear that hooded cloak Father's wife had made for me, but please, I must get out and breathe the fresh air…*please!*'

Nia closed her eyes so she didn't have to look at the pleading eyes now peering up at her. Would a few moments in the warm sun do any harm? Sir William would not question her judgement, but his wife would. If anything went wrong, she would be blamed. Gwenllian was too important now. Her marriage to Sir Rhys' son would make a strong alliance. This latest illness which caused severe stomach cramps, vomiting, and diarrhoea had weakened Gwenllian more than she'd care to admit, but she felt the intensity of Gwenllian's stare and couldn't stop herself from smiling.

Opening her eyes, she bent down and cupped the fragile cheek-bones in her hands. The child had become so thin, but nothing could stop the obvious transformation of this child. Eleven years old and her beauty already in evidence. So like her mother, poor lamb; a disadvantage as far as the new lady was concerned. How different might the household have been if Lady Jane had lived?

'Very well, but only for a short walk and no more.'

Jumping up, Gwenllian gave a whoop of joy and danced around the room. Unfortunately, this brought on a dizzy spell, and she crashed into the bed, swaying. Nia caught her and gently eased her into the chair. She hurried over to the small table on which a goblet and two beakers sat, and poured out some weak ale. By now, Gwenllian's cheeks were pale and she was sweating slightly. Nia pressed the goblet to her lips and forced her to sip the liquid slowly.

They both flinched as the door swung open. Lady Anne stood in the doorway. Her gaze took in everything: the child, half-dressed and extremely thin, her skin pale and grey. Dark circles under her eyes, which now glowered at her. Her long hair wild and unkempt and in need of a good wash. 'I shall have a hot bath prepared.'

Nia's increased pressure on her arm stopped Gwenllian from telling Anne just what she could do with the bath, and with one last hostile look, Anne went, the door firmly closed behind her. The message was clear: You will stay in here, but you will look respectable, ill or not.

Without words, Nia and Gwenllian moved closer to the fire and made themselves comfortable. The bath would take a while, so in the meantime they would sit and daydream together. Nia gently stroked the child's hair while she told her a story about the Welsh dragon, one of Gwenllian's favourite. The child sat quietly, staring into the flames, resigned to her fate, for now.

CHAPTER SIXTEEN

EIRA'S HANDS WERE SHAKING, AND she quickly stuffed them between her legs as she sat forward. Bronwen shifted uncomfortably in her chair and clung to her cup of half-finished tea. 'My dear...'

Bronwen waited expectantly, but nothing else came out. She watched as the elderly woman became flustered and took out a handkerchief and began mopping her face. She opened her mouth to continue, but no sounds came out except croaking noises. Eira crumbled and tears rolled down her cheeks.

Bronwen felt utterly horrified. 'Oh God! What is it? Eira, please, what is it?'

'You care...about me, of all people.' The words flew out of her mouth before she could stop them. Appalled, she quickly hid her face behind her handkerchief and harshly wiped her eyes and blew her nose, all the while keeping her eyes firmly fixed on the floor. Her mind raced. What had she said? What could she say? What should she say now? *Pull yourself together! You can't fall apart now, not now!*

Suddenly, the wave of nausea swept over her so quickly she barely had time to reach the kitchen sink. She had never managed to be this far from the village for so long and it was taking its toll, as it always had. After so long, the power of their hatred was still potent.

The chanting echoed around her head, feeling like her skull would explode from the pressure. Hatred burned in each person's eye as

201

spittle ran down their chins unnoticed; their full attention was on her. The power of that night had not diminished. Nia. The name echoed around her head. Murderess. Innocent. When would oblivion come?

***

Lady Anne found William discussing supplies with his steward in the Hall. Both men turned toward her as she entered, but only William smiled; his steward, Andrew merely bowed slightly and carried on looking through the lists. Ignoring him, she cleared her throat. 'William, I must speak with you.'

Andrew heard the real command of 'Leave us now!' but chose to ignore it until William gave him a quick nod. He waited until Lady Anne stepped farther into the room before gathering up the papers and without a backward glance left the Hall. Nobody liked her. She was known as 'that woman' amongst the servants, and he had no doubt that she knew it. Nothing passed her. Some whispered she was a witch, though no-one said it too loudly.

The woman was hard and cold. Perhaps that was why God had seen fit to keep her barren. But the one bit of gossip he did agree on was the hatred that smouldered in her soul. He saw the way she looked at 'little Gwen', as he called her. He'd watched the child grow and loved her as his own. She would come most days to play with his three sons, though they were all older. He had no doubt that the reason for her intrusion this morning would be about the child; sadly, it always was.

Anne waited a moment while William eased himself into one of the armchairs beside the fire. He looked tired and she felt a tinge of guilt, but quickly pushed it aside; things had to be said. 'I'm afraid it's about Gwenllian. I caught her running around her chamber half-dressed just now. She looked wild and dirty, my lord. I've ordered a hot bath for her, but this can't be allowed to continue. She must be made to behave like a lady.'

William didn't answer. He stared into the fire. Quietly, Anne poured him a goblet of wine and handed it to him. He took it without looking up at her but didn't drink. She sat opposite him, feeling the warmth touch her skin. She saw him frown.

'My dear William….'

'It's always about my Gwenllian.'

She heard the impatience in his voice and knew she was treading thinly. Her hand went automatically to her stomach and she felt reassured she was doing this for the best. 'I think she is feeling better, William; that is a good start. Perhaps now is the time to think about her betrothal as—

'Her betrothal? My daughter has been near death's door and all you can talk of is her damned betrothal?'

'Don't you think it's time? She is nearing her twelfth year. Sir Rhys has given you his word that she will marry his youngest son, but things change. What if he changes his mind?'

William drank deeply before answering, his anger evident though he tried hard not to show it. 'My friend will keep his word, as I will keep mine. Gwenllian will go to his son and we have already spoken and agreed their betrothal will be made this year. I have said nothing, as I have waited to see if I had a daughter to give.'

Ann reached out and gently touched his hand. 'I'm sorry, William. It is only that I worry about what will happen. War is so uncertain. We need to make a suitable alliance, and what I saw this morning hurts me. The child doesn't know the meaning of decency and respect. If we are not careful, no-one will take her as wild as she is now.' She could see she was going too far and she quickly added. 'Besides, her nurse is a bad influence. The bedchamber window was wide open. I could find someone who will help Gwenllian properly—'

'Gwenllian is in good hands. I have trusted Nia for many years.'

'Of course, William, but we do need Gwenllian healthy and lady-like for Sir Rhys' visit or I worry that he will see a wild, unkempt child and change his mind.'

'Rhys has known Gwenllian all her life. I am not worried; neither should you be. Gwenllian has proved yet again that she is a strong girl. You worry about your own health.' He regretted saying it the moment he had, but there was no going back.

He was so sick of hearing about her worries. The past few weeks, he had been hiding his own fears regarding his daughter as he'd sat watching her retching into a bowl after only a few sips of water. She hadn't eaten for a week, but Nia ordered the cook to make a watery broth, which she kept in the child's room. Gwenllian sipped it slowly and was finally keeping it down.

Of course, he wasn't stupid. As a knight, he knew what an alliance between both houses would mean. He was a knight in name only with a crumbling castle and a few acres of land. His tenants brought in a small sum, the battles he had fought helped his pocket, but there was never enough silver left over to rebuild his castle, and now the coming war would diminish more of his wealth.

The whispers of an invasion by Henry Tudor were rising; it seemed inevitable. His alliance with Rhys would put him in good stead—if the Tudor won. He was playing a close game, as was Rhys, but if they kept their heads, then victory could be theirs if the right man won the crown. King Richard sent word he demanded his loyalty, and he had given it freely years ago, but Richard never honoured him; he was more or less left to his own devices.

Rhys confided in him that he considered giving his allegiance to Henry as Richard was being harsh in his demands. The king's suspicious nature combined with his feelings of persecution and his constant habit of changing his mind made Rhys feel very uneasy and appalled at the King's behaviour. He expected the King to ask for some ridiculous amount of money to prove his allegiance. As yet, no word had reached either of them, but it was only a matter of days.

Word spread that this time Henry would land and many would rally to him. If he fought for Henry and they won, his prospects would be more profitable. Again, if Rhys also fought on his side, the future looked safe and profitable. He had to follow Rhys, but he was changing his mind with the changing of the weather. If their children were married, it would bind them more deeply, but his darling Gwenllian was only a child.

He slammed down the empty goblet and abruptly stood up. Anne hadn't moved or spoken since his harsh words, but sat quietly staring into the flames, lost in her own thoughts, no doubt. At his abrupt movement, she jerked back and looked up at him. 'William?'

'I'm sorry, Anne, it is only that I know you speak the truth. My Gwen is no longer a child.' Exhaling loudly, he poured himself another goblet of wine and drank deeply, finishing it before wiping his chin with the back of his hand. Looking around the stone Hall, he spoke almost to himself. 'Rhys will be arriving next week. Prepare for his coming and let us make it a celebration. It is time for Gwenllian to get to know her betrothed.'

***

Anne stood, turned away, and poured herself a small goblet of wine to hide her smile. Soon, she would be showing, another month, perhaps. If all went well, the marriage could take place in a year, maybe two. Perhaps earlier if politics made it necessary. Rhys's son was at least fifteen by now. He shouldn't have to wait for his bride too long.

And that old hag, Nia, could go and rot in Wales with that brat and be done with her. She was sick of the woman, always watching her, and she was always around. Everyone loved Nia; well, she did not. Why did she have to be the one to pull her dead babies from her wretched body whilst murmuring under her breath?

How could William stand the woman? He always spoke with Nia and confided in her, because she was another part of his history. She had been there helping when the midwife pulled him from his mother, and she had pulled that brat from Lady Jane. She could hardly bear to say or think the name. So yes, Nia could go. There was only room for one woman in William's life and it certainly wasn't some old Welsh witch.

***

She could feel the wet cloth and a cold drip of water running down her temple but she kept her eyes closed, knowing it would be too much of an effort to open them. Her senses seemed to swirl around, making her feel very dizzy. One minute she could smell wood smoke, wine, the straw that covered a stone floor, the next, spilled tea, lavender, and a cold cloth. She prayed for oblivion again, but it never came.

Bronwen peeled the damp cloth off Eira's forehead and dipped it into the bowl of cold water again. Wringing it out, she gently dabbed Eira's flushed cheeks and neck, all the time talking softly to her. She had no idea what she was saying, only that she needed to hear her own voice.

When Eira suddenly rushed away, she knocked over the tea and her first reaction was to save the cups. Following Eira into the kitchen seconds later and watching as she collapsed to the floor made her panic, which had surprisingly changed into automatic pilot. Turning Eira over onto her side, she ran for a pillow to place behind her back, and to get a wet dishcloth. After what felt like an eternity, Eira's eyes flickered.

It hadn't occurred to her to phone anybody until that moment. She was so used to being without a telephone, it was always the last thing on her 'need' list, until now. She contemplated leaving Eira and running the mile into the village for help, but just as she stood up, Eira opened her eyes.

Relief flooded her tense body. The fear of Eira dying, here, in her new home, alone, was an appalling thought on all levels, not the least of which was that Eira, at that precise moment, was her only friend in the world, however uncomfortable she made her feel.

'It's all right. I'm here.' She quickly knelt down. Eira was not going to die, here, in her cottage, not if she could help it. She saw a small bottle of lavender oil on her kitchen windowsill, which she used when cleaning. She jumped up and grabbed it. She let three drops fall onto the flannel and placed it onto Eira's forehead again.

***

Eventually Eira's head stopped spinning, and she became aware of her old, arthritic body and the taste of vomit in the back of her burning throat. Her head throbbed with each beat of her heart where she'd banged it against the wooden floor, and finally the cold, lavender-smelling cloth that now gently touched her hot skin awakened her.

Eira opened her eyes wider, and focused on the woman bending over her. She was saying her name over and over, something about it being all right. But it wasn't all right! 'Nia!' The name was torn from her throat in that agonising second as she saw the old woman's face bending close over her, her deep, dark eyes penetrating her soul, accusing her, mocking her.

There, in the corner of the room, movement. The child had come to partake in the mocking of her and take her away to burn in hell where she truly belonged. This living hell was never enough for what she had done. Now, please let it all be done. 'Gwenllian, Nia…forgive me!'

***

Jerking backward, Bronwen lost her balance and fell onto her bottom. 'What the hell? Eira. Please, Eira, it's me, Bronwen. Can you hear me?'

For a moment, Eira didn't move, only lay perfectly still, her eyes tightly shut. Then, she turned toward her and opened her eyes. 'Bronwen?' Her voice cracked with emotion and tears poured down her cheeks. 'Bronwen? It is you, isn't it?'

Feeling completely out of her depth, Bronwen nodded and eased herself into a more comfortable position. 'Yes, Eira, it's me. Are you okay?'

Eira only shook her head and wept. The whole episode felt so surreal that she couldn't form any words for a moment as her head tried to make sense of where she was. Her body shook, but as she had no energy left, she let it happen. Finally, Eira reached into her cardigan pocket and pulled out another tissue. She looked across at Bronwen whilst wiping her face and attempted a smile. 'I feel very embarrassed, my dear. I haven't had one of my funny turns for a long time.' Easing herself into a sitting position, she leant forward and patted her hand. 'I think I frightened you? Sorry.'

Bronwen didn't answer. Instead, she slowly stood up and began to rinse the sink of vomit. Opening the small cupboard underneath it, she took out disinfectant, a cloth, and a scrubber. Eira opened her mouth to apologise, but Bronwen knew what she was about to say and put up her hand to stop her. 'It's okay, I can do this. In fact, it will give me something to do, while I pluck up enough courage to ask you something.'

'It's all right, you know, it's just an old woman's thing, menopause or something, even at my age. Would you believe—?'

'No, I didn't mean that.' She interrupted and quickly carried on scrubbing the sink. 'I mean…you said some things…who is Gwenllian?'

***

The sun had barely touched the sky when William left their bed-chamber. She had lain for most of the night staring into the dark, listening to his tossing and turning. At some time in the night, he gently called out to her, but she continued to pretend to be asleep. Her fear of losing this child overwhelmed her and as much as she craved his touch, she would lie to keep him off her.

She waited until the door closed softly behind him, and then turned over and reached for the oatcake she had hidden beneath her pillow. Now squashed and a little stale, she nibbled on it regardless.

Her nausea hadn't been too bad so far and she found that if she nibbled on something dry before she sat up in bed, it was noticeably less.

Finished, she lay on her back, her hands slowly rubbing her stomach. She could feel a small, hard mound and rested her hand on it. Her third month had passed, but she wasn't showing yet. She knew she would not be able to feel anything, but just touching that area felt like she was having some kind of connection with her child, and it brought tears to her eyes.

Every instinct told her this child would be a son. Now all she had to do was do everything right so there could be no whisperings and no accusations. With all of the other babies, she had told William immediately that she suspected, so great was her joy, and seeing his pride was all that mattered in that moment. She prayed and looked for answers and, perhaps, it had been her vanity that God had punished, her need for approval from William. Maybe God took away her babies because of her pride?

Many times she asked these questions: How could a loving God take her babies? If it was for her vanity, why take innocent children? Why should his child live when all of hers died? How could that be fair? Was God fair?

She firmly pushed these evil thoughts away. God must not have any reason to take this one. This child, this son, would live. He would be born, but not by that Nia. She had heard of another woman in Shrewsbury, a good midwife who never delivered a dead child. When she felt ready to tell William about his son, she would mention this other woman and demand her presence. She was sure William would not deny her. Nia was bad luck. She was a curse because she hated her so much. Nia would not be present this time, of that she would make certain.

She swung her feet slowly out of bed, then she sat for a moment while a wave of dizziness swept over her. Today was not the day to feel dizzy. Today was a day of celebration. It had taken weeks to prepare and although Gwenllian still looked scrawny after her illness, she was to be presented to Rhys and his son. Nia had been ordered to keep a close eye on her and to bathe her completely.

Her betrothed, Alan, was illegitimate, although Rhys never turned his back on any of his children as long as an agreement was in place with his many mistresses. Gryffydd was his heir, no question, but he would do right by his other children too. Anne kept her opinion of Gwenllian marrying a bastard to herself. Nothing could stop her getting rid of the brat.

Alan was the son of Jenet, daughter of Dafydd Fychan of Maredydd. She had also borne Rhys a daughter who just turned ten. Both of these children visited with Rhys, as had many of the others. He displayed them like prizes, showing the world his virility. Of course, Janet, his new wife, didn't accompany him on these rare occasions. Rhys liked to believe he had some consideration for her feelings. She had as yet been unable to bear him children; Anne liked her.

Unusually, Janet arrived with Rhys yesterday evening; Alan had been kept out of sight as much as possible, riding with the soldiers, which of course, he'd loved. She listened to him telling some servant boys about his adventure during the ride from Dinefwr Castle where they had stopped for a few days' rest. Rhys was killing two birds with one stone. Whilst his journey to Derwen brought him up through his lands, he decided to visit his castles to be prepared for any outcome.

Now, weeks after leaving his home, he attempted to relax and enjoy the celebrations, but Anne had seen the whispered remarks between William and Rhys. She noticed the tension coming off her husband like waves. Janet felt and saw it too.

Calling her ladies, Anne made her toilet and nibbled on some fresh bread and weak wine brought up from the kitchen while they fixed her hair and gown. The dark purple velvet looked stunning with her oyster-coloured veil. The gold trimming finished the garment and she happily twirled. She felt beautiful and womanly. She confidently opened the bedchamber door. She could already hear the murmur of many voices as others broke their fast. She could hardly wait to see William's face as she carefully made her way downstairs and entered the Hall.

CHAPTER SEVENTEEN

GROANING LOUDLY, DEBBIE SLOWLY EASED herself off the crumpled, dirty bed and stood naked in the middle of her bedroom. She knew he'd left it but she glanced across at her bedside table to check. Yes, £200, as promised.

The bathroom seemed far away as she shuffled down the narrow hallway, grateful that it was empty; her roommate would either be at work or still in bed. Turning the shower on to very hot, she winced as she sat on the toilet seat and cried out as she peed. The urine made the lacerations burn like hot pokers between her legs. Once she gently wiped and eased herself into a standing position again, she stood for a moment, looking at her reflection.

The bruises on her arms and legs were already turning a deep purple. Turning to examine her back, her chin started to wobble and a big lump stuck in her throat. Why did she allow that bastard to do this to her? Some of the cuts looked quite deep, and when he had inflicted them, she screamed it was too hard; he'd just laughed. The deep red marks on her wrists from the rope chafed. She gently rubbed them as if that would heal them!

By now, the steam had all but made her reflection disappear and she abruptly turned away. She allowed it; she should accept the consequences, shouldn't she? Stepping into the hot shower, she winced as the water cascaded over her thin body. Her tears mingled with the soapy water, her sobs of pain and disgust lost in the noise of the spray. Before she could change her mind, she grabbed the large scrubbing brush, lathered it with soap, and scrubbed herself with all her might until she bled, until she was positive that no trace of James existed.

***

Adam was on the phone when Geoff returned from his ride. Leaving him to it, he unsaddled Fred and brushed him down. Satisfied, he walked him to the paddock and set him loose with the others. Fred didn't move off immediately, but nudged Geoff's pocket. Laughing, he found half a packet of mints and giving Fred one, lovingly patted him before returning to the stable-yard. Adam was still on the phone.

'Honestly, Joseph, stop worrying I…of course, I haven't…well, when I think she's ready for…I do know what I'm doing, you know… look, by all means…yes, you know you're welcome…yes, anytime… okay, I'll see you then. Give my love to Brenda…yes. Joseph, we'll discuss it then. Gotta go. 'Bye.' Exhaling loudly, Adam replaced the receiver and rubbed his ear. 'He's been talking for over an hour! I'm glad I didn't use my mobile or I'd have no credit left!'

Geoff set about making a coffee for both of them, then, sitting in the only other chair in the small room, he stretched his legs and sighed. They sat in mutual silence for a while, Geoff with his coffee mug resting on his stomach, his eyes closed, whilst Adam rolled himself a cigarette and sat back looking outside through the open doorway, enjoying the different sounds and smells that drifted in. Geoff finally broke their silence.

'So?' He nodded toward the phone. 'What's up?'

'Oh, nothing really. He just hadn't heard from me for a while, well, a week and he wondered if I'd decided to breed Scarlet this year or leave it for a while.'

Geoff took a sip of his coffee and smiled. 'You've already made up your mind. You said the other day you'd let nature take its course, and if it happened, all fine and well, but if not, you'd help it along next year.'

'I know that, but I'll be damned if I'll tell everyone my business. Besides, I've invited him and his wife to the Ball. I've already promised I'd not disappear this year, so it'll give me someone interesting to talk to.'

'Aye, that's a good idea. In fact, I guess this year will be interesting anyway, what with them, that new tenant, Rosalyn promising to come, it should be just about bearable.'

Adam's face clouded over. 'Yeah, I guess it will.'

Silence fell on the room again as each man drifted into his own thoughts. It was a comfortable silence that both men were glad for. Since Adam's insults, the air between them had been uneasy and then the situation with Mathew caused further awkwardness. They wanted to discuss Mathew and what he'd implied, but the atmosphere between them, as good as it was, also felt fragile, so neither one spoke about it, for now at least.

They both knew Mathew had finally arrived sometime that morning, but it became obvious almost straightaway that he wasn't able to work, and he had been sent to the Hall to rest. Perhaps Lucy could tempt him with something to put some colour back in his cheeks; he'd lost so much weight. Fat on Mathew had already been in short supply; now, if it were possible, he looked even more emaciated. It was a cause for concern. Worse, though, was the look of suffering that filled his deep, large eyes; he looked terrified.

**

Rose sat opposite Mathew in the warm kitchen. Lucy had just left to inspect the large pantry freezers in preparation for the immense feast she planned for the Ball. Rose sipped her fruit tea and tried to ignore her growling stomach. Lucy's descriptions of the buffet plus the plate of freshly baked cookies that sat in front of her were making her salivate, but she firmly remembered how stunning she would look for the Ball if she resisted. She took another large drink of tea.

She felt chilled to the bone. After leaning out of the window for a long time, daydreaming, she'd unenthusiastically gone about cleaning the small room. Twice she'd been convinced someone had been standing outside in the corridor, but when she'd gone to look, no-one had been there. She'd expected it to be Judith checking up on her, but then, the room had suddenly gone cold, so cold she could see her own breath. Rubbing her arms, she'd quickly grabbed her stuff and left. She'd heard old houses had cold drafts but that was daft.

She glanced across at her silent companion who sat hunched over an untouched mug of hot chocolate; she felt ashamed for trying to lose half a stone when Mathew looked like death. He really was too thin. She always felt a pang of jealousy that he managed to eat whatever he wanted and still remained so skinny, but, now, this wasn't right. 'Hey, that chocolate's going cold.'

His focus had been on the table, now he slowly raised his head and focused on her. His big grey eyes glistened with tears and then he looked away, toward the large kitchen window. For a moment, she thought he was going to speak, but he seemed to drift off instead, staring into space.

'Mathew?' She reached over and gently touched his hand still clasped around the lukewarm mug. He didn't move. 'Mathew?' She raised her voice a little and heard her own fear. He turned to look at her and it almost broke her heart. He looked utterly destroyed, and she wanted to run around to the other side of the big table and hold him. Instead, she held his hand. 'Mathew, can you tell me what's going on?'

He swallowed hard. His gaze looked down at her hand and he suddenly grasped it with all his might, making her jump.

'I can't tell you.' His face crumpled and the tears came thick and fast. He tried to get more words out, but he just couldn't. Letting go of her hand, he hugged himself and began to rock.

Rose flew around the table and took him in her arms. There were three years between them, yet he felt no bigger than a child.

Lucy was standing by the door silently watching. Their eyes met and Lucy nodded before disappearing again to phone Mathew's father. Rose held on tight and gently rocked him. 'It's all right Mathew… everything's all right.'

'But it's not all right.' His voice was barely a whisper, muffled against her chest, but she heard him and heard the despair behind the words.

'What do you mean, Mathew? Please, can you tell me anything?'

'It…it can never be all right now…because…because I've seen her.'

Gently disentangling herself so she could see his face, she made him look at her. 'Seen who, Mathew? Who is making you like this?'

'Now, now that I've seen her, now that I've been shown, it's my time. She only comes when it's your time. I see her every day, a little clearer, closer. She…she shows me things. Things no-one should ever see and now… now, I'm…dead.'

A gasp made her look up. Lucy and Judith both stood within the doorway, both pale, both looking at Mathew. Rose glanced back at him, but he hadn't noticed their arrival. He was again looking out of the window and far away, oblivious of the tears and mucus. She noticed the box of tissues on the sideboard. Judith beat her to it and handed one to her with a smile. Gently, Rose wiped his cheeks and his nose. Usually, this would have made her gag, but it didn't today.

The noise of a Land Rover pulling up outside broke the spell. Lucy rushed forward to open the door to Ron, Mathew's dad. He was a big, burly man, a farmer all his life, used to the ups and downs of farming life. But now, the man walking from the Land Rover was a broken man. He strode into the kitchen and took one look at his son and bowed his head, taking a second to steady himself.

'Ron?' Judith spoke softly and lightly patted him on his arm.

The man acknowledged her, but his attention was on his son. Putting his cap firmly on his head, he strode purposefully over to

Mathew, who hadn't moved or noticed his arrival. 'Mathew?' Without waiting for a reply, he lifted the boy onto his feet and effortlessly picked him up and cradled him in his arms. Mathew remained far away, his gaze inward.

Nodding his thanks, Ron then walked carefully through the door and carried his son outside. The women stood and watched as he laid Mathew in the back and covered him with an old blanket. He didn't look at them as he walked round to the driver's side or when he started the Land Rover and drove away.

The two older women shook their heads and went back inside. Rose walked outside, watching until she couldn't see the green vehicle anymore. What had Mathew meant? Was someone picking on him? Frightening him? That new woman who'd moved into the old cottage. Some people in the village had been talking about her; who was she? Where had she come from? Did she have anything to do with Mathew?

Feeling frightened, she slowly walked back inside and closed the door. She had a terrible feeling that she wouldn't see Mathew ever again. One look at Lucy and Judith now sitting at the table confirmed that they both thought it too.

***

When Sir Richard returned home later that day, it was Judith who told him about Mathew. He immediately telephoned his parents. Judith hovered around the study door while he spoke briefly to whoever had answered. From what she heard, it didn't sound good. When Sir Richard replaced the receiver, the look on his face confirmed her fears. Without hesitating, she quickly walked over to the drinks cabinet and poured them both a brandy. She wasn't really a drinker, but she guessed she'd need this one.

She handed one glass to Richard and waited while he gathered his thoughts.

He took a sip of the warming liquid and finally seemed to notice her still there. 'Judith, Mathew isn't doing too well, I'm afraid. It seems he has been taken to hospital and they've kept him in.' He leant against his desk and finished his drink in one gulp.

Judith hadn't touched hers, but cradled it, feeling comfort from the familiar smell.

'Is it serious?' Her voice cracked and she coughed to cover it.

Richard noticed and came to sit opposite her. 'The poor lad has lost so much weight in such a short period of time, his organs are failing. Judith, I think he's dying.' He put the empty glass on the table abruptly and fiercely rubbed his face. He had grown very fond of Mathew over the past year. He'd known his parents since they'd taken over the farm from Ron's father twelve years before. He could remember little Mathew, quiet and shy back then, aged about four. He'd always been a scrawny looking lad, even then. Oh God! Poor Mathew!

Judith picked up his empty glass and left her own in its place. She murmured something about the evening meal and quietly closed the door. She met Adam coming in looking for his father. She took him firmly by his arm and steered him toward the sitting room and calmly told him about Mathew.

Some of it he knew, but not about the phone call. He visibly paled as she told him and he got up and paced the room, needing to focus on something else. 'Will he die?'

She shook her head and sighed. 'We don't know. This has upset your father. He has a lot going on in his head at the moment, so perhaps give him a few moments alone?'

She stood and brushed down her skirt firmly; it wasn't a question, it was a request which she expected him to obey. He knew the voice and smiled briefly. 'I'll see how the evening meal is coming along.' Holding up her hand to stop him, she nodded. 'I know no-one is hungry right now, but it gives Lucy something to focus on…and me. Besides, starving ourselves won't help little Mathew, so I'll call when it's ready.'

She touched his arm reassuringly before briskly walking away down the hall. She dabbed at her eyes and blew her nose. She was frightened. Frightened by the look on Sir Richard's face when he came home from wherever he'd been. He looked worn out, like a man who knew his life was ending and had no fight left.

Then she'd had to tell him about Mathew, and the look on his pale face as he'd spoken on the phone frightened her even more. Instinct told her he wasn't telling her everything. What else could he have been told? Was the lad expected to die tonight? A possibility, but, surely, in this day and age, they can do so much in hospitals? If the patient had fight left, of course. Seeing Mathew today, it was as if he had given up. And who the hell was 'she'?

***

Richard stared ahead of him; his mind raced with possibilities. Ron had asked about some woman or girl. Mathew had become hysterical at one point in the hospital and they'd had to sedate him. 'He began to scream that she was there and she had come for him.' He'd listened as Ron attempted to pull himself together. 'It scared the hell out of his mother, and I'll not lie to you, Sir Richard. It broke my heart to see my son held by three men and a nurse, trying to hold him down while they...'

'Ron, it's all right. Is there anything I can do for you or Karen? I can try to find you the best doctor.'

There was a long sigh from the other end of the line and Ron blew his nose. Richard found that he was having difficulty himself and swallowed the large golf ball of emotion that clung to his throat.

'I personally don't think there is a girl involved here, but Karen did wonder if he was pining for someone. You know how sensitive Mathew can be. If there was someone he'd kept secret, do you think you might be able to find out who she is or was?'

It had been hard to try to keep his face blank while Judith had been with him. He'd been grateful for the brandy and been very surprised to see her holding one too, although he'd been unable to say anything at that moment. His mind whirled with thoughts and memories and past conversations and documents. Who was the girl? Could it be her? But why Mathew? He wasn't a Kenward.

Feeling sick with dread, he jumped up and rummaged around in his desks. Finally, he found the family tree of the Kenwards going back to the fifteenth century. It started with William Cenwearde and his two wives, but that line was broken, no heirs, so everything went to his brother, who by some accounts, was estranged, and it carried on down the brother's line. It had been his son, William's nephew, who'd finished building the original Hall on this site. Had his ancestors somewhere along the line become involved with a Morgan, Ron's family? He knew they'd been around for a while. Could it be possible?

He needed Geoff; he knew more about the local families…no, he needed Eira. She knew everyone and everything about them. She'd been around forever! A strange niggling concept tried to push its way to the front of his memory. Eira. Just how long had she been living in the village? He could remember an elderly woman when he'd been a boy, but it couldn't possibly be Eira. A relative, perhaps?

Ask Eira. She knows everything! He could vaguely remember hearing those jokes as a boy; had it been about her or someone else? Her mother, perhaps? Everyone would laugh and joke about it and all the women would flock to her home and ask advice about the War, rations, and babies. The men would see her in the village and would quietly ask about the harvest, the weather, and the homebrew she would make every year. Yet, surely, that couldn't possibly have been his Eira?

The thought was quickly replaced by another: why Mathew? The Kenward curse had never hurt children before, so far as he was aware anyway. But from their eighteenth birthday on, they were fair game.

He'd encouraged Rosalyn to go to University and she readily agreed, moving away as soon as possible; Adam had been harder to convince. Adam tolerated University for a while, but girls had been more his interest. Richard hoped that after gaining his degree, Adam would go on to achieve higher qualifications; he'd declined and returned home just as Rosalyn was leaving.

Every day, Richard's life had been a misery. He tried to ignore his fears and concerns and enjoy his son being home to help out on the estate, but even that had been a disaster, because Adam would disappear for days on end with one gold digger after another. He tried to ignore the fast cars, holidays abroad, and the stream of different girls that he'd find sneaking out early in the mornings. He'd wondered on many occasions if this was the curse; having a time-waster for a son. He'd put a stop to the money soon after and their relationship had taken a nosedive.

Picking up Judith's glass, he drained it before getting up and refilling it almost to the top. He'd hardly eaten all day. His head swirled with so many questions that he had no inclination to attempt to answer, which he knew was wrong, and yet, somehow it didn't matter. The brandy was slowly filling his head like a cosy cloud. Oblivion, that's what he craved right now.

He'd been too traumatised to eat during the lunch meeting, and now this. It felt like everything was falling apart and there was nothing he could do to stop it. This thing killed his wife and took a mother away from her two young children. For all he knew, it was involved somehow in the death of his sisters and his parents. His father had certainly believed in the curse. They had been helpless against it then. Mathew would die…and it would be his fault.

**

Adam stood for a long time staring out through the sitting room window. He didn't see the gravel or the grass or the shrubs that grew opposite and hid the view beyond; he was thinking about Mathew and the last few days. What had happened to him that could have changed the boy so drastically? Had it really been his awful bullying? His heart wrenched at the prospect that he was to blame and yet, something told him this had nothing to do with him.

What had the boy said? He's being haunted? By her, some woman who hanged or, no, she let someone else hang…or was it? Fuck! He raked his fingers through his hair and took a deep breath. *Now, let's think.* Hallucinations? A psychotic episode or something similar? He talked about seeing someone hang. He talked about hearing screaming and begging for mercy. Was it nightmares and if so, could they do this to a person? Or was the poor lad going mad? It was a possibility he didn't want to contemplate.

He believed the lad was having hallucinations, but from what, he didn't know. No-one could convince him that Mathew took drugs of any kind, but his ravings were proof that he was having some kind of episode, and the hospital were treating them. How awful it must be to be so terrified of a hallucination?

Memories of when his mother fell came into his head and he pushed them firmly away. The last thing he wanted to do right now was relive that terrible day. Storming away from the window, he ran two stairs at a time up to his room, Barnaby at his heels. From the corner of his eye he saw Judith coming out of the kitchen, no doubt to tell him dinner would be ready. Hunger was the last thing on his mind. He wanted to have a very hot shower, a change of his dirty clothes, and a stiff drink. He needed that, before he could go and face his father.

***

Judith watched silently as Adam ran past her and up the stairs. Glancing toward the closed study door, she contemplated knocking and asking if Sir Richard required a meal; she quickly decided against it, for now. She would give them an hour or so to think about the day's events and then quietly bring them something on a tray. She'd already checked the drinks cabinet, so she knew everything was in plentiful supply there. She didn't agree with drinking, particularly, although today she'd been tempted. Who was she to question Sir Richard anyway? If that's what they needed to get through this, then so be it, but tomorrow, she would find another way. Tomorrow, she was going to see Eira.

CHAPTER EIGHTEEN

ANNE RETCHED AGAIN OVER THE bowl but there wasn't anything left. Pushing her hair off her face, she sat back and tried to let her body relax. The two other women in the bedchamber watched her, one with concern, the other with contempt; Anne ignored both of them.

Her secret was out and she was furious. That damned child had announced it as she'd made her entrance. Everyone turned and looked at her, stunning in her finery, but no-one noticed her gown now, only what might lie beneath it. The sudden silence had quickly been filled with murmurs as people whispered their opinions. William rushed to her side immediately and gave her his broad arm. Together they walked to the main table and sat as one. He had kept his face outwardly calm and smiling, but she'd felt his tension; he was angry with her.

She barely noticed what she forced herself to eat off her plate or the conversation around her. Sir Rhys kissed her hand and whispered his congratulations, but his smirk never left his face; her embarrassment amused him. She saw him turn to Gwenllian and whisper something which made the child grin like a cat; she despised them both.

It had been very difficult to control her emotions, but Anne managed fairly well considering Gwenllian, the brat, had ruined everything by taking away her secret. Anne was surprised and, from the gloating look on Gwenllian's face, she knew what she'd done, and Anne hated her even more.

Forcing herself out of bed, she held onto the back of a chair while she waited for the dizziness to pass. William had hardly spoken to her the rest of the day or at last night's feast, but could she blame him? How could she explain that she had kept it secret out of fear? It sounded too unbelievable, even to her, but if God had taken her children because of vanity, then she would attempt to behave in the complete opposite and then, this child, his son, would live.

'You, come and do my hair.' Her barked order made both young women jump. They had been whispering near the fireplace. 'I can guess what you're both talking about. Save your dreary assumptions for the kitchens. Now get on with it and don't do it so tight this time.'

The two maids hurried to her side. One began to braid her long hair while the other washed her hands, neck, and face. Their exchanged looks went unnoticed; Anne had her eyes closed, enjoying the feeling of warm water on her cool skin. Once dressed, she would find William. He would no doubt be in the Hall or courtyard with Sir Rhys. She would take him to one side and make him understand. Gwenllian would not win this one. She had to explain her secrecy and make amends for William's embarrassment of his daughter's untimely proclamation yesterday morning.

Sir Rhys' loud teasing of William's lack of knowledge encouraged many bawdy comments from a few men. William had taken them with a grin, but sitting next to him, she saw his discomfort and wanted nothing more than to defend her decision to keep her pregnancy hidden, for a while at least, but she'd kept her eyes lowered and her mouth firmly shut. Refusing to discuss her pregnancy with anyone, yesterday had been a long and arduous day. Now, she would remain silent no longer. She would wipe that smile off Gwenllian's face if it was the last thing she did.

***

Gwenllian nibbled on her apple without much enthusiasm. She was bored, angry, upset, and frightened, but she'd tried to hide all of these feelings; only Nia guessed. Since her declaration yesterday morning during the breaking of their fast, her father had more or less ignored her. He sent orders that she should remain in her bedchamber until she was called for.

The new gown lay across her bed; she'd hardly glanced at it. It had been made especially for today, her betrothal. Crushed pink velvet with silver trimmings. She'd tried it on last night and stood passively while the women crooned and fussed. Nia had said nothing. They'd made her walk up and down the chamber while they admired their work. The hem trailed along the floor behind her a little and one of the women had rushed forward and picked it up. 'We don't want to dirty this, do we?'

Frankly, she couldn't care less and from the way Nia watched her, she knew it too. All this silly fuss over a boy! She'd known Alan for most of her life. They had played in the woods a few times when he'd visited with his father years before and he'd shown her how to brandish a wooden sword. They'd watched in awe as a cat gave birth to kittens and the blacksmith had given Alan one to take home once it was weaned.

On this visit, Alan more or less ignored her, preferring to stay with the men. He looked different, especially in the face. Was it stubble on his chin? He had definitely grown since his last visit. He looked to be at least three feet taller than she.

'Nia, why has Alan changed? He hasn't once wanted to see the new foal or come out riding with me. All he does is speak with his father or my father and look sullen.'

Nia grinned. 'Oh, my dear child, I knew this day would come, but I have to admit to dreading it. You do understand what is happening today?'

'Of course! Alan and I are being betrothed. That is why I have to wear that foolish thing.' She angrily pointed at the dress. 'Why I have to get all dressed up to see Alan I don't understand, it's only Alan.'

'Child, you do understand what being betrothed is, don't you?'

Gwenllian crossed her arms. 'Well, yes. It means that I have to marry him when we are older.'

Nia watched the child fight back her tears. She knew Gwenllian was frightened, not just of today, but also of leaving her father, of what was happening around them, of Lady Anne, and what she had done to her. 'Gwenllian, do you understand what happens in a marriage between a man and a woman?'

'Well, they get married and a baby comes if she's a good wife. If not, they die. She runs the household while he does man things like hunting and fighting and drinking and telling stories of battles fought.'

Nia sighed; her heart felt heavy with guilt at not having spoken about babies before. The child had not started her courses, so she'd said nothing, wanting her to enjoy her innocence that little bit longer. Now, she realised, she had left it too late. She eased herself down in the chair next to Gwenllian and wrapped her arms around the child tightly for a moment before letting go. 'Gwenllian, it seems there are a few things I need to tell you.'

***

William sat back and stared across the room. Anne's explanation helped to ease his anxiety a little, but not much. Already fearful of what was happening in the country, Rhys had confirmed Henry Tudor was intent on invading and reclaiming the crown. Rhys hadn't made a move for or against it yet, although he had been sent word that King Richard expected his loyalty.

He needed an alliance with a powerful family. Rhys was an obvious choice, having been friends for many years. Also, an alliance with the South of Wales meant more leverage. Battles fought and won meant honours bestowed, and he needed those. Battles fought and lost meant death and humiliation for his family, but to have a powerful family behind him could mean the difference between life and death. Secretly, he agreed to follow Rhys, but no-one knew that, yet.

But, his heart broke every time he thought about his Gwen being married and living far away. He knew it was irrational and he felt weak thinking it, but now he had found out his wife was with child. A possible heir? A son? Would this child live? The choices he made had to be safe choices, for their sake and so far as he could see, an alliance with Rhys was his best option.

'What are you thinking, William?'

He glanced over at Anne who still stood behind the opposite chair. She looked pale and frightened and looked like she was clinging onto the chair for her life. He hated himself for putting her through a day and night of uncertainty. He held out his hand to her. She almost ran to it and clung to him.

He forced himself to smile. 'I was just thinking about our future. So much is changing, becoming uncertain. Gwenllian is growing up and I have to prepare myself to let her go and live in someone else's house, in another land. Now you are carrying another child. I pray so hard, Anne, but I wonder what I have done so wrong that my children keep dying. Has God forgotten me, do you think? Could I have been a better father, a better husband, a better master to my tenants?'

'No, oh God, have mercy, no!' Anne squeezed his hand hard. 'He hasn't forgotten you, my love. You are not a bad man. You are good. Perhaps too good to some people. This alliance with Rhys will strengthen our future. Gwenllian and Alan get on well enough. She will be fine.'

One quick glance showed her they were alone, so she quickly settled herself onto his lap and rested his large hand on her womb. This had been the closest contact between them for a few weeks and she felt the stirrings of his arousal. 'I have to believe this child will live. Our love will make it so. I dare not allow you to possess my body, but if you will allow me, there are other ways of pleasuring my lord.'

Easing herself onto the floor, she glided her hands along his thighs. She felt him shiver and looked up at him. His blue eyes gazed down at her with such a hungry longing that she felt very powerful, his manhood within reach, so close, she brushed against it, teasing, and then back down his quivering thighs. Every ounce of his body was tensed as her hands slowly moved toward his erection. She eased it out into the open and deliberately placed it inside her mouth. She heard him groan and used the tip of her tongue to tickle the end before moving slowly down the shaft. After a minute, she noticed his breathing had quickened and his hips now tried to push deeper. Taking his cock out of her mouth, she began to use her hand, moving slowly and deliberately, until, finally, with a low grunt, his seed spilled over her fingers. She quickly wiped it off and knelt back down and waited while he composed himself. 'There are many ways to love a man, William. Never forget that I am yours, whichever way you choose. Now, if you'll excuse me, I need to check the preparations for tonight.' With a slight curtsey and a wanton smirk, she left.

William stared after his wife, shocked at what had just happened. Quickly rearranging himself, he poured a large goblet of wine, draining it quickly; he knew what had to be done. Not all his unease had left him, but he certainly felt calmer about the prospects before him.

***

Gwenllian sat on the bed, her legs drawn up, her arms encircling them tightly. Nia thought that if she could, she would have disappeared inside herself. As she'd explained what marriage was and how babies are made, the child had grown paler and slowly curled into herself for comfort. It hadn't passed her attention that usually when Gwenllian was upset, she'd shout and scream before running to curl up on her lap. This time she remained firmly detached, and it broke her heart.

She waited for some response, but when none came, she reached out and gently touched the child's arm. Gwenllian jumped as if she'd touched her with a hot poker. 'Don't touch me! No-one can touch me!' Gwenllian's cheeks flared and her eyes stared coldly. 'If I say no, then not even Alan can touch me. He tried to kiss me once for a dare and I hit him with a big stick. I can and will do it again!'

'Darling, Gwenllian, as his wife you must obey him and have his children.'

'No! Never! If he tries to put his…his thing anywhere near me, I'll…I'll chop it off!' Gwenllian flew across the bed and stood, legs apart as if ready for a fight. 'You can't make me go through with this…can you?'

Slowly, Nia sat down on the edge of the bed and sighed. 'I'm sorry, darling, but they can. It's all arranged and has been for many years. This union between your families will help your father and if this war happens, he'll need all the friends he can get. You must get ready, Gwenllian. It's nearly time.'

'I won't! Alan and Sir Rhys and Anne and…and…they can all go to hell!'

'Even me?' The gruff voice from the doorway made them both jump. Nia gasped and froze, but Gwenllian, after a moment's hesitation, ran to her father and flung her arms about his neck. 'Oh no, Father, not you! You wouldn't make me marry Alan, would you? You love me, don't you? Please don't make me!'

He felt her tears soak into his tunic. He cleared his throat as he fought with his own emotions. He disentangled himself gently and knelt before her. 'You are only in your eleventh year, my dear Gwen. This is only a betrothal with a fine gown, your favourite food, and good company. I promise you, I won't let you go until you're a woman and ready to make Alan a good wife.'

'I'll never be ready, Father. Please…'

William stood straight. 'I've made my promise to you, Gwen, and I mean it. We all have to do things we don't want to.' Reaching out, he stroked her cheek 'Besides, in a few years, you may change your mind. Alan has already grown into a fine young man, eh?' His eyes met Nia's. 'Have her ready within the hour.' His gaze travelled to the pink gown. 'Make my daughter into the princess I know she can be.'

***

Bronwen stirred the tea and stared out of the windows. It was getting dark but she wasn't really looking outside. She was busy thinking about Eira and what she'd said. Glancing up at the ceiling, she wondered if Eira was awake yet. She'd been loath to let her walk home and insisted that Eira have a rest. That had been four hours ago. There was no way her conscience would allow her to let Eira walk home now at this time of night and there was no way she was walking back in the dark alone, so Eira was stuck here and she was stuck with her.

Gwenllian. The name rang around her head. She said it out loud to the empty room and it sounded so strange to say it, yet comforting in a bizarre way. It was a beautiful name and Bronwen hoped it was the child's name, but Eira had clamped shut, saying she needed to rest for a while. If it was, how the hell did Eira know it? Perhaps other people had come into contact with this ghost. Of course, that had to be it. It was inconceivable that she, a stranger, should be the only one to have ever seen her. That would be ridiculous. So who else had seen her and where and how had they reacted to seeing her?

'God forgive me!'

Bronwen jumped violently, spilling her tea. Cursing, she threw the cup into the sink and ran up the stairs to her bedroom.

Eira sat upright in bed.

'Eira, are you—?' she started, but realised Eira wasn't focused on her or anything in the room; Eira was staring at something else and the hairs on the back of Bronwen's neck stood up. Daring herself, she turned to look behind her, half-expecting to see the child, but there was no-one there.

She rubbed her warm, wet jeans as she moved slowly into the room, checking the corners before gently sitting down beside Eira, who hadn't moved. 'Eira? Can you hear me?'

Her head turned and her eyes focused on her. For a moment, she looked positively terrified, but after a few minutes, she finally seemed to see her, and she visibly relaxed. 'Bronwen, my dear.' Looking at her surroundings, she blushed. 'Oh dear, I was dreaming…I'm so sorry. I'll just nip to the loo and then I'll be on my way. I'm so sorry about this…I feel very embarrassed.'

Hesitantly, Bronwen reached out and touched her hand; it was frozen. 'It's all right, Eira, but I must insist on you staying here. I'll sleep downstairs on the couch or in the spare room. No, no, I'll be fine, really. I have a sleeping bag somewhere.'

'Oh, Bronwen, you're too kind, really, I can hardly bear it.' Eira's voice cracked and she sniffed loudly. 'I'll be fine walking home, really, I have things that have to be done and I have the shop, people will wonder where I am and—'

'Eira,' Bronwen interrupted. 'Do you have any idea what time it is? It's almost eight. I can't let you walk home, especially in the dark, and I'm certainly not walking around on my own either, so…' Standing up, she started sorting through the wardrobe and found her old sleeping bag dumped at the back. Helping herself to one of the pillows on her bed, she smiled, hoping it looked encouraging. Finally, she headed for the door, and turning back to her guest, she tried to sound as confident as possible, although inside she was dreading every minute. 'So, are you hungry? I have some eggs. I'll make us an omelette with a small salad?' Without waiting for a reply, she quickly headed downstairs, away from the sad, staring eyes.

***

As he neared the village, he slowed the car down to a crawl. He could see lights on in the pub and most of the little cottages. Farther up the lane, the houses were in darkness; so was the shop. He stopped outside it and leant over the passenger seat to have a better look. No, definitely no lights on in the back, either. Where was she?

He turned left, down the lane, stopping outside a tall, wooden gate with high hedges on either side that blocked his view into her garden, but he already knew it would be empty. Maybe she was dead? Save him the bother, a nice, quiet death in her sleep.

With one last look, he drove away and headed for the cottage. He smiled to himself and glanced at the wine bottle rolling around the passenger seat. He'd surprise her with it, wave it about, catch her off-guard and force his way in and then…oh God, he could hardly contain himself.

***

Martha heard the car and rushed to the window. She watched as the white car stopped outside the shop for a few minutes and then drove around the corner to Eira's gate before speeding off down the lane. She was sure she'd seen the car before. Yes, she had! It belonged to that horrible estate agent who worked for Sir Richard occasionally; vile little man.

She watched a while longer to see if he'd come back this way; he didn't and there was only Kenward Hall and Oak Cottage farther up the lane, so, where had he gone? For that matter, where was Eira? She had needed some rice, but when she'd found the shop shut, she'd borrowed some from Elizabeth, who'd delighted in telling her the terrible news about little Mathew. She'd been thrilled at being the first one to know. It had annoyed her.

Picking up her telephone, she dialled her friend's number. 'Elizabeth? You'll never guess what I've just seen. I think it could be the possible mystery man of our mystery lady up at Oak Cottage.'

***

Geoff ached all over and his eyes stung from lack of sleep, but he needed a damned drink. He knew Richard would have wanted, possibly expected, him to call for a long chat, but he couldn't face him right now. He needed to be with men he'd grown up with. Men who worked the land, and for whom life was simple. Men who knew him and knew to keep their mouths shut.

The heat from the roaring fire hit him as he opened the pub door and strode in. Five steps took him to the small, curved bar behind which Ian, the landlord, greeted him with a nod. 'Usual, Geoff?'

He waited patiently while Ian pulled his pint of ale. There was a strange pleasure in hearing the soft whoosh and glug as the brown liquid slowly filled the glass. The smell filled his nostrils, and the anticipation of the flavour made him salivate slightly. Placing the exact amount of money on the bar, he nodded his thanks and took a long drink, enjoying the smoothness of the ale as it slid down his dry throat.

'How's things then, Geoff?'

The intrusive voice came from one of the two elderly men sitting on a bench near the window; they must have been nearing ninety. Geoff slowly lowered his pint and sighed. It was wishful thinking on his part to think he wouldn't be questioned. It seemed he couldn't even have a quiet pint.

'Things are not too good, Joe, but then, you'd know that, eh?'

Unfazed, the elderly man grinned. 'Aye, I've heard the story, poor lad. Have you any idea's what's caused it then?'

Geoff looked around the small room. The two men sitting by the window and a farmer he recognised sat in the armchair near the fire, all looking back at him expectantly. Ian leant forward, his elbows on the bar. It occurred to Geoff that people would consider him to blame somehow, and he considered it as well. After all, he'd been the one to suggest Mathew for the job, and everyone knew it.

He cleared his throat and had another drink before answering. 'Well, Joe, I can honestly say it has nothing to do with the Kenwards, they've treated him like a son, as have I.' Hugh, the man sitting beside Joe, mumbled something into his glass of beer and Geoff waited for him to speak out loud; he didn't.

'Everyone loves that boy, even Adam. I know you've all heard how he may have been overly strict with the lad, but he isn't to blame for any of this.'

He took another long drink and watched them exchange knowing glances. Oh yes, he could guess what exaggerated tales they heard from their wives who in turn would have heard some wild story from Lucy. He had no doubt from the look on their faces that Adam had been painted as black as they come, who probably beat and tormented the lad to sickness.

'I'll bet you haven't heard that Adam has found Mathew a good place at the racing stables up near Ludlow.' The silent looks confirmed his theory and Geoff grinned. 'He surprised him with the news and when Mathew is better, Adam will help him become the jockey he's always wanted to be.'

He swallowed the lump in his throat and finished his pint. He knew in his heart Adam loved the boy and wanted the best for him but it wasn't so long ago that he threatened to leave because of Adam's temper. Didn't that mean that somewhere in his heart, he believed Adam was guilty? No, Adam wasn't responsible for this. She was.

He suddenly felt very claustrophobic. He needed some air. With a curt nod at the barman, he left, hoping his own fear wasn't showing on his face.

It was almost dark. The three streetlights glowed orange and he could easily see the layout of the whole village. He purposefully strode over to a bench next to the small park and sat down. Searching for his tobacco, he noticed his hands were shaking slightly. It took him two goes before he had rolled a cigarette and gratefully, he lit it and inhaled deeply. Sitting back, he watched the pub.

'Evening, Geoff.'

He jumped at the sound of the man's voice. 'Ron! Jesus, man, you scared the hell out of me!'

'What are you doing out here? Has Ian barred you or something?'

Geoff noticed how thin Ron had become and even under the street lamp, he could see how pale and worried he looked. He also looked like he'd fall over any minute. Geoff indicated the bench; Ron almost fell onto it. 'I just needed some air. You know how it is, eh.'

'Aye, I do.' Ron stared at the ground. Geoff let him be and quietly smoked his cigarette and waited.

'How's everyone up at the Hall, then?'

Geoff heard the slight quiver in the man's voice and knew how hard it was for him. Torn between wanting to be with his son and the need to be with men and have some normality. He caught a strong whiff of alcohol and wondered how many he'd had. 'They're fine, thanks, Ron. Worried, obviously.'

He saw the farmer nod slightly. 'I saw Lucy today, busy woman getting ready for the Ball. It's good for the village, you know. They need this, to keep in touch with each other…and have something familiar.'

'To be honest, Ron, I'm not sure if it will take place…I mean…'

'No. It must take place…whatever happens. The villagers need this, don't you see. So many things happen here. We see things. We hear things, but we never speak about it, do we? My father used to say this village was cursed and the May Ball was the only way to keep the evil at bay; it's the treaty. Do you see?'

Geoff stared at him for a long time while he digested his words. Ron stared down at the ground, his head in his hands. Geoff reached out and touched his shoulder; he was shaking. 'I think I know what you mean.' He purposefully ignored Ron's last comment and tried to sound enthusiastic. 'It gives the villagers something to look forward to, especially the wives. A good old tradition dating back hundreds of years and…'

'Yes. And why is that? Why did the lord of the manor decide to give his poor tenants a party every year? Have you ever wondered why? I have, so did my father. He went looking once, said he'd found some old document, a letter, something about an evil that lurks in the shadows and has to be contained within the boundaries of Derwen. The trees that circle the village are the boundaries; so, maybe it's still here? The lord placated them with this May Ball and gave them more rights so they wouldn't curse his family anymore or something like that anyway. But, there are always sacrifices…is my son a sacrifice?'

The question took Geoff by surprise. 'What do you mean? Mathew is ill and...'

'No, Mathew is dying, you know it, I can tell. Bad things have happened to the Kenward family over the years, haven't they? Deaths, mostly. Take Helen, for instance. You remember what they said in the village, they said it was her. They said she'd come for another victim in revenge. Mathew has talked about nothing else except a woman or a girl when he's been coherent. Something terrified him, Geoff. Some woman has terrified him and I can't find out who or if...if she's actually real. Do you know? Geoff, do you know anything?'

Startled by the sudden desperation in Ron's voice, Geoff sat stunned, trying to form words but nothing would come out. 'I... I...' Eventually he took a deep breath and tried to calm himself. 'Look, I think we've all heard one story or another about this evil witch that wanders around the village late at night or screams revenge for her murder as she glides around the old castle ruins. Are these ghost stories true? I honestly don't know, but do they have anything to do with Mathew? How could they? From what I have heard over the years, it is only the Kenward family who are supposed to be haunted by the ghost for something that happened hundreds of years ago. What that was? I don't really know that either, although I've heard many variations. What is happening to Mathew couldn't possibly have anything to do with this ghost story because he isn't a Kenward for a start and besides—'

Ron stood up abruptly. 'I have to get back. I'll see you.'

Geoff watched him walk fast back up the dark lane toward his farm, his head down, hands in his jacket pockets. For an instant, Geoff considered running after him and asking why the sudden departure, but a nagging feeling he'd tried to ignore over the past week wouldn't let him. Ron's behaviour sadly answered the burning question: was Mathew a Kenward, but who and when? He'd never believe Richard would have had an affair. Further back, then? But that would make Ron or even Karen a Kenward.

He slowly wandered back toward the stables; he was trying to remember anything that might help. The Morgans had had some deaths in the past, which wasn't unusual, and from what he'd gathered, they'd been fairly natural, or at least, not unexpected. Ron's uncle had gone bankrupt and killed himself, which was why Ron bought the farm. Karen had had a few miscarriages before and since Mathew's birth. He was fairly sure he'd heard that Karen's parents had died in a car crash. For once, he wished he'd listened to gossip.

CHAPTER NINETEEN

B RONWEN DRESSED QUICKLY AND ALMOST ran downstairs, her mind made up. Today she would go to Shrewsbury and find out what she could. Nothing was going to put her off, nothing. The weather was cloudy but warm, the bus went through the village in just over an hour; she had plenty of time.

She made herself a cup of tea and toast, then ate and drank as she stared out through the windows into space. Her mind was racing over yesterday's events and last night's guest.

At dawn, she'd heard Eira quietly slip away.

She had awoken from a fitful sleep, confused and on alert hearing the front door shut. She'd quickly sat up and debated whether to go after her, but just as quickly decided against it. She didn't have the energy to deal with any more dramatic events at that moment. Instead, she'd lain on her back staring up at the ceiling and tried to think about everything since she'd moved in over a week ago. Had it really only been that long? She'd tried to go back to sleep because thinking hurt her head, but she'd only dozed, giving up an hour later and heading for the shower; it was time for some answers.

The memory of last night, the awkward silences while they ate, the chitchat about the weather and Eira telling her snippets about the village, punctuated by the television to break the tension, and then the horror of that estate agent turning up; she shuddered at the thought of him.

Eira had called to her from the kitchen where she was doing the dishes she'd insisted on washing. Bronwen hadn't argued since it gave her the chance to relax for a moment and attempt to get her thoughts in some kind of order. Walking into the kitchen, she saw Eira looking out of the window. 'What is it?'

Without turning round, Eira answered. 'I believe you have a visitor.'

Joining her at the window, she gasped when she saw the white car parked outside the garden gate. It was too dark to see inside, but she knew who it was—that awful estate agent. 'Oh bloody hell! Why is he bothering me? He keeps turning up. What the hell does he want? Is Adam Kenward trying to scare me because I'm not moving? I've paid for this cottage for a year, you can bloody well tell him I'm not moving out. He can send as many lecherous estate agents as he likes.'

'My dear, I don't know why you think Adam has anything to do with this man, but believe me, he wouldn't send him. This man has a different agenda, nothing to do with the Kenwards.'

Bronwen felt herself blush at that and her stomach lurched at the very idea. She was his agenda. At the same time, she was horrified at how relieved she was that Adam Kenward had nothing to do with his previous visit. He wasn't trying to scare her out. Maybe he'd learnt something from their encounter?

'What are you going to do about him, dear? I know he's seen the kitchen light on and I know he's seen me with you or he would have got out of the car by now.' They both turned away from the window. Eira crossed her arms and waited.

Flustered, she'd looked out again and knowing he was sitting there looking at her, she'd quickly turned off the light, leaving them in the semidarkness. 'I guess we'll go back into the lounge, leave the dishes, and have a drink, watch television, and forget about him.'

'And if he knocks?' Eira asked.

'Well, I don't have to answer my own door now, do I? If I ignore him, then surely he'll get the message that I'm not interested…right?'

240

'Yes, perhaps.'

It was obvious that both of them knew he was going to be a problem, but one neither of them wanted to talk about, just then anyway.

She'd led the way back into the lounge and abruptly closed the curtains over the French doors, remembering the last time he'd come unannounced; there was no way he was going to get a chance to spy on her. Switching on the television, she'd flicked around until they agreed on some old film that hadn't long started. Neither one was really watching it; they were half listening for the car or a knock on the door.

It was late when Eira finally said she'd go and rest. Bronwen stood and waited, but halfway up the stairs, Eira turned back. 'I want to thank you for your kindness, Bronwen.'

Holding up her hand to stop any interruptions, she continued. 'I came here to give you answers, but, I think you need to find them on your own. Go to Shrewsbury, the library should still have what you need.'

'I don't understand, Eira, what answers?'

For a moment, it looked like Eira was fighting to breathe as she licked her dry lips and fought hard to compose herself.

'Eira?'

'Yes, yes, my dear, I'm fine. Listen to me, all will become clear, very soon, just be patient.'

With a nod, Eira had slowly turned to carry on up the stairs. 'Wait a minute! I don't understand this. Eira, I have to ask, do we know each other, because sometimes you look familiar and I don't know why.'

'You will understand, Bronwen, soon, I promise. The answers you want can be found. Look for Gwenllian. It all begins with Gwenllian.'

***

Quickly finishing her breakfast, she grabbed her jacket and keys and trying to ignore the butterflies in her stomach, she walked fast to the village. On the way, she tried very hard not to think about the quiet lane, or the Kenward Estate, which she hurried past, but no white car came speeding up behind her. On reaching the village, she saw four women standing at the small bus shelter; they were all chatting excitedly, until they saw her approaching and silence fell. She kept her eyes on the road.

She stood slightly apart with her back to them, praying very hard that the bus would be on time; it was. A small one, barely big enough to hold more than a dozen people and it was already half full. Her stomach churned as she paid the driver and walked up the narrow aisle, all eyes on her. She sat down gratefully in an empty seat near the back, kept her face turned toward the window, and waited for the vultures to start picking; they didn't.

Once the bus moved off, the chattering began, but none of it was aimed at her. She was aware of some sidelong glances of curiosity from the women who'd already been on the bus. No doubt the gossip about a new woman moving into the village hadn't reached them yet, but she had no doubt that by the end of the journey it would.

She found herself relaxing as she listened to the excited prattle of the women and the movement of the bus as it meandered through narrow lanes, stopping now and then for more passengers, all women. The constant drone of their voices had a motherly sound to it, which she found strangely comforting. Even when an elderly woman came and sat next to her, she smiled back politely and realised how nice it was to be with these people. No words were exchanged, but it felt okay not to. She felt secure in their presence and that did come as a surprise to her.

A few months, even a few weeks ago, she would have been in a sweating panic about being surrounded by strangers. The possibility of their intrusion into her life, wanting to know every detail, would have made her cringe away from doing the journey. Had she changed then? Had she finally found the strength everyone had always said she had in her?

Three quarters of an hour later, when they finally reached Shrewsbury, she felt the churning fear rise inside her and something else too: disappointment. The small bus, filled with chatter and warmth and mothers, had felt safe, and she wanted to keep hold of that feeling. Just for a while, she'd felt a sense of belonging and now it was over, she felt quite sad and deflated.

She was the last to get off, and she smiled her thanks to the driver, who nodded back. Standing on the pavement, the first thing that hit her was the noise. The cars, lorries, buses, and so many people. She'd only been away from the bustle of a city for a short time. The noise and busyness was an intrusion; she hated it.

***

Gordon slammed down the telephone and paced his office floor before finally flinging open his door and bellowing, 'Paula, has James come back yet, or phoned?'

The receptionist shook her head and carried on typing, flinching as the door slammed shut again. She secretly hoped James had died horribly in some accident, or chopped his cock off and was bleeding to death somewhere. She could just about tolerate Gordon, but sometimes even he could be a dirty bastard and she'd had enough.

Switching off the computer and the printer, she signed the piece of paper, put it into an envelope, and left it on the desk. She picked up her cardigan and hesitated outside the door, but eventually knocked lightly. Not waiting for a reply, she opened it and stood in the doorway, her hand still holding the doorknob.

'I'm leaving. You'll find my resignation on the desk. You will be hearing from my solicitor regarding the sexual harassment I've endured.'

'What? Hey, come on, Paula, we just had a bit of fun, that's all, come on, let's talk about this.' Gordon took a step toward her. She quickly let go of the doorknob and backed away. 'Come on, as if I'd hurt you. Would I?'

She felt the tears pricking the back of her eyes and sniffed loudly. She could feel her resentment slipping. He saw it too and tried again. 'Paula, you know I respect you. You're our best receptionist. Can't we work this out? A misunderstanding, I mean, I'm married, hmm?'

At that moment, James came storming in, making them jump and turn toward him. Ignoring both of them, he pushed past Paula and headed for his office. He smelt of sweat and sex, and she just stopped herself from gagging. She glanced between James's office and back at Gordon before she turned and stormed out, banging the door shut behind her. Her mother was right. She didn't have to work in those conditions. She did deserve better.

***

Gordon stood staring after her. If she did make a complaint, there would be hell to pay. She was their third receptionist in the last year. Damn everything! He could do without this bullshit. His wife had informed him that morning over breakfast as calm as you like that she was divorcing him, after seventeen years, two boys, and an expensive holiday every year, the bitch! Was it his fault she'd let herself go? Wasn't he a hardworking man who deserved a bit of fun?

Two sales had fallen through. He had furious clients phoning him, expecting him to know all the answers and now an irrational receptionist up and leaves, where the hell was he going to get another one and quickly?

His fury erupted when he walked into James's office and found him sitting with his feet up on the desk, a smirk on his face, cradling a cup of coffee. 'Where the fuck have you been? You turn up late, I've had to make excuses to your nine-thirty appointment and what the fuck have you done to Paula? She's left.'

James ignored him and sipped his coffee. He was going over the last hour in his head; he loved every second of it. The woman's terror as he'd grabbed her from behind and her pathetic attempt at fighting back. The submission as her need to survive took over and she became compliant. The staring eyes, the beating heart, the shaking limbs; nothing changed, but he loved it all. As always, it was over too soon and he'd left her there, in the field barely conscious, his semen carefully wiped away, her clothes neatly piled next to her battered body. It was his calling card so they knew it was him; no other predator could take his credit.

No mention of the clothes was ever in the newspapers, but then, only half of his victims reported their shame; he often wondered about the others. Did they want him to come back, was that why they'd never reported him? It was as he'd always known: Women wanted it, even if they said no.

'James, are you fuckin' listening to me?' Gordon stepped forward and banged his fist down on the desk. James glared at him. 'As I said, I had to move your nine-thirty; they'll be here in twenty minutes. I suggest you clean yourself up, wash off the whore you've been with, and get to fuckin' work, because if you push me anymore, James, you and I are in serious trouble. Have you got that? Now, I'm off to try to find someone who's willing to come and work in this shithole.'

Slamming the door behind him, Gordon stood for a moment in the reception area and looked around him. He'd worked damned hard to get this business up and running. He was getting sick and tired of James's bullshit. He turned up when he wanted, and stinking; it wasn't fun anymore. Had he been with this mystery woman? James had been with someone that morning and rushed away, from the smell of him; not even a shower…perhaps she was married?

Suddenly, he felt terribly randy. If James could have his oats this morning, why couldn't he? Glancing at the wall clock, he knew Susan would be finishing a class in half an hour. Would she be up for a quickie? It was only a slight detour to the college from the agency. She would help take his worries away.

CHAPTER TWENTY

WALKING A FEW PACES FROM the bus, Bronwen became overwhelmed by the bustling of the people, their energy and total oblivion to each other as they rushed to wherever they were going. Everyone pushing and jostling in and out of shops. It made her feel very vulnerable. She stepped off the pavement and stood at the side of a doorway, slightly sheltered from the main throng of people. She took a long, deep breath, watched, listened, and tried to decide what to do and where to go.

Looking up and down the main street, she was hit suddenly by the lunacy of what she was doing. She had come to an unfamiliar place with no idea what she was looking for or where to find it. Idiot! *Look for Gwenllian*, Eira had said, but where?

'Are you all right?'

She jumped at the light voice next to her. A very old woman stood beside her, a basket over her arm and a kind smile. 'Sorry, you just look a bit lost. Are you foreign?'

The last three words were said slowly, which made her smile. 'No, but I am lost.'

This statement seemed to relax the woman and she edged closer. 'Lived here all my life. It's a lovely place, of course...' She nodded her head toward the mass of hurrying people. 'It's become a nightmare these days to get from one place to another, so many people.' Looking her up and down, she continued. 'Here on a holiday?'

Bronwen blushed. 'Well, no, I live nearby.' To say this out loud gave her a strange, comforting feeling; she was a local! 'It's my first time here though. I don't suppose there's a library close by?'

'Yes, there is a good library, near the castle. Just head straight along this road and the library is on your left, you can't miss it. Are you a student then?'

Looking at where the woman pointed, she nodded absentmind-edly. 'Yes, I suppose I am. Thanks.'

***

The woman watched as she carefully stepped onto the pavement and became a part of the crowd, before long, she disappeared from view. The old woman sighed and shifted her basket. *Poor woman looked terrified*, she thought, *a haunted look in her eyes. I hope she finds what she's looking for.*

She suddenly clutched her coat closer to her as a freezing chill surrounded her body. It felt so dense, separate from the cool breeze of the day; it made her shiver with fear. And then it was gone, over in just moments, and left her feeling quite breathless. She reached out and touched the solid wall of the shop, grateful for it. It felt like she'd been touched by death. She thought of the young, frightened woman, closed her eyes, and prayed.

***

Bronwen tried to keep to the inside of the pavement, her shoulder near the walls of the buildings, but it became impossible and she was manoeuvred into the middle, jostled into the road and back again. She hated it, remembering Liverpool.

She hardly glanced at the shops and businesses she walked past. Clothes and knickknacks were never her thing. Well, actually, thinking about it, they were never allowed to be her thing, because she wasn't allowed to have anything of her own. She slowed down outside a shop that sold kitchenware and other household things. What would it be like to choose stuff for herself? She could do it. She had the money and the freedom. What on earth would she buy?

She walked on. The cottage wasn't hers. Everything in it was someone else's. It hadn't occurred to her to buy anything because the cottage was fully furnished. Perhaps it was time to begin buying things she wanted, but what? It crossed her mind before moving that buying anything of her own might 'jinx' the place! She smiled to herself at such lunacy; after all she'd experienced since moving in, her own hi-fi or couch couldn't do any harm!

***

Eira sat staring into her cold fireplace long after she heard the bus rumble through the village. Bronwen was on that bus. Bronwen was going into Shrewsbury. Would she find it? She'd sent the documents anonymously years ago and asked that they be kept in the records office for anyone who might want to do research in the future. What she'd actually meant was, in case a woman should come and want information on the Kenwards of Derwen.

She thought about opening the shop, making a cup of tea, sorting out deliveries, but she didn't move. The shop, once she opened it, would be full of nosy women wanting to know why she'd shut early and where had she been. The cup of tea, like opening the shop, meant moving and her legs ached something terrible. After being so close to the boundaries for so long, her body felt like it had been pulled apart, so the deliveries could also wait. She thought about hiring someone part-time and sighed; no, what she really needed was to die.

The air in the room changed suddenly, and her gaze fell on the corner of the cold room. 'Please, let me die now. No more…I'm so tired. Haven't I suffered enough?' Her voice cracked and her face crumpled as she gave way to the tears. She involuntarily curled into herself and gently rocked, trying desperately to find some comfort. The icy fingertips slowly traced the line of her back and she cried out for mercy…no-one heard her.

***

James stood mesmerised, unable to believe his own eyes. The damned woman was standing on the opposite side of the road, staring into a shop window. She looked absolutely delicious in her tight jeans, black boots and a black top, her jacket over her arm. He'd cursed his luck last night on seeing the old hag from the shop through the kitchen window. He'd driven off to wait farther down the lane, but on returning an hour later, he'd peeped through a crack in the curtains and had seen Bronwen was still not alone.

He rubbed his chin and wiped his sweating hands on his trousers. Okay, she hadn't seen him. He had clients in five minutes. Could he try to get hold of them and cancel? No, he'd already annoyed them this morning and his clients needed this deal to go through. Where would she be going? There wasn't much down here except a few more shops. The castle? That had to be it; she was sightseeing, of course.

Watching her slowly walk away, he felt a stirring in his trousers and tried to ignore it. He could see his next appointment walking toward the door and he cursed them under his breath. As they walked in, he fixed them with his best smile and held out his sweaty hand. Indicating his office, he glanced once more through the window; yes, she was heading for the castle. Half an hour, would she still be there?

***

Her head was whirling with thoughts and wishes and needs, and she didn't really take much notice of her surroundings until she became aware of fewer people. She saw she was right. It had thinned out considerably, and there before her was the entrance to the castle, a tarmac driveway on one side with grass, benches, and flower arrangements on the other. She could see the ruins beyond, shrubs and small trees dotted everywhere; it looked quite nice. The flower display was very pretty, but this wasn't why she was here. Looking across the road, she saw a large building. It looked more like a college to her. A large statue of Darwin stood in front of it. Crossing the busy road, she wasn't surprised to find it had been a school once. It had that feel about it, but now it was the library. Her stomach knotted; this was it, hopefully the answers she needed were inside. She headed for the front doors and stepped inside.

**

Ron held Karen's hand tightly while the doctors tried to explain the treatment being given their son. None of it made any sense, but he nodded in the right places and signed the forms and tried to look like everything would be fine.

Karen clung onto him and whimpered against his chest. He was glad she couldn't see his face. He swallowed hard and coughed; he had to be strong, for her. She'd hardly eaten since Mathew became ill. She'd hardly slept, wandering the house like a ghost clutching his photograph or sitting next to his hospital bed, watching him toss and turn in his own nightmares.

Nothing they could do. There was nothing physically wrong with him, so it all had to be psychological. Did they have any idea if he had experienced anything traumatic lately? Did he take drugs? Was there a history of mental health issues in the family? Questions, so many questions, and no answers.

A few minutes later, he was slowly walking along a white corridor, his wife walking unsteadily beside him. Their anxiety and fear seemed to isolate them from the other people who walked quickly past them. They were united in their confusion; he desperately wanted to turn and run. To remember his beloved son as a happy, loving boy, not the terrified skeleton that he knew awaited them.

They heard his screams long before they reached his room. He saw the nurses running in and out of his son's room and then he felt his wife slump against him and his attention became fixed on her. He was grateful for her faint as his tears fell, splashing soundlessly on his wife's unconscious head and the cries of his son finally died away as the medication filled his veins…and the room became silent.

**

Martha turned off the television and sighed. She loved hearing the news and hearing about other people and their problems; it made hers seem so unimportant. She looked across at her sideboard where the four pictures of her late husband sat in a row. Polished every day and kissed each morning and evening. Even after six years, she still missed him terribly, although she'd never tell anyone.

She picked up her empty cup. Of course, Derek had had no time for other people and their problems. All he'd cared about was his fruits and vegetables and his customers. She missed the market stall with its hustle and bustle, the organising, the trips to the wholesalers, and so many people to talk to. She missed the rituals of the day, the first cup of tea and a muffin; Derek loved his muffins. Missed the exchange of gossip with the woman in the next shop, and the people watching, working out who was thieving and alerting the security. Sadly, there was always one a day.

Amongst the fruits and vegetables, she'd have a small area to sell her homemade cakes and tarts that she'd baked. She hardly ever came home with leftovers; her cakes had always been snatched up. She never baked anymore.

Movement outside her front window made her glance sharply toward it; a child, at this time of day? Shouldn't they all be at school? She hadn't heard of anyone being sick. Peering through her net curtains, she looked left and right, but whoever it had been had gone. In her kitchen, she began to do the washing up. She had half an hour before the old film began, maybe she could go over to the shop for something and find out if Eira knew where the new girl was going and where Eira had been yesterday. Yes, perhaps she could bake herself a cake after all these years and…what was that?

She removed her marigolds and placed them on the sink. She could hear whimpering coming from her lounge; it sounded like a young child. Her heart thumped loudly in her chest and she drew her cardigan closer as the temperature dropped and she could see her own breath.

Her heart skipped a beat as she peered around the kitchen doorway and her chest tightened as she saw the small figure sitting on her couch, curled up, her face hidden in her hands. The long golden hair told her that this was a girl. The fact that she could almost see through her told her this apparition was not of this world.

And then, the child's hands fell away from her face and she turned to look at her. The scream that desperately wanted to escape died in her throat, she only managed a strangled sob as the piercing blue eyes filled with hate and despair blazed into her own. She vaguely became aware of the pain in her arm as it spread through her chest and she tried to catch her breath, but none came.

'You did it wrong.' The voice was that of a child, but the venom behind it was ancient.

CHAPTER TWENTY-ONE

ADAM LOOKED UP AS HIS father walked into the kitchen. The look on his face told him this was bad news. Lucy saw it too and immediately stood up and set about making another pot of tea. Adam stopped putting on his boots and pulled out the chair next to him. 'Dad? Sit down.'

He sat with his head in his hands for a moment; everyone waited. The kettle boiled, Lucy made the tea and came back to the table, and no-one rushed him. It was obviously about Mathew and some part of them didn't want to know. Adam cracked first. 'Dad, is it, Mathew?'

Richard looked up and nodded. 'Yes, I'm afraid it is. Mathew has been sectioned, he...he tried to kill himself last night.'

Judith gasped. 'Oh God! But why? How?'

'Apparently, he managed to get hold of something sharp. I don't know too many details. Ron was...well, you can imagine how he was.'

Lucy poured out the tea; her hands trembled badly and it took a few attempts. 'How's Karen?'

Richard shrugged and accepted his cup gratefully. 'I don't know. Ron didn't mention her.' Pouring milk into his steaming hot cup, he absentmindedly stirred it, staring at a crumb on the table. The room fell silent for a while as they tried to come to terms with the news.

Adam moaned loudly and pushed back his chair. Grabbing his other boot, he pulled it on and paced the floor. 'Why, Father? What the hell has happened to the boy? Oh, I know you all think it's me, but I spoke to him and…something has happened to him. Something frightened him to—' He was about to say 'death', but he couldn't bring himself to say the word, as if it would become true somehow. Instead, he turned and slammed his fist into the doorframe.

'Adam!' Judith jumped up and grabbed his hand before he could protest. 'You've cut it.'

He pulled his hand away from her grasp and sucked the small wound. 'Doesn't matter. The point is, someone is doing this to Mathew. He spoke about some woman. He told me about his nightmares, about a hanging and seeing the blood and hearing screaming…'

'Oh stop it!' Lucy covered her ears.

Adam ignored her. 'Whatever is happening to him, he believes it is all real. Is it?' He was looking at his father, who had paled visibly. Returning to his seat, he slowly sank into it. 'Is it?'

Richard looked away. He could see the many questions left unasked over the years about his mother and the circumstances of her death. He could see that Adam guessed that he knew more than he was saying about Mathew, but what could he say? Tell them the terrible truth? That they were cursed? That the ghost of a murdered child had killed his mother and was right now tormenting Mathew?

***

Entering the large building, Bronwen found she was in the wrong department, but the kind woman behind the desk guided her round to the side of the building to the Records Office. When she explained her enquiry, she was shown to an empty table. 'You can work here. I'll see what we have on the village and the ruins. If you look over there, you'll find the births and deaths records; that's a good place to start.'

Looking at where the woman pointed, Bronwen nodded and walked over to the shelves. Quickly glancing around the room, she was relieved to see that the other people in the room were too engrossed in their own research to be bothered about her and she slowly relaxed. She liked it in there; it felt cosy. Books lined the walls, and she wondered about the history that each one might contain. Did any of them have what she needed?

After a while, she came across a large book containing copies of marriage certificates dating from the sixteenth and seventeenth centuries. '*Sir James Cynward married Catherine Mills on this 12th day of June, 1674*'. 'Wow!' She blushed when she realised she'd spoken out loud, but a quick glance showed her no-one had taken any notice. 'So, the Kenwards have lived here a long time.' She wondered just how old the Hall was and when they moved from the castle, if they had owned it, of course?

After another twenty minutes of reading through older reference books, she came across an older marriage of a '*Cynwearde to firstly an Eliza and then to a Dorothy Barnett in 1588*'. She felt she was getting closer and needed to find earlier documents. The ruins looked old; how old, she had no idea, but surely older than 1588. It was also interesting to see how spellings of the Kenward name had changed over the centuries.

Going back to the shelf, she finally found a book on old halls and castles of Shropshire. Flicking through it, her heart stopped when she fell on a page about Kenward Hall. '*The building we see today was built around the late 16th Century during the reign of Elizabeth I by a David Cynwearde, a favourite at the time. He re-built it for his new wife, Dorothy Barnett, who gave him four children. His first wife had died in childbirth.*'

Her interest grew as she read about the family's fortune. How they had become loyal friends to the Tudors and how it started with a William Cenwearde who had been born in 1451. He'd fought for Henry Tudor at the battle of Bosworth and he had been granted title and lands for his loyalty. Some believed it was his sword that killed King Richard. There was a brief description of an old fortified castle, built on an Iron Age hill fort, but no pictures. On the same page, there were three black and white photographs of Kenward Hall, one taken in the nineteenth century and the other two taken during the 1950s.

She stared at the pictures; it looked beautiful but she needed more. Going over to the woman, she asked if there was anything else.

'If you fill out the cards with what you specifically want, I can get it from storage. Here, I've found this; perhaps this will help for a start.'

Bronwen took the thick, heavy book, smiled her thanks, and returned to her table. Her heart raced as she turned the pages. It contained references to old photographs of the village of Derwen, paintings of the Hall and the village and old original letters written during the First World War and copies of older letters dating throughout the centuries. One of them, dating from the sixteenth century, stopped her. It was about the old family home. It mentioned the old castle and how well the new home compared. Another letter dated 1789 was about the May Ball. Had they really been going on that long?

Then, there it was. Reference to the family tree of Cenwearde, and it began with William. The spelling had changed around the time of the Battle of Bosworth; she wondered if that was significant. Her hands trembled as she wrote out her slips of paper. Taking them to the woman behind the desk, she swallowed the bubbling nerves. The answers were here, and it excited and terrified her at the same time. William. What was it about that name that made her feel uncomfortable?

***

William and Rhys rode through the gatehouse entrance and stopped their horses in the small, square courtyard. William dismounted and tried to ignore the feeling of inadequacy that always filled him whenever he rode into his courtyard. It was really nothing more than an area between the front of the castle where the kitchen and guard rooms could be found and beyond this, the tall gatehouse and the back of his home with the great Hall and private bedrooms. He'd added bits and pieces over the years, but it still embarrassed him.

Slapping his favourite brown mare on the neck, he searched for his wife among the people who were busy working in and around the courtyard. Some bowed slightly in his direction before continuing their labour. He'd always liked to keep a fairly relaxed house, although he knew Anne didn't approve. 'They should show more respect to you as their lord. They owe you their loyalty. After all, you own the lands they use.' She'd corrected herself. 'It is only right that they should bow to you, and me.'

He'd laughed at this, knowing it had more to do with her own feelings of the household and tenants not liking her. He'd tried to make her understand that he knew he had their loyalty and respect because they paid their taxes on time. He held a monthly court where the tenants could come and speak freely, and it worked. Any grievances were worked out and any injustices were dealt with satisfactorily.

He'd had to punish a few people along the way, mainly men who'd been passing through his lands causing trouble or stealing. The tenants appreciated his quick justice and the openness of their relationship. In return, they did their best and were loyal to him. He preferred it this way. He didn't want to be a tyrant and hated. He believed that to bring the best out of a person, regardless of status, he would treat them with respect. If he carelessly beat a man for something unimportant, then the people would hate and fear him. William firmly believed that if he cared for a man, that man would respect him back.

Anne appeared at the top of the steps looking a little out of breath. Halfway through her pregnancy and she was looking radiant, but tired. Many nights he'd woken to find her sitting by the fire, softly singing to her swollen belly, unable to sleep. He knew she was worried that she'd lose this baby, but he prayed every day, and all looked well.

Sir Rhys saw her and bellowed his greeting. 'My Lady Anne, what a delight to see you again.' Running up the stairs, he bowed low over her hand and gently patted her stomach. 'I hope my friend's child is also doing well?'

Anne smiled. 'Yes, my lord, he is doing well. Keeping me awake most nights with his constant kicking, though.'

He saw the dark circles under her eyes and grinned. 'So then, we have a male heir who can keep the ladies up all night already! I can't wait to meet him!'

William, who had followed Rhys up the stairs, slapped him on the back and gently pushed him forward through the doorway and into the Hall; he was laughing. 'Neither can I my old friend, neither can I.'

Rhys moved away to the far corner of the Hall while William kissed his wife. She was a real beauty, but there was something about her that made Rhys feel uneasy. Something in her look, perhaps? Sometimes he felt as if her smile hid her true feelings toward him and his family. Women! More trouble than they were worth.

At that moment, the servants brought in wine and bread and cheese, a bowl of apples, and small bowls for the broth that he could smell bubbling away in the large cauldron over the fireplace. Relaxing into a chair, he felt his muscles slowly melt and his cares disappear. He never told William, but here, he felt completely at ease.

The King never bothered him here, but he had no doubt his scouts would have informed him where he was. He would attend the King soon, but not before he was ready. Henry Tudor's spies hadn't contacted him yet, so for now he could allow himself the small pleasure of peace, and it felt good.

He and William had spoken for hours on end about the dilemmas that faced them both. William pledged his loyalty to him and would follow him to either side, although he knew which side William preferred. Uniting their families would strengthen William as long as they fought on the winning side. Could Henry defeat Richard this time? It looked possible and now that Richard had made some demands testing his loyalty, he was infuriated enough to fight with Henry, but caution held him still, for now.

'Uncle Rhys!' Gwenllian flung herself into his arms and kissed him on both cheeks, before turning to see where her father was. Rhys saw the flicker of hatred in the child's eyes when she saw him with Anne and frowned. He kept his concern for the child to himself, but he was aware of the tension between Gwenllian and Anne, as everyone was.

Hearing his daughter, William turned and extracted himself from his wife's arms and held his own out to Gwenllian who ran into them. Rhys saw the look in Anne's eyes and felt his unease swell. Perhaps the sooner she was married to his son and away from Anne, the better for everyone?

His spies told him that Henry would land very soon. The outcome for himself would depend entirely on if he sided with the right man, and if he did, and they won, then the sooner Gwenllian could marry Alan and be safe. He didn't dwell on the idea that if William died in battle, Gwenllian would be left alone with Anne. Such a possibility filled him with dread.

The rest of the evening was spent in long discussions, swapping gossip from his journeys around his estates across Wales. All the while, he watched the sparks fly between Anne and Gwenllian who knew exactly how to annoy her stepmother. Curled up on her father's lap, she only moved long enough to eat her broth and then returned to eat an apple and feed William some cheese. He laughed and joked about his little kitten. He could see that William sensed the tension too, but he didn't push Gwenllian away. Aged eleven, she should have been acting like a lady, but she was still so small and petite, barely any weight to her, it was easy to forget that she was nearing womanhood.

He glanced across at Anne, whose fixed smile was beginning to crack; her nerves looked shattered, and he wondered what would break her? She was getting heavier. She couldn't do much harm at the moment, and once the child was born, her attention would hopefully be fixed elsewhere. That was, of course, if the child survived. He knew William hated the idea of being away in battle while Anne was pregnant, but God and hopeful kings didn't wait for anyone.

The conversation gradually turned to the betrothal and how it all seemed a long time ago. 'Only two months gone. Did you enjoy it, my dear?'

Gwenllian shook her head. 'Of course not, I had to wear a dress!'

Rhys laughed loudly. 'Would you be more content if, as my son's bride, you didn't have to wear beautiful gowns, but dress like a boy?'

Gwen frowned and thought for a moment. 'I think, maybe, I've been told by my nurse, Nia, that when I get older I will enjoy looking beautiful and graceful, but I think that I will be content if I don't have to marry Alan, though.'

Anne gasped and William started to speak, but Rhys interrupted him. 'Why don't you want to marry Alan? Has he been mean to you?'

Gwenllian looked at her father and grinned sheepishly. 'Well, he used to throw mud at me and pull my hair and hold me down sometimes and tickle me or try to put insects into my ears.'

Rhys guffawed, leant forward, and patted Gwenllian on her knee. 'Oh, my dear child, you do amuse me. If I promise that Alan will never do any of those things again, will you consider him as your husband?' Ignoring the fact that they were already betrothed, he waited, looking imploringly at her.

Eventually she smiled. 'Of course. I will be nice to him as long as he is nice to me. Is that fair?'

Rhys held out his hand and shook her proffered hand. 'Dear Gwen, you are a treasure. I swear to you now that my son will act properly, as a husband should. There will be no hair pulling or throwing of mud.'

'Good, that's settled, then. In a few years, I'll be his wife. Until that time, I will be helping to look after the new foal as Father has given her to me because I became betrothed to Alan.' She grabbed a large apple from the nearby bowl and smiled. 'I like getting presents too. Tell Alan that!'

All three adults watched her skip away and saw a figure came out of the darkness and join her. Nia was never far away. The three fell into silence, sipping their wine and watching the darkness slowly gather strength before Anne excused herself and left the Hall, leaving the men to talk about the possibility of war. For Anne, the only thought running through her mind was the idea of Gwenllian marrying in a few years. A few years? No, she would be rid of her sooner than that.

***

Bronwen leant back in her chair and stretched her legs. Rubbing her eyes, she wished for the hundredth time that their writing hadn't been so bad. She had been trying to read letters from various family members from the nineteenth century regarding one thing or another. Out of the vast array of letters dating back centuries, these were the easiest to read. Some mentioned their delight at having some guests over for the weekend. One or two talked about the Ball. One letter caught Bronwen's attention. Written to someone living near Ludlow, it asked why they left in such a hurry the night after their arrival.

'17th day of May 1855

> *My dear friend, what has happened to make you leave in such haste and without an explanation? Has someone within my household insulted you? I will be travelling down your way in a week. May I call on you?*
>
> *Your most concerned friend,*
> *Lady Francis.'*

Bronwen scrutinised the letter over and over. What had frightened this person, if anything? Wasn't it rude in those days to leave without any explanation?

'Here you are. I've found it.' The librarian gently placed a large roll of paper on the desk. 'It dates from the late eighteenth century, so please be very careful.' With a glance at the precious parchment, she walked away to help someone else. Bronwen watched her leave as her hand gently touched the rolled paper and she felt sick with both responsibility and excitement at what it might contain. It had taken her a while, but the librarian finally found the Kenward family tree, written by a lady from the village.

Moving the other books and letters to one side, she very carefully pulled on the string that held the paper in place. She unrolled a little and tried to read the heading. *The family of Cynwearde's family tree to the present day of our Lord, 1799.* And there at the top of the page she could clearly read, *William Cenwearde, born 1451, died 1498, married to Lady Jane, 1468, born unknown, died 1474 after giving birth to a daughter Gwenllian. His second wife Anne, born 1460, died unknown.*

She vaguely read the rest, but none of it really mattered, this was it, the time of Gwenllian, the time of her death. A quick glance confirmed she died in 1485; that made her eleven or twelve years old. The emotion she felt surprised her. She rummaged in her jeans for a tissue and wiped her eyes and nose before anyone noticed.

How daft was she? Getting upset over a death that happened hundreds of years ago, yet, it felt so personal. The myriad of strange occurrences since moving to Derwen connected her to this child's plight whether she liked it or not. Why show her all these things and make her feel these emotions if the child didn't want someone to help her to—what? Bring justice?

She sat staring at the yellowed paper, hardly noticing the other names that ran down it. Like spiders' webs, the names spread out like a pattern. She focused in on a name, Mary, died 1643, then another Joanna, died 1689, and then another and another. All Kenward wives seemed to have died quite young, and not long after they married into the family. She began to wonder about Adam's mother. She was dead. Eira had briefly mentioned it. What was it about the Kenward women?

Deciding to dig deeper, she handed in her slips of paper and waited, her heart pounding with excitement and anticipation. Could it be possible to solve a murder? Would she find the answers? Had the woman been brought to justice? She guessed not, but someone had been hanged; she'd been shown the whole, horrid scene. She shuddered at the memory and forced the image from her mind.

Lady Anne. William's second wife. The name, only recently read, felt so familiar. Seeing the name written on that family tree hadn't surprised her, and it brought with it so many questions and emotions, but why? The librarian headed toward her with more papers and a book; she quickly made room on the table. She would help Gwenllian and find the answers to these riddles about Lady Anne, and she hoped more than anything that the outcomes were favourable.

***

Alone in William's private chamber, Rhys and William finally allowed themselves to relax. Rhys wandered over to the window and looked out at the grey sky while William poured them each a goblet of wine. Taking the offered refreshment, Rhys returned his gaze to the outside world. 'I believe Henry will arrive soon with the coming of better weather, especially after his last failure.'

William didn't answer; he was waiting to see where this conversation would lead. He had been waiting all day for the obvious conversation the men needed, but they hadn't had a chance to be alone. Stretching his legs, he watched his friend form his thoughts.

At last, Rhys turned away from the window and did not come to sit beside the fire, but leant against the windowsill, keeping a distance between them. 'I hear you had a visitor last month? Sir Thomas Mydden? What could that man possibly have to say to you, I wonder?'

William frowned; he didn't like his tone. 'Yes, your spies are correct, my old friend, he did surprise us with a visit.' Damned if he would tell him everything outright, though. He sipped his wine and held Rhys' stare.

Rhys laughed first. 'All is well, William, no tricks, no interrogation, but I do want to know one thing, if I may, as your friend. Who are you loyal to, Henry or Richard?'

William stretched his arms above his head and used the time to think about his answer. Sir Thomas had asked him the same question, but more bluntly and with his usual arrogance. He informed William that if Richard felt that he needed persuading, then Gwenllian might enjoy a trip to London for a while. Damned devil!

The fury he'd felt at being threatened by a pompous upstart like Sir Thomas Mydden was carefully controlled and hopefully hidden well enough to convince his uninvited guest that he remained loyal to the King. Of course, he hadn't said which King. Sir Thomas had heard of Gwenllian's betrothal to Alan and he'd implied that Rhys was loyal to King Richard, but William wasn't so sure. King Richard had also demanded Gryffydd, Rhys' heir, as a hostage, and there was a rumour he'd been asked to swear an oath of fidelity.

William sighed heavily. 'I am in the same position as you. The King has demanded my loyalty and my sword, if it comes to that, though he is almost sure it will not. He has threatened to take Gwenllian as hostage, though he has not asked me to swear anything other than this.'

Rhys grunted. 'Ah, so you've heard the rumours then? Yes, it's true, he's asked me to swear an oath of fidelity upon which I promised to guard Milford Haven, hence my reason for being this far away from it. I am here, amongst other reasons, to give myself some extra time to see what may happen. I have no doubt his spies will have informed him that I moved up the country and not down it, but I felt I needed time to think and here I can always be allowed the time to do that. Am I right, or have I overstepped our friendship?'

William grinned. 'So, that's why you come here so often. And I thought it was for our cook's excellent food and my homemade wine!'

Rhys finished his drink and poured himself another. His smile faded. 'Food and excellent vintage aside, I need to know, who are you for?'

Returning his stare, William exhaled loudly. 'I am for Henry, Sir Rhys. I have been for a long time now. King Richard has shown himself to be incompetent and since the rumours of his being involved in his nephews' disappearance, his taste is sour in my mouth. To murder children is unforgivable; there is no honour in it.'

Nodding, Rhys came to sit opposite his friend. 'Yes, I agree. His view of children is appalling to me. He thinks he can use them as pawns, which is inconceivable. I love all my children but to use my heir as a hostage…I cannot bear to think about it. As far as I am concerned, he has insulted my family name and honour.' Standing abruptly, he held up his half-empty goblet in a salute. 'May the Lord help us in our fight. Long live King Henry. May he succeed.'

William stood, clinked his goblet with Rhys' and they finished their wine. 'Now, my dear friend, I will return to my home and make swift preparations, although, I will admit to you, I had already begun them before I left for here. I expect to know soon how and when Henry will arrive on our shores. If my spies have done their jobs well, he will know by now that Milford Haven will be unprotected.'

William slapped his friend on the shoulder and embraced him. 'You play a dangerous game, Rhys. The King will not tolerate anything that might cause any kind of unsettled feelings. You must have learnt that, especially after your skirmishes with the Duke of Buckingham—and look what the King did to him. I would prefer not to have you dragged away and your head become nothing more than a trophy. Now this, you have taken up where Buckingham left off, where he failed, but you can rely on me to join in when you need me. I will talk to our Sheriff at Shrewsbury and see where his loyalties lie. Oh, don't worry,' he quickly added, seeing his friend's raised eyebrow, 'I am discretion itself. I will be ready.'

Within the hour, Rhys had gathered up his small entourage and was saying his goodbyes to the women. William stood motionless at the top of the stair and watched. He understood his friend's regret at having to leave so soon. He looked forward to moments of peace.

Gwenllian questioned Rhys about his abrupt need to leave and he ignored the question with flattery. He gently kissed Anne's hand, complimented her on her hospitality, and left with a quick nod in William's direction.

***

Bronwen rubbed her eyes. They felt hot and sore from trying to read the faded handwriting. There wasn't much left of the letter, but she had just about managed to understand that she was reading a photocopy of a letter dated 1485 from William to Sir Rhys thanking him for his visit and he looked forward to their meeting again very soon. Perhaps he would honour him with a visit from a friend? He hoped to expect them within eight days. The original letter was one of a kind and was being held in the British Museum.

Everything about the letter said that it had an underlying meaning. After further reading and talking with the helpful librarian, she managed to find out that Sir William had indeed helped bring down King Richard and had fought alongside Henry at the Battle of Bosworth. History said that Sir Rhys, his lifelong friend, was supposed to have been the one who actually killed King Richard, but it was never proved.

Sir Rhys' son, Alan, a bastard from one of his many mistresses, was betrothed to Gwenllian, William's daughter.

She tried to imagine what it must have felt like being betrothed at such an early age. Did she know the boy? Had she agreed to the betrothal? Did she know what she would be agreeing to? Whenever she saw Gwenllian, she looked so young and frail. How could anyone expect her to marry someone at that age? Then again, she would never marry because she'd been murdered. The thought just popped into her head and the emotions that came with it were overwhelming. She needed a break.

She'd noticed the coffee machine when she'd come in. Checking her purse for enough money, she slowly wandered over to it, stretching her legs as she went, feeling the warmth rush down her cramped thighs. Suddenly, she felt a freezing chill run down her spine. She spun round and gasped, quickly choking it off. Her gaze darted around the large room. There was nothing, but she could have sworn…feeling flustered and a little out of breath, she made her way to the entrance and took deep breaths of cool air. The answers were hopefully coming. *Gwenllian, try to be patient…please.*

***

The small figure moved away from the many papers and went to stand by the large window. She knew no-one could see her now and in a way was grateful for it. Her tears fell silently. William. Her father. Oh how she missed him. To see his smile, hear his voice, to feel his strong arms keeping her safe. She frowned. But they hadn't kept her safe, had they, not from *her*.

'Librarian, is that window open? I'm getting a chill, it's so cold.' The elderly woman shivered and rubbed her arms. 'Never mind, it feels warmer again now…how strange.'

***

Bronwen watched people coming in and out of the building. She'd hardly touched her tasteless coffee as she pondered over what she'd read and possibly seen. Her stomach growled loudly; she was starving but she couldn't face the dinnertime rush, pushing in queues and vying for the few benches dotted around. Glancing toward her full table, she couldn't bear returning to the warm room, either. Her head felt too full of information; she needed time to sort it all out and get it straight.

Decision made, she threw the remains of her coffee into a bush and dropped the small cup into the bin. After a brief check with the librarian, she photocopied the family tree and a few letters. She wrote down the names of the books with the information she'd found, then returning everything, she left. It seemed plausible that Sir Richard might be able to fill in some gaps about his family. Maybe she could talk to him at the ball and then leave. It certainly gave her something to talk about instead of standing awkwardly in a corner. Did he know about Gwenllian? That was the million-dollar question.

The warm sunshine was blinding after the interior of the reference library. She shielded her eyes and walked quickly toward the statue where there was a space to sit. Looking around at the people who now occupied the benches, happily talking and eating their lunches, she wondered if their lives were as weird as hers. Would anyone believe her if she told them? Here she was, feeling anxious about being surrounded by people, yet she was haunted by the ghost of a murdered child and trying to find information about her family.

It felt crazy! It was crazy! But, sitting here in the sunshine, thinking about William and Rhys and the two kings, all dead but in some way, they affected her. In a strange way, she felt a connection with them, especially William. She could picture him. Tall, broad of shoulder, muscular, with thick, wavy brown hair with streaks of silver, kind, hazel eyes and a smile that lit up the room. A deep voice that held command and respect, but a tone that let people know he was generous and kindhearted. He had a heart that felt remorse for those he'd slain and carried the guilt of it. A father, a husband, and a lover.

She shook herself; what was wrong with her? There was no way she could possibly know what he looked like. Fantasising about what she'd like him to look and act like wasn't helpful. A picture of his friend, Sir Rhys, also came into her mind, rather good-looking too in a roguish sort of way. She pushed him firmly away too and stood up.

'Miss Mortimer! Bronwen!'

She turned toward the voice calling her name and stiffened.

He walked quickly toward her, grinning like a Cheshire cat but his gaze travelled over her body like a snake. She rose abruptly and took a step back when he stopped and stood too close for comfort.

'Bronwen, I thought I recognised you, what are you doing here, then?' He looked around at the library behind him, but immediately turned back to her and waited.

She glanced at the library. There was nowhere to run. If she excused herself and went back inside, he'd follow her and she'd be trapped indoors with him no doubt breathing down her neck; as it was, he wasn't hiding his feelings well at all. He looked both annoyed and excited at the same time.

'I…just…sightseeing. Excuse me, I have to go.' Backing up, she turned and walked away, anywhere, the town, the castle, anywhere was better than being near that revolting man. She knew he was watching.

***

Adam barked instructions at David, who merely shrugged and replaced his headphones over his ears and carried on washing down Daisy's legs. Adam watched him for a moment, deciding whether to pull the headphones off his ears and stamp on them until they broke into tiny pieces or whether to just walk away and hit something; he chose the latter. He pummelled the saddle until he finally felt the pain in his knuckles and licked his skin. Even that didn't make him feel better.

He'd been foul to everyone ever since they'd learnt about Mathew, but on hearing from Lucy that the Ball was still going ahead, he'd been furious. He'd followed his father into his study, slamming the door behind him.

'What do you mean by this? It's appalling! How can you expect—?'

'I don't expect anything,' Richard interrupted. 'But Ron and Karen have asked that life go on. The Ball is an important part of life in this village and—'

'Life! This village is dead, always has been. Come on, Dad, you know this is in bad taste, to continue with it is just… just awful!'

Richard nodded and slowly sank onto his bed. 'I know, I know, but it's what is happening and that's that.'

Adam stared at him for a moment and shook his head. 'This Ball thing is a bloody farce, always has been. Why the hell do you do it? So what if some ancestor decided to connect with the villagers. Who cares these days? You've got to stop it, Dad, you've got to.'

He'd stormed out just as the phone rang. It was probably Rosalyn, no doubt asking about the stupid Ball. She always considered it pointless and dull, and had managed to wangle her way out of many over the years. He'd admired her for it. Good old Rosalyn, he missed her. Chester wasn't too far away, but either her hectic timetable got in the way or his did. He'd last had a quick lunch with her just after Christmas and spoken to her twice on the phone. Both conversations had been brief and awkward, with neither of them saying what they really wanted. Life was too short; maybe he should make more of an effort. Glancing at his watch, he made a decision: He'd speak to her at this stupid Ball. Now, it was visiting hours, and he was no good to anyone here while he was in his foul mood. Jumping into his car, he skidded out of the stable yard and headed for Shrewsbury.

***

Bronwen knew without a doubt he would follow her. So she wasn't too surprised when she heard someone run up behind her.

'Bronwen!'

She stopped and swung round to face him, her arms crossed to protect herself and to try to stop him from seeing how much she was shaking.

'Did I frighten you? You *do* remember me, don't you? I'm James. I helped you with your cottage. I was hoping you and I could go to lunch?' He raised an eyebrow in a questioning manner, his arrogance evident; he expected her to say yes.

She licked her dry lips and quickly looked around her. Two young girls walked past sharing a packet of crisps; they'd be no use to her. She took a deep breath and tried to stare him out. 'Yes, I…do remember you and I'm not interested in lunch. Leave me alone, please.'

She felt scared and flustered, and flounced away in the direction of the castle. Walking under a stone archway, she stopped and looked around at the large, circular garden that it opened onto. There were many people sitting around here on benches, and some sat on the grass. Trees and large overgrown bushes gave shade. A large rectangular building stood opposite. She felt a little steadier seeing people, but she was still too aware that he was close by.

Narrow steps led upward to her right; she decided to climb them. Anywhere that got her farther away from that man. A sign said it led to a tower; after a steady climb, she reached a small doorway that led onto a platform where there was indeed a small tower. What must have been the original castle wall surrounded it and enclosed the platform. She felt trapped.

***

A wildcat! He watched her walk away and felt aroused by the sight. After his clients meeting that went on for much longer than expected, he'd been caught in other meetings Gordon had forgotten to tell him about and with interviewing potential new receptionists. He'd run out of the office as soon as he could, fearful Bronwen had long gone. He couldn't believe his luck seeing her sitting there in the sunshine. She was beautiful.

Some of her long hair had become loose, and it shone golden in the light. That slim waist and rounded arse—he couldn't wait to get hold of her. He hoped she'd fight, so he could subdue her. They all came across as demure, but just as he'd witnessed, underneath they were all wildcats. It was something all the quiet ones kept well hidden, but deep inside, they craved excitement. Seeing her storm off now only made him ache for her even more.

He looked around at the people eating their lunch; he considered none of them a threat. No-one would rescue her; they all looked too passive, stuffing themselves. No-one ever intervened. People were too engrossed in their own lives. He began to walk toward the stone archway. He'd seen her turn right, and he knew that it went nowhere. She was up there, and if luck was on his side, he would make a start on his little wildcat. He would make her purr.

*****

Her heart beat so fast she thought she'd never get her breath back. Her body shook with adrenaline, and her throat felt dry. Looking over the castle walls, she couldn't see him below, but the bushes obstructed some of her view. Satisfied he must have left, she leant against the stone and tried to relax. Another major confrontation. How well was she doing?

Her counsellor would be pleased, she thought. Was she really starting to come out of her own shell that she'd made herself? Was now the right time? Her counsellor had told her it would happen when she was ready. Was she?

'Let me ask you this,' her counsellor had asked on their last session together before she'd left Liverpool for good. 'Could you have seen yourself doing this major thing nine months ago?'

'No way. She would never have let me and I...I would have believed I didn't deserve it.'

'And now? Do you deserve it now?'

Bronwen had wiped away the flowing tears and sniffed loudly. 'Yes, I deserve it now.'

Looking out at the railway tracks and the river, she looked beyond, as far as she could see. Yes, she deserved this. She deserved to be happy and free. Slowly, she became aware that she was no longer alone and she turned toward the intruder. Her heart hammered in her throat and she found it hard to breathe.

'What's wrong, darling?' he drawled. 'You look so tense. Why don't we go somewhere? I can help you unwind.'

Her breath quickened. There was nowhere to run. He leant against the small, narrow doorframe stopping her escape; he looked completely relaxed. She took a few steps back, but stopped when he grinned wickedly. 'Do I make you nervous, darling? No need, I am good with women, I can teach you all kinds of things. You'd love it.'

She found her voice, but it was barely a whisper. 'You leave me alone! Go away! I…I'll…scream!'

He raised an eyebrow and carried on grinning. He took a step forward. 'Why would you do that? I've done nothing to you…yet.'

She felt cold and hot at the same time. He'd whispered the last word, but she'd heard him perfectly and knew his implication. She'd known since meeting him what he was; evil, like her father. A tear trickled down her cheek and she abruptly wiped it away. He was enjoying this; damned if he would see her cry too.

Fifteen feet lay between them. Their eyes locked together. For a few minutes no-one moved or said a word until finally, he took another step closer. She still didn't move. His gaze travelled over her body, resting longer than necessary on her heaving breasts. He licked his lips. 'Come on, Bronwen, let me have you. I'll make it a pleasure, I promise.'

His sickening request revolted her and she swallowed hard to stop the rising bile. He saw the movement and smiled; reaching into his trouser pocket, he massaged himself. 'I have something for you to swallow if you'll let me.'

Her body began to shake uncontrollably as slowly he walked toward her. She could see his hand touching his erection and her fear and revulsion turned to pure anger and a will to fight to her last breath. She braced herself against the wall and kicked out, missing. He dodged to her right and made a grab for her, but in that last second, she turned and kicked out again. He dropped like a sack of spuds.

As he dropped to his knees and rolled onto his back, clutching his groin and making wheezing noises, she dodged past him and ran for the doorway. She heard him cry out something incoherent but she flew through the gap and ran down the steps. Oblivious to the bushes on either side and the rough-cut steps, she prayed she wouldn't fall and break her ankle. She wasn't sure how long a man was incapacitated when kicked in the balls, but not as long as with a broken ankle, that was for sure.

Her luck ran out as she turned a slight corner and collided with the person coming up. Falling headlong into what she assumed was a man, although she didn't have time to think as together they rolled down the last few steps and collapsed entangled on the gravel. With the wind knocked out of her and her eyes blurred with tears of pain and panic, the voices she heard didn't quite register as she lay on her side. Her main focus was how to remember to breathe. In…out…in… out. Trying to assess the damage to her body, all the while waiting for him to appear at the stairs.

Moving slowly, she managed to get onto all fours and gasped as pain shot up her leg. Gingerly, she checked and noticed a large graze on each knee; her hands were also in the same condition, and her head hurt where she'd banged it against the other person. She looked across, and saw the back of a man, sitting on the gravel, rubbing his head. She tried to speak, but her lips felt numb. She needed to reassure the elderly couple who now bent over her that she didn't need an ambulance and warn them about the possible rapist who could come and find her any second. She was also trying to get herself together enough to ask if the other person was all right.

Easing onto the gravel path, the man lay on his back, winded himself. He couldn't form words, but turned his head to look at her. Both froze. Adam's expressions on his face changed rapidly from disbelief to fury and then to concern as she collapsed sobbing.

This was the last straw; she couldn't fight them both. Her battle left her.

CHAPTER TWENTY-TWO

EIRA SIPPED HER CHAMOMILE TEA while she sat in her garden, trying to enjoy the warming sun; it wasn't working. Everything ached regardless of the handful of painkillers she'd already taken. The shop hadn't been as busy as she'd expected, though she'd had one or two outright enquiries as to her disappearance. 'I had a bit of visiting to do and decided to stay over; you know how it is?' She must said that sentence at least seven times in the last four hours; she knew it wouldn't end, either.

Of course, in a way, she couldn't blame them. She'd spoilt them over the years, being there all the time at their whim. Often she'd enjoyed the company and feeling needed, but now she'd had enough of the gossiping, the nosiness, and the ever-watchful eyes. Now, she wanted oblivion, peace, and love, real love.

She sighed heavily. Someone was coming to ruin her peace and quiet; a woman. She longed for a whole day to be by herself. Before the last war, she remembered an afternoon when she'd been left to herself to plant her flowers and herbs; they knew to leave her be in those days at least. A sharp pain shot through her back as she eased herself off her chair. Damned arthritis and damned old age!

As she rubbed the small of her back, Judith appeared at her garden gate. Without waiting for an invitation, she opened it and walked in, closing it softly behind her. 'Everything all right, Eira?'

Eira nodded. She looked concerned, and berated herself for being nasty. 'Please, sit down, kettle's not long boiled. I'll make you a cuppa.' Indicating the bench opposite her own chair, she was about to go into the kitchen when Judith stopped her. 'No thanks, at least, not just now.'

Eira searched her face and slowly sat down. 'So, not here for pleasantries, just come to ask my advice, eh?'

Judith blushed and rubbed her hands nervously. 'Well, I, yes, I suppose I have.'

Eira reached forward and, wincing with the effort, patted Judith's lap. 'I'm sorry, feeling a little bit irritable today, God help anyone who crosses my path.' Seeing Judith's hurt expression, she quickly continued, 'But, you're not here to do that, are you?'

Judith attempted to smile. 'I guess that depends on…well, I came to tell you that the May Ball is still going ahead, even after Sir Richard heard about dear Mathew. Don't you think that's awful? Personally, I find the whole thing grotesque, but, I was hoping you might talk to him, he…he listens to you.'

Eira remained silent while Judith hunted inside her handbag for a tissue. She waited while she dabbed at her eyes and gently wiped her nose. Eira's mind was racing, but she'd mastered the art of hiding her emotions when a need called for it; so, outwardly, she appeared calm and serene. Of course the Ball must go ahead. There wasn't any question. Damn this interfering old bat. Bronwen had to be introduced to the Kenwards, there was no other way, and the Ball was the perfect opportunity.

'I understand your concern, Judith, but, surely, Mathew is on the mend? This is only temporary, isn't it? Why stop a very old tradition, which I believe the majority of the village are looking forward to?' Seeing Judith wasn't convinced, she quickly added, 'And, I believe Ron specifically asked it to go ahead. If you like, it can be in Mathew's honour.'

'You make it sound as though the poor lad is dead. He could…I mean…he tried to…oh God, Eira it's so awful! What has happened to him?'

Eira shook her head slowly as she leant back in her chair. 'I don't really know, but perhaps the village needs the Ball to cheer everyone up a little. It's not about ignoring what happened, only that, perhaps, we could all do with some release from the tension. Do you know what I mean?'

In answer, Judith blew her nose and silently shook her head. Eira left her there while she slowly made her way into her small kitchen. The pain in her legs was almost unbearable, but she clung onto the kitchen sink and waited for it to subside. Darling little Mathew; it was such a shame that he'd been chosen. She was fairly sure that he wasn't attached to the Kenward family except as an employee, so why him?

The tears fell unexpectedly; another innocent life damaged because of her pain, the guilt. It never went away. It was so close, the end, she could almost reach out and grasp it, but to take another innocent was devastating. It should be her, never Mathew. Could he hold on to life? Would he live if she died first, or was his end inevitable? She sobbed as quietly as she could, not so much for the boy, though it broke her heart, but for the mess she had caused.

***

Judith sat still, listening to the faint noises coming from the kitchen. So Eira hadn't known anything new about Mathew, which was odd. Eira knew everything about everyone. Outside life never interested Eira, or so she said whenever anyone invited her out on a day trip. In fact, she didn't think Eira ever left the village, which was very odd.

She stood up, but remained in the garden. She'd give her a few minutes before going inside and helping her with the tea. Besides, she had no idea what to say to her. Perhaps she should just go? She glanced at the closed gate and decided against it; that would be rude. Damn this May Ball! Why keep up the stupid tradition anyway? Okay, most of the times she'd enjoyed them, but no-one was looking forward to this year's, surely?

The sunshine warmed her face, and she closed her eyes against the sudden glare. She gently rubbed her fingers against the large bush of rosemary and sniffed. The garden always helped her feel calm, but not today. She suddenly shivered despite the warming rays and went back to her seat to wait for Eira to compose herself.

***

William stood by his chamber window staring out at his property. From here, he could survey everything he owned. The small courtyard that encompassed his stables and his horses, the adequate shelter that also served as a smithy and a workshop, depending on what was needed. The double-storey guardroom that he knew was overcrowded, but his men never complained about its cramped conditions, at least, not to his face.

They took it in turns to sleep in large tents in a sheltered position behind the castle. Of course, he knew they didn't really sleep but took their pleasure with willing women from the surrounding areas. If it kept them happy, fine. It also meant that he had men front and back of his property and he knew they rarely went anywhere without their weapons. It gave him an extra sense of security, though how secure a lust-filled soldier could be was another matter entirely.

His attention suddenly focused on his daughter. She sat in the dirt, in the shade, her back leaning against the storeroom door, giggling happily as she teased two kittens with a piece of string. The stable cat had done well again and four kittens had been born to her five weeks before. Sadly, two had died under mysterious circumstances. He had heard the whisperings about sorcery and the devil's work, but as only pools of blood had been found, he couldn't agree with the village gossips.

A moan from behind him turned his gaze away from outside, to his bed, where his wife still lay sleeping. Tiredness overwhelmed her lately and she had taken to her bed more often. It was late morning and she had barely risen when she insisted on returning to their bed to rest. Of course, he encouraged it, but if she slept, she wasn't eating, and Nia said food passed on to the child, which helped it grow strong. Whilst sleeping, Anne was denying their child nourishment.

She turned in her sleep and her bump came into view. She was now in her sixth month, but she looked too thin. At mealtimes, he tried to encourage her to eat more, but she complained of being unable to breathe with such a full stomach and a child pushing upward. Nia advised him to leave it be; small meals more often were advisable, and she had of course been right. Anne managed to keep most of the food in, but still she looked as if she'd not gained weight.

He'd confessed his fears to Nia and he realised, as she had, that his main concern had moved from his wife to the need for a healthy son. Nia had already confirmed that Anne carried a boy, in secret of course; she was always right. He could hardly contain his excitement and nerves. It was so close now, if anything went wrong…no, he couldn't think like that.

It had been over a week since Rhys had ridden back to his lands. Not much after, it became common knowledge that Henry was going to cross the Channel. There was no doubt that it would be soon. Henry might already be on his way, but as yet, no news had reached him. William hated waiting for news; the outcomes were too unpredictable. He had heard that the Earl of Shrewsbury rallied to Henry's banner, but he wasn't a powerful man, so he had to keep his feelings to himself, for now.

Could Henry really win and become king? Would he be a better one than this man who stole the crown from two innocent boys? Was he as ruthless? There was still no evidence to suggest King Richard had had anything to do with their disappearance, but the rumours were flying strong.

He forced the thoughts away; it didn't matter. He had pledged his oath to his friend Rhys, and would rally to him when the time came, but it was like an itch he couldn't scratch. His men were restless too, practising their swordplay whenever a quiet moment presented itself. Swordplay and quiet contemplation, making their peace with God.

Perhaps it was about time he did the same. He glanced out of the window and then at his wife, he thought that it was also about time he made his peace with the two precious women in his life.

The arguing had begun as soon as the cloud of dust had barely settled after Rhys' departure. Anne was furious that he would even consider war when his child could be born while he was away.

'What if you don't return? What will happen to me and our child? You don't care about me anymore. You'd rather fight for a man you've never met and you might lose!'

He tried very hard not to think about losing. He'd held her close, attempting to reassure her, but Anne pulled away and kept her back to him. 'I'll win…we'll win, and then Rhys and I shall return with a new king and he will honour me and all will be well, I promise'

But, he knew that if he didn't win, King Richard would not be merciful, to him or his household; all would be forfeit. Gwenllian might be safer if she went to live with Janet; at least then she'd be deep within Rhys' lands, a far safer place than here.

Faithful, loving, stubborn Anne. After screaming at him and calling him many hurtful names, 'deserter' being among them, he'd finally managed to calm her down, using the unborn baby as a reason. She'd stormed off and had barely spoken to him since. His frequent attempts at placating her came against an icy wall, so he'd given up. He'd met many women, but none as headstrong as Anne. She could be, and for the most part was, a loving wife, but cross her, she was like a whirlwind.

He reached out and gently touched the cold, grey stone of his chamber. Perhaps, if Henry did win this war, he might gain favour. Rhys promised him that he would be recognised for his loyalty. If he could prove himself in battle, would Henry reward him?

He hadn't shared his hopes with Rhys as he'd listened to his friend talk of expanding his lands and property and of rebuilding his favourite home, Carew Castle, and his hopes of acquiring many others. He did not care for others, but he did dream of rebuilding his home and making it more hospitable.

If Henry did win and became king and he was rewarded, he wanted to build a new home, a home befitting his status, a home Anne would be proud of. A castle with a large garden. A home where his children could run about and play. His children and, perhaps, grandchildren? He looked down at his Gwen. Her giggling reached him and he smiled; a home where his daughter would always be welcomed.

Suddenly, she jumped up and ran away in the direction of the meadow. He was about to call out when he noticed Nia, slowly making her way after her. Poor woman! She was getting old now; perhaps Gwenllian's marriage would be welcomed by everyone. He tried not to dwell too much on that. To think about her marriage meant thinking about the future and he couldn't be sure he would be in hers.

His thoughts strayed to Robert, a prophet who worked for Rhys. It was he who finally persuaded Rhys to change sides and fight for Henry, having reassured him Henry would win. Reassuring him Henry's landing would be without problems this time and the Duke of Buckingham's fate would not be shared by Rhys. What a mess that had been. King Richard had been overly ruthless in his dealings with the Duke. People still talked about the monstrosities before he was finally put out of his misery and beheaded. Only three years had passed, but it still remained fresh in his mind.

Had Rhys talked to Robert about other parts of his life? Decisions he had to make? Alliances? Had he asked the prophet about joining with his family? If that were so, what would have happened if Robert had said the union between his Gwen and Alan was ill-favoured? Had he asked his prophet about his friendship and loyalty?

Pushing himself away from the window, he gently closed the wooden shutters against the glare of the warm sun. Prophet or no, he had no-one to help make his decisions, so he had to make sure everything was in order before Rhys' messenger came. He would ride into the village and survey his lands. Speak with a few of the older villagers, check the mill, and, perhaps, look for a suitable spot for a new home.

He stood for a moment longer, gazing down at his sleeping wife and his unborn child. He saw a slight movement and his heart surged with joy. He reached out to touch her swollen belly, but withdrew his hand and quickly strode out of the silent chamber, closing the door softly behind him. He was so aroused. He had every intention of visiting a woman he knew, a woman who allowed him use of her beautiful, plump body. She never questioned him, or complained. She never argued or asked anything in return, she was just there. He never said her name, for to say it and touch his own wife would be too shameful. Knowing he was going to visit the woman had made him withdraw his hand. He didn't want to take any chance of reprisal from God, but he was a man with men's needs.

***

Anne slowly opened her eyes and listened to William's departure. She knew of his plans to ride over his lands and visit the small village, which usually meant he was going to see her. She felt guilty for having spoken so angrily and for her actions since, but her body ached and her head reeled with alternative endings to this possible war.

How could he contemplate going away to fight for a man he didn't know or know for sure his politics? He only had Rhys' word on the matter. Damn the man to hell for putting her William in this position! She was carrying his child, a son for sure; it was folly to fight now. The dangers outweighed everything else.

As if in answer to her thoughts, her child squirmed uncomfortably and she had to roll over onto her back and lie full length to accommodate it. She could feel the pressure on her rib cage increasing, and she fought for breath, slowly rubbing the area and willing the child to move; it did. She could almost imagine him curl up again after his big stretch and she smiled warmly, softly caressing herself. How could William consider throwing all this away on the word of his damned friend?

CHAPTER TWENTY-THREE

BRONWEN'S HANDS SHOOK; THAT'S ALL that registered for a few minutes as her brain tried desperately to take in the morning and the last twenty minutes. The library, the attack, the escape and now this, talk about frying pans and fire!

She became aware of gentle hands and a strong smell of mint as she was carefully helped up. Through her blur of tears, she saw that the two main people who helped her were quite elderly, so as graciously as she could, she allowed them to escort her to an empty bench, most likely the one they quickly vacated on seeing her fall, as an opened packet of Polo's lay on the seat. The woman picked them up before helping her sit down.

'There now, you just take your time. Kenneth, go and check the gentleman. He looks hurt.'

She kept her head down and her hands clasped tightly between her legs. She did not want to look up and see Adam Kenward. His anger had been clear as he'd been about to shout, but on seeing her, he'd stared wide-eyed, his mouth open, before something like disbelief followed by concern had flashed across his face, quickly followed by pain.

She dared herself to turn her head slightly and take a quick peek. The elderly gentleman had his back to her, and Adam stood with his left side to her. They were both looking up the narrow stairs from where she'd run. Adam was slowly rubbing his right shoulder and she could see a scrape on the back of his left hand. She quickly looked back at the tarmac path

She heard their approaching footsteps and tried not to be sick. The shaking now spread through her body and she clamped her lips together to stop them from trembling. *It's just shock. It'll go.* She repeated this in her head to help focus. It was a technique she found useful in times of stress, and this was certainly one of those times. The horror she felt at that moment was overwhelming, and she tried to concentrate on the breathing techniques she had been shown. Breathe in, two three, and out, two three, breathe in, two three…and out, two three, breathe in…what?

'Do you think she's all right? She's very pale and I can see her shaking from here.'

The elderly woman sat down and gently placed an arm around her shoulders. This was the final straw. Bronwen, so unused to any show of affection, fought the panic, the fight, the flight, and as various parts of her body began to sting and throb with pain, much to her utter horror, she started to cry, uncontrollably.

'Oh you poor lamb.' As any loving grandparent might do, the woman gently pulled her toward her. For a split second, Bronwen felt her body tense at the sudden contact, but she couldn't fight anymore. She released herself into the woman's embrace, and let her hold her tightly, gently rocking her as she murmured. 'It's all right now, everything's all right now. That's right, let it out. It's the shock. It's all right.'

'Should we take her to the hospital, do you think? We're here for a holiday, so I don't know if…'

'Yes, there is one, nearby. I'll take her.' Adam's voice sounded strange. Was it concern or duty because he knew her?

She heard the hesitation in Kenneth's voice. 'Well, I don't know. She looks pretty shaken there and you don't look much better off. What was she doing, running like that down those steps, madness?'

Adam didn't answer straight away; he was looking toward the bushes. 'I'm not sure, but something frightened her. We're… neighbours.'

Finally, she managed to quieten down and gratefully took the offered tissue. Carefully avoiding Adam's gaze, she wiped her face and blew her nose. She was conscious of people passing by and looking at her; apparently, so were her rescuers.

'Come on. Let's get her away from here. I can't stand people who just gawp at others and do nothing.' A little louder the woman said, 'Especially those who've just witnessed an awful accident but carry on eating their chips.'

Bronwen grinned; she liked her saviour. She allowed herself to be pulled gently to her feet and found she was grateful for Kenneth's appearance on her other side. Any other time, she might have flinched away or run a mile, but now she allowed him to put his arm through hers and his wife did the same. Adam hovered at Kenneth's side. He looked uncomfortable, but she couldn't think of anything to say; 'sorry' sounded absurd.

Without rushing, the foursome slowly made their way toward the big arch. Passing the steps, she averted her eyes and swallowed hard; he had to still be up there, or was he nearby? She let herself be guided down the driveway and they all stopped opposite the library where she was relinquished into Adam's custody. He didn't attempt to touch her, but after a brief swapping of phone numbers and best wishes, he led the way, away from the town.

She followed him slowly, only once turning round to check her rescuers were still watching; they were. They waved and smiled reassuringly; she missed them both already. Alone with Adam after their kindness felt terrible, and she wanted to cocoon herself in their grandparent-like warmth. These two strangers would never have allowed any man to hurt her. Their concern for her wellbeing was evident when they'd insisted that Adam give them his home address and phone number and prove who he was before allowing their ward into his care.

Now, slowly walking behind Adam, she felt mixed emotions that she'd agreed to go with him. She didn't want to be alone, knowing James could be nearby, but she'd have preferred to stay with her saviours. It was her pride and embarrassment that had made up her mind; after all, they were on holiday and strangers. Adam was not. But was she safe with this Adam? She quickly glanced at him and bit her lower lip and winced as she bit into a small cut. She had to admit that he felt slightly safer than the damned letch she had escaped from.

Slowly, they made their way along the narrow pavement and she began to feel nervous as she saw fewer and fewer people. Adam gathered speed and he now walked a few feet ahead; she had slowed down. 'Where are we going?' It came out as a croak, but he heard her and stopped.

'My car's parked just over that bridge. Five minutes? I'll take you to the hospital.' Seeing her shake her head, he shrugged. 'All right, I'll take you home…to the cottage.'

He turned and walked at a steady pace. She kept a few feet behind him. She didn't want to have to speak to him; it would be bad enough on the drive home. She calculated about a twenty-minute journey. Could she do it? She briefly considered the bus, but that wasn't due for another few hours and she desperately wanted to be safe, within her own cottage; she had no choice.

**

Adam sucked on his lower lip, tasting the blood. He'd obviously cut the inside of his cheek and lips. His shoulder throbbed and the minor scrapes on the back of his hand and his right arm stung. The shock of it all had worn off. The shock of it being the woman from his cottage was still nagging him.

At first, he'd been angry that some fool had flung herself on him. His first thought had been a thief, and been about to fight back, and make the person wish he'd never considered him as a target. Then he'd seen her. The look of terror on her face jolted him into reality. She hadn't thrown herself at him, she'd fallen, running pell-mell from something, or someone.

As they'd walked her back toward the road, he was convinced someone was watching them from the shrubbery. A slight movement in the corner of his vision had made him walk a little faster, encouraging the others to follow suit. Whoever it had been, he was determined to get her away. And that annoyed him too. She meant nothing to him, right? She'd taken his home. Yet, seeing her there, battered and bruised, big, blue eyes wide with fear, he'd felt an overwhelming urge to protect her.

He didn't need to turn around to know that she was following him. Part of him wanted to stop and check her injuries and her wellbeing, but another just wanted to get it over with. He was feeling chivalrous, that's all, nothing more. He was a gentleman; he wouldn't leave any distressed woman alone, would he?

Finally, they reached the car. He glanced at her as he opened the passenger side for her. She had a nasty scrape down her temple, which by tomorrow would be an ugly bruise. He noticed a tear on her top and blood on her jeans. He had no doubt that there were other injuries beneath her clothes and, for a fleeting moment he would have liked to have seen them, cleansed them, and made her feel better. She was a good-looking woman.

She kept her head down as she climbed into the car. She avoided his gaze as she reached for the seatbelt. He closed the door and quickly walked to the driver's side. He looked around the full car park and wondered if whoever she'd been running from had followed them, but he saw no-one looking suspicious. Exhaling loudly, he opened the door, climbed in, and slammed it shut. Best get this over with.

She was crying, silently, her hands clasped tightly in her lap. Only the constant fall of her tears betrayed her emotion. He didn't know what to do or say. Should he take her to the hospital? Perhaps if he asked her what she was running from? But, why would she tell him anything? Eira. Take her to Eira. She'd know what to do. He started the car.

***

Rosalyn sat at her office desk and sipped her black coffee. She stretched her legs beneath the large, solid wood desk and kicked off her high-heeled shoes. She could hear her two assistants tidying things away in the large shop; the door that separated her office from them stood slightly ajar. She contemplated joining them, to giggle and gossip about the day's customers. Sometimes it could be the highlight of the day if they'd had some interesting women in, but she didn't move.

She'd not long come off the phone with her father who'd filled her in over Mathew, poor little sod! She was sure he'd had a crush on her last year. He'd followed her about, staring at her, blushing and stuttering whenever he'd brought her horse, Daisy. It was a nuisance and not one she'd have liked to experience again, but she'd never have wished this on the boy.

She guessed by her father's tone that she hadn't been the first to point out that the Ball going ahead was in very bad taste. He'd told her about Mathew's parents wanting it to go ahead and spoken about tradition and the village needing it, and she'd heard what he'd really been saying: 'I hate this, but please come home, I need my family around me.'

He'd spoken of the need to keep things as normal as possible. What the hell was normal about a young lad suddenly going cuckoo? So she'd agreed yet again and reassured him that she'd be there on the Friday night and yes, she'd stay until Sunday night and yes, they'd have a nice family meal and everything would be great. Boring!

She rubbed her eyes as she slowly began to read through the accounts for the past month. It was looking better, at least. She'd opened this shop three years ago and had been talked into opening another in Liverpool just over twelve months ago. At last, she was seeing profit; the bank manager would be pleased. Perhaps she could think about a small holiday? She pushed the idea away as soon as she thought it. Better not get too complacent.

She jumped as the phone rang. 'Hello. Rosalyn Kenward speaking.'

As the caller spoke, she listened attentively; at one point, she began to bite her nails, realised, and stopped herself. Her heart beat faster as the person spoke, until finally, she replaced the receiver with a bang. Damn it!

She felt no guilt or remorse for what she'd done, felt nothing but revulsion after what she'd just heard, and gave herself a triumphant pat on the back. She'd hesitated only briefly after hearing about this stranger moving into Adam's cottage, but the more she thought about it, the more it made sense. Finding a private detective had been surprisingly easy and this had helped her feel justified in what she was doing.

She pulled a face as she realised her coffee had gone cold and put the cup down. What did this Miss Mortimer look like? Adam hadn't given anything away when he'd told her about it and neither had Father, as he'd never met her—which she found very odd. How could a tenant keep herself to herself for so long? Did she have something to hide? Well, yes, she did, as she'd found out. Why hadn't Father checked this woman out? She was sure he'd get rid of her once he found out what she was. She was doing them a favour hiring this detective, and he'd only just begun; what else would he find out about her?

***

Judith stood and was about to go inside to find Eira, who had been in the kitchen for a long time, when she came out carrying a large tray of freshly brewed tea and a plate of her homemade shortbread. Judith heard her stomach growl and they laughed together, the uncomfortable grief for Mathew hidden behind pretence. To hide her shame, Judith busily admired the bright purple lavender while Eira placed the tray on the small, round table. They sat quietly, enjoying the warm sun and the fragrant flowers, sipping their tea and occasionally munching a biscuit. They passed the time of day talking about this and that, both staying away from the topics which would cause them harm: Mathew, the Ball, and the Kenward family. Company was what each one wanted and for now, that was enough.

***

The small figure watched the two women from the upstairs bedroom window. Her pale cheeks flushed with anger, and a burning rage ran through her thin body. The visitor, she was one of them; she would be punished.

***

Martha lay on her lounge floor. She couldn't feel her body anymore, only a strange numbness. She wanted to try to move her hand, to touch her face, as she was sure she had tears rolling down her cold cheeks, but nothing would move; her will had left her. She would die alone.

As her breath started to leave her, she was aware of a slight warmth on her legs and she knew she'd wet herself. For a fleeting moment, this disgusted her, but then nothing mattered. Dying while she lay in her own piss didn't matter. Dying without saying goodbye to her friends didn't matter. Nothing mattered but a strange sensation, like floating on a warm wind and a knowing that she wasn't alone after all; her husband was waiting.

***

Anne managed to eat breakfast, but within minutes, she had vomited and was left with an aching stomach, a raw throat, and a vile temper. Megan, one of her ladies-in-waiting, received the brunt of it. Having cursed her for being useless and uncaring and complaining about the freshness of the bread and the bitterness of the wine, she physically pushed Megan out of her bedchamber, slamming the door in the girl's face with the last ounce of strength she had.

She sat on the bed, enraged, and attempted to calm herself. The child kicked from within her, which helped a little. How dare that damned man leave his son! Would he ever forgive himself if she lost this child too? She clasped her hands over her mouth as if she'd spoken the words out loud and prayed to God to take them back.

She gently rubbed her womb and eventually the child stopped writhing and settled down. She let out a deep sigh. She had to remain calm, or at least as calm as possible; her son was too precious.

She couldn't help her thoughts returning to the men who ruled her and her son's fate. What of Henry Tudor? Could he really cross into this country to take it by force? If Henry failed, William would most likely die, or they'd be forced into exile with no prospects and little money. All William's wealth lay in his home and the surrounding lands; it was not much, but it was all his. If Henry won, what favours would he grant? It was all a great risk and one that William was obviously prepared to take regardless of how she felt about it.

And what of the King? Of course, she'd never met him but had spoken with those who had. They all whispered that he was a bad man and rumours were rife of his involvement in the disappearance of his nephews. Had he killed them or had them taken away? She believed they were dead, as did William. And what of Richard's wife and son? Some believed they had died from a curse placed upon the King in revenge for the two boys. Could curses really work?

She suddenly stopped rubbing her womb and stared into the fireplace where the fire had dwindled into a warm glow. Was it possible? She slowly crossed herself for thinking such a thought, but only half-heartedly. Wouldn't she do anything to save her husband and indeed her son? She would kill for them, she was sure of it. Could she curse someone and save those she loved?

She sat unmoving as she contemplated all the obstacles that might lie between William's and her happiness. She didn't care that he was only a knight, but the castle was something else. It was cold, uncomfortable, and old. So many parts needed attention but there were always other needs that had to come first. She dreamt of a fine house with a grand staircase and warm rooms with glass windows.

Her gaze had fixed beyond the fire; now her gaze turned inward, remembering an old woman from her childhood. An old nurse who had told her stories and rhymes, rhymes to help with life, she'd said. Rhymes and rituals that could heal or hurt. She'd thought them nothing more than fun games, until one night, the old nurse had disappeared. When she asked, she'd been told she'd gone back to her own people. She'd believed for years her own people must have been the fairies. Could she use these to help Henry win the crown? Did they really work or had her silly rhymes to get William been nothing more than coincidences?

***

Adam manoeuvred the car through the afternoon traffic, which was slow going; it was making him more and more wound up as each minute dragged on. Now that he'd made up his mind to take her to see Eira and hand over responsibility, he wanted it over and done with. Besides, he wanted to get back to the stables, he'd been away too long; he also wanted to check the damage she'd done. No broken bones, but a possible bruised rib or two, a bruised shoulder, and raw scrapes that hurt more than the bruises.

He risked a quick glance across at her. She'd stopped crying, that was a small relief, but she looked very pale and she still clasped her hands tightly together in her lap; her gaze had never looked up. What was she thinking? Finally, they were out of the town and on the dual carriageway, heading for Derwen, only ten minutes and then…

'Stop the car!'

Her scream made him jump violently and he jerked the steering wheel. The car overtaking him blared its horn, but he ignored it and slammed on his brakes. At the same time, he indicated his intentions. More angry horns ensued, but he ignored all of them as he watched her wrench the door open, stagger onto the grass verge, and vomit.

Minutes passed and he sat listening to her retching over and over, but when she fell silent, he turned to look. Quickly undoing his seatbelt and getting out of the car, reaching her just in time as she stumbled backward. She was shaking so violently, he suddenly felt very scared that he'd done the wrong thing. Hospital was the best place for her, what an idiot! 'God damn it to hell!' he muttered, one arm around her waist and the other trying to stroke wisps of loose hair off her face. Her eyes were closed, but she hadn't fainted completely.

Within seconds, she was coming round and pulling away from him. At last, she stood, a little shakily, but disengaged herself from his arm. She looked awkward, but he tried to give her a reassuring smile, which didn't seem to help. She dug around in her jeans for a tissue and he waited while she gingerly climbed back into the passenger seat. Getting behind the wheel, he took a deep breath and exhaled loudly. 'Okay, then? Let's go.'

But, instead of heading for Derwen, he acted on impulse and turned left, down a narrow lane. He saw her reaction and wondered if he'd made another foolish mistake. 'It's all right. I just thought you looked like you could do with a drink...I know I could. If I've made the wrong assumption, I'll turn around; it's not a big deal. I just thought...' He shrugged. What else could he say? He knew he'd made the wrong decision about the hospital. Why not make it worse and get some alcohol down the woman?

'Oh...' She looked across at him. He could feel her uncertainty. 'Oh, right...I...well, yes, I suppose I...could do with a drink. Thanks.'

He quickly glanced over and saw the deep crimson blush before she turned away and looked out of the window. What the fuck was he doing? Hospital was the best place for her, not a fuckin' pub! But he calmly parked the car in the small car park a few minutes later and led the way into the old inn.

***

Bronwen stared at her reflection in the oval mirror in the spotless, musty smelling bathroom. *What are you doing? Fire, frying pan, definitely!* She didn't feel as queasy now; her stomach felt like a bottomless pit. Her heart felt like it would burst through her chest, and her mouth felt like moss. It didn't smell much better, either.

She washed her face with cold water and soap, rinsed her mouth over and over, using her finger to rub her teeth and gums. She undid her hair and plaited it, blew her nose again, and used the toilet. Washing her hands and face helped her feel a little more human. But was she ready to face Adam Kenward? Not likely, and her stomach dropped beneath her.

***

He'd ordered two whiskies and was standing by the bar when she walked in looking uncomfortable, so he picked up both glasses and led the way into a little alcove. She nervously sat opposite him and said nothing as she twiddled with her fingers, her head down. What was he supposed to do now? Stupid idiot!

'I ordered a whiskey. I'm told it's good for shock, or a brandy if you prefer…or something else?' Was he rambling? He sounded like it.

She looked up and reached for her glass. Taking a sip, she looked like she enjoyed it as she put it back on the table. He did the same and an awkward silence followed. He tried not to look directly at her, but he couldn't help glancing at her. She smelt of apple soap and she'd tidied her hair. He wondered again how long it really was.

He coughed nervously and glanced around the room. He'd been here before; they always had a nice selection of whiskies, which was what had made him think of this place. Also, no-one was likely to bother him here, or know her, for that matter. He doubted very much if she ever went anywhere, she looked so anxious.

He finished his drink in one gulp and stood up to get another. She didn't move and he didn't ask; he got her another too. When he returned, she was staring at an old photograph on the wall but he wasn't sure if she was really seeing that, or something else. The look on her face made him feel uncomfortable.

He leant forward and saw her flinch. To hide it, she quickly finished her first whiskey and looked at him, questioning the second. He just shrugged. 'Right, well, this is the thing. I'm not used to women throwing themselves at me without some explanation...' He waited to see if she'd say anything, and when she didn't, he carried on and said, 'So, perhaps you would do me the honour of telling me what happened today?'

She sat with her elbows on the table and her hands covering her mouth. He could see she was trying to think of something to say, so he waited, but after ten minutes of silence, he reached out and gently touched her arm. The flash of anger as she cringed surprised him. He stared at her, confused for a moment, and then realisation flooded his head. 'Was someone up there? Did they hurt you?'

He watched horrified as her face crumpled and fresh tears fell down her cheeks. What the hell had he got himself into? Getting up, he found some napkins and brought them back to her. She took them without speaking and frantically wiped her face. 'I...I'm sorry. You're being...so kind...' She said it as though surprised, and that stung a bit, but he couldn't really blame her after their last meeting.

'You know, I'm not such a horrid person, but you didn't have to use me as a soft landing, you know!' His attempt at lightening the mood was rewarded with a thin smile.

She reached for her drink and drank it back in one.

'I guess I do owe you an explanation, but...did I hurt you?' Her voice was barely a whisper. He had to lean closer to hear her.

He was surprised by her question. 'God no! Made of steel.'

'No, you're not. I saw you rubbing your shoulder, is it…badly bruised?'

He grinned. 'No, really, I've had worse. Falling off horses gives nastier bruises than these. Look, you look like you need something to eat, perhaps—'

'No, really I…I'm not hungry.' She quickly interrupted, 'Thank you…for…being my soft landing. I…' Fresh tears welled up in her eyes and she quickly dabbed them away.

She started fiddling with her jeans pocket and he realised she was looking for money. He put his hand up and shook his head. 'Please, it's on me today. Come on then, I'll take you home, unless you want to tell me something?'

She shook her head and stood up, a little unsteadily. He hesitated briefly before leading the way out of the inn. Whatever had happened to her, he wasn't going to find out today. Besides, he'd had enough; he just wanted to go home, check his own bruises, ride Scarlet, and not think. He wasn't responsible for this woman. He'd done his bit. The sooner he got her back to Derwen, the better. Maybe Eira would have better luck?

***

James managed to get back to the office without attracting any attention. He knew he must have looked flushed and possibly walked a bit strangely, but the office was thankfully only a few minutes from the castle. It had taken him a good ten minutes before he'd been able to hobble slowly down the steps. He'd stopped dead when he'd seen Adam Kenward of all people walking with that bitch. Two old people walked on either side of her, but why Kenward? Had she told him?

He settled himself in his chair. Checking the office door was locked, he undid his trousers and cautiously withdrew his flaccid penis. Checking it, he sighed with relief when he found it looked and felt okay. Of course, he knew the only way to really test it and reached for the phone.

Minutes later, he replaced the receiver with a smile. Two hours, just two hours. All he had to do was get through three clients and he could leave early. Readjusting himself, he glanced at the clock; his first potential buyer was due any minute. He straightened his tie and slicked back his hair.

Bronwen Mortimer. Just thinking the bitch's name brought a mixture of pleasure and pure hatred. She'd made him look like a fool, acting all coy, when all the while she was a wildcat. He should have remembered that, but regardless of his lapse in memory, no-one, especially some dumb bitch, made him feel foolish; she would pay. Debbie would be her substitute. He paid her well enough, but he looked forward to the real thing.

***

Judith didn't feel comfortable leaving Eira, but after nearly two hours and four cups of tea and a bucket full of shortbread, she felt she'd neglected the Hall and its occupants for too long. Besides, Eira looked like she needed a rest; she wasn't looking her best lately.

It took about ten minutes to walk back to the entrance to the Hall, but her legs felt heavy and she was sweating profusely. She stopped and wiped her forehead and neck with a handkerchief. She hated the thought of getting old like Eira, and the menopause had been the starting point. Since finishing HRT, it felt like her symptoms were returning, not as often, but often enough to inconvenience her.

It seemed her whole life had been spent in the service of the Kenward family, not that she begrudged it, of course. She regretted not having children of her own, but once Sir Richard had come into her life, no other man could compare as a potential father. She reached into her handbag for a fresh handkerchief, as the other was sodden with her sweat, when a slight movement near the bushes to her left made her look up and freeze.

***

Debbie grimaced as she replaced the receiver and quickly lit another cigarette. Her hand shook as she reached for her beer. Finishing it, she went to her small drinks cabinet and took out a three-quarters-full bottle of gin and an unopened bottle of tonic. The sleeve of her shirt fell back, revealing a wrist burn that had hardly healed, and farther along her arm, a bruise still purple and tender. She could feel the others on her body and quickly poured a large measure of gin, ignoring the tonic. She drank it all down, and poured herself another.

James Hawthorn. He paid her rent. He paid for her habit. He paid for the luxuries. Was it worth it? She gasped as the alcohol warmed her throat. If nothing else, at least she'd be pissed when he came to torture her.

CHAPTER TWENTY-FOUR

WILLIAM STAYED AWAY FROM HOME for most of the day. He surveyed his lands and listened to his tenants about various problems such as leaking roofs and damaged crops. He listened patiently while neighbours argued over missing livestock, debts owed, and fighting children. Although it wasn't the usual way of doing things, he felt it was necessary to try to bring a little order in his part of the world. Knowing he had assisted in settling disputes and organised help with crops and leaking roofs eased his worries about leaving. If he weren't coming back, at least the tenants and serfs would be happy!

He grinned to himself as he vaguely listened to yet another complaint about pigs getting out of the pen and causing damage to a vegetable plot. He liked these people. They were skilled men and women who worked the land and had skills to use in trade. He would happily sit with the blacksmith for hours watching him mould horseshoes and trinkets for the ladies. The basket weaver was another man he liked to talk to, the smell of willow in his nostrils. They were people, like himself, with problems. Although theirs were different, they weren't strangers to it; in a way, he envied the villagers.

He wondered if they envied him, his castle and land and servants. He doubted they could even contemplate what it was really like. The crumbling walls of his home, the endless worry of finding money to pay for food, clothing, the King's taxes, wages, politics, backstabbing, it never ended.

At last, he couldn't find any other reason not to return home. His lust had been sated, his duty as lord of the manor had been honoured, his lands, such as they were, were in order. If he didn't return from the battles, he could die with a clear conscience, as far as the village went anyway. Anne, Gwenllian, and his unborn son were another matter.

Turning his horse back toward the track that led to his home, he could just see the two towers of his old ancestral castle. From here, he couldn't see the crumbling walls and thought about how he'd change the design, if the right man became king. The fashion was changing, yet without money and rewards, he could barely afford to live in it, never mind restore it.

He knew Anne wished for better comfort, though she'd never said anything. But he'd caught glimpses of her inspecting the walls when she thought she was alone. Her face flushed with hope and imagination of what their home could really be like. She'd come from a family known at Court; she was used to better. Her cousin's home was a fine house with a large lawn, a small maze, and secret alcoves where he had first courted Anne. The hunting lodge once owned by Anne's mother was also impressive. When they'd married, he'd been given a share of her mother's lands in England and a small dowry; it hadn't been nearly enough.

Rhys promised him that Henry would reward him well for his help in Henry's march up the country. He had already visited his friend, the Sheriff of Shrewsbury, who informed him of the King's orders: Henry was not to be allowed to enter the city at any cost.

'Where do your loyalties lie?' William asked as casually as he could muster.

His friend had smiled and poured some more wine into his goblet. 'I told the King I would not allow Henry to enter the city. He would enter over my dead body.'

William reached for some bread and played with it, needing time to get his thoughts into shape. He managed to keep his expression as plain as possible. 'What did the King say to that?'

'He didn't say much, he never does say much. And you? What will you do?'

William didn't answer immediately, chewing on a piece of bread and forcing it down with his wine. His mind raced with potential answers. He'd rehearsed what to say for every question, but now that the time came to it, he wasn't sure. He'd known John for a long time, but could he really trust him? 'I…haven't decided yet. Besides, I've other, more important, things on my mind like a young wife and a new betrothal. Politics will have to wait.'

They laughed together and ordered more wine. They spoke of other matters, both aware that each man was watching, listening, and circling around the real questions. *'If I betray the King, will you kill me?' 'If I betray this King, will the other make it worth my while?' 'Can I trust you, old friend?'*

As he slowly rode toward his home, his thoughts turned to battles he'd fought and the feel of his sword piercing the flesh of another man, the look in his eyes and the sound that escaped him as death came for him. One day it would come for him, but in what manner? Through the clash of steel or through illness? He hoped he would not linger on his deathbed. He was a fighter, a killer who had killed in battle without mercy, knowing that his opponent was thinking the same. It was the one thing he was good at, and he had fought his way into better lands and wealth. Could this be his last battle that might save his dwindling fortune? Bring him the luck he deserved?

Not for the first time, he wondered if his children dying were not his punishment for the lives he'd taken in battle, and if that were indeed so, then what of this child? As Anne had screamed at him in anger, if he went to fight with Henry, he might not be back in time for the birth, and what if something went wrong again? It would be more blood on his hands, but his hands were tied.

In the distance, he saw a small group of men riding toward him. He recognised Rhys' banner. He reined in his horse and watched them approach. He looked up at the blue sky and breathed deeply, saying a silent prayer for the safety of himself and his family. Clicking his horse into a trot, he kept his expression blank. So it had begun. Henry had managed to land safely. By tomorrow, he would have to leave.

***

Gwenllian watched from the battlements as the five men cantered toward her father returning from the town. She knew these men and knew it was time for her father to leave. She'd worried about him all day and had watched for him in between playing with the new kittens and helping in the stables. Anne had tried to make her do some of her embroidery but she'd only stayed long enough to make a nuisance of herself before fleeing from Anne's wrath, giggling as she ran from the chamber.

She'd heard some of the arguing between her father and that woman and she'd felt nothing but delight in hearing it. The War and the parts about going into battle didn't appeal to her greatly, but she understood it was her father's honour and she must be brave about it. Why couldn't Anne see it was her duty to honour her father's wishes? Stubborn, spoilt woman!

She cried herself to sleep some nights, but sometimes dear old Nia heard her and offered comfort and reassurance. If Nia said it would all be well, she believed her. Nia never lied. Her father would fight for this man Henry, and he would help him win. She believed this because she had been allowed to watch her father and his men practise their swordplay many times, and her father was very good. She'd marvelled at the swinging of his heavy sword and she'd imagined many times all the bad people he would send to their deaths. No, she had every faith that he would return. As much as she believed Nia, she believed her father more and he had promised her that he would return.

She watched as the group of Rhys' men met her father. She watched as they talked for a long time, and then she watched as they trotted toward the castle. She watched from above as they rode beneath the gateway, and she watched as they all dismounted and walked toward the great Hall together. She quickly wiped a tear from her cheek before briskly heading for the Hall as well.

A movement above her in the tower made her smile to herself. So, Anne had seen his return too. Gwenllian hoped she was crying and hurting, stubborn woman. 'But, God, don't hurt the innocent baby!' Crossing herself, she quickened her pace; she would reach the men before Anne did.

***

'Richard!' Judith stuffed her soaking handkerchief inside her sleeve. Flustered and hot, she quickly corrected herself. 'I mean, Sir Richard, what are you doing here?' She straightened her skirt, conscious of the sweat running down her thighs. She glanced around for anything that might distract him while she composed herself, but nothing sprang to mind.

'I fancied a walk, that's all. The house feels quite claustrophobic at the moment, don't you think?' As if realising her dilemma, he walked away and examined the black gates. Gratefully, she whipped out her handkerchief and wiped herself dry, although within seconds she knew she'd be soaked through again. She eventually joined him at the gate, then realised she might smell, so she backed away a little.

'It's hard to believe sometimes that I own all this.' His hand swept over the field and the lane. He looked toward the village and sighed. 'I wonder how much it's all worth?' Realising she was listening, he laughed. 'Do you think it's worth anything? What would someone give me for this entire village, do you think?'

She shrugged; she didn't want to stay here and get into this conversation. She wanted to get back and change and cool off; she was beginning to feel dizzy with her inner heat.

Richard smiled and offered her his arm. Reluctantly she took it. Could he see how sticky and sweaty she was? Her legs felt wobbly and she became grateful that she had taken his arm. Her gallant knight walked slowly and talked about the weather and the food Lucy was preparing and the nice cup of tea he fancied. Not once did he mention her sodden skirt, or the large patches beneath her arms, or the river of sweat that cascaded down her face and between her breasts.

As they walked, Richard began to quicken the pace. 'Please, Sir Richard, I can't walk so fast.' Judith puffed beside him.

With a brief glance behind him, he grinned. 'Sorry, I just really need that cup of tea!' He smiled reassuringly and linked their arms again. She noticed he was trembling slightly, but she didn't ask why. They remained silent for the rest of the way until they parted company when he headed for the kitchen and she headed toward her room. Not once did she look behind her. She didn't need to; she knew without doubt they were being watched, but by whom?

***

Her eyes burned with hatred for the man who carried her family name, his arm hooked by that old woman. He had seen her, she was sure of it. His being here only added to her energy. For a fleeting moment, she felt pity for this man, but he had quickened his pace and the moment passed. They always turned their backs to her. They always betrayed her. He'd promised he'd return and protect her. He'd promised that he loved her. The liar!

***

As he approached the village, Adam glanced across at Bronwen. She hadn't spoken since they'd left the pub, ten minutes before. She sat still, her head slightly turned away from him, so all he could glimpse was a bit of chin, an ear and a cheek; the cheek was wet. He slowed down as the village opened up and he looked across at her again. This time he took in her golden brown hair, plaited, resting on her shoulder;

he could see her slender neck. He pushed all thoughts of kissing it out of his head and slammed on his brakes harder than he intended outside the shop. She didn't move or say anything. Impatiently, he leant forward so he could see her face better. 'Look, I know Eira. She's a kind old lady who could help you.' He waved at her bruises. 'Would you like to meet her?'

She didn't answer, but shook her head.

'Right, then, I'll take you back to my—to Oak Cottage, then?' He was out of his depth with this woman. Something had frightened her, that much was obvious, and he felt a strong need to protect her, but she'd pissed him off by taking his cottage. Okay, technically, that wasn't her fault, but without her, there wouldn't be a problem. He knew nothing about her, which he'd never encountered before. All the other women he'd known flung themselves at him and were open books; this woman gave nothing away. Even her accent was odd. She had a slight Welsh tone when she was angry, but not a hint of a Liverpudlian accent, so he didn't believe that she'd been brought up in Liverpool. So where?

She was pretty. In fact, he found her deep blue eyes beautiful. They betrayed her in that they showed everything. Her emotions ran deep, but it was in her eyes that she held her emotions. They flashed in anger. They swam in tears. The sorrow in her eyes now made him mad with frustration. He wanted to slap her about until she told him what had happened and he wanted to hold her close against his chest and rock her gently, telling her everything was okay. He did neither.

Passing the Kenward Estate, he glanced up the lane that led to his stables and wished he'd never left that morning. He didn't need all this complication, what with Mathew, the ball, Scarlet, and now this woman. He thought of the cold beer he would treat himself to once he'd dropped Bronwen off, but then considered leaving her alone might be a bad idea. He didn't know what to do for the best.

When he pulled up outside the cottage, he saw her quickly glance around the area and guessed what she was doing. He turned the car around so it faced the way they'd come and parked, keeping the engine on. 'Shall I come in and check everything's all right? I mean, it doesn't look like anyone's around.'

She blushed and shook her head. 'I'll be fine.'

She was about to get out when he stopped her. She jerked at his touch, and he quickly withdrew his hand. 'Look, it's probably some male macho thing or something, but I'm not comfortable leaving you like this. Let me fetch Eira...or somebody else?' He waited for a response; none came. 'Do you know anyone?'

She met his gaze briefly before looking back at her lap. He could see she was thinking about what to say. Finally, she opened the car door. 'I'll be fine. I...like my own company, thank you.'

Closing the door, she marched into the garden, opened the front door, and slammed it shut. Stunned by the sudden departure, he watched her and then the closed front door for a moment. 'Ungrateful bitch!' He felt hurt and he didn't like it. Driving away, he looked back once, just to be sure, but the road was empty. At least he knew where he stood with the woman and he could forget about her. As he turned into the Kenward Estate, he knew he hadn't convinced himself of that at all.

***

The little girl watched the Kenward drive away. She turned her back on him once he was out of sight and returned her gaze to the cottage and the one within it. Even from where she stood, she could feel the old connections and it felt good. For now, her anger was contained, spent, and she was enjoying the moment.

Walking slowly, she entered the garden and stood beneath the bedroom window. The feelings that swept over her were so raw. As if time had stood still and she had but walked through a doorway into this world. Time had changed the face, the body, but the energy was the same; it felt good to be so close again. This was the one who could help her. This was the one who would set her free, but would she remember?

***

Bronwen yanked off her clothes as she stormed up the stairs, leaving them wherever they fell. Rushing into the bathroom, she turned on the shower and turned the knob to hot. She winced as the water touched her skin, but she made herself get under it a little at a time, until it cascaded over her head and down her body.

Reaching for her scrubbing brush, she savagely cleansed every inch of her skin. Ignoring the throbbing sting, she scoured herself with every last bit of energy she had left. The cuts to her knees and hands stung, as did the large graze across her thigh which she hadn't noticed, and her body ached with bruises not yet showing. Then she collapsed in a heap at the bottom of the shower and sobbed her heart out.

After a while, she forced herself to move. Shaking, she turned off the water and wrapped herself in a large towel. Stumbling across the hall into her bedroom, she climbed into bed and pulled the duvet over her head, cocooning herself from the outside world. The doors were locked and bolted. The windows were shut and locked. She would be safe here, away from that lecherous bastard and all foul men. Curled up in a ball, she gently began to rock herself and try to clear her mind of it all.

***

Eira remained standing by her garden gate for a long time. She stood very still and listened to everything around her. She could hear the bees humming around her rhododendrons; she heard the blue tits singing nearby. She heard three farmers laughing and chatting outside the old pub. She heard doors opening and closing as people went in and out of their homes. In the distance, she heard a car coming along the lane and knew it was Adam returning home; he hadn't stayed with her, then.

She'd known something was wrong when she'd seen them park outside her shop, but then he continued to the cottage. Bronwen hadn't looked well at all. Had she found the book? Had it triggered her memories? She quickly dismissed that. She doubted that a book would trigger her memory. Then again, the woman was very sensitive...

Stepping out into the lane, she smiled back at the farmers who saw her and waved. Something else felt wrong. She could feel the residue of energy; it felt like black treacle in the air, making it hard to breathe. She looked toward the park, nothing. Her gaze travelled over the chapel, the new houses, the pub and the farmers walking away toward their farms. The ten little cottages, neat and...her eyes rested on Martha's door. She felt a wave of remorse, and tears sprang to her eyes...it had begun.

***

Mathew sat silently staring at the blue button on the psychiatrist's cardigan. He vaguely heard the slowly asked questions, but he couldn't answer. It was not that he couldn't speak; he just couldn't be bothered forming words anymore. Why bother? He had tried to find the words to tell them what was happening to him, the images, the horror, the blood. He was a seer now, not good old innocent Mathew, and not one of them had believed him. She'd said they wouldn't; she was right.

***

The eyes watched as she crawled through the dark tunnel on her hands and knees. As she slowly forced her way forward, she could feel the damp earth beneath her hands. She could smell it as it filled her nostrils, so much that she could taste it in her mouth, which she kept clamped shut.

She could see a dot of light in the distance and knew it was her way out. She could escape and be free if only she could reach it. She scrambled faster and faster, but she never seemed to get any closer to the light. And the eyes just kept on watching.

Suddenly, she knew it was there behind her. She could feel its hot breath on her legs, her backside, her back, but she couldn't turn around to face it, to fight it. It was closing in, ready to pounce, to hurt her, to use her, to make her feel pain and bleed, oh God! There would be so much blood!

Looking down at her wet hands, she could see them glistening as she turned them this way and that and all the while she could feel the hot stinking breath behind her. Peering closer, she could see something pouring off them and the smell of it made her retch, blood, black blood. It poured off her hands and she was covered in it. It started to drip from her eyes and her ears and her nose and her mouth filled with it and she opened her mouth to scream, but only the black blood oozed from it. She tried to swallow it, keep her mouth shut, but it kept coming and she couldn't stop the blood.

And the eyes kept watching and the breath grew stronger and she knew it was over. She knew him. He'd betrayed her.

***

Bronwen banged her head on the floor as she tumbled out of bed in a heap of bedclothes and towel. She fought against the duvet for a moment as her body battled to wake up. She sagged against the bed in relief and sat wrapped in her warm bedding for a long time, staring into space, thankfully seeing nothing at all.

Eventually, she slowly stood, the blanket wrapped around her. She could see that it was almost dark; she'd slept a few hours. Still wrapped in her duvet, she shuffled to the window and peeped out; the road was empty. Pulling the curtains across, she grabbed her dressing gown and opened the bedroom door: no noises.

The lure of the warm bed was inviting, but so was a cup of tea and biscuits. She hadn't eaten since that morning and thrown up everything anyway. Her stomach growled loudly. How could her body be so pathetic at a time like this? The nightmare still fresh in her memory, she shivered and drew her dressing gown tighter around her. She hadn't dreamt that since she was young. The trauma of the day had obviously played with her head.

She pulled on clean knickers, trousers, and an old jumper, wincing as the cloth touched the raw skin and bruises. Damn that letch! Hadn't she been through enough shit? Why couldn't men just leave her alone? Lecher wanted to rape her! Kenward wanted to save her or something! Who else? Her father popped into her head and she yanked open the door; no way, he wasn't getting into her head again, and she rushed down the stairs to run away from the image of him. Listening, she heard nothing and checking the bolts proved everything was still locked and barred against all intruders, including the bastards who invaded her head.

Stomping into the kitchen, she set about making tea and found some chocolate digestives and an apple and forced all thoughts out of her head. No way was she going back to that part of her miserable life; it had no place here. This was hers and nothing and no man or ghost was going to ruin it.

***

He watched as first the lounge and hall lights came on and then the kitchen light. He could see her silhouette and he stepped back behind the hedge just in case. Damn the woman! What the hell was he doing here anyway? Throwing his half-smoked cigarette on the wet grass, he quickly walked away before she saw him.

Thrusting his hands in his pockets, Adam forced himself to keep walking and not to turn round for one last look. He tried to remind himself that he didn't care about this woman. He had only come to check if his cottage was okay and not destroyed by some thug looking for his old girlfriend. He'd convinced himself that was what must have happened up at the castle; she was running from some boyfriend who had found her hiding place, or something? Lame, so pathetically lame, and he knew it.

***

Rose watched from the shadows as Adam walked over the cattle grid and onward toward the Hall. She'd been about to run and catch him up, but something about him made her stop and hang back. He looked angry. What was on his mind? Mathew, perhaps?

She glanced back up the lane in the direction he'd come from and frowned. Nothing up there except his old cottage, and there was some woman living there now. Could he have been to see her? No way, surely. She'd heard how he felt about the new tenant. Why would he go and see her?

Sighing loudly, she walked onto the estate. Judith had asked if she could stay over for a few nights, as it would be easier to finish the work. She'd be paid overtime, of course. Damn right she would! Of course, Judith hadn't known the real reason for her accepting; it meant being only one floor above Adam's bedroom. To be so close and, maybe, if she could show him she was his, just maybe…the rush of warmth between her legs made her feel dizzy with lust. She hurried on.

The light had almost faded as she stood outside the Hall. The outside lights suddenly sprang to life and for a moment, she was blinded. Shielding her eyes, she looked up at the attic windows. One of them was now bricked up and the other had metal bars across it. Was someone there? She stepped closer to the wall, out of the glare of the lights and looked again; she could have sworn she'd seen someone looking at her. With one last look, she walked away and headed for the kitchen where she could smell steak and ale pie cooking for their evening meal. It was a welcoming odour, but suddenly, she felt uneasy, and for the first time since being asked, dreaded sleeping at the Hall.

***

Eira stood, unsure what to do. It had been ten minutes since Adam and then Rose had walked nearby and the sounds of approaching steps made her hastily walk into her garden and shut the gate. Rose, as always was complaining to herself about the weight of her bag, poor girl! In a way, she felt sorry for Rose. Brought up on the outskirts of Derwen, she'd never really fitted in, always needing excitement. Her poor mother constantly complained about the trouble Rose got up to in school and dropping out of college. The job up at the Hall had been the last resort. Rose had taken the job. Anyone with eyes could see how she adored Adam.

Would the girl never learn that only cheap boys liked her behaviour? Real men would see beyond her makeup and short skirts and see the real woman. Sadly, Rose was destined to be pregnant at an early age, if she didn't change her ways. The father unknown, and no doubt drugs and alcohol would play a large part in her life, if not death; she'd seen it all before.

She hadn't forgotten Martha. The poor woman wasn't going anywhere, but she'd need a few minutes to prepare herself. Hearing others walking had given her the excuse she needed to gather her thoughts. Thinking about Rose, even for a minute, had helped. Slowly, she walked around her garden, trying to find comfort in its familiar surroundings and smells. She rubbed various herbs between her finger and thumb and sniffed their fragrances. She picked a sprig of lavender and kept it in her hand while she contemplated what to do.

At that moment, she heard the familiar rumble of the Shrewsbury last bus. It stopped, as always, outside her shop. She held her breath, but no-one came in. She heard them talking about various things, the day, their goods, who they hadn't seen and then she stiffened as she heard one of the women mention Martha's name. It was too good to be true!

She moved as swiftly as she could and stood by her gate. She could hear at least four women chatting as they made their way along the road toward the cottages and the pub. She knew they wouldn't go into the pub, they never did; it had to be the cottages. She recognised Elizabeth's and Hilary's voices, the others were too faint. They would find Martha, she was sure, and she didn't envy them one little bit.

***

The muffled scream came again. 'Yes, come on. Do it again, bitch!'

This time it was just a muffled groan. 'Not good enough, you whore. Scream for me!'

James tightened the cords around her wrists and pulled. Her arms stretched to almost breaking point, but he slackened the tension just in time. He was too good at this to break her arms, but it was tempting. He let go of the cords and her arms went limp. Coming around the bed, he straddled her waist and began slapping her face. She was awake, but groggy. He slapped her harder and without knowing why, he head-butted her, hearing the crack of her nose as it broke. Seeing the blood run down her mouth and chin only heightened his desire to hurt and he took hold of one of her arms and twisted it. She yelped. Good.

He untied both her wrists and stood back and watched the pathetic whore wipe her face. One of her eyes was almost closed from where he'd punched her over an hour ago when he'd found her drunk. It was not how he'd imagined it. He could see all the old bruises, now mingled with all the new ones. He smiled. So much pain, so much degradation; he loved it.

He stood naked, his erection having returned almost at once after he'd had her quickly the first time. She'd been unconscious and that had really annoyed him. This was her punishment. She wore only a pink bra and one strap had been torn off; the other he'd snipped off. The cups hid nothing. They had slipped down so that they rested just beneath her breasts; her tits were her best asset.

Reaching for the whip, he moved closer to the bed. She saw the movement and jerked away; her eyes widened when she saw the whip.

She whimpered. He grinned. 'Please…James…no more. Fuck me if you must…but…no more. Please…I've had enough. You…you've broke my nose. I want extra for that…please, James…'

In answer, he grabbed her arm and flipped her over onto her front. She raised her head in protest and tried to lift herself up, but he put his foot on the small of her back and pushed her down. 'If you move, I will kill you.' She didn't move again.

A while later he surveyed his handiwork, a tumbler of brandy dangling between his fingers. He stared at Debbie as she painfully rose to her knees on the bed. Every movement was agony for her; he loved to watch. He'd let her think it was all over and then he'd have her on her back, knowing that with each thrust, she was enduring the pain of the lashes and the pleasure of him.

She refused to meet his gaze and he quickly finished his drink. 'Can I have a drink now…please, James?' Her voice was barely a croaked whisper. He handed her his empty glass. He looked down at his erection and smiled wickedly. 'Of course, my darling.' He indicated the floor. 'Get on your knees and drink from this.'

As she carefully inched her way onto the floor, grimacing with every movement, he sighed with pleasure as she took his rigid cock in her mouth. It really was too easy. This whore had lasted longer than the others, but perhaps now was the time to find another. He looked down at her pathetic body. Yes, her addiction was becoming too noticeable. He didn't like that. They started to look too sluttish and he liked them to look at least half decent. Images of Bronwen Mortimer flooded his head and he grabbed Debbie's hair and forced her to move faster. Yes, there was no doubt about it, he definitely needed someone else and he knew exactly who that could be.

***

The knock at the front door got no response. Frowning, Elizabeth peered through the letter box and recoiled as the smell of urine reached her. She found Martha's set of emergency keys behind a plant, quickly opened the small door, and went inside. Moments later, she was shuffling down the garden and shouting incoherent words, trying to get someone's attention. She quickly glanced around the empty village, but the women had already gone inside. Not a soul could be seen, except...

She stared at the small figure, not quite comprehending what she was seeing at first, only knowing something was wrong. The child didn't move from the road and it was then, she could see it, the road, the grass behind, all of this was visible, through the child. She began to scream, for Martha, for herself, for anybody, but the child just stood silently watching and smiled.

CHAPTER TWENTY-FIVE

WILLIAM SAT IN HIS FAVOURITE chair. The warmth from the fireplace eased his aching muscles, but it made his eyes feel heavy and tired. He rubbed them.

His steward sat opposite, waiting for William to finish his sentence. 'My lord?'

William stopped and let his hand fall heavily onto his lap. 'I have so many feelings about this, Andrew. My wife hates me, my daughter tries to understand, and my friend wants my loyalty for a potential new king. King Richard demands my obedience and questions my loyalty, which, as it happens, if I continue with this, would be right. I feel so torn. I am excited about the possibilities, yet I fear what may happen if I am on the wrong side.'

His steward laughed. 'My lord, isn't every man torn between his woman and his king? At the end of the day, are we not hunters, my lord? We are men, we need the thrill of the battle, makes our blood hot, and our loins!'

William laughed heartily. 'Old friend, I can always count on you.' Suddenly sober, he leant forward. 'Can I count on you now, to protect my wife and child? If I fail in this task, will you carry out my orders?'

Andrew knelt before William. 'I swear by Almighty God, I will do my duty and protect your womenfolk. My only regret is that I cannot go with you.'

William sighed and leant back in his chair; he waited until Andrew also returned to his. 'I would have you at my side in a heartbeat, if I could trust any other man with my family. As it is, danger lurks nearby and you will need your wits about you. Richard has many spies. For all I know, he may send his men tonight and stop me. Or he may come while I am away and hold my family hostage. Nothing is certain…'

Andrew nodded and for a while the two men lapsed into silence, each one lost in his own thoughts. Finally, it was William who broke the silence. 'Will she ever forgive me, do you think?'

'I believe she will.' Andrew knew he spoke of Anne. 'After all, my lord, she is carrying your heir. All this wandering the corridors at night and refusing to eat will pass. It is a woman's folly to tempt you to stay, but her duty as a mother will win over. She will not do anything that would harm the child.'

William stared into the fire. 'But will I? Are we madmen?'

Leaning forward, Andrew looked William in the eye. 'I think, my lord, that if we are madmen, it is God that has made us so to defend our lands and our families. To have the ability to be animal-like and mad with rage, yet keep our wits about us while fighting for our lives, can make us richer men, gain us more lands and honours and title, so in this way, we are helping our families. How can that be wrong?'

William raised his eyebrows in astonishment and grinned. 'You have really thought about this?' Standing up, he slapped his friend on the shoulder. 'Then come, my fellow animal, let us find the men who have declared their loyalty to me. We have until dusk tomorrow, when I shall ride out and meet Rhys and this Henry Tudor on their march northward. Together, we will march into Shrewsbury and if all goes to plan, who knows?'

Gathering their cloaks, the two men walked swiftly outside into the courtyard where a few men had gathered at the blacksmith's. Some sharpened their swords and knifes while others stood about talking and checking saddles, bridles, horses' hooves. 'How many men does Sir Rhys have, my lord?'

William smiled. 'Well, he was boasting about nigh on a thousand, but...' He shrugged and led the way down the stairs, wiping his forehead with his cloak. 'I'll tell you this, Andrew, it is getting warmer. If it gets any hotter I'll have to fight the damned battle naked!'

The closest soldiers heard his remark and guffawed loudly. 'You won't need to draw your sword my lord,' shouted one soldier. 'Once they see your cock it'll scare them off anyway!'

'No, riding bare-arsed will ruin his manhood!' shouted another.

'I know someone who can fix that!' Shouted another and all the men laughed, including William, who nodded enthusiastically.

Anne stood just within the doorway and heard a few more ribald remarks about her husband's anatomy before turning away. She slumped into a chair in the Great Hall, but unable to bear being still, she quickly stood up and paced the floor. Granted, he hadn't known she was listening, but laughing about her with his men showed her he had no respect for her feelings. She felt torn; her body yearned for him, but recoiled from him also. The fear that it might harm the child was only an excuse; she felt betrayed by him. That he should choose to leave her and fight for this man whom everyone had doomed to failure, it was madness. Yet, he would choose him over her and their son.

A glance down at her round bump quickened her decision. She walked briskly along the corridors and out through the kitchen. She ignored the quick curtseys and bows and stares and left the castle through the back. A few soldiers stopped their chatter and stared at her for a moment as she stood waiting for them to open the big heavy door of the gatehouse that guarded the rear of the castle. She noticed one was about to ask where she was going without her ladies, but decided against it and ordered the door to be opened.

Once on the other side, she climbed the slight incline of the old fort that had once stood there and hurried on toward her meadow. It was on the other side of a small wood and she considered it her sanctuary and a place where she could think without being interrupted, most of the time. She wasn't stupid; she knew that right now someone would be aware of where she was and would have ordered her servants to be nearby.

The grass was getting long and it tickled her calves as she lifted her skirt slightly. She wandered into the middle, and here she eased herself down and looked in the direction she'd walked from. From here, she could see most of the castle between the trees, and the ramparts higher than the trees. She could see people milling about, doing their work. She caught movement within the trees and knew someone was there, watching, guarding. It wouldn't do for the lord to come back from joking with his men about his virility to find his young wife taken, or worse.

She picked a blade of grass and twiddled it between her fingers. She had come here to think about her possible predicament with her child, and William. She gently stroked her stomach and tears sprang to her eyes; she didn't need a midwife to tell her she wasn't as big as she should have been by now. The child moved, but was it frequently enough? She would often try to coax him to move, by pushing one side of her womb and he would push back or suddenly squirm against the pressure and she would be both satisfied that he was still alive and worried that her pushing might be harming her child.

She began to hum to herself quietly. A tune she heard many times as a child. A tune sung to her by her old nurse. A tune she remembered finding soothing. Her mind drifted and soon she felt calm and able to think clearly. But, the thoughts that popped into her head would not be smiled upon by the church; she would be branded a witch for them, more so if she acted upon them.

She began to remember the words her nurse had taught her. Words and tunes which, when said over and over, healed and brought comfort. But, there were those words that when repeated brought the demons from the dark places. They brought harm and bad luck, even death if the desire was strong enough. Was she strong enough? Was she able to kill Henry Tudor before her husband made the wrong choice and killed himself, putting her and their child at risk? She gently stroked her belly and smiled and knew the answer as she felt the tiny life stir within her.

*****

The evening was chaos with an ambulance crew and the police buzzing around poor Martha's cottage and talking to everyone in the village. Eira heaved a long sigh of relief as the policewoman closed the shop door behind her. What could she tell her? The spirit of a vengeful child was determined to balance an injustice done hundreds of years before? She'd be locked up.

Poor Elizabeth. She'd been found muttering gibberish, curled up in Martha's front garden, and lashed out at anyone who came near her. It was obvious that she'd found her old friend but as the policewoman said, she'd never seen anyone behave that way before, so what had terrified the lady?

Eira knew the answer, but instead of telling them the truth, she'd shaken her head and looked genuinely concerned. And concerned she was, but for other reasons. She watched the vans and cars and people, and then looked beyond them all and her eyes rested on the small figure that stood motionless by the chapel, silently watching the village. Was she pleased with herself for killing one and terrifying another? Was it all a joke to her? A child's prank? How many more? Who would be next? They were all to blame in her eyes. She was an innocent.

*****

Turning her back on the castle and the prying eyes, she started to gather the materials she'd need. Her gown had deep pockets and she stuffed the grass inside them. She already had stalks of corn and small twigs hidden inside her private chest, beneath the bed. The twigs made a good imitation crown and the corn made sturdy bodies; four bodies. Each one needed clothes to represent them and the grass and earth would add bulk to each doll.

Henry Tudor had to die now, before King Richard found out about William's loyalty to him; then William would be safe and he could come home and be with her. That whore in the village had to die for lying with her William. Nia had to die for being a part of William's past, always watching, always mothering that brat. And the fourth doll?

Gwenllian? They would have a son. Was there any real need for the girl? She was either wed soon or Anne would use the other option. There had to be no more obstacles. Once everything was over, nothing would stand in the way of their love and happiness. She would show William that she loved him, and he had no need of another female in his life. She would be his life and William would be grateful for it.

***

Bronwen opened her eyes and tried to focus on the noise. The television came into view and she groaned; she'd left it on. The morning news was always depressing, and she reached out and switched it off. The silence was eerie. She pushed herself up. Standing in the centre of the lounge, she had a strange feeling that something was wrong. She glanced at the couch where she'd fallen asleep and at the large knife lying on the floor. Yes, something was wrong, but she'd survived it and was still alive and unmolested.

She yawned loudly, not bothering to cover her mouth, then wandered into the kitchen and switched on the kettle. What she needed was some breakfast, tea and supplies. Opening the cupboards, she huffed loudly. 'And the cupboards were bare.' She sang out loud and clucked her tongue. Better get supplies before she starved to death and Adam got his cottage back! She wondered if Adam had spoken with Eira about yesterday's horrors. He'd seemed genuinely concerned for her wellbeing: bloody men. She checked her cuts and bruises; not too bad. She stretched and winced. Her lower back ached, as did both of her shoulders, her knees, and her right calf. Could have been much worse, she reminded herself and quickly made the tea.

Taking the last piece of bread into the lounge, she couldn't help but think about the previous day. It made her feel quite sick, but it wouldn't go away. Perhaps she could confide in Eira and tell her about the estate agent? Eira was the only thing close to a friend she'd ever had. Wasn't that what friends did, confide in each other? Share secrets? Yet, even as she thought about it, she shied away from doing it. As much as she liked Eira, there was something very odd in her behaviour and not just the other night. Whenever she was near her it was like a memory she couldn't quite place. As if she'd met Eira before somewhere, but she knew logically she hadn't. It was her eyes, perhaps? Or the shape of her face, the tilt of her head?

Pushing thoughts of Eira aside, she remembered all the information she'd read yesterday. After her trauma, she hadn't had time to process it all as she'd wanted to do, about Gwenllian and all the other Kenwards she'd found in the library. She had no doubts now that the ghost of the murdered child was Gwenllian, but why had she been killed? There seemed to be so many why's but no obvious answers.

It had all begun with Sir William and his family, but what of his wife, Anne? What had she been like? There had been a small paragraph written next to the family tree and it had mentioned Lady Anne and listed the children she had lost. Poor woman! The death of her children must have been hard. How had she coped?

'Witch!'

Bronwen froze. The whisper came from behind her. Beads of sweat gathered along her upper lip as icicles on the back of her neck made her hairs stand on end. Forcing herself to look, she slowly turned her head and jumped up off the couch to face whatever it would be.

She was alone.

CHAPTER TWENTY-SIX

ADAM HEARD THE SHOUT BUT ignored it and ducked into Jack's stable. Lifting a pitchfork from the wall, he began to muck out. He'd managed to avoid everyone last night, keeping himself to himself in his room or walking around late at night; he didn't want to engage in conversations and explanations.

Dear old Judith had sent up a tray for him. Rose had knocked on his door with it. When he'd shouted to leave it outside, he'd listened for her retreating footsteps; it was a few minutes before she did leave. He was grateful for the thought of food, but his appetite was minimal, and he hardly touched it.

After his attempts at eating, he'd had a shower and taken stock of his injuries. His shoulder was the worst, cuts and minor bruises everywhere else. Seeing them had made him wonder about Bronwen and her own injuries, physical and emotional. Thoughts of her big blue eyes and that look full of pure terror as she'd crashed into him at the bottom of the stairs were the reasons why he'd crept out and wandered down to the cottage again, just to be sure.

'Hey, I've been shouting for you!' His father stood within the doorway. Adam didn't respond, but kept on shovelling. 'Look, I know you're avoiding me and I know the reasons. I'm concerned, that's all.'

Adam stopped and leant on the fork, and waited.

Sir Richard saw his chance and stepped into the stable. 'Talk to me, son. I know you went to see Mathew yesterday, and you were gone for most of the day. Judith said you looked a mess. She thought perhaps you'd been in a fight. You looked bruised. Did he attack you, or something?'

The look of genuine concern for some reason made Adam laugh out loud. 'Mathew didn't attack me. It was something else.' Shaking his head, he shuffled a few more forks of dirty straw and stopped when he realised his father was still waiting for some explanation. 'Look, it's nothing to do with Mathew, anyway. He wasn't great and I only stayed a few minutes.' Needing to change the subject, he chose the only other thing he could think of. 'Dad, please explain to me why we're still having this Ball?'

His father looked annoyed. 'Because it's bloody tradition and we've not missed one yet, okay?' His tone matched Adam's. 'You think I like this? What with Martha being found dead yesterday evening and that friend of hers needing to be sedated? As well as little Mathew? I bloody well hate this too, but it's going ahead.'

'But why? It can be cancelled. It could be postponed if everything you said is true. You know how it looks, Dad.' Adam was breathing hard as he gripped the fork handle.

Richard glared at him for a moment, and then collapsed onto a hay bale, deflated. 'I can't really explain...not right now, but this is important, to Mathew's parents, to me.'

Adam sighed heavily and sat next to his father. After a few minutes of silence, he quickly rubbed his face as though making a decision. 'I guess you could do with more support than I've been giving you. Sorry, Dad.'

His father looked so surprised at this that he wasn't sure how to react himself. He shrugged and let the statement go. He picked up fallen brushes and dropped them into the bucket they used to keep the grooming equipment in.

'You know what, you're right. I could do with a supportive son, but I'll settle for whatever you can give me. I'll explain everything; just give me a couple of weeks. The Ball will be over. We should know if...'

Adam heard his father's voice break with emotion and knew what he meant. Would Mathew still be alive? Adam busied himself with setting things straight in the large chest of drawers where they kept bits and pieces that might come in handy. Old bridles, odd stirrups, old brushes and other odds and ends for the horses were all placed in the chest. He wanted to allow his father time to compose himself. He heard him sniff and blow his nose.

'Adam?'

He turned and faced him, an old horseshoe in his hand.

His father glanced at it and grinned. 'We might need one or two of those, for luck.' He walked to the doorway and stopped. 'Thanks.' And he was gone.

Adam stood still, listening to his father walk away. He twiddled the horseshoe around his fingers, thinking it felt cool against his hot skin. What had his father really come to talk about? Mathew? Yes, but there was something else troubling him. His old friend, John, had been visiting more often lately. He hadn't given it a second thought, but now wondered if something was wrong financially.

Paying off that ex-wife of his had drained them of a lot of money, but that had been eight years ago. He wasn't blind. He could see every day the odd jobs that needed doing around the old place, but if he were honest, he hadn't given it that much thought, either. The business had taken up everything.

He thought about all the possibilities of selling the old Hall and cringed away from it. His father would never do it, and he certainly had no intention of ever selling his family home. If they were in financial difficulties, perhaps they could sell off a few acres of land, or the cottage?

It surprised him that he hated that idea too. The cottage had become an embarrassment, a reminder of his pathetic attempt at marriage and look how that turned out. He loved and hated the place in equal measure, yet the possibility of losing it, even for a year, had infuriated him. How would he feel if it belonged to someone else forever?

Thinking about families and couples got him thinking about Bronwen and the Ball. Was she coming? He doubted it very much. He'd been thinking about the way she'd behaved. Something created that fear in her and the only situation he could think of was abuse of some kind.

She reminded him of a broken foal he'd helped rescue years ago. The foal had known nothing but abuse since being born nine months before. It was starving, injured, and terrified, and it had a look in its eye. Bronwen had that look, a haunted look of someone who survived something horrific. Her defences were up so high, any show of vulnerability was seen as a weakness, but she could fight. He'd witnessed that, and he liked it. Just like the foal that Rosalyn had adopted. Following months of love and care between them, the foal had survived and was named Daisy. He glanced out at the paddock where he could see the horse happily nibbling on grass. A happy ending because Daisy learned to trust another human being. Could Bronwen do the same?

***

James sauntered into the office on time, whistling to himself; he felt good. His administrations to the whore had left him feeling much better about losing to Bronwen Mortimer. He'd come to the conclusion that her behaviour had been quite a thrill, except the kick to his balls.

He never kept a woman for longer than a few hours; it was too risky. Now that Miss Mortimer had decided to behave in such a manner, it gave him another good reason to show her who was master. The thought of having her for a weekend of pleasure was so arousing. He made a list of all the things he was going to do to her and in what order. The A4 paper was now hidden in his drawer. He liked his women to attempt to fight back; it was pitiable of course, but it added to the fun and humiliation when he overpowered them.

330

He would make her submissive and he would watch her anger and frustration and fear and, finally, he would watch her realisation that his body would be the last she would ever see. He would have her soon. Part of the thrill was the anticipation, so, perhaps, he wouldn't rush into it just yet...

He hadn't realised that he was absentmindedly rubbing himself until a loud knock on the office door brought him back to reality with a jolt. He quickly straightened himself just as Gordon walked in.

'James! Good news! The Montfords, yesterday, they came to see the old...ah, you remember, well, they want it; they're coming in later this afternoon to sign the papers. Well done.'

James shrugged. 'I knew they would. I didn't show them anything else with the amount of land they wanted except that house. They talked non-stop about their grandkids, so I knew they'd want it once they saw the playroom attached to the garage. It was a done deal.'

Gordon poured himself a cup of coffee and sat opposite the desk and smiled. 'Ah yes, but a profitable done deal. This one will bring us a tidy commission, which I have to say I could certainly do with, thanks to that wife of mine. Talking of bitches, fancy celebrating?'

'When? I might have plans.'

Gordon smirked. 'Oh yeah, with who? That mysterious woman?'

'As a matter of fact, I might be seeing her at the weekend. Although...' James pursed his lips and clicked his tongue. 'I could always come and play first...'

Gordon smacked the table. 'Good man! Susan has a mate. Saturday night all right?'

James nodded and picked up his pen. 'She better not be a dog or I'm having Susan!'

'Don't worry. Susan says she's a filthy little bitch who's up for anything, apparently. Maybe we could swing a group, what do you say?'

James leant back in his chair. He knew Susan didn't think much of him and the idea of forcing her into an orgy she wouldn't be

331

completely comfortable with was exciting. 'Yes, sure, sounds good. What's the woman's name?'

Gordon grinned and stood. 'As if you cared! Her name's Clare, so I'll call Susan for Saturday night. About eight o' clock do you?'

His next appointment was coming in ten minutes. He looked around his office and sorted the files of the houses he knew would interest these people. Some people had more money than sense, which suited him. He'd help them spend their money and eye up any potential love things whilst doing business. Most of the wives were dogs, old and plain, but just occasionally, a treasure would arrive. Bronwen Mortimer was one such treasure and soon, he would take and take and take again, and he had to plan it right. So, firstly, he'd keep himself satisfied with a few practices. This Clare would do for the weekend, but what about tonight? There was always Debbie, but for once, that idea didn't excite him.

***

Judith sat down heavily and smiled her gratitude at the cup of tea thrust into her hands. Lucy smiled and went back to her baking. Judith watched her and tried to calm down. Her body felt like a roaring fire was burning inside, and her heart felt as if it would thump its way through her chest. Sweat poured from every orifice, and she knew she looked a terrible sight and that made her feel much worse.

She desperately wanted to get up, go to her room and shower and change, and open the bedroom window and let the cool air rush over her burning skin, but there wasn't one ounce of energy left in her body. She felt completely drained.

She heard his footsteps long before he appeared in the kitchen and quickly mopped her face and neck. Lucy saw her agitated state and opened the large kitchen window. Richard walked in and poured himself a cup of tea, appearing none the wiser as he smiled at the two women and bent down to admire the pastries fresh from the oven waiting to be cooled and then frozen, ready for the May Ball.

The cakes would be baked the day before and the multitude of sandwiches, pasta, and rice dishes would be made on the morning; Lucy ran it like a military operation.

'Well, all this looks marvellous, Lucy! You've done us proud again.' Turning to Judith, he continued, 'And the Hall looks lovely, as ever. It's just the lights to sort out and I believe it's more or less done, isn't it, ladies?'

'Yes,' replied Lucy, busy kneading the dough for her crusty cobs, which she'd also freeze and then bake on the day. 'You and Adam can do that.'

Judith clutched her cup, watching the two talking about the preparations and whatever was in the larder. Their voices seemed to be moving in and out and the room felt as if it was spinning. She was aware of a slapping sound and saw it was Lucy slapping Richard's hand as he reached over and pinched an oatmeal biscuit. Why couldn't she be so relaxed with him?

It was an effort to raise her hand to her forehead; it felt like lead as she tried to rub her eyes. It didn't help. She only saw black spots in front of them, while the room seemed to rock, backward and forward.

'You stole my time.'

'What!' She dropped her cup onto the saucer and it clattered loudly in her ears. It seemed to vibrate and join with the roaring noise that suddenly filled her head, and then blackness took her.

***

Richard stood motionless as Lucy ran to her friend who lay slouched in her chair. It was only when she shouted him to come and grab Judith, his legs moved. He caught her under her arms before she slithered to the floor. He picked her up with some effort, and carried her into the small sitting room and laid her down on the couch. Lucy immediately took over and unbuttoned her blouse to the chest and picked up her hand and rubbed it.

All of this Richard watched, detached from it as he stood stunned and heaving for breath. He shook from the effort of carrying Judith, but more so with fear. He'd heard it, felt it, seconds before Judith fainted.

Lucy was talking to him, but he didn't register what it was at first. 'Pardon?'

'Could you fetch a drink of water, please?' Which she quickly followed with, 'Are you all right, Sir Richard?'

He felt far from okay but he tried to smile reassuringly and nodded. Forcing his legs to move, he walked briskly back to the kitchen, stopping abruptly at the door. The room felt very cold. He quickly glanced around but it all looked normal. Rushing to the glass cabinet, he took down a large glass and filled it with cold water, and ran out of the kitchen, hating that his back was to it. One quick glance behind him showed him no-one was there, but right then, he didn't trust his own eyes.

***

Rose heard the door slam shut downstairs and froze, listening for any other noises that would indicate someone was coming upstairs. She heard nothing else and heaved a sigh of relief. She hadn't meant to stay in his room long, but once inside, it was too much of a thrill to just leave immediately.

She held Adam's pillow in her arms, and gently fluffed it, kissed it and sniffed. Sadly, it smelt of detergent and not of him. She clutched it to her breasts and froze again as she suddenly saw a shadow pass beneath the bedroom door; someone was outside. She quickly looked around, nowhere to hide. Throwing the pillow back on the bed, she grabbed the polish and the duster and stood by the door. Whoever it was, she had an excuse for being in there ready, but no-one came in.

Peering beneath the door, she couldn't see anyone. She strained to hear; nothing, but every nerve told her someone was out on the landing, waiting. Was it Sir Richard? Judith would have stormed in and given her a tongue-lashing by now. Lucy, perhaps?

She placed her ear next to the wood and listened; a faint humming came from the other side. Who the hell was humming? She licked her lips nervously. There was no use for it; she'd have to brazen it out and use the excuse of polishing as planned. Taking a deep breath, she flung open the door, ready to confront whoever it was. There was no-one.

She quickly stepped out into the corridor and closed Adam's bedroom door behind her. Looking up and down the gallery, she shivered as a blast of cold air hit her; there had to be a window left open somewhere. Well, damned if she was going to go and find it. She quickly headed downstairs in search of company.

From behind her, the humming began again. An old tune. A pleasant tune; a child's soft lullaby.

***

By the afternoon, Bronwen had quickly cleaned the place, made a list of all the things she needed, and now sat on the porch doorstep, the sunshine on her face with a cup of black coffee; milk was most definitely on her list. For the first time ever, she wished there was a supermarket nearby, unsure as to how Eira might be feeling on seeing her again; besides, she had mixed feelings about seeing Eira too, but it was inevitable.

She sipped her coffee and screwed up her face; black coffee was not her favourite drink. She knew she was trying to delay the obvious, but why? After the other night with Eira, it was hardly surprising she felt embarrassed about seeing her again, but there was also something else she couldn't quite put her finger on; it was there simmering just below her consciousness.

She was about to take another sip, then changed her mind and threw the coffee away. Dangling the mug in her finger, she tried to clear her head and think. Everything felt as if it was going too fast and she was stuck in the middle. This was not what she had in mind when she decided to leave the city. Being attacked by a vile, loathsome man, being rescued by a man she hated, her only friend the strangest woman she'd ever known, and now she was expected at some Ball! Not to mention the haunting…her life was quite bizarre.

Her stomach lurched and she let out a slow deliberate breath to try to still it. She could deal with only one problem at a time. So, which one to focus on today? Looking around at the tall grass, the broken gate, and knowing the shed still stood open around the corner, it would all have to wait; the Ball was at the weekend and so, unless something else happened, that had to be her main focus right now.

She couldn't help giggling to herself. How would her counsellor have reacted to that?

'You have to try to put things into perspective, Bronwen,' she could hear her counsellor say. 'It's no use to you if you're worrying about absolutely everything when you don't have control over everything. What can you control?'

The Ball. She had control over whether she went or not, didn't she? She had control over how long she stayed. She'd formed a rough plan in her head and although it terrified her to go, she felt better knowing she could think of a variety of excuses to leave. Now all she had to contemplate was what to wear? Eira would know.

Adam Kenward, her hero? His concern for her had been nothing more than chivalry to his new tenant, surely? She'd seen the real side of his nature outside his gates. Perhaps he'd forgotten that, or, perhaps he was making up for that. Whatever his motives, she had no intention of being in his company for longer than needed.

Gwenllian. The name brought tears to her eyes. Why would anyone want to kill her? She was sure that she'd heard the word 'witch' and she'd been thinking about Lady Anne at the time. Was there some connection? She was almost positive it had been a woman up on the tower. Was it Lady Anne? A mother wouldn't kill her own child, surely?

No, stepmother. Of course, Gwenllian was Sir William's child from his first wife, but still even as she tried to deny it, she knew it was right. Mothers killed their babies. Children killed their parents. Daughters killed their fathers.

Her thoughts returned to the estate agent. What the hell was he about? Rape. She had no doubt that was his intention, and it made her feel sick. What if she hadn't had that lucky kick? What if he'd managed to grab her? What if he'd…raped her?

She swallowed hard to stop the rising bile and quickly stood up. Moving briskly, she took the cup into the kitchen, grabbed her purse, her key, thought about her cardigan, but changed her mind.

Pulling the door closed, she locked it. Moving helped dispel some of the disgust and fear that threatened to overwhelm her, but it still lingered. He had wanted her from the first time she'd met him. He'd never made it a secret.

She walked to the gate and made a mental note to paint it and fix it. It looked like all it needed was a couple of new screws. Looking up and down the quiet lane, she stepped out onto the road. The lane was lined with yellow dandelions and white cow parsley. The wet April had ended, and now May brought a slightly warmer atmosphere; everything flourished and filled the air with sweet scents. She stopped and looked back toward the old stile that led to the castle. She couldn't see it from where she stood, but she could picture it as clear as day. What if she were to go back?

It had crossed her mind before, but she'd shrunk away from it; it was just too ghoulish and terrifying. Yet, somewhere within her, she knew that one day, she'd have no choice but to go back. It lay maybe a mile away, across the fields. Was she never going to walk that way ever again? Was she mentally going to diminish the area she would explore? She'd become a recluse if she began to do that. She laughed to herself. Wasn't she that already?

Maybe the answers did lie in the Shrewsbury library? If she could find those answers, perhaps she could return to that castle and, somehow, exorcise it and help Gwenllian move on? She had been loved once; she was sure of it. Didn't love conquer all?

***

He knew the one he wanted the moment he saw her standing three people in front of him at the Chinese takeaway. He listened to her order: sweet and sour chicken, with rice and some prawn crackers. A meal for one, surely?

After ordering his own beef curry, he waited outside and watched in which direction she walked. Popping his head into the takeaway, he told them he'd be right back and quickly followed her. He stayed out of sight, but close enough that he could watch those legs. Good calf muscles; she worked out. Good; a fighter, perhaps, or at least, one who thought she could fight back. Even better.

She hurried away from the town and turned into a small estate of newly built houses for first-time buyers. James sniffed; he wouldn't be seen dead with this rabble on his books. First-time buyers were only worth knowing if they had a rich family. He watched to see which house she let herself into and smiled. He'd seen all he needed to see. Big breasts, long legs, lived alone, or at least tonight she might be. His erection was hurting; he licked his lips and ran his hands through his hair. There would be time. Anticipation was half the fun, but first, he would eat.

CHAPTER TWENTY-SEVEN

WILLIAM SAT COMFORTABLY, HIS LONG legs stretched out, crossed at the ankles, a full goblet of his favourite wine in his hand and his sleeping daughter curled up on his knee. Nia had come once to try to detach the child, but William waved her away. He enjoyed the warmth she brought, but, more importantly, he wanted to remember the feel of her, the smell of her, and to know she fell asleep into peaceful dreams, contented at being with her father. He wanted to give her that memory, if it should be her last of him.

Most of the Hall had either drifted away to their own beds or had fallen into a drunken stupor where they sat. Seven men gathered around his table and shifted into comfortable positions as each man sensed the talk would continue long into the night.

'So, my lord, I've heard tales of Sir Rhys and his thousand-strong army. Is it true?'

'Aye, I've heard this also.'

There were murmurs from around the table at this and William grinned. 'Does it really matter? It is our group, the men of Derwen, who will be triumphant in the battle to come. Richard will flee!'

The men laughed loudly. Gwenllian stirred, but didn't wake. William drew her close, settling himself more comfortably. 'This Henry has already landed. Rhys will either meet with him tonight or by tomorrow, for sure. We ride out tomorrow at dusk and meet them on their ride northward. Scouts tell me King Richard has not moved. He is showing himself to be a fool.' The men nodded at this, so William continued. 'You are my most loyal friends. Men I have fought with before, men I can trust. I can't say the same for this Henry, but I can assure you all that Sir Rhys is as trustworthy as my own hands.'

'Aye,' called Martin, 'but we all know where your hands have been, my lord!'

'Well,' laughed William, 'that's true.' More sombrely, he gazed down at his sleeping daughter. 'But, it's not my hands I'm worried about. Our plans to unite with Henry don't seem to be known. However, if they are…?' He shrugged and drained his goblet.

The men understood perfectly well what would happen to them if their treasonous behaviour was discovered. A few touched their necks as if in reassurance that they still had them unscathed.

Andrew leant forward and in a whisper said, 'I've heard Henry has over three thousand mercenaries.'

William waited while a page filled his goblet. 'Yes, I've heard this too and that worries me. If I, a mere knight, have heard these stories, Richard must have. Yet, I am aware that if Richard knows of Henry's plans, why am I not dead, or imprisoned, or worse, my family…?'

'Wasn't that the reason of the King's messenger?'

'Aye, it was, testing my loyalty, but since then, I have heard no news of gathering forces to stop Henry's march. Rhys will meet him near Welshpool, and return through my lands and onward to Shrewsbury. I am not naïve enough to believe that I know of these plans only because of our friendship. I cannot fathom it.'

There was a long silence as each man thought about the possible future and the possible consequences. William's three dogs enjoyed the absentminded attention as their ears were tickled or their bellies stroked.

'Let us hope this Henry is grateful.'

Each man jumped up and turned toward the voice. Two men drew their daggers, but quickly sheathed them and bowed with the others. They all visibly relaxed as Lady Anne stepped out of the dark doorway.

'Did I startle you?'

William frowned at the intrusion and at her obvious taunt. 'What is it, Anne?'

She took a deep breath and bit her lower lip while she stepped farther into the Hall, her eyes fixed on the sleeping child. 'I've come for Gwenllian. She should be in her bed this late hour.'

She managed to keep her voice steady, although he could see a pulse throbbing in her neck and her colour had risen, flushing her neck and cheeks.

She made to reach out for Gwenllian, but he held up his hand. 'She's fine where she is. I'll bring her to her bed soon.'

She lowered her eyes and he saw her clench her fists at her side. Realising he had sounded too harsh, he softly said. 'Go to bed, Anne. You're right, it is late. I'll follow soon.'

He watched her nod once. She did not look him in the eye and she quickly walked away, her back straight, her hands clasped in front of her. He was tired, worried, and weary of her anger toward him. Perhaps, though, he should have been kinder; after all, hadn't she come down in search of Gwenllian?

His attention returned to his men, who finished their drinks and were now stretching, yawning, scratching, heading toward their own beds, as if Anne's arrival had been the excuse they all needed to move. He didn't blame them; after all, most of them had a wife or a sweetheart of their own.

He sat watching the fire after they'd gone. The dogs remained, as did the page until he sent him away. Poor lad was falling asleep where he stood against the wall. He was left with his thoughts and his beloved child wrapped in his arms. He thought of carrying her up to her bed as promised, but just for a while, he wanted that connection. He couldn't understand it, but it felt important to hold Gwenllian one last time, before he left. A cold shiver ran down his spine and he shuddered. He would see her again, he was not destined to die, yet, but he drew his child close and silently listened to her steady heartbeat.

***

Anne flounced up to her bedchamber. Dismissing her waiting ladies, she slammed the door behind them and stood in the middle of the floor fuming with anger. How dare he treat her like some serving wench? Dismissing her to bed like some paid whore to wait on her master! 'Bastard!'

Saying the word out loud shocked her into stopping. No, she loved him. He was her William. He was her everything. It was this damned uncertainty that was bad. Damned men and their wars!'

She moved to the window, opened the shutters, and gasped at the cool breeze that stirred her clothes. It felt stifling inside the room and the air felt so refreshing. So much so that she slowly undressed, letting the dress fall to the floor. She began to unravel the braid in her hair. Soon, she was completely naked; her brown hair hung past her breasts, and the breeze gently lifted strands to play around her erect nipple. She moaned with pleasure at the sensation.

Knowing no-one could see her—the candles had extinguished themselves as soon as she'd opened the shutters and the moon was barely new—she idly played with her breasts, her thumb gently gliding over her nipples, making them stand out even more. The tightening around her breasts made her stomach contract, but also caused sudden warmth between her legs. One hand groped blindly over her small bump and entered the slippery crevice. Her lips felt so much fuller and sensitive with her growing son inside her. Within seconds, she could feel the building of an energy that promised so much pleasure, she could not stop.

Afterward, her legs could barely hold her up as she stumbled to the bed. She felt languid. Her hand felt heavy, like a rock, as the pulsing between her legs stopped and her heart slowed. A sudden lurch from within her womb made her gasp for breath and, for a moment, she froze, but the child was only turning. She watched in fascination as her skin rolled and dipped and settled again. Gently, she stroked her womb and smiled with the responding kick. *Soon, my darling boy. Soon.*

It was a long time before William joined her in their bed. She lay still, her back to him. She felt his scrutiny in the darkness and then he lay on his back. A memory wormed its way into her head and she fought to remember it. Acts that could be done to help labour, a gentle ride, eating certain foods were supposed to bring on labour, though she doubted it. The most common act, her nurse had told her, was sexual contact.

'If the babe is strong enough, the man's seed will not harm it, but encourage the child to come out,' she'd told her.

She'd shaken her head in disbelief that any woman would want to endure a man moaning and thrusting on top of her when she had a child within her belly. Her nurse had laughed. 'There are other ways!' But she'd refused to tell her more, on that subject anyway.

Some herbs had the same effect, but she wasn't sure of those. Besides, he left tomorrow morning; there wasn't any time to go and find the herbs, even if she could remember the names. Granted, they were specifically for late babes who refused to enter the world, but wasn't her son healthy?

As if in response, her son kicked her and rolled and punched. A sound escaped her lips as she attempted to get comfortable again, but it was no use. William heard her and sat up. Turning to him, she silently reached down. His feeble attempt at stopping her was over in seconds as he groaned with pleasure. Lying on his back, he allowed her to excite him further, but within moments, unable to stand it any longer, he pushed away her hand and gently turned her and entered her from behind. She gasped with the intrusion, but fell silent.

She was concentrating inward, imagining that with every thrust he was weakening the sack that kept their son safe. Fear mixed with an urgency to hold their living child and show William what he would be jeopardising filled every pore as William's seed exploded inside her. Their son wasn't due for another month. Was he strong enough to be born now?

She listened to William's heavy breathing as he gently withdrew from her. She could feel his seed, and prayed that she hadn't endangered their son. A sudden kick made her smile proudly and she laid a hand over her belly. Reaching over, William covered hers and together they fell asleep, their son protected under their hands.

***

Adam wiped his face with the old towel he kept in the office. His shirt hung over the back of the chair. He could feel the sweat trickling down his spine. He was examining his bruised shoulder and noticed he'd caught the sun; he liked that. He knew he looked good with a tan. He flexed his arms and grinned. 'Yep, still got it!'

Movement noticed from the corner of his eye made him swing round embarrassed and walk the few steps to the doorway. The setting sun was in his eyes and he tried to shield them from the glare. He looked around the stable yard, but he saw no-one.

Puzzled, he walked out into the yard and looked at the closed doors, the paddock; the place felt eerily quiet. He looked at his watch and was surprised to see it was gone six o'clock. David would have already left but Geoff was usually around.

'Barnaby! Roger! Henry!'

He waited for the sound of running paws; none came. Where the hell was everyone? He walked back into the office. He had a load of paperwork to finish. Joseph and Brenda would be arriving sometime tomorrow, depending on who they could trust to watch over the stables. He was looking forward to seeing them again.

Bronwen Mortimer. His thoughts travelled back to her again as they had done since their first meeting. He couldn't decide how he felt about the woman, which was not something he'd considered for a long time. He sat back and put his hands behind his head. She was pretty, but in the right dress, he reckoned that she could be beautiful. He'd never seen her in anything other than jeans and shapeless tops and wondered, not for the first time, what kind of body she was hiding. He shook his head and reached for a cigarette. He didn't need that kind of hassle…but, he couldn't ignore it anymore, either. He liked her.

On the one hand, he wanted to protect her. Wrap her up in tissue paper and carry her around in his pocket, like a helpless kitten. On the other, he'd seen the spark of fury when they'd first met; she could and would fight if necessary, and he admired that. When he'd reached out and touched her, he'd seen fear and repulsion at his touch. Or, he was completely wrong and she was a lesbian?

A loud knock at the door made him jump. 'Yeah, what is it?'

'It's me.'

The woman stepped into the office. With the sun behind her, he thought for a brief second he'd conjured Bronwen here. But as the woman walked farther inside, he beamed warmly. 'Rosalyn!'

Pushing himself away from his desk, he rushed round it and hugged his sister tightly. He held her at arm's length, and noticed the black eyes, the pale skin, the bones sticking out from beneath her white, cotton blouse. Hugging her again, he didn't squeeze quite so hard this time. 'God! It's good to see you. It's been too long, sis.'

'Okay, all right, let me breathe!' She disentangled herself from his grasp and straightened her blouse, smoothed down her navy skirt, and stepped back surveying him. 'You look as knackered as I feel! Got a drink?'

Smiling, Adam hid his concern for her as he put his shirt back on. She'd lost even more weight since Christmas, he was sure of it. Now wasn't the time to ask, but he'd make damned sure he'd speak to her about it sometime during this weekend. To change the subject, he flicked her short bob. 'You've dyed your hair?'

She smoothed it back down and nodded. 'Yes, what do you think? It's ruby red.'

It made her look too pale, and her eyes looked big and bulgy. Her neck looked as if any moment it would snap. 'Yeah, suits you.' *Coward*, he thought.

She didn't look fooled. 'Oh yeah, well, nothing else has changed, except the hair, of course. I'm still a skinny wench who ran away to the city, opened a couple of shops, drinks like a fish, smokes lots of grass and fucks anything that says yes and stays still long enough.' She gave him a devilish grin. 'And that's all. Now, can I have a bloody drink? The drive down was shite!'

Adam laughed and put his arm round her, leading out into the yard. 'All right, interrogation over, but you and I do need to talk. Have you seen Dad?'

They walked slowly, arms linked. 'Yes, he sent me to find you to tell you we're all having dinner together and you are to come and get washed and dressed. Lucy is preparing a slap-up meal for my homecoming! You have an hour, I think.'

'Oh good, I'm starving! Haven't had time to eat properly all day. So much to do.'

***

Rosalyn nodded, but said nothing. They walked in companionable silence till they reached the kitchen door. She watched him playfully tease Lucy, and smiled where appropriate, but her thoughts were elsewhere. She hadn't eaten all day, either. The meeting that morning would have taken her appetite, even if she'd had one. The information she'd been given angered and disgusted her, making her fearful. She'd left as early as she could, feeling a strong urge to be with her family, something she hadn't felt for a very long time.

She took a deep breath and let it out slowly. She also had another strong need and for the first time since her teenage years, she was looking forward to the Ball, when she'd finally see this Miss Mortimer woman, the tenant with a big, dark secret. A woman she wasn't prepared to take a risk with. After the Ball, she would tell him everything.

CHAPTER TWENTY-EIGHT

JAMES LISTENED TO THE RADIO. His car stank of his beef curry but he didn't really care. He wound down the window a little farther, sat back, and watched the sun. Another hour or so and it would be quite dark. He did enjoy this time of day, especially if the sky was interesting, as it was now with streaks of blue and dark grey and hints of orange and pink. He often wondered, when he looked at dusk skies, why, if there was a God who could make something so beautiful and interesting to watch, he had made him a monster.

Looking at the car clock, he chewed his lower lip. He still wore his work trousers, but he'd changed into a black T-shirt he liked to keep in the boot. He sniffed it and grinned; he could smell the last bitch he'd taken. The memory aroused him and he fidgeted with himself to get comfortable. *Calm down, James*, he thought. *All in good time.* He patted his groin and smiled. He might be able to get into her house earlier, if he was lucky.

***

Melissa was bored. Friday nights had always been pub night, but tonight, she was alone. She hadn't been in the mood to play gooseberry with her mates. She sighed loudly and poured herself another glass of white wine. For the hundredth time that day, she wondered what Keith was doing.

Picking up her dirty dishes, she carried them into the kitchen. She saw the bottle of wine was almost empty and decided to open another one. 'Might as well get pissed!' She spoke out loud to the ginger cat that sat watching her from the top of the fridge as she threw away the remaining Chinese meal. *Keith would have finished that*, she thought. *What a waste.*

Realising the bin was full, she glanced at the cat. 'You're not going to have this either, it'll make you sick.' She smiled as the cat meowed back. 'I'll give you something in a minute.'

She flung open the back door and carried the bin out onto the narrow path where the rest of the rubbish was kept. She looked up at the darkening sky and groaned; she should have gone out after all! She jumped as a large hand clamped over her mouth, at the same time pulling her back toward her open door. She was so shocked that for a second, she thought it might be Keith playing a trick on her, and then she tried to struggle.

The hand that grabbed her arm and twisted it behind her back felt like a vice, and the pain that shot up her arm and along her shoulder made her wince, but the hand clamped tightly over her mouth muffled sound. She tried to kick back, but he dodged her feeble attempts.

She realised it was pointless as he dragged her into the kitchen, kicking the door shut. Forcing her onto the floor, face down, he lay fully over her, his weight pressing down; breathing was a struggle. Lifting her head, he crashed it down onto the hard wooden floor, once, twice, making her eyes water and blood gush from her nose. Had he broken it? She felt his hot breath on her neck and her stomach clenched with fear as he whispered into her ear.

'Tonight, my darling, you are mine.'

***

Gordon heaved himself off Susan and rolled, breathless, onto his back. Edging away from his sweating body, Susan reached out to the small bedside table and quickly lit a cigarette. For a long time, both of them were silent, basking in the glow of sex. In reality, Susan knew he was too exhausted to speak.

She was starting to notice little things like that. Sweating more, taking longer, if he could actually manage it. He had definitely put on weight since they'd first got together and sometimes it was like being shagged by a very large, hairy pig grunting and wheezing above her. The shine was definitely wearing off, especially now that she was seeing a new bloke.

Keith was fit, energetic, handsome, well, sort of, but he was also a lorry driver; she wasn't naïve to believe that she was his only bed partner and he was the same. He'd recently finished with a girl she vaguely knew in Shrewsbury. As he'd said himself, he could never have two vixens in the same bed. He liked his life uncomplicated and easy, which suited her.

She glanced across at Gordon and grimaced; he was becoming a bore these days. He had his eyes closed and she wondered if he was asleep. She wouldn't have been surprised. She only bothered with him because he had money, and he wasn't too mean with it. He'd helped with fees and weekends away when she'd just needed a break, but was that enough?

Tomorrow. She would make her decision tomorrow. Clare could get anyone in a good mood, and a filthy one. Maybe a foursome was what was needed to add a bit of sparkle to their love life? Although the thought of James in that foursome wasn't a nice one.

As if reading her thoughts, Gordon turned onto his side, surprising her. 'So, looking forward to tomorrow night?'

She turned to him after extinguishing the cigarette. 'I thought you were asleep, and yes, I suppose I am.'

'I can't wait to meet this friend of yours. You say she's filthy? A naughty little girl? Is it wise to introduce us?'

Susan grinned. 'Gordon darling, she'd eat you alive. You wouldn't last two minutes with her. She's a hungry lady, is Clare.'

'Are you saying I couldn't satisfy her?' He looked hurt for a moment, but quickly brightened up. 'Perhaps two men could though, eh?' He was getting aroused just talking about it.

Seeing his excitement, she smiled seductively and gently wrapped her hand around his growing erection. Leaning forward, she whispered. 'Two men and a woman might!'

***

Bronwen picked at her pathetic meal of half a tin of beans, a few mushrooms, and a tomato and wished for the hundredth time that she'd made the effort and gone to the shop. The television was on, but after a while, she switched it off. It was only background noise, something else to keep away the thoughts of tomorrow night.

Pushing away her nibbled food, she poured herself a small whiskey. She'd have to be careful; she only had one more bottle and this one was getting very low. Where else would she find a decent whiskey? Sipping it, she savoured the amber liquid as it gently warmed her stomach. Deciding on a CD, she sat back and let the haunting melodies of violins wash over her. Tears welled in her eyes, but she blinked them away as memories of her past involuntarily flooded her mind.

She loved the sound of violins, always had. An old memory formed in her head and she grinned. As a child, she and her mother would watch them playing on television or listen to the music and dance around the room like ballerinas. Her mother had confided in her that she learnt to play the violin, but had given it up when she'd married. Years later, she'd found her mother's violin hidden away. She'd known by then that her mother hadn't given it up; she'd been forced to give it up by him.

How furious he'd been when he'd found her with it. He'd smashed it to small splinters of wood before her eyes, all the while daring her to cry, daring her to stop him. She'd done neither. She'd stopped listening to music from then until now, her time of escape. There hadn't been room for music in his house, or his sister's. She hadn't been worthy enough to enjoy music or dance or sing. They were for free people. People who deserved to live. She hadn't fit either category. They'd been sure to drum that into her, every day.

Gulping back the rest of her drink, she gasped as the warmth hit her. She quickly poured another, berating herself but unable to stop. She sipped it this time and settled down again and tried to shake herself out of her melancholy. She knew it was because of the recent events, and because tomorrow night was looming and she had absolutely nothing to wear. Jeans and a shirt didn't seem satisfactory if it was a Ball.

He'd never bought her any new clothes, his sister refused to spend perfectly good money on new clothes, so most of the time she'd worn jeans from charity shops and old shirts or blouses. Most of the time that suited her, as trousers made her feel safer, but, just every now and again, she'd longed to wear something pretty. She realised that she wanted to look nice for tomorrow night.

Thoughts of Adam involuntarily brought thoughts of her father, and she shied away from them. She did not want to go down that road, not here in her beautiful, if a little scary, sanctuary. That lecher had caused these memories to flood her brain and she fought against them. Memories of her mother always brought him too, and she hated him all the more. He didn't deserve to be there, in her head and definitely not with Mother.

Trying to find middle ground, she thought of Eira, but was she middle ground or something else? Tomorrow she would visit her, ask her advice on suitable clothes, and fill up on supplies. Both were essentials. She definitely needed supplies, and she had to fit in with the villagers. She knew how important it was not to look like a tramp or the tongues would never stop wagging. She had no other options left. After all, she had to trust someone; Eira was as good a person to start with as any other.

***

Geoff sat on his front doorstep smoking, watching the stars as they came out. He loved the night sky. The dogs lay around his feet and everything was quiet except for the occasional neigh from one of the horses and dog farts breaking the silence.

He belched and patted his stomach; he felt full after Lucy's meal. Roast beef with all the trimmings had gone down a treat, as had her homemade lemon meringue pie, of which he'd wolfed two slices. Oh yes, sometimes life could be good, even for a few hours. It was what they'd all needed, a little respite from their worries.

He now felt a bit guilty. Mathew had no respite; neither did his parents, and they didn't deserve that. No-one had spoken about the Ball until he'd been about to leave; it was only then Richard had shouted after him. 'See you bright and early. I need those bulbs changed, if that's all right with you?' he'd quickly added, as if realising he'd broken an unsaid rule.

Geoff had merely nodded and bid everyone a good night's sleep. Times like that, he was glad he didn't live in Kenward Hall. He much preferred his little bungalow behind the stables. Here, he was close enough if needed, but far enough away when he needed time alone. The dogs generally split their time between the bungalow and the Hall, which suited him.

He reached out to stroke Barnaby, when the dog suddenly stiffened. Looking round, he noticed all the others did too. Roger sat up, his gaze focused beyond the hedge that separated him from the stable-yard. Geoff felt the hairs on the back of his neck rise. He reached out and touched the dog, needing contact with something real.

The dog's reactions told him this was nobody from the Hall. The dogs would have gone berserk by now; not one of them moved. He strained his ears to hear anything that might have alerted the dogs, but the night was silent and he couldn't see anything beyond the hedge. 'What is it, boys?'

His voice sounded strange in the silence, but none of the dogs responded anyway. There was a light switch a few yards from where he stood, which would flood his small garden with light. He was just standing up to flick the switch when he realised the atmosphere had broken. Whatever it was had gone, and he felt his body relax. The dogs wagged their tails and licked his hands and arm as he fondled their necks until they settled back down, but he noticed that each one had moved just a little bit closer to him, and for this, he was grateful.

***

Gwenllian sat on the slight rise of the earthwork, her legs bare, already covered in mud, her skin beginning to turn brown from the sun. She rolled back her sleeves to catch more of the sun's rays. She was concentrating on her daisy chain, which now stretched along the length of one thigh. Gwenllian wanted to make one as long as herself to give to her father. Nia sat quietly beside her, sewing and occasionally fanning herself as the warm sunlight beat down on their bare heads.

'You look like a pair of travellers!'

Nia dropped her sewing in fright, looked up and shielding her eyes, gasped as she saw Lady Anne glowering down at them. She heaved herself to her feet and curtseyed, which wasn't an easy thing to do standing on a small hillock.

Anne turned to Gwenllian who returned her attention to the daisy chain. She hadn't stood or acknowledged Anne's presence beyond a quick glance up. 'You, child, you should be ashamed! Baring your legs in such a way, and betrothed! You are a child of a decent family, behave in a proper manner!'

Getting no reply, Anne stepped forward and yanked the daisies apart. 'I said, cover yourself girl. Have you no respect?'

Nia stepped forward as though to go to Gwenllian's side, but Anne's scowl stopped her. She looked from one to the other, unsure what to do. Gwenllian hadn't moved, but now sat staring at her broken chain in her small hands. Anne stood above her, hands on her hips, glaring down at the bent head, waiting.

'I'm busy…Anne.' Her voice was calm, no trace of emotion. She took hold of both ends and managed to bring them back together. Letting go of the middle, she found the end she had been working on and continued with her task.

Anne stood flabbergasted, unable to form words, her mouth opening and closing; then, as if realising how she looked, she turned to Nia. 'It is your duty to care for this girl. This is *not* proper behaviour for a betrothed child. I'm sure Sir William and Sir Rhys will be disappointed. You have failed in your duty.' Anne grinned maliciously. 'Things are going to change.'

Slowly, she made her way back to the castle walls, all the while feeling Nia's eyes on her. That little urchin was probably watching her too, and mocking her. Damn the pair! She'd only come out to gather some more grass; her dolls were not as plump as the subjects. It had to be right, and she was panicking.

After last night, she'd felt a few twinges in her back and a tightening around her belly, but nothing else. She whispered the words and made an offering of a newborn kitten as the gods demanded, but William was still leaving and her son hadn't been born. She had hoped the gathering of more grass would help bring on contractions, and if not, she had been prepared to run around and hope her exertions would help. The brat and her ever-watchful nurse had ruined it.

She gently rubbed her swollen belly and frowned; she was his wife. Much more important than some child. Married off or killed off, either was acceptable to her now. Her panic that William was leaving in a few hours was beginning to show. She had to get rid of all competition, the King, the whore, and those two. Nothing must stand in the way of his loving her child. And definitely not some battle he might never walk away from. She had to have this baby now, within the next few hours, today.

She had almost collapsed with joy when just before dawn a messenger arrived, a scout coming to tell William that King Richard's men had been seen near Ludlow. William immediately called a meeting and it had been decided to act as normal as possible. The horses were hidden in the stables and the excess men despatched to the village under strict instructions not to get too drunk. If all went to plan, they'd leave under the veil of night.

Richard's spies were everywhere and riders had been seen, but they had left to report back to the king. A couple of spies lingered nearby; these could be dealt with quietly. William had barely spoken to her since their union last night. He'd been busy with his men, his horses, and checking the castle still had adequate guards, which proved that he was worried about any reprisal. This angered her intensely. But now, God had answered her, surely. She had some extra hours to make this child come, then, perhaps, seeing his son, he wouldn't get involved.

***

Sir Richard sat quietly in his study, the door slightly ajar. He sat comfortably, staring at the French doors, his legs stretched out before him, his hands behind his head. He was so tired, but he knew he wouldn't sleep. His head swam with worries, conversations, his children—he listened to them race upstairs, giggling and out of breath as they tried to push the other out of the way. They'd done that as small children; he smiled as they repeated an old game as adults.

He heard the murmur of women's voices and knew it to be Judith and Lucy, who had agreed to stay at the Hall until after the Ball as she'd done every year. She liked to be near her creations and oversee their defrosting and baking. Should he tell them he'd spoken to Mathew's dad and asked again if he considered the May Ball to be in bad taste?

'Of course it should go ahead. Mathew is stabilising, we think. They've sedated him, for a while. If I thought I could make her, I'd bring Karen for a drink. As it is, have one for me, eh?'

Sir Richard assured him they would drink a toast to Mathew and his speedy recovery.

He listened to doors being closed and Judith and Lucy walking into the hall and up the stairs. He listened to Kenward Hall settling down, the creaking of the old wood as it slowly shut down for the night. It felt like a thick blanket had gently covered the Hall as sounds became muffled until finally, everything was silent.

He yawned. God, he was tired! He stretched and stood up. He was about to make a move toward his own bed when his gaze fell on the chimney breast where his coat of arms hung. How could he tell them this might possibly be the last May Ball? Would they care? Everyone always believed that just because he had a title and a Hall, he automatically had the money that went with it; not so. His friend John understood and he knew he wouldn't rush him, but he felt that the sooner the decision was made, the easier it would be. Listening to the sudden bang from upstairs as either Rosalyn or Adam bounced on their bed, he wondered if his children would ever understand if he made this terrible choice.

It was wonderful having both his children around him again. He doubted that Rosalyn would blame him. She'd see his decision as purely a good deal, but then, Kenward Hall meant nothing to her. Adam, on the other hand, would mind considerably. Creaking floorboards, carpets in desperate need of repair, out of date plumbing, a roof that probably wouldn't stand another harsh winter, he loved it all. Even when he'd re-built Oak Cottage, he'd always had in mind to return to the Hall when Catherine had children. Thank God she hadn't.

That bitch! Would things have been different if she hadn't taken them for a very expensive ride? He'd never know for certain, but he knew that money would have come in handy to do some of the repairs.

He wondered where she was now. No doubt screwing some other poor man for all he was worth. She'd certainly screwed Adam, in more ways than one. Since her, his son hadn't had a decent relationship with any woman. Would he ever see grandchildren running up and down the stairs? Bouncing on the old beds?

Rosalyn didn't have one maternal bone in her body, too bloody skinny a body, he'd noticed. Did Adam have a paternal instinct? He knew Adam would make a great father; all he needed was a decent woman. Geoff told him about his new tenant, Miss Mortimer, and Eira had assured him she was coming with her tomorrow. He was dying to meet her. Was it wishful thinking? Was he hoping Adam would fall in love, move to Oak Cottage so he wouldn't feel so guilty about handing over the Hall to the National Trust? Another loud bang from upstairs made him flinch; when would his kids grow up?

***

Rose jumped at the noise and cautiously opened her bedroom door. It had come from Adam's room. Were they jumping on his bed? She yearned to jump around his room, especially his bed. Closing her door, she leant against it, hugging herself against the chill. Damned old houses, why weren't they ever warm?

She touched the old radiator; it was cold. Adam could keep her warm in his strong arms, his big hands roaming her body; she trembled with possibilities and crept back into bed. Tomorrow night, she would make her move tomorrow night! She played with the idea, considered the pros and cons, but in the end, life was for living. She had to make a move, or at least show him how she felt and let him make all the moves.

The problem had obviously been that she had been too subtle in her approach. He was a strong businessman, he liked strong, powerful women. Not too sluttish or too country-girl innocent, she had to find that in-between. The dress she'd chosen had cost her most of her week's wages, but if she could get Adam's attention, it was worth every penny.

Wrapping the covers closer around her cold body, she flicked through a woman's magazine and tried to concentrate on the pages, but her attention was inward. Her stomach lurched with the possibility of asking Adam to dance; no, she would make it a reality. His eyes would follow her around the room; he would not be able to resist asking her to dance. He would be overwhelmed with lust, his need to touch her dress, explore the body underneath…she gasped with pleasure as her fingers explored her body intimately. Perhaps, tomorrow, it would be his fingers, and she groaned with anticipation.

***

The room was silent. A few candles flickered on different surfaces, giving a romantic feel to the bedroom. Suddenly, soft music played from a small stereo in the corner. The room was a picture of romance; perfect, he thought.

The naked woman on the bed stared up at him, her arms and legs tied so that she was spread-eagle, her mouth covered with tape and a gag. Slowly, he undressed, his eyes never leaving hers, watching her reactions, seeing her fear, her resignation to what was to come. Her dismal attempts at pulling on the ropes all helped arouse him more. If only she knew that.

'Now, my darling,' he spoke softly, as a lover might. Reaching out, he gently stroked the inside of her thigh. 'What shall we do first?'

CHAPTER TWENTY-NINE

'**M**Y LADY…MY LADY, ARE YOU well?'
The voice sounded distant as the wave of pain and dizziness forced her to cling onto the back of the chair. The concern for her sounded feeble and she wanted to shout, scream, and scorn their attempt; she knew they didn't care if she died.

Focusing on the floor, her head lolling between her arms, she considered the irony; William had ridden out of the gate only an hour before. She'd stood alone, watching him ride out of sight and long after, until a wave of giddiness came over her, followed quickly by a tightening of her womb and a trickle of warmth between her legs. Panicking, she managed to fumble her way down the stairs of the tower, through the courtyard, and back into the refuge of the Great Hall.

Someone saw her. She heard questions, voices ringing in her head, but none of it mattered. Only the hot, burning pain that gripped her womb, her thighs, her vagina, and took her breath away mattered. She heard a woman's voice, but didn't register what was being said until a pair of strong arms carefully picked her up, ignoring her cries and carefully carried her to her bedchamber. She heard words like sheets, hot water, fire, and then another wave of pain shot through her and she screamed with fear as darkness took her.

***

William rode silently for a long time. His own scouts told him that a small band of the king's men still lingered nearby, no doubt to watch his home discreetly. They had been dealt with, but he was still wary. He had to make good time to reach Rhys by dawn. He knew the route they planned, but he also knew plans changed. Henry Tudor would be somewhere on his way to the Preseli Mountains, and then he was making his way to Cardigan. The plan was to meet up with Rhys and then head toward Machynlleth to meet with Henry's army. They would then return and head toward Shrewsbury, gathering men along the way.

It was hoped that by the time Henry reached Shrewsbury, he would have such a number of men that the sheriff would not fight him. His friend had assured him of his loyalty to the king, but his decision would be made at the time of Henry's arrival at the city gates.

He knew men's loyalties changed on a whim, but in some way, he felt responsible for the sheriff's behaviour. After all, it had been he who'd reassured Rhys that Shrewsbury would not fight. If it went wrong, it would not look good for him and he needed to make a good impression with this Henry Tudor.

He ordered his men to ride in silence. Through experience, he knew that thoughts came unbidden during the quiet moments and he had made his peace with that over the years. Anne, Gwenllian, his unborn child, all flooded his head as he now relived his goodbyes to each one. Gwenllian had clung to him tightly, whispering over and over again how much she loved him. Her gift of a very long daisy chain hung around his neck. Although it was now broken, half having been torn in their embrace and the small fragile flowers almost dried up and dead, he touched one of them and said a prayer for his little angel.

Anne had been a little more reserved in her embrace, but after last night's surprise, he understood and let it go. Her fear of the unknown outcome of the battle and her fear at being so close to the end of her pregnancy and her anger and hurt at his leaving, he understood, because he felt them all too.

Her kiss had been brief, her arms around his neck tightened once and she had released him and they stared at each other for what felt like an eternity. He couldn't read anything in her eyes except love and sorrow before she turned away first and walked toward the tower. He kicked his horse into a fast trot. His farewells had been better than he had hoped for and he hoped his homecoming would be just as sweet.

***

Rose huddled beneath the covers; she had hardly slept all night. The dawn light was a comfort as its grey fingers groped their way into her small room and illuminated every corner. Peeping over the covers, she tentatively reached out and switched off the bedside lamp she'd kept on.

Her gaze darted around the room. She strained her neck, as she had last night, to see the dark corner beside the wardrobe. She sat up and forced herself to peer beneath the bed; only once she saw that everything was empty and safe did she let out her breath. She realised she was shaking and not just from the chill in the room and curled back down under the covers, wishing not for the first time that Adam was there to protect her.

She must have dozed off as a voice drifted into her dream, which she tried to ignore, turning away from the intrusion and moving farther down the bed. A firm knock on the door, its opening, and a loud cough made her groan with fatigue, desperately trying to cling onto the residue of sleep.

'Rose! Come along, girl, breakfast will be ready in ten minutes. There's a lot to do. Rose!'

She grunted, but it seemed to be enough for Judith. 'Wonderful! You're awake. I'll see you in ten minutes, or else…'

Rose eased herself into a sitting position and noticed that she'd slept two hours and desperately needed more. Forcing her body out of bed, she shuffled over to the dressing table and looked at her face in the small oval mirror. 'Bloody hell!' She looked pale with dark rings beneath her eyes; this was not how she wanted Adam to see her.

A sudden drop in temperature stopped her dead. She looked around the room, but couldn't see anything. Rose knew she wasn't alone. Her nails dug into the old wooden dresser. She wore nothing except a pair of black knickers. She could see her skirt, blouse, and bra hanging over the end of the bed where she'd flung them the night before.

She stepped away from the dressing table and quickly reached for her clothes. While yanking them on, her gaze darted around the room, searching for any sign of…of what? She didn't know what 'it' was. Only that 'it' had kept her awake for most of the night, making noises, breathing heavily, and pulling on the bedcovers. At one point she was sure she'd felt a small hand play with her hair. She quickly headed for the door, almost stumbling against it in her haste to leave. A scratching sound behind her, made her yelp with fright, and she pulled open the door and fled.

Coming to a halt outside the closed kitchen door, Rose double-checked that no-one and nothing else was following her. Taking a deep breath, she let it out slowly and tried to restore a feeling of calm. Tonight was the Ball. The very thought gave her huge butterflies in her stomach and she took another long, deep breath. Opening the door, the smell of bacon and eggs, toast and coffee hit her. Smells that brought both comfort and nausea, regardless of how much deep breathing she could do. The butterflies refused to disappear, or the fear that she'd spent the night in a haunted room. She firmly blinked away her tears as she determinedly closed the kitchen door behind her.

***

The small child giggled to herself, shrugged, and quietly closed the bedroom door.

***

Placing a full plate in front of Rose, Judith noticed how pale she looked. Exchanging glances with Lucy, she poured a large glass of pure orange juice and handed it to the silent young girl.

She took it without comment and sipped it while she stared down at her breakfast.

'Everything all right, dear?' Lucy eventually asked as she stood watching her cooking going cold.

Rose raised her head and nodded before returning her attention to her untouched plate.

'Come on, eat up, you'll need extra energy today, it'll be a long one.'

Judith sat opposite Rose and slowly buttered her own toast and sipped her tea. She was aware that some people weren't morning people, but Rose looked like she was in shock.

Leaning forward, she made Rose look at her. 'Rose, do you feel unwell?'

Before Rose could answer, the door opened and Adam and Rosalyn entered, both chatting excitedly about some past event. Judith and Lucy's attention shifted to accommodating the new arrivals. Plates of bacon and egg were placed in front of them, mugs of coffee, and fresh toast. The stilted atmosphere lifted slightly as the pair of them talked with Lucy, complimenting her on her cooking, though Rosalyn hardly touched her breakfast, letting Adam polish it off after finishing his own. Judith was also included in their reminiscing about past childhood follies. Rose remained silent, picking at her plate.

***

Judith half-listened to the conversations going on around her, nodding when appropriate, but her thoughts were on Rose. The girl's behaviour troubled her. From a selfish point, it was hardly good timing if the girl felt too ill to help with decorating the Hall; then again, she did look genuinely upset and hadn't had much sleep judging from the dark circles.

A nagging fear crept into her head, but she forced it away. She'd never really believed in ghosts, but since living and working at the Hall, she'd had to come round to the possibility that there might be something walking around the old place. Had Rose encountered something?

Being so busy lately, she had almost managed to forget the strange incident in the kitchen, what with poor Mathew and the Ball and Sir Richard worried about something else, most likely financial. Would he sell the Hall? Was that why this Ball was so important? Would it be the last?

Rose eventually excused herself and headed for the back door just as Geoff was coming in. Pushing past him, she disappeared outside. Everyone watched her leave.

'What's up with her?'

Adam shrugged. 'Who knows, Geoff…who knows?'

Rosalyn grinned and dug Adam in the ribs. 'Maybe Cinderella is excited about the Ball and is hoping for a dance with her Prince Charming!'

Adam hunched over his coffee. '*Humph*! It's probably boy trouble, or hormones. I can never work you women out!'

Judith smiled and sat back, cradling her own hot drink, enjoying the feeling of fullness, the calm before the storm. Another ten minutes and she'd make a move. She glanced toward the back door and considered going after the girl, but decided against it. She'd make a start without Rose, but she'd get an answer from her at some point, that was certain.

***

Rose hugged herself for some reassurance as she slowly walked round the walled garden. She felt afraid. The thought of having to go back to her room was not one she relished, yet, if she thought about it logically, whatever it had been, it hadn't hurt her, only scared her. Besides that, did she really want some spook to ruin a perfectly planned evening? The answer was most definitely 'no'!

***

She could see their fear and the need for answers as people came into her shop. Some came and bought a few odds and ends, but it was obvious that these were not needed; the need was companionship and the shop was the centre of the village.

They asked her advice, her theory, and her feelings on Martha's death and Elizabeth's reaction, the circumstances surrounding the death, and the police and forensic activity since. Foul play was mentioned more than once, but quickly dismissed. It was a known fact Martha had a bad heart and had had a small stroke a few years before. Elizabeth's reaction and subsequent breakdown was the most natural thing to happen. After all, they had been good friends for many years, helping each other through the deaths of their husbands. They found comfort in the art of gossip and though harmless, most of the time, they had become something of a legend throughout the village. Now Martha's demise was affecting everyone else.

Eira considered people's reactions very strange. How many times had she listened to these people whine and moan about 'those gossiping women' and now, one was dead and the other sedated; they felt their loss.

Mathew's illness was the start of it; it had unhinged everyone's safety. The suddenness of it astonished the village, and as all good villagers did, they rallied to help and support. Martha's death and Elizabeth's hysterics had shaken the very foundations a little more as each villager felt the order of things shift. The young and the old were being affected and that was not right.

For the most part, she was able to contain her hatred of the villagers. After all, they were not to blame; their ancestors were. She could feel it creeping in as the innocent paid the price of a terrible injustice. She could not be blamed for it all; it was time others had to accept their own parts in it. Fools who thought they knew what they were doing. Fools who thought they knew how to wield such power, but in reality, they could not. They had condemned themselves and their children; innocents, condemned with the damned; such a mess.

Her attention was brought up quickly as three boys dived into the shop, heading straight for the sweets aisle, their mother following them reluctantly. She smiled her greeting at Eira, who watched her silently, waiting for the inevitable question that would come at any moment. 'I see the police have gone again. What do you think happened, Eira?'

She sighed, resolved to having the same conversation yet again and the sun had barely come up. She answered the questions and listened to the theories and the worries. She could hear the excited tones of the three young boys and she tried to push away the feeling of dread. Surely not all innocents would suffer? Even as she thought it though, she already knew the answer and swallowed the sudden lump in her throat.

CHAPTER THIRTY

BRONWEN STOPPED FOR THE FOURTH time and made as if to turn around. She was nearing the gates to the Kenward Estate and she felt very uneasy. At quarter past eight in the morning, she doubted anyone would be around, but she had to be careful. The last thing she needed was to bump into Adam, or anyone from the estate for that matter. That frightening prospect was tonight. She forced herself not to dwell on it since there would be time enough to fall apart later.

She ran past the gates, refusing to look at them or the land beyond. From the corner of her eye, though, she was aware that only one gate was open—did that mean someone was about? It made her run faster, almost a sprint as she neared the village, because if she ran, she wouldn't have time to think about changing her mind.

The urge to return to Shrewsbury and its library hadn't left her since Adam had dropped her off; she would not be frightened off by a man. She had every right to be in the town and damned if some lecherous estate agent would stop her. If she didn't go back now, she never would and she'd be on the road to living a recluse's life.

She knew the answers were in the library, somewhere; it was a certainty that frightened her with its knowledge. The rest of last night had been spent in turmoil and worry and fear that she'd not go through with it. Then, what if she did? What would she find? So many what ifs, it hurt her head and she firmly refused to think about the Ball—that was something else entirely.

Reaching Eira's garden gate, Bronwen stopped to catch her breath. It was a warm day and a trickle of sweat ran between her breasts. Her back felt sticky. The bus would be here any minute. She walked quickly around to the front door, pushed it open, and shut it behind her. The loud noise made her cringe, but she stepped away from it searching for Eira. Her eyes finally rested on the figure and she stopped dead. 'Eira?'

She knew it was her even as she asked, but the figure of the woman didn't move for a moment, staying in the back of the shop, remaining in the shadows. Bronwen stepped forward, breathing heavily with excitement and exertion. 'Eira, have you a moment?'

The figure moved; for a brief second, she looked like someone else, someone she thought she should know. Then the moment was gone as Eira stepped slowly forward into the light, a smile warming her face. Bronwen frowned, the smile could not hide the change in her friend's face—she looked haggard, pale, and sick. The thought of losing her only friend was so horrible, she quickly walked forward.

'Eira, you don't look well. Is there anything I can do?' She tried to sound as concerned as she felt, but her awareness of time running out was pounding her head.

Eira shook her head and reaching out, patted her hand that lay on the counter.

'If there is, let me know. I just have to ask, this Ball tonight, what do I wear? I'm sorry, that sounds so selfish, but, I haven't got a clue and I'm catching the bus…'

Eira held up her hands to stop her floundering and gently patted her on the arm. 'I'm all right, Bronwen, just a little tired…and, I must say, I'm surprised and glad to see you. You've been okay? You look a little bruised, dear…'

Bronwen blushed. *She knows what happened*, she thought and dug around in her pocket for the long list of groceries she needed. 'Yeah, I'm fine, dreading tonight, actually.'

Eira's hand rested on her arm. 'I know, dear, but really, it won't be that bad.' Looking at the piece of paper, she smiled. 'Is this everything you need? I'll get it boxed up and send one of my lads to deliver it before you return from Shrewsbury. As for what to wear, it's decent and best clothes. It's hard enough getting a farmer to change out of his tweeds and wellies, so Sir Richard makes it worthwhile. Men are in suits, no, no, not black tie and dinner jacket, but best suits and nice frocks. Is that any help?'

Bronwen nodded mutely. She felt that she should stay and help gather her requirements or make Eira a cup of tea or something, but the rumble of the coming bus broke the spell and she quickly thanked Eira and opened the door. 'So, I'll see you there, then?'

Nodding, Eira stepped forward and held open the door. 'Yes, my dear, I'll be there around eight. I'll look out for you?'

Bronwen had time to nod before she ran across the road and joined the other women waiting to get onto the small bus. She found an empty seat and looked out of the window. She caught Eira's eye and gave her a small wave. As the bus moved off, she knew that Eira was watching it go and wondered why leaving her behind should make her feel sad.

***

Eira watched the small bus until it had disappeared from sight. She knew its journey and could visualise the lane, the fields on either side, the large, old oaks standing to attention, guarding the way into the village. That was as far as she could remember. She knew of and had seen pictures of the dual carriageway, but she'd never bothered to try to see it. All of her knowledge came secondhand from others who travelled to the town and beyond. Most days, she felt resigned to her fate, but sometimes, like today, she yearned to journey beyond the barrier and see for herself the many changes.

Bronwen's concern had brought so much emotional turmoil, it now stuck in her throat like a golf ball, and she tried to stem the flow of tears. It seemed so wrong that Bronwen should care for her in this lifetime. To help occupy her mind, she slowly walked across the road to the Morris family and asked for help with the deliveries. She stayed awhile, patting the two dogs and stroking the cat, passing the time so she didn't think about Bronwen too much.

***

Bronwen was the last to get off the bus and stood more or less where she had the last time. Gradually, the bubbles of anxiety crept into her stomach. Somewhere in this town, that lecherous bastard might be lurking. She'd be more careful this time and check every shop before passing it.

She glanced both ways, half-expecting to see his smug little smile, beady eyes, and sweating hands. When she didn't, she quickly walked toward the town and prayed she'd find a shop that sold decent dresses, so she could get to the library and leave. She took a deep breath and followed the crowds toward the main high street. Surely, luck had to be on her side this time?

An hour later, she was smiling to herself as she walked toward the library; she had found a suitable dress in a New Age shop. She'd actually gone to look in the charity shop next door, but had come out disappointed. She'd stared at the window display for a while, trying to pluck up enough courage to go in, as she'd never ventured inside one of those types of shops before. It all looked a bit weird! But, wasn't her new life weird? It certainly couldn't be classed as normal.

She'd been pleasantly surprised to find a lovely selection of velvet dresses at the back of the shop, amongst many other shirts and skirts of various colours, and what she'd describe as New Age hippie stuff, but she liked them. Would she have the courage to wear them? Now that was another matter entirely. She'd gazed at the variety of multi-coloured wall hangings and breathed deeply the gentle aroma of a burning incense stick while she considered how far her courage went. Glancing slowly around at all the various displays of tarot cards, incense burners, and statues of weird looking animals, her eyes rested on a stand covered with various stones and crystals.

One purple coloured one, about the size of her palm, was jagged on one side and smooth on the other. She read the label next to it. *'Amethyst, a good healing stone, helping to release past hurts, and a good dream stone to help you remember your dreams'.*

She gently picked it up, unsure what to expect, but it felt warm and safe and perfect. If nothing else, it represented her life right now, unstable, unsure, frightening, yet smooth compared to her other life back in Liverpool and before that. She had to believe her life could become smooth, or else what was the point? And besides, she could certainly do with some healing; that might be helpful. Though she wasn't sure about remembering her dreams. Her nightmares were not something she wanted to remember.

Decision made, she carried the stone to the shop assistant who smiled warmly, which helped her feel reassured. She asked about the dresses.

'Can I try one on? I have a party tonight and I don't know what to wear.' Bronwen felt her cheeks going crimson, but the woman quickly moved from behind the counter.

'Of course, please, let me help you. We'll have some fun. You try on anything you fancy.' The assistant's enthusiasm was contagious.

Bronwen slowly relaxed as she paraded in front of the full length mirrors while the assistant picked out other dresses to try. *I look pretty,* she thought and that astounded her.

The fifth dress made them giggle as Bronwen got stuck trying to wriggle into a bodice and they gave up. 'I'm not a skinny woman.' Bronwen shrugged as she pulled the tight corset over her head.

The assistant shook her head. 'No, you have a curvy shape, which is much better. Try this one; the colour would suit you.'

The velvet dress was a forest green colour with wide straps which covered the tops of her shoulders, but her arms were bare. The bodice was styled like a corset in the front with a full length skirt. It stopped just below her ankles. She looked stunning.

'Some black sandals with a heel will finish that off, or a pair of Doc Martens boots?'

Bronwen grinned. 'I've never worn sandals but I have black boots that should be okay.'

The assistant brought her a lovely cream coloured shawl to wrap around her shoulders to finish the ensemble, which she'd be grateful for later in the evening. It was warming up, but the nights were still cool. She decided to keep her hair simple and put it up in a soft bun; she was actually feeling a little excited at dressing up and looking beautiful. Nervous, but excited nonetheless.

The library was in sight. A quick glance round and she darted across the road, past the statue, and stopped outside the door. Catching her breath, she straightened herself and went inside, double-checking that she hadn't been followed.

'Can I help you?'

Bronwen turned to the women who watched her, a pile of books clutched to her chest. She was sweating, and she flapped her shirt to try to cool off and managed to smile shyly at what she presumed was the librarian. 'Yes, please, I was here last Saturday doing research. Another lady helped me. I'm sorry, I left in a bit of a hurry and—'

'Ah, I see. That will have been Shirley. Tell you what, let me sort these out while you cool off. It looks nice out there for a change?' She inclined her head toward the door.

Bronwen blushed and wiped her forehead on her sleeve, flapping her shirt a bit more.

The woman shifted the books to one arm and indicated the large book on the desk. 'Just sign in and I'll be back in a minute. Find yourself a seat.'

The large room was almost empty again. Four people sat around one large table, poring over various books and what looked like an old photo album. She could see black and white photographs stuck to the yellowed pages. She walked to the table she'd sat at before, farthest from the group. Here she was sandwiched between two high bookcases, each one jammed with books of varying size. Some looked quite new while others looked old and torn.

'Right.' The woman stood on the other side of the table. 'What can I help you with today?'

Bronwen explained why she was there and what she'd had last time. The librarian nodded. 'I'll look on the computer and see if my assistant found anything else for you. It will have gone back into the storage room, so you'll need to fill out the slips again, but it shouldn't take too long.'

Half an hour later, Bronwen was surrounded with books, diaries, photograph albums, accounts, and a few historical documents, all on the village of Derwen. Some she recognised from her last visit. She quickly flicked through them and then set them to one side. The diaries looked interesting; some dated back to the eighteenth century from some occupants of the village, but one in particular stood out: the diary of Mary Kenward, 1799. Sitting comfortably, Bronwen began to read.

***

Her scream vibrated around the large room, stopping everyone in mid-activity as they all turned at the sound. Anne gripped the sheet and twisted it as another searing pain shot through her body. She felt the force of the contraction and tried to focus on pushing, but it was like pushing against a solid wall and the dagger-like agony vibrated through her groin and back into her burning womb. 'William!' She screamed his name with the last ounce of strength she had before she turned her face into the soaked bed-sheets and let the dark carry her away again.

***

James strolled into the office just before lunch. Gordon glanced up, the phone balanced on his shoulder while he waited for Susan to pick up. His first thought was, *James looked like the cat that definitely got the cream*; the next one was, *Smug little prick!* His new woman must be good to make James look like that! 'Good night, was it?'

Without a word, James winked and poured himself a cup of coffee.

Giving up, Gordon replaced the receiver and sat back. 'Well, did you get cream?'

'I got more than cream. I got the whole three-course meal with extra dessert and a free liqueur coffee, my friend.' Sipping his coffee, James sauntered over to his own office and flicked through his appointments: a couple this morning and a busy afternoon with plenty of time to wind up Gordon.

Gordon followed him and now leant against the doorframe. 'Dirty bugger! I suppose you'll not want to go out tonight, she'll have tired you out?'

James grinned. 'Not at all. I'm raring to go, if this Clare isn't too bad looking. It's the girls I feel sorry for. I hope they can keep up.'

Gordon laughed. 'It's not them who've got to keep up!'

James watched his partner walk back to his own office, still smiling at his own pathetic joke. He was interviewing all morning for a new receptionist; none so far had been adequate. They had one from an agency during the week, but she refused to work weekends. Desperate, Gordon had agreed, but it left them running around the office, which wasn't professional. Their clients had serious money, and they expected everyone to jump when they told them to. They needed a good receptionist. After a lot of deliberation, they both decided they would need a good, ugly, receptionist so they wouldn't be tempted.

James had seen the written complaint of sexual harassment from Paula, informing them she was going to take it further. He'd tried to contact her to talk about it, but she'd refused to speak with him on the phone. Either he 'paid her compensation or she'd talk to the appropriate authorities'.

They'd already decided to pay her, depending on how much she wanted; a couple of grand should do it. Her threat helped them make a decision they'd discussed on a few occasions: getting rid of one shop, most likely Liverpool. They employed eleven people in Liverpool, Chester, and Shrewsbury. Chester was doing very well, covering a large area in England and Wales. After doing his calculations, James had worked out that Liverpool was the worst of the three.

Gordon's wife was going to bleed him dry if her lawyers got their way, and Susan was becoming more demanding. If they had to pay Paula some money too, they would need the extra that getting rid of Liverpool would bring. The door of the office opened and a rather large, plump girl walked in. Nice smile, generous tits, curves. James hid his smile in his cup of coffee; he'd have his hands full with this one. After introducing himself, he showed her into Gordon's office, wondering how long it would be before he got a feel of this one?

**

She lay perfectly still; even breathing hurt. Only her eyes moved as they looked around her bedroom at the candles. Some of them had long since gone out, but she could count six that still burned. She could hear next door's television blaring and she felt utter loathing for the couple.

Sandra and Chris were supposed to be good neighbours, weren't they? They'd shared the occasional bottle of wine and a couple of beers in the summer while sitting in the garden. Sandra invited her to an Ann Summers party last year, so why hadn't they heard her last night? Why hadn't they come to check on her? They knew Keith had left.

No-one heard her. No-one had come to her rescue. No-one heard her whimpering and begging and choked sobs as the pain and humiliation went on and on and on. Someone should have saved her.

She stared up at her bedroom ceiling and wished she was dead. She could smell him on her, mixed with her own piss and blood. Worse though, she could smell the scented candles that she'd bought with her mum last week. The scent of roses filled the room, a room that was supposed to be filled with love and desire, with Keith. Not this vileness. This room and everything she held with love had been destroyed by his filth, by his despicable acts. His violation destroyed everything she was. She had to destroy everything.

Rolling onto her stomach, she cried out as a burning sensation ripped across her back. Her groin felt slick, and she gagged, knowing it was from him. Her body burned with pain; she couldn't think of anything else except everything had to be destroyed; she had to burn him out of her.

Reaching out, she just managed to push the nearest candlestick over. She heard it hit the floor and waited. When nothing happened, she wormed her way farther up the bed and reached down to the floor where her discarded knickers lay. A magazine peeped out beneath them. She barely acknowledged it as she held it to the flame, and waited.

***

Bronwen rubbed her eyes as the fine writing began to blur. She had moved on from Mary's diary to reading what could only be described as memoirs of a wise woman. After rummaging around the large pile of books and documents, she'd found references to the diaries from an old W.I. history book dated 1955 where some ladies of the village had got together and written a compact history of Derwen. Bronwen found it very interesting, but the memoirs were so much more.

She only gave her name as Anne of Derwen, but strangely, Mary had also mentioned her in her own diaries, referring to her as 'the wise woman' who the locals went to for help, but the dates didn't tally. It would make this 'Anne' too old to be alive. Perhaps they were a family, mother passing down knowledge to daughter, perhaps?

As Bronwen flicked through it, the librarian came up behind her and commented on the woman's handwriting. 'It's remarkable, really, women in those days could rarely read, never mind write. This woman's hand is very neat.'

It hadn't occurred to Bronwen before, but the librarian was right. The handwriting was very neat and the more she read, it was obvious the woman was educated. So who was she? A wise woman, for sure, but weren't they old hags who were bent over with arthritis and looked like your typical witch? Whatever the general thought, this Anne was not a conventional woman of the eighteenth century.

It did cross her mind that she had encountered two Annes: William's, and now this woman in the village. Obviously, a common name. It was frustrating not having a surname for this wise woman, but it did seem quite common not to have one unless you were rich. From what she was reading, this Anne was definitely not.

'Margaret of Derwen came today. Silly woman demanded I cure her sore feet. I bathed them in Rosemary and gave her an onion to rub on her warts. I also told her to buy better shoes. As payment, she gave me a chunk of cheese and a bottle of ale.

'Sir James came to see me in the dead of night as always. His son has another fever and a sore throat. I gave him a tincture of honey and lemon and a small bag of lavender to warm through with warm water and soak a cloth in and place on his son's forehead. He was to allow air into the room and his son would be fine in a few days. Sir James did not like the idea of fresh air being allowed into the room, silly man.'

Bronwen scanned the small book and grinned when she found the entry four days later.

'Sir James sent his manservant to me with a note of gratitude and a leg of mutton, two bottles of his finest wine, and a large loaf of bread. His son is well. I am safe.'

Frowning, Bronwen gently closed the book. *Safe. Why would she put that in?* she thought. Did they still burn witches in those days?

Unable to resist, she picked it up again and flicked through the pages. The book was full. The woman must have had a lot of customers. Near the end of the book, she noticed something quite odd. Three pages from the end, this woman had written the date 1830. She must have been very old by then. Flicking back to the beginning of the book, the first entry was dated 1732. That would make Anne ninety-eight years old. She'd always assumed they died quite young because of poor health and hygiene. This woman must have been very wise to live that long. She felt a stir of pride for this lady and smiled to herself. She wished she'd known her.

Something caught her eye at the end of the book and she sat forward. It didn't have anything to do with anyone's ailments in the village; this piece of writing, written on the last page, seemed squeezed on, quickly added. A strange thing to add onto a diary of a healer woman of sorts, it read,

'I am lost. It has failed again. I attempted to walk toward the ruins today but the trees hold fast and I failed. I wept, remembering how it had once been my home. I yearn to touch its walls and walk amongst its rooms, now open to the sky.'

Bronwen read it again, staring at the page, trying to understand its meaning. She obviously meant the castle ruins, but that had been ruined for hundreds of years, even by 1830; how could the castle be her home? Had a small part of it still been standing in the nineteenth century? That was possible, but why couldn't she go and visit it? What had she meant about the trees, or was it a metaphor for something else? Was she forbidden to visit the castle? After all, it must have belonged to the Kenwards.

If the Kenwards were mean landowners, perhaps they stopped anyone going on their land. Maybe they'd threatened to shoot anyone who trespassed? That sounded like something rich landowners would do.

Her thoughts returned to the Ball tonight. She would be mixing with rich landowners, and she clenched her fists to try to control the anxiety that flooded through her. To take her mind off it, she put the book to one side and sorted through the marriage and birth certificates and finally stopped at an old photograph album. The label on the front read '*1888, the village of Derwen*' and she opened it.

She scanned the fuzzy black and white pictures. Some were torn, and others were water damaged, and only half the picture had survived. She saw men in flat caps and breeches, women in long skirts, children everywhere. Pictures taken of the village showed the same row of cottages and the pub at the end. Eira's shop looked different, but unbelievably it was there. There wasn't any park of course, or a particular road, just tracks leading past the cottages. There wasn't a road leading to Kenward Hall, either, just another dirt track. She could see where carriages had made ruts in the mud.

She vaguely heard a siren scream past the window, followed by another and subconsciously registered a fire engine and an ambulance, but her whole attention was focused on a small photograph taken outside the original shop. It showed a group of boys. Two were in flat caps and shorts. The others stood behind them and were wearing white shirts with their sleeves rolled up. They were all smiling and posing for the camera, leaning forward in anticipation for the click. It was the woman who stood behind them who Bronwen was staring at. The woman was Eira.

CHAPTER THIRTY-ONE

ER SCREAMS HAD DIED AWAY. Now all she could manage were groans. Her throat felt hot and raw. As if sensing it, Nia stepped forward and held a cup of water to her dry lips. Anne drank thirstily, but spluttered as another contraction ripped through her exhausted body.

A wet cloth was plastered to her forehead, and water dribbled into her eyes and down her hot cheeks; she didn't care. She knew she was dying and didn't care. William was gone. Their son was gone, she was sure of it. She'd heard the hushed whispers and the glances, but even without those, she knew. No child, however strong, could withstand this ordeal. She had condemned her son to die; now she wanted to follow him.

Nia began wiping her arms, her chest, and face, wiping away the sweat and hair that was plastered to her burning skin. The midwife stood at the end of the bed, wringing her hands as she watched the contractions. She had arrived to the sounds of Lady Anne's screams. Now, hours later, nothing had changed. With a sudden decision and a quick nod to Nia, she knelt down and oiled her hands. She waited for a contraction to end before deftly rubbing oil between Anne's legs; she set to work.

After another contraction, she roughly began to massage Anne's belly before applying more oil to her hands and rubbed oil around Anne's stretched vagina, making her gasp with pain. Another contraction and the midwife stopped her administrations and waited; once over, she began again, rubbing and gently pulling and turning, and then everything seemed to fall into place.

As another contraction reached its peak, the midwife pushed down on Anne's stomach. 'Come, my lady, push!'

Anne grunted with the effort and cried out as the taut skin tore, but the midwife encouraged her to keep pushing, and to breathe. She kept pushing and gasping for air between contractions, and for that longest of time, nothing mattered, until she felt the familiar sensation of a sudden release and she knew her son was born.

***

Bronwen squinted at the photograph. It couldn't possibly be, of course. Yet, the resemblance was uncanny. She had to be a relative, but she looked like Eira did now. The bun piled high, her oval face, her plump physique. If only it wasn't black and white. She'd love to know if this woman had the same intense green eyes as Eira.

The group was standing outside the shop, so perhaps the shop had been a family business. It was interesting to know it had been going for all this time; Eira must be proud. Not for the first time, she wondered just how old Eira was. Seventies, maybe?

Looking around at the small pile of papers and books, she sighed heavily; she felt very weary. Most of the Kenwards' history lay before her, from William right through to the twentieth century. Nothing had been found on the present owners of Kenward Hall; she'd asked, but nothing was written since 1929. The last had been a letter from an Arthur Kenward; she presumed him to be Adam's grandfather. He was writing to a friend, telling him about the failure of the stables.

'The structure is too unstable these days and the few horses that are left have been moved to a barn for their safety; God forbid that I should lose them too. We still use the buggy on occasion, but I am

hoping to afford a new vehicle very soon, which, I am assured, will reach my destinations quicker. I look forward to seeing you once again and hope that your business venture does not delay your coming to our annual May Ball.

We have discussed your sudden departure and the reasons behind it. I trust that your wife will feel able to accompany you and that you have assured her that the stories that surround this house and those who dwell within it are false and nothing more than nonsense.

Your dearest friend,
Sir Arthur William Kenward'

Staring at the spidery writing, Bronwen tried to think of any possible reasons for a friend's swift departure. Could it be Gwenllian? Why not haunt the Hall as well as the cottage and the scene of her murder?

It was too much to believe that she only haunted her. Why would she do that? Unless ghosts could pick their victims. Did ghosts have a conscience, a train of thought to help them to decide to haunt someone and no-one else? She doubted that; after all, they were dead. Surely thoughts didn't come into it. Perhaps she had no choice who she showed herself to? Perhaps it was just coincidence that she was around when the energy of this child had manifested itself?

Even as she considered it, she dismissed it. It felt personal, or did she just hope that it was because that would make her special somehow? Her counsellor would have a field day with that! But, did they have some connection? Two abused children, perhaps? She was not a murderer, she was a victim, just like the child. Was that a possible connection?

***

Nia leaned against the outer stone wall of the castle; her hands clutched the dirty rag now covered with stains. It had been over an hour since she'd left the bedchamber, searching for a place to wash off the blood, sweat, and dirt. It wouldn't come off. It felt ingrained into her skin, embedded forever as a reminder that she had failed in her duty. What would Sir William say?

She breathed deeply of the cool night air. She could smell the sweet grass and the piles of hay nearby, along with the sweat of the few horses left behind and the dung. All familiar smells. Nia hoped they would ground her, but they didn't. Her fear of what might happen was overwhelming, and her legs finally gave way and she slid down the wall, landing in a heap. Huddled into herself, she finally let the hot tears flow and trembled with fatigue at the horror she'd left behind.

Gwenllian stood in the shadows and watched her nurse weep silently. She had been waiting outside in the corridor for her brother to be born, but after hearing the screams coming from inside the bed-chamber, she'd retreated to her favourite tree and waited there, instead. Andrew watched her go with a nod before returning to the castle.

After what seemed like forever, she'd noticed various people moving about. Some were crying, others, mostly the men, looked sombre and went about their duties, staring down at the ground. She saw the midwife leave the castle gates, her box of medicines in her hand; Andrew had touched her shoulder in reassurance. She was pale and visibly shaking with fear and exhaustion.

Now, she edged her way toward Nia. Squatting down beside her, she gently touched her nurse's arm. 'He's dead, isn't he?'

Nia nodded and a fresh wave of anguish took over. Sighing, Gwenllian slowly stood up and squared her shoulders. 'I want to see him.'

For a moment, Nia wasn't sure she'd heard her correctly, as she'd spoken so quietly, but now, watching the child walk purposefully back toward the courtyard, she scrambled to her feet and hurried after her. She finally caught up with her at the bottom of the stairs that led up to the private chambers. 'Gwenllian, you can't see him! Let's go to the chapel and pray for his little soul instead.' Her beseeching voice sounded too loud in the quiet of the evening and she lowered her voice to a whisper. 'Let the babe rest. Let us go to the chapel.'

Gwenllian looked down at her restraining hand and pulled her arm out of her grip. Before Nia could protest, she ran up the winding stairs as fast as her little legs could manage, knowing Nia was following. She knew she wouldn't catch her. She wanted to see her brother before her nerve left her. It was her duty, as her father's daughter, to be able to tell him how beautiful his son, her brother, had looked. Everyone else would tell him anything to make him happy. At least he could rely on her to tell him the truth, and she would.

Reaching her father's chamber, she took a deep breath and opened the door. The smell of blood filled her nostrils and she gagged. Gwenllian forced herself to step into the room, barely lit by three candles. It took a few minutes for her eyes to adjust to the dim light. The figure lay unmoving on the bed and, for a moment, Gwenllian thought Anne was dead too.

Then the figure moved slightly, curling into herself, and she could hear whispering. Stepping closer, she coughed. 'Anne? I...'

It was as far as she got before the figure on the bed heaved up and turned, screaming at her. Anne's eyes were wild and wide open, glaring at her with so much fury and despair, Gwenllian stepped back. She cradled something in one arm, something covered in blood and gore and filth. She realised with horror it was her brother.

Gwenllian stared wide-eyed at the corpse held tightly against Anne's heaving chest. She managed to swallow and took a step backward before she looked up at the woman who now pointed a long, bloodstained finger at her.

'*You*! You are to blame for this! You should die, not this perfect son. *My son*! It should be *you*!'

Gwenllian stumbled backward to the doorway and collided with Nia who just reached the bedchamber, her chest heaving from the effort. She grabbed Gwenllian and held her in her arms, slowly backing away from the vision of madness that now knelt upon the bed, her insane eyes never leaving them.

The blood-soaked linen lay around her, her chemise covered with her blood and her own filth, her hair matted and wild about her pale face. Her stare darted from one to the other, then suddenly, her attention reverted to the dead child she held in her arm, and she gently eased herself onto the bed and crooned softly to her son. Anne offered her breast to the child whose mouth would never open willingly, and all the while, she spoke to him, her voice, barely a whisper, and full of love for a son who lived only in her demented mind.

Nia pulled Gwenllian out of the room and closed the door softly behind them. Without a word, she pushed her along the corridor to her own room. It wasn't until the door was closed behind them that she let out the breath she had been holding. With a loud sigh, she sat down in the chair beside the unlit fire.

Gwenllian sat down on the floor by her nurse's feet. 'It will be all right, Nia.' Gwenllian spoke more to herself that to her nurse. 'She'll have another once this madness has gone. Father will know what to do.'

Reaching out, Nia gently stroked the top of Gwenllian's head. 'No, my dear.' Her voice was calm and quiet. 'Lady Anne can never have any more children…it is finished.' She spoke the last three words to herself.

***

Adam flung himself down next to Rosalyn on the grassy hill. Their horses munched grass nearby. Watching them, Adam felt compelled to follow suit. He picked a long blade of grass and stuck it into his mouth.

Rosalyn took off her long brown cardigan and lay back on the cool grass, her eyes closed and her hands clasped together resting on her stomach.

Adam watched her. Her arms were nothing more than twigs. Her stomach was non-existent. He could see her collarbone protruding beneath her round-neck T-shirt. Her long legs, crossed at the ankles, were no bigger than one of his arms. He noticed the belt she was using to hold up her jeans was on the last hole. She looked fragile, weak, and ill.

'Your silence is so deafening, I can hardly hear myself think!'

He pulled the grass stem from his mouth and let it fall. 'Sorry, Sis.'

Sitting up, Rosalyn turned to look at him. 'Well, what's the matter? You've had something on your mind since I got here.'

Adam shrugged and refused to look at her; instead, he played with the grass between his fingers. 'Not much. This stupid Ball tonight, Father is acting weird lately, Scarlet hasn't got pregnant from Dulas and not through lack of trying on his part.' Rosalyn giggled at this, but he continued, 'Geoff is looking very old lately and that is a worry. The good news is Mathew is finally stable. Then, there's you.'

Rosalyn looked startled. '*Me*! What the hell have I done?'

'Well,' Adam began cautiously, 'you do look like you're auditioning for "who can impersonate the best skeleton" act. You don't phone, and when I finally do manage to track you down, you blow me off saying you're too busy. I'm worried about you. So is Father. In fact, so is everyone.'

Rosalyn glared at him before jumping up and putting her cardigan around her waist. 'Women just can't win with people like you! A tiny bit of fat and she's told to slim down and be thin and only then will she be gorgeous and desirable, but that's still not good enough, is it?'

Adam flinched at her venom, but remained sitting, looking out at the village. 'There's thin, Rosalyn, then there's ill and besides, I've never called you fat, have I?' He said quietly, 'Are you anorexic or something?'

He heard her *humph*. 'Don't be so bloody daft, of course I'm not. I ate a cooked breakfast this morning, didn't I?'

Slowly, Adam stood and faced her. 'No, you didn't, you hardly touched it, besides, there's also a condition called bulimia.'

Rosalyn looked away first and walked over to her horse. 'You really do worry too much, Adam.' Her voice quivered with emotion. 'You should be worrying about other things. I'm fine…give us a bunk up?'

He quickly clasped his hands together and heaved her up into the saddle; she was barely any weight. He looked up at her questioningly. 'What do you mean? What else should I be worried about, besides the list I gave you?'

She averted her eyes while busying herself with her stirrups. He noticed she was chewing her inner cheeks, something she'd always done as a child when thinking about something. 'Nothing. It just seems to me, you have rather a long list, that's all.' She clicked her horse forward and turned back to him as he swung himself into his saddle and caught her up. 'Come on, let's not fight. Let's go over that way.'

Adam looked to where she pointed and shook his head. He could see the back of Oak Cottage on the left and beyond, on a small hillock, the clump of trees and part of the round ditch were visible. 'No, let's go over that way, past the village and follow the track back to the stables. It's a good hour's ride. It's almost two now, we'll need time to freshen up and no doubt Judith will find us something to do to help out.' He swung his horse in the opposite direction, but Rosalyn didn't follow him.

'What is that over there?'

Impatiently, Adam glanced over his shoulder and sighed. 'Those are the ruins, don't you remember? We don't go over there.'

Without looking at him, she asked quietly, 'Why not? It's our land, isn't it?' When he didn't answer, she continued. 'Have you ever wondered why we never went there as children? That's a bit odd, isn't it?'

'We did go there once.'

'Did we? I don't remember.'

Adam swung his horse around and came to a stand next to her unmoving horse. 'You were very young, only three, I think. I had taken you on an adventure, but you got tired and fell over and hurt your head and I wouldn't leave you. They found us eventually, it was just going dark.'

Something in his voice made her tear her eyes away and look at him. She glanced back at the mound. 'Okay, scary stuff, but what exactly is it?'

'It was an Iron Age fort, a settlement or something. Our ancestors built the first wooden castle in the middle of it, using the ditches as a kind of defence. Ingenious really, and then the stone castle was built around the beginning of the 1300s, and then another of our wonderful ancestors rebuilt it as a fortified house about fifty years later, digging the ditches deeper. I think the idea was to make it into some kind of moat, but I don't think that actually happened. It must have looked amazing once, with its high banks and fortified stone walls and the tower...'

Rosalyn glanced at him, then back at the trees. She couldn't see any ruins from here, only a round mound, which must have been the top of the outer ditch, and the trees, oaks mostly, mixed with a few chestnuts. They all looked very old.

Glancing left and right, she could see the oak trees that as children they had climbed and built dens around. From her vantage point on the horse, she could see six. As children, they'd raced from one tree to another, but she couldn't remember if they'd finished the whole circle. A circle of oak trees. Some ancestor's idea of art, perhaps, and if Adam was to be believed, over three hundred strides apart, in the steps of a twelve-year-old boy anyway.

A sudden chill down her spine made her shiver, and she rubbed her shoulders to warm up. 'Come on, then, let's do this track of yours and then I'm going to have a long soak. It's been ages since I've been riding and I don't just mean horses!'

Adam pulled a face and kicked his horse into a canter headed for the village. He was glad to leave. He'd felt a strange sensation looking at the ruins. The horses never strayed to that end of the field, nor did any of the farmer's sheep.

His sister might not remember the ruins, but he did. He had lain curled around Rosalyn next to a large piece of stone wall that had fallen into the ditch. It felt like hours and he silently prayed for his father to find them before night came; he had. He found out later it had been Eira who directed them to their hiding place, just in time, because something had been there with them. Something who hated them, something all children fear: the bad thing.

***

Eira sat rigid against the cottage wall, the rosemary clasped tightly between her hands, forgotten. She could smell the horses' sweat, the grass beneath their feet. She wanted to scream at them to leave, but some corner of her brain told her it was useless anyway; this was nothing more than a vision, a picture. Adam and Rosalyn were moving away from the ruins; they were still safe, for now.

CHAPTER THIRTY-TWO

BRONWEN STRETCHED HER ARMS ABOVE her head, then realised people could see her doing it; she quickly stopped and put her head down. The glare of the sun after the library was intense and she wished she'd bought some sunglasses as well. She clutched her bags, ignoring her growling stomach as she walked quickly in the direction of the bus station to the safety of the bus that would take her home.

She watched people walk by, mostly the women. She watched how they walked, how they dressed, and wondered if she'd ever be confident. Buying the dress had proved to her that she could be brave if she tried; tonight would be a big tester on that.

While she waited for her bus, she thought about balls throughout the years and contemplated what women might have been like in Gwenllian's time, right up to Eira's generation. Women had changed quite a lot in those centuries. Attitudes had changed considerably in some ways, but not all. Men used girls as pawns in the mediaeval times, hadn't they? Selling them off to make alliances, not caring one way or the other about how the girl felt about it. That still happened in some countries. It made her think about men's attitudes toward women, and the thoughts made her feel very sad, because, in reality, had anything really changed at all?

***

News reached them days later that Henry Tudor was only a few miles from Shrewsbury. He was expected to arrive at the town's gates by dusk. A rider had been sent out to find Sir William and tell him the news of his son's death and the unsettling behaviour of his wife. Nia listened to the arguments against telling him but, in the end, Andrew had asked her advice and she'd not hesitated in her reply. She'd simply said, 'He must know.'

She'd watched the rider leave the castle, knowing that her life depended on his return. She hadn't eaten for days; neither had Lady Anne, who still remained in her chamber. Nobody dared enter the room anymore and avoided it at all costs. Everyone, that was, except Nia, who stood outside the door twice a day, morning and night, leaving a fresh tray of food and attempting to talk to Anne through the door. As yet, the food remained untouched and her coaxing remained unanswered.

Nia knew someone would pay for this mess. The midwife had fled once the child was born. Megan flatly refused to go near the closed door of her lady's bedchamber. They had all witnessed the horror of Lady Anne. Some whispered about devils and demons taking over her body. Her bloodshot eyes and wailing were certain to be devils claiming her soul. Her son should have been baptised and buried by now. People were questioning why that hadn't happened. It had been four days. The poor innocent child was doomed to Hell, and his mother too.

Nia's last hope was that Sir William could sort this mess. More than aware of Lady Anne's feelings toward her, she was terrified that she would be blamed somehow. Only Sir William could save her. He would see that none of it was her doing. He would see that she had tried her best to save his son, but had she tried hard enough to save his son's soul? She had promised him that she would protect Gwenllian and his unborn son. He made her swear on the Holy Bible that she would bring his son into the world.

'Nia, I've brought you some food.' Gwenllian climbed the last step onto the tower and held out a plate of bread and cheese. Nia took it, forcing herself to smile, but she couldn't eat. Gwenllian walked around the battlements and shielded her eyes against the glare of the sun. 'Is Father coming home?'

Coming to stand beside her charge, Nia put an arm around her shoulder. 'I don't know, child. I hope so…for Lady Anne's sake.'

Gwenllian nestled her head into her nurse's chest and chewed her nail. 'Is my brother in Hell, Nia? Everyone is saying he is, but he is an innocent. The devil can't take innocents, can he?'

Nia held her tighter. 'No, he can't. Your brother is in Heaven. Don't worry about it. Your father will sort it all out, soon.'

'Lady Anne hates us. Has she gone mad?'

Wrapping her arms around the child, Nia held her tightly as Gwenllian returned the bear hug, both needing the comfort. How could she tell her that Lady Anne was indeed mad with rage, and that soon that evil rage would find a victim? She had seen it in Anne's eyes. All rational thought had left her. Gwenllian had to be protected at all costs.

***

Anne sat wrapped in a bed sheet stained with blood, urine, and faeces. She'd flung off her soiled chemise days ago, and it lay where it had fallen. She felt the warm sunlight trickling in through the window on her face as it intruded on the dark room; she turned her back and kissed the soft fuzz of her son's head. She jerked away as her lips touched frozen skin and the stench filled her nostrils and she turned her head and retched.

Drawing the child's rigid body closer to her own, she could feel the cold, dead skin but she couldn't pull away, believing her own warmth could fill his frozen blood and make his tiny heart beat once more. Contact with her child was all that mattered.

Her mind turned away from what she knew to be real. If she could just pretend a while longer, it would be well. God would not take her child, not again. She had been a good wife, a good mother. Her God would never punish her for being desperate and trying the old ways to save her baby's life.

She became aware of a dripping sound and a smell she recognised but for a while, her confused mind refused to understand. Finally, it dawned on her what it was, and slowly, she looked down on her breasts. Her milk, her son's milk, dribbled onto the rancid sheet that covered them both. She watched as it collected next to her son's ear and dripped down onto his neck. Her son's lifeless eyes, half-closed, stared back at her. His small, perfect mouth had frozen in a grimace of her own doing as she'd tried to force-feed him. She opened her mouth and screamed.

***

The bus journey home was in itself uneventful, except for the multitude of butterflies that hammered against her empty stomach, and she felt nauseated. She drank the last of her bottled water, hoping to drown the butterflies, but her stomach was too acidic and she felt faint. Bronwen just wanted to get home, eat something, and get the evening over.

Her thoughts raced between scenarios where she was made to look foolish in some way in front of the whole village, to Adam Kenward being shamed by her in some dramatic fashion; neither image was helpful. Instead, she tried to imagine May Balls through the ages: the dresses, the transport, the music. It helped a little. Then, from the blue, she wondered what Adam would think about her in her new dress. Why did she care? Pushing that out of her head, she focused on the diary extracts she'd read until they arrived at Derwen village.

***

James slammed his office door behind him and sat down, running his fingers through his hair a few times to try to gain control; he was furious. He'd been looking forward to leaving the office early and getting ready for his night out with Gordon and the girls, but a potential client telephoned, demanding a meeting at his home, today. He'd arrived promptly at three o'clock, to be informed by Mr Collins that his mother would show him around his six-bedroom house as he had another appointment. This wasn't unusual, but on seeing the state of the mother, he'd known for sure the appointment would take longer than expected.

The mother looked more like his grandmother, doubled over, small, and almost blind. She'd shuffled along slowly from room to room. He'd almost run into her twice in his haste to leave. He'd have seen the house in half the time, but this house and the four acres attached to it was worth a lot of commission so he'd persevered. Over an hour and a half later, he'd finally left, with no definite deal, caught in Saturday traffic, and it was nearly six.

'What's up with you?' Gordon stood in the doorway fiddling with his tie. 'I said we'd meet the girls about seven for drinks. I've booked a table for eight as planned. We could go on somewhere else if we want…or we could see how we feel after drinks…' Gordon gave him a knowing smile.

James nodded and scratched his chin. 'I'll need a wash first. I've been stuck in the car.'

Gordon paced the floor for the ten minutes it took James to clean himself, emerging with a grin, the hand towel in his hand.

'You'd better put that in the wash. I'm not drying my hands on that thing if you've been using it on your cock!' Gordon shook his head while James pulled on his jacket and checked his wallet.

Gordon suddenly looked serious. 'Well, whatever happens tonight, I hope it cheers Susan up. A friend of hers died this afternoon, a fire or something.'

James looked at him questioning. 'Fire? Where was that, then?'

'In one of those new estates built last year, you know, near the castle. A young woman, apparently. I asked if she wanted to cancel, but Sue said she needed to get out and her friend Clare didn't know her. James, did you hear me?'

With an effort, James pulled himself together and grinned sheepishly. 'Sorry. Drifted off there, must be tired from today. Need a drink. Shall we go?'

While Gordon went round the office and reception, checking everything was off, James went back into the bathroom for another quick piss, or so he told Gordon. What he needed was a minute on his own to think. Could it have been his bitch from last night? He'd left some candles burning. Could one have fallen?

He liked to fuck them, hurt them, and humiliate them, but to kill one? He'd had to once, but only because she'd made too much noise. He didn't care that they saw his face; it was rare that they remembered properly. He'd always found that strange, but he never let it bother him. He'd seen the so-called sketch of the 'mad rapist' who preyed on young woman; it looked nothing like him. It looked like any man in his early thirties. He was safe.

How would it actually feel to kill another one? It crossed his mind with Debbie from time to time, but she was a whore, not a woman, she didn't count.

'Come on!' Gordon's sudden knock on the door made him jump and he instinctively flushed. Opening the door, he found his partner grinning at him. 'What's wrong with you? Cystitis, or are you nervous? By the way, what happened this afternoon? Got a deal?'

'I'll tell you on the way to the pub and you can tell me about our new receptionist.'

The two men walked slowly toward the city centre. People milled around them and soon they were lost in the crowd. James looked once behind them, toward the outskirts of the city, toward the new estate for first-time buyers; she had been most obliging. He hoped this Clare was just as good, if not better.

***

Mathew forced his eyes open and tried to focus on the small, white room. Everything looked blurred and distorted, but he blinked hard to try to remove the groggy weight that tried to pull his eyelids down and send him back to oblivion. Someone was in the room with him. He couldn't see them, but he knew. He felt the surge of panic but his body refused to react to it. He could do nothing but lie there, knowing he should be running or hiding, but he couldn't. His drugged body refused to obey his screaming instincts.

'Hello, Mathew.'

The soft voice came from near his right ear and he forced his head to move, he had to see, to know, but he didn't want to. The small face before him smiled and he attempted to smile back, but even as he tried, the face slowly changed into a grinning skull and it reached out for him. *Why? Why?* he screamed inside his head, his mouth refusing to do anything other than dribble.

'I can't help it, Mathew. It was you and yours that did this…you and yours. I am bound now, until she saves us.'

The voice drifted away, floating in the air as she moved to the door. He watched her progress, unmoving from his small, narrow bed. He waited until she evaporated before his heavy eyes, and only then did he allow himself to be taken back to oblivion, his last thought: *Who is she?*

***

Geoff whistled to the dogs to heel. All four came running and waited until he threw the two balls in the same direction. He smiled as they all rushed for the prizes. He walked fast, enjoying the exhilaration of being out in the fresh air; the Hall had been too stifling. Everyone was on edge. Judith was having one of her hot flushes and taking it out on young Rose, who was sulking and not pulling her weight. Richard was just getting in everybody's way and had finally gone out for a drive. Lucy was shouting at anyone who dared to enter the kitchen area, even for a cup of tea; he'd had enough.

He'd checked on David, who was finishing mucking out the stables; he'd told him Adam and Rosalyn had gone out for a ride an hour before. Geoff looked for them, but they must have gone beyond the village. Without thought about where he was going, he just walked and pushed himself on, up the meadow and to the fields beyond. Past Oak Cottage, he walked on toward the old ruins.

He could see the mound of earth and the old trees that covered it. Approaching it slowly, he glanced down at the dogs, which now stayed close to him. Two had a ball in their mouths. 'What is it, Barnaby boy?'

The dog looked up at his name and wagged his tail, but his attention returned to the ruins in front of them. Little Toby gave a low growl. Geoff felt the hairs on the back of his neck rise up and he shook himself. It was only spooky because no-one ever came here, he told himself. He stopped a few hundred feet from the outer ditch. He could see the remains of the gatehouse and the castle ruins beyond it. Nothing much was standing except one of the towers, but even that looked unstable and covered with ivy. He walked the perimeter, keeping his distance; he had an overwhelming curiosity to walk among the ruins, but the behaviour of the dogs warned him it wasn't a good idea.

He looked over his shoulder; he could see the village about a mile away, and to the right stood Kenward Hall. He couldn't see the stables as they were in a slight dip, but he could see where they were supposed to be. It really was a beautiful spot. A shame it had such a bad reputation.

He'd asked Richard and Eira, of course, about the old ruin and its neglect, and he'd listened to their lies and stories and allowed them to change the subject and let it go. Years later, Richard confided in him about the curse of the Kenwards and the ghost that walked among them. He hadn't believed him at the time, but now he did. He'd seen things, heard things; watched death stalk the village and sadly the Kenward family. He was positive the evil spirit of the child had killed the children's mother.

He looked back at the ivy-covered stones and marvelled at its construction. It was amazing architecture, even after five hundred years or more. He stepped a little closer, one foot on the outer bank; Henry howled, which made him jump back and turn to the dogs. They were all restless and fidgeting to go. He looked around, but he saw nothing. A slight breeze moved the branches in the trees and stirred the long grass around the fallen stones, but nothing else moved.

Backing away, the dogs around his heels, they suddenly froze. Every hackle was up. As one, they stared toward the tower. At its base, a dark doorway. Geoff instinctively knew someone was there; so did the dogs. He found his voice at last, and he barked his command. 'Come away, then.'

It was like the starting pistol each dog had been waiting for. They turned and fled, Geoff with them.

He ran as fast as his legs could carry him, the dogs urging him on. He could think of only two things as he fled: *I hope the dogs don't leave me* and *what the hell is coming after me?* The dogs didn't leave him, and as they neared the end of the field, he could see an old stile in the middle of the hedge. Half of it had broken away and was hanging awkwardly to the side. The space, though, was just wide enough to run through and he did, as did the dogs, but he almost stumbled down the slight incline into the lane, the dogs landing neatly on the grass verge.

He stared back at the narrow opening, half-expecting something to appear. Nothing did. He was bent over trying to catch his breath when the dogs began barking. Whirling round, he was confronted with a young woman, a shopping bag in her hand, frozen, staring at him, then at the dogs, then back at him. 'Be still!'

His firm command brought instant relief and the dogs backed off, coming to sit beside him, only Barnaby edged forward, tail wagging slightly, sniffing the woman and her bag.

'I'm sorry I startled you, miss. The dogs won't bite.'

She looked like she wasn't too sure, but she lowered her large shopping bag and attempted to smile.

He realised who she was almost immediately and smiled. 'You're the new tenant.' Without waiting for a reply, he continued, 'I'm Geoff, I work up at the Hall.'

'Oh. I…erm…Bronwen.' She cleared her throat. 'Are…are all these dogs yours?'

He turned and slowly began to walk toward her. 'God, no, these belong to Adam. That's Barnaby. He's a big old softy. That's Toby, Henry, and that old boy there is Roger. You like dogs?'

Bronwen nodded and bent down and let Barnaby lick her hand; she ruffled his ears. 'He's lovely.'

Geoff could see how uncomfortable she was and didn't really blame her. Some strange man comes stumbling out of a hedge with four mad dogs. No wonder she looked scared to death. Did she know what lay beyond the hedge? After all, it wasn't far away. Surely she must have been exploring since she's been here?

He glanced across at her; she was pretty. Not too skinny either; this was nice. 'Are you coming tonight, miss?'

He noticed she blushed at the question and he warmed to her. 'Yes, I'm meeting Eira. Are you going?'

'Aye, I'll be there, stuffing my face with Lucy's pastries. I'll look out for you and, perhaps, I'll save you one!'

His attempt at lightening the mood worked as he was rewarded with another blush and a shy smile. With a wink, he whistled to the dogs and hurried away. At least there would be someone interesting to watch tonight and for the first time in ages, he actually looked forward to the Ball.

**

Bronwen watched him go, her heart finally slowing down to a steadier beat. When he crashed through the hedge with those dogs, she thought her life was over and the hounds of hell had come for her; nothing would surprise her these days.

It hadn't been a conscious decision to get off the bus a stop early, but when she'd realised where she was; it seemed daft to wait while it meandered around for another ten minutes or so to get to the village. Getting off at the side of the dual carriageway had meant a twenty-minute walk straight up to the cottage, avoiding the village, and Eira. The last thing she needed was someone fussing over her tonight. She wanted to arrive and say 'Hello' and leave, not think about it too much.

She smiled to herself as she stared after the man and the dogs. He seemed nice and she did like dogs, just not when they were hurling themselves over stiles that led to haunted ruins. It felt extremely strange being in that lane again in bright sunshine with company when only a couple of weeks before, she had been running for her life, or so she'd thought.

Her legs finally stopped shaking and she walked up her garden path. It was only as she unlocked her front door that she suddenly wondered what had frightened him and the dogs so badly that they'd behave like the Devil himself were after them. If they had come from those ruins, she had no doubt what they might have encountered, and yes, it probably was the Devil, but not Gwenllian…surely?

CHAPTER THIRTY-THREE

ROSALYN STOOD MOTIONLESS AS SHE read through the file given to her by the investigator; it was riveting stuff. She wasn't stupid enough to believe this kind of thing never happened. The news was full of similar stories, but to have the person involved with her own family was too close.

She read it through again, then slowly closed it. Letting her arm fall to her side, she absentmindedly tapped the thin file against her thigh. What was she going to do? She'd come with the intention of telling her father and Adam everything, showing them the file as proof, but now that she was here and having reread the file a fifth time, she was having doubts. The woman had been a child. The case said it had been self-defence, but some people, an aunt, had been convinced that she'd meant to kill. Was this woman really capable of planning a murder and conning the authorities?

She was dying to meet her. She glanced at her watch and realised in a few hours she would. She left the file on top of her dresser and dug out her towel. She'd best get into the bath before anyone else took all the hot water. She needed a good long soak, especially after the hot ride. She felt nervous, excited. And hungry. Looking down at her flat stomach, she cringed; they'd expect her to eat tonight and the thought made her feel sick.

Locking herself in the bathroom, she ran the water and added jasmine bubble bath. She thought about her brother. He was hiding his loneliness very well, considering. If only evil bitches had some kind of mark, everyone would see them for what they really were; perhaps, then, he'd be safe from them. Catherine had been a real professional bitch. No-one had seen that one coming, well, no-one except Eira, but then, she saw everything. Would this one be easy to spot? Was she fat and smelly, with sweat patches under her arms, smelling of piss and body odour? Would she have eyebrows that met in the middle and huge forearms and tattoos? Digging out a half bottle of brandy and her diet pills, she took out two and poured herself a small amount and drank it back in one gulp, for courage, she told herself; she'd never met a killer before.

How would Adam react if she went ahead and told him? She'd left him at the stables with some giant man who'd just arrived with his wife as they finished removing the horses' tack. She'd stared unashamedly at the man, who laughed at her reaction before engulfing her in a gentle hug. She thought her ribs were going to break.

She'd walked back to the Hall with his wife, Brenda, who Rosalyn liked immediately. Judith met them and she'd shown Brenda to their room on the top floor. Slowly easing herself into the hot water, she smiled to herself; if nothing else, this Ball certainly felt as if it was going to be interesting.

**

Eira sipped her chamomile tea and waited impatiently for the pain-killers to work. Her body felt like it was on fire and any movement sent boiling hot pain through every muscle, so she sat very still and waited.

It was half an hour or more before she felt able to continue getting herself ready. Her long, pale blue dress hung on the back of the bedroom door, and she winced as she reached up and got it down. Laying it on her bed, tears burned her eyes. Would this be the last Ball she ever saw? She hoped more than anything that it was.

So many years had passed since she'd found happiness in getting ready for a celebration. The days when men were gallant and gentle-manly, asking the ladies to dance, escorting them onto the floor. Only one man had ever mattered to her, and she'd lost him.

'He was mine first.'

Eira didn't turn around, but continued to stare at her dress. Reaching out, she gently touched the soft cotton fabric. 'Yes, he was.'

'You took me from him.'

Eira didn't answer; there was no need. The answer was always there. She picked up her dress, held it tightly to her body, and let the one runaway tear fall.

***

Bronwen stepped out of the hot shower. She was shaking as she dried herself. She let the water cascade over her for nearly half an hour and now felt sticky and was freely sweating from the heat.

She wiped away the condensation from the mirror and stared; she looked like a big sweating pig. She threw down her towel and stepped into the shower again, yelping as she turned the water to cold.

A few minutes of that was all she could manage, but she felt much better afterward. Her cheeks were still bright pink, but the shock helped her own anxiety about what she was about to do. Quickly drying herself again, she walked naked into her bedroom and sat down at the small dresser. Drops of cold water dripped from her hair and she shivered as they touched her warm back. She stared at her reflection; what was she doing? She didn't have a clue how to behave at these things.

She glanced at the small, red bag in which she kept her makeup collection, which consisted of one black eyeliner, black mascara, and a small, square eye-shadow case that hadn't even been opened. The brown and gold colours shone slightly in the light. She picked up the unused matching lipstick and groaned; she never used make-up.

No-one had ever shown her how to apply it. 'No better time to learn, lady…' She smiled at her reflection, remembering her aunt's opinion on makeup.

'*Only whores paint their faces.*'

Her aunt would glare at her, ranting and raving about 'whores and women these days'. '*No morals…no dignity, it's no wonder men treat them like the whores they are.*'

She stared now at the black pencil in her hand. She knew she wasn't a whore, or a bad girl, for wanting to make her blue eyes look a bit better, but it was hard not to ignore all those years of verbal abuse. Her hands shook as she began applying it to her face, and twice she had to stop and wipe it away as she'd made a mess. The end result wasn't that bad and she turned her attention to her long hair.

***

The large camp was bustling with men. Some played cards around the many fires that littered the field, while others chatted about the day and what was to come. Others took advantage of the women who frequently followed camps to earn a penny or two. Some men sat alone, silently staring into the embers, a tankard of ale in their hands, contemplating their life and death if they failed in their quest.

William had seen it all before. He wandered around his men and many others, introducing himself and exchanging banter, but on the inside, he was screaming. His thoughts raged around his head, about Anne, their dead son, and his Gwenllian. How could it happen again? Hadn't he prayed enough? Had his union with his wife brought on early labour? Was it his fault? Was it hers?

Every muscle in his body wanted to ride like the Devil to his home, to see his son before they placed him in the earth, but he could not. He wanted to take Anne in his arms and comfort her. At the same time, he wanted to beat her senseless; if indeed they were partners in crime for his son's death, then they should pay. His torment might be death on the battlefield, but hers should be from him for failing him in her duty yet again.

He loved her, of that he had no doubt. It burned within him as he fought with his desire to beat her half to death. How could he love a woman so madly if she was so useless to him? He needed sons. His wife was not helping his ambitions. Rhys didn't have problems with raising bastards as his own. Why should he? Anne wouldn't like it. Damn the woman. If he couldn't rely on her womb, then he should find another who would give him an heir.

'My lord!' Dafydd's shout broke into his thoughts and he turned, unsmiling, to the soldier. 'I've just heard that the Sheriff of Shrewsbury did indeed lie down in the dust and allow Henry to walk over him. Is that true?'

William nodded slowly and sat down next to his tent. 'It is indeed. He had told King Richard that Henry would only get into Shrewsbury over his dead body. He may not have been dead, but he found a way to keep his honour. Thomas is a good man.'

Dafydd sensed William's low mood and quietly went to fetch a jug of ale. A pig roasted on a spit nearby and he cut a few slices for both of them. Bringing the small meal back to where William sat unmoving, he thrust the jug and the plate of meat at his master; William took them without a word. 'My lord, do you wish the messenger to take back a message from you? I know he is waiting nearby.'

William looked up at where Dafydd indicated and saw a young boy waiting, a chunk of cheese in one hand, standing near a large cauldron of steaming stew. 'No, there is nothing to say. Perhaps he could send a kiss for my Gwenllian.' He hesitated. 'And, perhaps, tell my steward, Andrew, I will be home as soon as God allows...' He knew the message would also reach Anne. It was all he could give her for now.

Dafydd nodded once, went over to the boy, and gave him his instructions. William stared at the food and the ale and put the plate down. If nothing else, he would get roaring drunk, perhaps find a wench who was willing, and forget his useless, adorable wife. If he was to die on the battlefield, he should at least try to enjoy his last days on the Earth.

***

Her heart was racing as she walked along the lane toward the Kenward gates. They were wide open and small white fairy lights were hung along the top spikes. As she reached them, a car passed her with five people crammed into it. Another car drove into the estate and she quickly followed over the cattle grid before another one came. She could see small groups of people ahead of her. The butterflies that had been flapping inside her stomach suddenly got bigger wings. She felt physically sick.

'My dear, slow down!'

She turned, relieved, as Eira walked toward her.

Eira grinned as her eyes travelled over her dress and back up to her hair, which she'd managed to put up into a loose bun.

Wisps of hair floated around her face and tickled as the breeze caught them.

'You look amazing, Bronwen!'

Bronwen blushed and looked down. Her hand immediately covered her mouth as she tried to hide a smile. Eira reached over and took hold of her hand and pulled it through her arm. Linked, they turned as one toward the Hall. 'How do you feel? You look absolutely terrified, my dear.'

Bronwen knew Eira could feel her shaking, so there wasn't any use in pretending. 'To be honest, I feel like throwing up, I'm so scared. I...I don't do this type of thing.'

Eira tutted. 'A young woman like you! Well, all I can say, it's about time. You look good enough to eat, that dress is lovely!'

'That's what I'm afraid of.' It came out before Bronwen could stop herself.

Eira stopped and turned to her. 'My dear, no-one is going to hurt you here. I don't know what life you've had, but tonight, it will be different. Now, come on, we'll walk slowly so I can catch my breath, what do you say?'

Taking a deep breath, Bronwen let it out slowly. 'Okay, let's do this then.'

'You know, you look so lovely, your dance card will be overflowing tonight!'

'Dance card!'

Eira laughed and clung tighter. 'I'm only kidding. I won't leave your side, unless, of course, you want me to!' she said with a wink.

They carried on walking. People passed them, and Eira nodded and smiled but didn't stop to introduce her, which Bronwen was grateful for. If she was going to have to meet these people, she preferred it to be in a big crowd so it was over and done with, then they had other people to talk to when conversation ran out with her, as it always had. After all, what did she have to talk about?

Eira was still talking about the various people who lived at the Hall. 'Do you know, everyone goes on a diet after tonight as they all put on a few pounds! Lucy is a wonderful cook, but a terrible gossip!'

Bronwen giggled, but said nothing.

Eira continued. 'There's Judith of course, lovely woman, been with the family for ages. And there's Rosalyn, down from Chester for the weekend.'

Bronwen frowned. 'Who's Rosalyn?'

'She's Adam's younger sister. We hardly see her anymore. She has a couple of shops, selling clothes and accessories. Perhaps you know it?'

Bronwen shook her head and carried on walking; they were almost up to the front garden.

Eira watched her closely for a moment before carrying on. 'Then there's Sir Richard, of course, he's a lovely man, and Adam, who you've met. Oh, don't look like that; he's nice once you know him! Here we are.'

Bronwen stopped and looked up at the front of the three-storey building. Its black and white timbered frame was stunning. She noticed it had been rebuilt at both ends with stone and had mullioned windows on each floor. She could see where a few windows had been bricked over and thought that was sad. She could see funny-shaped chimneys and wondered why they were spiralled. Eira was ahead of her in the front porch, itself a dark oak timber frame and beyond it, a huge wooden, front door with studs all over it. 'It's beautiful. When was it built?'

Eira grinned. It was a lovely house, sometimes she forgot. 'The foundations go back to the fifteenth century, but what you see is mostly sixteenth, with a few additions over the years. I believe Sir Richard's great-great-grandfather did rather a lot of alterations in the late eighteen hundreds. If I remember correctly, he modernised the kitchen and brought the toilets inside the Hall!'

Eira bit her tongue. It would be so easy to tell her, here and now, how she knew that. Not from some book, but how she'd helped him choose the colours and been the one who'd finally persuaded him to bring the bathrooms inside. After his wife died, it had only been she who could persuade him to do anything. He'd have let the Hall go to ruins.

She was looking up at the windows, now ablaze with lights. They could hear classical music and Eira sighed. Bronwen raised an eyebrow. Eira smiled. 'I like the waltz. Come on, it's time. Take a deep breath and you'll be fine.'

Walking onto the porch, the huge door opened as if by magic. Taking a deep breath as suggested, Bronwen followed Eira into the brightly lit hallway and tried to ignore her butterflies.

They were met by an elderly gentleman with white hair, bright, gentle eyes, and a warm smile. He greeted Eira with a hug before turning to Bronwen and offering his hand. Taking it gingerly, he smiled as she quickly let go. 'Fabulous to finally meet you, Miss Mortimer. How's the cottage?'

Bronwen could feel her cheeks getting warm and cleared her throat. 'Fine, thanks.' She met his gaze for a moment and quickly looked away at the dark panelled walls and the various pictures, a deer's head and antlers, and a shining coat of armour with two swords crossed above it. She knew she was being watched by Eira and Sir Richard and turned back to them. 'It's…lovely.' She nodded toward the swords. 'Are they real?'

Sir Richard smiled warmly. 'Yes, they are. Come from the First World War, so they're not that old, but we do have older ones if you're interested in antiques?'

Bronwen knew what he was doing. No-one knew anything about her history, her work, or where she'd got her money from. She couldn't blame him, really. It was only natural to wonder how a non-working tenant paid for a cottage for a year. He was digging and he knew she knew and he grinned mischievously. 'Sorry, I won't pry. Enjoy your evening.'

'Oh, Richard! See to your other guests. I'll look for you for a dance later.' Eira winked at him and led Bronwen down the hall and into a large room. 'He's a good man, you know.' Eira whispered. 'He's one of the good guys.'

'Yes, I believe he is.' Bronwen looked back as Sir Richard greeted another couple. He caught her watching him and smiled; she couldn't help but smile back. He was a good guy and, for a brief moment, she was very pleased to have come.

***

Rosalyn stood on the gallery looking down at the arriving guests. She held her breath when Eira walked in followed by a stranger; this had to be the mysterious Miss Mortimer. Her father's greeting confirmed it. She looked nothing like she'd expected. She wasn't particularly stunning, but she had to admit, she was pretty, curvy certainly, not skinny. Her hair was piled on top of her small head in a loose bun and it really emphasised her face and slim neck. The green velvet dress she wore was lovely. She wondered where she'd got it.

Rosalyn sipped her red wine and frowned. This woman looked uncomfortable, not confident in the slightest, and certainly not the type of woman Adam would go for. He liked strong women, not this frightened pussycat. Or was it an act? It was possible. She had been hiding a secret for many years; perhaps she'd become a finely tuned actress? If so, she was doing a bloody good act.

Eira was escorting her. It almost looked like she was holding her up. From her vantage point, she thought the woman was shaking. She was about to make her own entrance when she saw Miss Mortimer look back at her father and smile. So, she wasn't a frightened rabbit, after all. Walking quickly down the stairs, she saw her father smile back. She would put a stop to that as soon as possible.

**

As they stepped into the large room, the live band was playing a jazz number. Eira told her that it was the Great Hall and explained that Sir Richard's father had separated the room with a wooden partition, which was wide open. She could see that whatever furniture had been in there had been removed and wooden chairs were against the walls. Groups of people talked and laughed. Many glanced her way and then resumed their conversations. Bronwen kept her gaze on the wooden floor.

She allowed Eira to lead her into the farthest corner where a small bar had been set up. Glasses of white and red wine stood on silver trays. Bronwen took a glass of red, while Eira ordered a gin and tonic from one of the two barmen. She could feel eyes burning into her back and she pulled the cream shawl closer around her shoulders.

Eira noticed her doing it. 'Don't worry, my dear, they're all willing themselves to come over and talk to you. Once they've done that, you'll be fine. It's a bit like a pack of dogs. They'll sniff round you, see if you're acceptable, and then they'll accept you!'

Eira laughed at her own joke.

Bronwen smiled, but she looked worried. 'I don't want to be sniffed at, Eira, I just want to be left alone. Why did I say I'd come?'

Eira gently patted her arm. 'You said you'd come, because deep down, you knew it was the right thing to do. If you want to live here, you need to meet these people, get to know them, so you're not living in perpetual fear all the time, eh?'

'I suppose you're right.' She took a sip of her wine and tried to relax. Turning to face the other guests, she found it strangely easier if she could imagine them as dogs; she much preferred animals. She caught the eye of one woman and smiled at her. The old woman immediately smiled back and whispered to her male companion who in turn looked and smiled. *Perhaps this isn't going to be too bad after all*, she thought.

'Bronwen, this is Geoff, he works here. Any odd jobs, like that garden gate, he's your man.'

Bronwen turned back to Eira and quickly shook the offered hand of the man in the lane.

Smiling, he turned to Eira. 'We've already met. I scared the living daylights out of this poor lady this afternoon.' Turning back to Bronwen who was blushing crimson, he spoke softly. 'I hope you recovered from my sudden appearance with the dogs.'

'Yes, I was fine, thanks. Where are the dogs now?'

'Oh, they're all down at my bungalow, behind the stables. They'd eat all the food if we left them up here.' Leaning forward, he whispered, 'Besides, Judith would have a screaming fit if the dogs were allowed in the Hall and made too much mess!'

'Where were you, Geoff, to be frightening my poor friend?' Eira was listening with interest.

'Oh, nowhere really, just up the lane, near the cottage.' Looking in the direction of the buffet table, he smacked his lips together. 'If you'll excuse me ladies, I see a pork pie with my name on it. Oh, Miss Mortimer, I couldn't help noticing your hedges. Perhaps I could help you with those? Just let me know.'

The two women watched him go, nodding his head to those he passed on his way to the long table groaning with food. Bronwen wondered why he'd been reluctant to tell Eira where he'd come from? Were the field and the ruins out of bounds or something?

She had no time to dwell on it; as soon as Geoff moved off, another person took his place, then another, and another. All used the excuse of saying hello to Eira, but it was obvious it was Bronwen they wanted to meet. After the first few initial enquiries and digging into her past and present, she found it easier to step back and to just be a part of a group of people. They were all talking about people and places she didn't know, but it felt quite comfortable after a while to be a part of something. She actually felt herself start to relax by the second glass of wine.

***

Adam watched her from the corner of the room. He was surrounded by people, just as she was, and he was pretending to be listening, like she was. She looked nervous and completely out of place, but beautiful in that velvet gown and the cream shawl emphasised her breasts and shoulders. Far longer than decent, his attention fell on them.

He could hardly believe that this was the same woman he'd first encountered outside the Hall gates and then again at Shrewsbury Castle. He could see elements of the same frightened rabbit he'd rescued. He could just see a slight bruise on her arm, almost faded, and had a sudden urge to kiss it better.

'...so, that's when he hit it full swing and damned if it didn't go for bloody miles, eh, Adam?'

'I'm sorry, what?' He pulled his attention back to his friend who laughed and looked over his shoulder. 'Oh, I see what's got your attention, quite a filly!'

414

Adam glanced back at Bronwen, but she had become lost amongst the growing crowd. 'She's our new tenant up at the cottage. So, Graeme, you were saying about the cricket?'

'Oh no, no, no, I want to hear about this new filly you can't keep your eyes off.'

Adam finished the last of his pint and quietly belched. 'There's nothing to say. Her name's Bronwen Mortimer, not sure how old she is, and she's a tenant for at least a year.'

Graeme playfully punched his arm. 'Oh come on. You must know something about her. Where does she come from? What does she do?'

Adam shrugged and lit a rolled cigarette. 'Haven't a clue. Come on, fancy another?' He waved his empty pint glass at his friend and without waiting, made his way toward the bar; he knew Graeme would follow. Bronwen was amongst a large crowd gathered in the middle of the room. He felt grateful that she wasn't anywhere near his old mate. As a drinking friend, he was fine, but he could be just a little bit tactless sometimes, which had got them in a few brawls over the years. He didn't want him blurting out anything untoward at Bronwen; he instinctively knew it would frighten her, and strangely, that was the last thing he wanted.

***

Bronwen sat down. Her feet were killing her and her stomach was growling so loudly, she knew everyone would hear it, even over the band. They were pretty good, playing a few slow ones, and then moving onto a few faster numbers. They'd just finished a jive, and couples were making their way off the dance floor, fanning themselves as they flopped down in any empty seats.

A few people smiled politely in her direction and she found herself smiling back. She knew she looked flushed and should probably slow down on the wine, but holding her third glass gave her something to focus on. She desperately wanted two things: the toilet and food.

She was trying to pluck up enough courage for the first one when Eira came toward her, a young, skinny woman in tow.

'Bronwen, let me introduce you to Rosalyn.'

'Erm, pleased to meet you.'

'How do you like Oak Cottage?' Rosalyn's tone was blunt.

Bronwen flinched. 'Fine, thanks.'

'So I've heard. Paid for a year, didn't you? Not many people can do that.'

The animosity was clear in Rosalyn's voice and Eira stepped forward, but Bronwen abruptly stood and smiled as sweetly as she could. 'Yes, I did, and I'm enjoying being there, makes quite a change from the palace I'm used to.' Turning to Eira, she continued. 'Could you show me where the toilets are, please?'

Without waiting, she forced her wobbly legs to walk toward the farthest door where she noticed other women heading and hoped she was correct; she was. Eira caught her up and together they joined the small queue outside the downstairs bathroom.

Eira was laughing to herself. 'I don't think I've ever seen Rosalyn lost for words before, well done!'

Bronwen leant against the wall. 'I don't know what came over me. Perhaps I should apologise?'

Eira stopped laughing and stood in front of her. 'You dare apologise to her. She was being downright rude, for some reason, I'll be finding out why tomorrow. Go on now, toilet is free. You look a bit flushed. Cold water will do you good. I'll wait for you here.'

Thankful, Bronwen locked the door behind her and felt a mixture of relief as she emptied her full bladder and horror at what she had just said to Adam's sister. Okay, her tone hadn't been very nice, but did she really care?

The cold water on her cheeks felt good. It also felt good to have answered back, if she were honest to herself; none of this turning the other cheek nonsense her aunt had always drilled into her. Where had her courage come from? Two glasses of red wine probably helped. She shook her finger at her reflection. Naughty, naughty!

Checking her dress, she hitched it up slightly; even though it hadn't moved, it clung to her bosom like a glove. Rosalyn didn't have much of a figure. Very flat, too skinny, anorexic, most likely. She stared at her reflection. *At least I've got my health*, she thought and felt quite sorry for Rosalyn.

She found that she was actually having quite a nice time. The villagers were friendly, a bit pushy, but nothing she hadn't expected. Sir Richard had come over a few times and exchanged pleasantries with Eira and tried to involve her too. The only person she hadn't spoken to yet was Adam. Would he show up? Why would she care?

Refreshed, she'd joined Eira, who was still smiling. 'Feel better? Good. I think it's time to eat. You've done very well, considering; you've worked up an appetite, I'll bet.'

Bronwen allowed herself to be led back into the Hall. She followed Eira toward the long table of food. Picking up a plate, a napkin, and a fork, she slowly walked along the table.

At one end were a variety of meats, slices of beef, ham, turkey, and chicken wings, a large salmon, prawns in garlic butter and scampi with lemon wedges. There were different types of salad, including a large bowl of potato salad, a bean salad, and what she'd call a usual salad, and every type of fruit she could possibly think of cut up and arranged in the shape of a huge flower. In the middle were baskets of crusty cobs that smelt fresh. Beside these were knobs of butter in a long dish. Next to these were homemade pork pies, Cornish pasties, spinach and cheese lattices, and three types of quiche. There were various types of cheeses and crackers, rice and pasta dishes and, at the farthest end, her mouth watered at the variety of fresh cream delights on offer. A large lemon meringue pie, a chocolate gateau, strawberries and mango, a large bowl of trifle, and a pyramid of profiteroles with chocolate sauce cascading down them. A large jug of cream finished off the ensemble. She agreed with Eira; she would be going on a diet after all this.

'Looks wonderful, doesn't it, ladies? Eat up or you'll have us men down at the gym working it all off!'

'Richard! As if you'd go to a gym!' Eira replied, laughing.

Bronwen smiled and started putting some pasta on her plate. The band stopped for a break and most people were making their way toward the table. She felt the familiar panic begin to rise. She always felt hurried and went to pieces if there were too many people waiting for her to finish. She followed Eira along the table, slowly filling her plate, but then she began to think people would say she had too much!

Eira seemed to sense her change in mood and looked back at her. 'Take your time, there's plenty for everyone.'

Sir Richard heard her comment and came over. He gently patted Bronwen's arm. 'I get nervous too. I always think I look greedy if I pile my plate high, but I still do, because this is Lucy's cooking and everyone in here will do the same. So, you go ahead and have what you like.' He squeezed her arm affectionately and moved on to another person. Bronwen watched him as he moved from one person to another, always smiling, having a joke. She smiled; if only she'd had a father like that.

Her smile froze on her face as she met Adam's stare across the room. He was standing with his sister, who was busy talking to an older woman whom she recognised as Judith. Adam wasn't listening to their conversation, he was watching her, a strange look on his face. She looked away first.

CHAPTER THIRTY-FOUR

S IR RHYS AP THOMAS STRODE into the chamber confidently and poured himself a goblet of wine. Seeing his friend's face, he poured him one too and set it down in front of him. Sitting opposite William, he drank his down fast and reached for another. William hadn't touched his or seemed to notice it was there.

It had been two months since the battle of Bosworth. Two months since Rhys had been made a Knight Bachelor and William given the honour of becoming Sheriff of Shrewsbury. There had been a great celebration, but later that night, in private, William gave back the title, against Rhys' advice. King Henry had been offended by his behaviour, but had had more important issues to deal with and had granted Sir William's wish that the old Sheriff should remain as a loyal subject. After all, he allowed Henry into the city without a fight.

Henry had glowered down on William who knelt before him. He didn't need this fuss over honour and whether or not he had earned it. He had a country to subdue and those living in it to accept him as their King and his darling wife, Elizabeth, as their Queen. He quickly glanced across at her and she smiled, giving him a slight nod, before turning to face the room.

She contemplated the man kneeling before her husband. She understood his problem and felt pity for the man. Henry was a soldier; he would never understand William's dilemma. William was an honest man. She hadn't met many of those in her lifetime; she liked him. What

419

had to be done in the name of politics was too horrible to dwell on, but it was done and there was no going back. He had followed his king's wishes and it now haunted the man. His grief was etched on his face.

'My Lord Henry, perhaps we can find another honour to bestow onto this worthy man. After all, his was the hand that killed your foe. Some land, perhaps, to build a new home that isn't tainted by… by this tragedy.'

Henry turned to look at his wife, and she was right, of course. The sooner he gave this man something, the sooner he could forget him and get on with being King. 'Very well, you are right. Sir William, I understand your predicament regarding your actions, but you were the man whose blade cut down my enemy. I cannot forget that, so I give you the village and all the lands between it and Ludlow. I also grant you the title Governor of Ludlow and you will help oversee its growth and the restoration of the castle there.'

Crouching down, he whispered in William's ear, 'I give you this, but do not reject my offer again, or you will have nothing regardless of what you did for me. Grieve your children and move on.'

William slowly stood up and bowed low to his new King and Queen. Turning to leave, he caught his friend's eye, who was nodding and smiling at him. He acknowledged him before leaving the chamber with a heavy and broken heart.

Sir Rhys had now come to find him and to celebrate their honourable titles. Rhys poured another and slammed it down in front of his friend, who jumped back, surprised.

Rhys was trying hard not to lose his temper and was breathing heavily. 'Damn it, man! The King has given you riches and power and you sit here as if he ignored you. After all that you did. I don't understand you! He's changed your name from Cenwearde, which you told me meant "*bold guardian*", to Cynwearde, which means "*royal guardian*". You are a hero, William, whether you like it or not.'

'I don't like it!' William swept his hand across the table, sending the goblets and the jug to the floor, spilling red wine everywhere. 'I hate this. I wish I had died on that battlefield and not come home to…to this.' His face crumpled and he finally let the tears fall. 'How can I live with myself? My boy, my darling Gwenllian…my…wife… Nia. Oh God! What have I done?'

Rhys watched his old friend for a long time, his own emotions close to the surface. He forced them back inside. He would never forget the scene that greeted them as they rode into the village of Derwen or what waited for them at William's home. A hero's homecoming had been tragically snatched away. Instead, a murder trial and a hanging awaited.

'It will haunt me until my dying day and beyond for what I did, and I want it to, I deserve to burn in Hell for it.' William sniffed, but the tears kept coming and eventually he couldn't talk anymore.

Rhys' hand shook as he picked up the goblets and placed them on the table. He left the shattered jug and went in search of another. William remained unmoved until Rhys returned and poured himself another goblet full. 'William, it had to be done. Justice had to be seen to, don't you see? Henry could not have tolerated such a scandal. His enemies would have used you as a pawn against him. Can you not see how it could have been used against our King? He could not honour the man who'd slain Richard when that man's wife was a…'

'Murderer.' William finished the sentence for him.

Rhys nodded slowly and sat down heavily beside his friend. Silence fell as they remembered the horror that had awaited them. There was nothing Rhys could say to ease his friend's burden. A sacrifice had had to be made, plain and simple. He had nothing personal against the woman, but sadly, politics demanded it and so it was done. Now, it was time to move on, gain power, and help bring peace to the country; that would be their penance.

'You know what might do you good, old friend? Seeing life as it can be. You have brought happiness to these people by slaying that tyrant King Richard. The people hated him for his arrogance and his greed. You should celebrate that, with your people, your tenants, show them that you can be merciful and kind, but also show them that you are not someone to be afraid of, a man of the people…what you need, my friend, is a celebration of some sort.'

***

'Adam!' Eira saw him and called him over. 'Have you been avoiding me? You've met Bronwen, I believe.'

He nodded in her direction, then turned his back on her and gave Eira a big hug. 'Of course I haven't been avoiding you, just busy. What are you having? It all looks so good, doesn't it?'

Lucy heard his comment and gave him a beaming smile. Bronwen saw it; did everyone like this man? Determined to ignore him and keep well away from him, she walked away from the table and headed for an empty seat, followed closely by Eira. 'Didn't feel like talking to him, dear?'

'Certainly not!' She could feel herself blushing and put her head down, concentrating on her food. She became aware that Eira was still watching her and she sighed. 'He isn't a very nice person, you know.'

Eira raised her eyebrow, questioning. 'Really?'

Bronwen forked a piece of pasta, but after a moment, let it fall gently back onto her plate. 'Well, I guess, he can be nice. He helped me…you see, I got myself into a bit of a dilemma.' Seeing Eira's concern, she quickly added, 'Oh, it's all right now, but, you see, Adam was there, in Shrewsbury and, okay, I will concede, he can be a gentleman… perhaps…' Needing to get off the subject of Adam and his sister, she quickly added. 'The only Kenward I do like, which did surprise me, is Sir Richard. He seems so kind and—'

'I am glad to hear it. I rather like you too.'

Bronwen jumped and turned to find Sir Richard smiling down at her, a piece of ham in one hand, a large brandy in the other. 'Seems we like each other so much. Perhaps I can claim a dance later?' His slurred speech made her wonder just how many brandies he'd had in the past hour.

'A dance? No…I don't…'

Ignoring her, he grinned. 'I'm so glad. Looking forward to it.' Bending down, he whispered. 'I'm sure my moody son will be delighted too.'

'Oh go away with you.' Eira shooed him away. 'Poor woman's trying to eat. She doesn't want her food pickled in brandy fumes!'

Richard laughed loudly before stuffing the slice of ham into his mouth as he wandered over to the band, just coming back from their half-hour break.

Bronwen watched him go; suddenly all hunger had gone, and she felt sick with fear. Eira patted her knee. 'Don't worry, dear, he's so drunk, he'll probably forget. He was right, though, you should dance. You're young and alive. Might as well enjoy life while you can.'

Something in her tone made Bronwen turn to her but she let the question go. She didn't want to dwell on the possibility of making a fool of herself on the dance floor. Instead, she nibbled on a piece of salmon and looked around the room. Above Eira's head was an old picture of the Hall, painted in watercolours; it was pretty good. 'That's good,' she said quietly, pointing to the picture.

Eira glanced over her shoulder and smiled. 'Yes, that was painted by Rosalyn when she was fifteen, I think. She did it for the Ball held that year. For something different, everyone was to make something that could be sold at a fair. Not many villagers bothered, but Rosalyn did that. Richard said it was too good to sell and hung it there.'

Bronwen looked closer at the painting. 'It is very good. I suppose she is talented, then.'

'Yes. Besides her manners, Rosalyn is a talented lady.'

'How long has the May Ball been held, then?' Bronwen tucked into a chicken and cheese quiche.

Eira watched her for a moment before answering. 'It started in the fifteenth century, not long after Henry Tudor came to the throne, and carried on ever since.' She looked down at the plate on her lap.

Seeing the sudden change, Bronwen reached out tentatively and touched Eira's arm. 'Why did they start?'

Eira's head snapped up and she seemed to shake herself out of her sudden low mood. 'Oh, I don't really know, Bronwen. I need another drink. Fancy another wine?'

Without waiting, Eira stood up quickly and put her untouched plate on the chair. Bronwen watched her go. Had she said something wrong? She decided to do a bit of digging. If she could find enough courage, she'd ask Sir Richard about these May Balls; perhaps it might lead to some answers.

***

Adam found Rosalyn sitting at the bottom of the stairs and sat down beside her. He had his own beer in one hand and a glass of white wine in the other. He offered this to his sister. She took it with a grateful smile and sipped it. He'd been watching her to see if she'd eat anything; she had, but disappeared into the bathroom soon after. One look at her pale, clammy face told him she'd thrown it all up. 'Hey, sis, will this put a smile on your face?' He indicated the glass of wine.

'You can talk! You've been moping around since this stupid Ball started,' she snapped back. 'The only time I've seen you smile was with Eira and that Mortimer woman.'

He was shocked by the venom in her voice. 'What the hell is this? If you had been watching my mingling, you'll have seen me smiling and laughing with Joseph and Brenda, who I've talked to almost nonstop since they arrived this evening. I also laughed loudly when Graeme told a funny joke. I've even had a small flirtatious moment with Lucy over her pork pies. If you say something funny, I'll smile at you.'

He watched her fighting the urge to smile; she lost and punched him in the arm.

'All right, I'm not feeling too good, that's all.' They sat in silence until she broke it and asked, 'Do you know this woman?'

He knew she meant Bronwen and shook his head. 'Not really, met her once or twice.'

He could see her from where he sat. So could Rosalyn and she was watching her intently. 'Do you know her or something, 'cause you're acting like you hate her.'

Rosalyn sipped her wine and didn't answer straightaway. He could see her fighting with what to say and it puzzled him. Rosalyn had been acting secretive and hiding papers from him when he'd entered her room unannounced. Was she in some kind of trouble? He was about to ask her when he heard Bronwen's name being mentioned for the fourth time by another small group of villagers who stood near the doorway; they hadn't noticed Adam and Rosalyn. He glanced at Rosalyn and noticed how she behaved when she also heard Bronwen's name, and he frowned. 'Come on then, spill the beans.'

'It's nothing, really. I just don't like her. She's jumpy and acts all shy and coy, but she doesn't fool me.'

Adam laughed. 'Bloody hell! So you don't actually know her?'

Rosalyn shook her head.

'Well, I don't either, but...' He was about to say that he believed that she was frightened for real, but decided not to. 'I haven't heard one bad thing about her. She's definitely the topic of the evening, which isn't a bad thing, considering I thought everyone would be sad and depressed talking about Mathew. Perhaps we should give her the benefit of the doubt?'

'The benefit of the doubt! Jesus, Adam! That's not like you!' Rosalyn looked astounded and shook her head. 'I never thought I'd see the day my brother would give some stranger the benefit of the doubt.'

Adam drank his beer. 'I think you've had enough. The wine has obviously gone straight to your head and bypassed your empty stomach.'

Rosalyn abruptly stopped laughing and was about to retaliate when she noticed Eira staring at them from the Hall doorway.

'You two should be ashamed of yourselves.' She spoke in a hushed voice and came toward them, two glasses of wine in her hands. 'It took a lot of guts for this young lady to come tonight. You should know why, Adam. I must say, I'm disappointed in you both.'

Adam frowned and opened his mouth to ask if she knew about Shrewsbury but Eira turned to Rosalyn. 'Go and get something to eat, dear, the skinny, malnourished look is definitely not the fashion.'

Rosalyn flounced off toward the bar looking indignant. Eira turned her attention to him. 'The band has started up again. Perhaps you should start the ball rolling and ask Bronwen to dance?'

'What? I don't think...' Adam stood up, towering over her.

Eira stood her ground. 'She's finished her food and I was getting her another glass of wine.' Thrusting the red wine into his hand, she grinned sheepishly. 'But I think you'd prefer to take it to her and ask her to dance.' She turned and walked away before he could argue.

He felt very foolish at being caught bitching about Bronwen. He finished the rest of his beer in three mouthfuls and left the empty pint glass on the stair. If he was going to do this, he might as well get it over with, and besides, if he allowed himself to be completely honest, the idea of holding Miss Mortimer wasn't a particularly horrible one.

***

Bronwen saw him from the corner of her eye and knew instinctively he was coming over to her. She felt eyes watching both her and his approach, and the food she'd eaten suddenly became a heavy weight in her stomach. He stopped in front of her, saying nothing. She knew she couldn't ignore him as everyone was watching them, so she forced her head to move and she looked up at him. He held a glass of wine, but he gently placed it on the table beside her.

He grinned. 'Can I have this dance, Miss Mortimer?' He held out his hand and waited, his eyes never leaving hers.

Her glance darted left and right; they were all watching and waiting. She could feel herself sweating. 'I…erm…no, thank you, I don't—'

It was as far as she got before he bent down and gently pulled her to her feet. A few people nearby clapped their approval and smiled warmly as he escorted her onto the wooden floor. Other couples were also dancing slowly around them as he wrapped one arm around her waist and clamped the other around her hand. The music was some slow number, but she wasn't focused on what it was, only where she was.

'What the hell do you think you're doing?' she snapped through gritted teeth

He smiled sweetly at her. 'Dancing with you. I thought it was the least you could do.' The heartrending look on her face made him wish more than anything he could take it back. 'Look, I was being hassled to dance with you. One dance and they'll leave us alone. I thought I might have been doing you a favour as well as myself.'

'I don't need any favours from you.'

Their eyes locked and he saw the flash of anger. For the first time in his life, he was annoyed with Eira for putting both of them in this situation. Why had she done it? Why had he allowed it?

'Let go of me,' she whispered at him.

He quickly glanced around the room, then back at her upturned face. 'If I let you go now, they'll all be talking about it. Is that what you want?'

He felt her stiffen in his arm and he thought she was going to fight her way out, but then she sagged against him and shook her head. He held her tighter. 'The song's almost over. If you can keep your defences up for just a little bit longer…'

'I hate you!' she mumbled and stared at his shoulder as he shuffled her around in a slow circle. He could feel her heart hammering against his chest. She was hot, her palms were sweaty, her neck and face were flushed, but he couldn't help it. He enjoyed holding her. It was like holding a terrified kitten but he didn't doubt either that somewhere within this kitten a fire burned. She had been hurt in some way, he was certain of it. Why else would she be so frightened and defensive? He wanted to protect her.

Suddenly, she broke free. The band started into a faster song. With as much dignity as she could muster, she walked quickly out of the Great Hall, her back straight, looking at no-one. He watched her leave and felt tempted to follow her, but Joseph strode purposefully toward him, two pints in his hands and he was dragged into a conversation about fillies and stallions. Bronwen would have to wait.

***

'Bastard! Bastard!' was all she could mutter under her breath. How could he do that to her after rescuing her? Men just wanted to touch and humiliate her; she'd been right all along about him. The thought hurt more than she'd expected. She deliberately walked toward the main front door, which now stood ajar to let the cool air in. Wrapping the shawl tighter around her shoulders, she stepped out into the porch. It felt a lot chillier after the heat of the room and her sweat-soaked body quickly cooled enough to feel comfortable again. Stepping farther away from the Hall, she wandered from the front garden and walked around to the side of the large house.

It was quiet. She could see quite well, as four large lamps illuminated the front of the Hall and their light reached parts of the sides too. They gave off a warm orange glow that made Kenward Hall look rather beautiful. 'Damn Adam Kenward!' She let her breathing slow and tried to rationalise what he'd done. He'd rescued her again, she knew that now, and he'd been right. But she couldn't decide if he'd done it out of spite, a drunken joke, or a desire to actually dance with her. This was all too new to her...

The hand that suddenly clutched her arm was icy cold and completely surprised her. The shock of contact took her breath away;

all she could manage was a croaked sound as her throat closed over and she couldn't breathe. Her eyes bulged as she fought for oxygen. She stumbled to her knees. The hand never left her arm; it gripped like a vice.

She stared into the eyes of Gwenllian.

A flash of red-hot pain shot through her body and she convulsed. Falling, she lay on her back, fighting for breath; she felt the world spin faster and faster, and it felt as if she were falling, yet, somewhere deep in her logic, she knew she couldn't be as she was already on her back.

Her fingers tore at an invisible obstruction wrapped around her neck, but they touched nothing but her own skin. She heard voices, shouting and screaming, and smelt fire and its thick, acrid smoke. She fought against it, but it was no use and she knew it. This was her nightmare, but she was awake and this time, she couldn't escape. Her last sensation was the cold, wet grass beneath her body and then the darkness came.

***

The child sighed. Eira promised she would find a way to get this woman alone. Bending down to the unconscious body, she gently stroked the pale face. 'It is good to see you again, my dear friend…it is time to remember.'

CHAPTER THIRTY-FIVE

DESPITE JAMES'S INITIAL PROMISE TO himself that he wouldn't get drunk, by the time the two women finally arrived an hour late, drinking on an empty stomach made him feel quite tipsy. Looking across at Gordon, who every now and then would stare off into space, he realised he was much worse and wondered if anything would actually happen tonight.

He staggered slightly as he heaved himself up, Gordon met the girls enthusiastically, groping Susan's arse and winking at the woman next to her. He turned to James and flicked his head in the direction of Clare's breasts. 'Fine specimens, eh, James!'

Susan slapped him playfully. 'Gordon! Stop it! Drinks, meal, and then you can admire Clare's tits!' She gave James a quick smile before she walked off with Gordon in tow to the bar. Clare squeezed in next to him in the booth.

He eyed her openly and liked what he saw. Gordon was right. She was very well endowed and what she wore hardly covered any of it. She was a bit chubby for his usual taste and the clothes she wore looked cheap, but tonight wasn't about class It was about having fun. She certainly looked the type of woman who liked fun.

She watched him looking her over and leant forward so her cleavage showed off its full splendour. 'Like what you see, then?'

He swallowed and tried to avert his eyes from her bosom. He felt a stirring in his trousers and shuffled in the seat. Clare grinned and laid a hand on his thigh. 'I can ease that for you.'

He looked at her creeping hand as it slowly made its way toward his groin. Placing his own over hers, he smiled. 'Ah yes, but the expectation is just as sweet.'

She removed her hand as Susan and Gordon returned with a pitcher of something blue and a round of beers. She giggled. 'Oh, I quite agree. So, can we eat soon, I'm hungry?'

***

Rose glanced down at her blue strapless dress; she knew she looked amazing, but up until now, Adam hadn't said one word to her. She picked another grape and popped it into her mouth. She was starving, but she didn't dare eat too much. The dress fitted perfectly; the last thing she needed was to bloat up. The underwire bra was digging into her ribs and her thong felt as if it would cleave her arse in two.

Adam had just finished dancing with that new tenant and he was engaged in a conversation with that giant man and his wife. She stared at him, willing him to turn and look at her and fulfill her dream, and her plans that she'd had filling her head for weeks. He should have spotted her by now, realised just how beautiful she was and whisked her onto the dance floor, holding her close whilst staring into her eyes with such longing. Without a word, he would lead her out of the room and up the stairs to his bedroom, where he would strip her slowly before making love to her all night, worshipping her body with his own, the light of the full moon radiating down on them through the open window...

Damn it to hell, who was she kidding?

She had stood and watched him for nearly three hours. She'd turned down a dance with David as she'd been waiting for Adam, but, perhaps, he should see her dancing and then he'd be smitten? She looked around for David, but couldn't see him. Turning back to Adam's group, she panicked, realising he'd gone. She had to find him and make him dance with her if necessary.

The dance floor was full of jiving bodies and she squeezed along the wall. Outside in the Hallway, she heard a few drunken villagers talking as they waited for the toilet.

'Oh, aye, that Mortimer woman, lovely…quiet, but lovely.'

'I know what you mean, not ugly. Adam seemed to like her…'

'Lovely dress. Velvet, was it? Lots of nice dresses…Annabel looks nice…'

'Who the hell is Annabel? You mean the young maid who works here? Rose…'

'Nice girl… lovely dress…'

'Where did that Mortimer woman go, anyway? I fancy asking her for a dance…'

'Ha! You're too drunk to dance, Eric, go an' piss before you have an accident.'

Rose stepped back into the Great Hall and grinned; at least some people had noticed her, but not the right person. She scanned the room, but he wasn't there; had he gone for a piss too? She suddenly chewed her lower lip. She was gone and he was gone. Were they together?

***

They hadn't got as far as the restaurant before the two women were groping the men and vice versa. Deciding to order a Chinese take-away instead, they headed for Susan's flat. Dumping the food in the kitchen, they started eating the prawn crackers as the women found plates and forks. They were about to serve up the food but Gordon couldn't wait any longer.

He rushed up behind Susan who was reaching up into a cup-board for some soy sauce, then reached around her and grasped her breasts. Kneading them, he pushed his erection against her bottom; she answered him by pushing back. He pulled her round, and began kissing her passionately while fumbling with her bra and yanking her top over her head.

James and Clare stood rooted to the spot, watching this performance until she broke the spell and dived on James with a guttural sound and thrust her tongue into his mouth. Clasping her tightly, he moved his hand to her heaving breasts and yanked the top downward in one pull, revealing them. He bent his head and licked and sucked them as she clung onto the kitchen sink behind her.

Suddenly, he was pushed aside as Gordon rushed past him, his trousers around his ankles. Stunned, James stared at the bathroom door where Gordon had disappeared, but within seconds, it all became clear as all three listened to the retching sounds of a man who had drunk too much.

Susan picked up her discarded bra and wandered out of the kitchen. James looked back at Clare who was pulling a disgusted face before she broke away from him and followed Susan into the lounge. James stared around the kitchen at the unopened silver cartons and the half-eaten packet of prawn crackers and sniffed. Damn Gordon!

He waited until Gordon staggered out, reeking of vomit, before he left the kitchen and followed him into the lounge where the two women sat on the brown couch.

'You're fuckin' disgusting!' Clare spat at him.

Gordon shook his head. 'I'll be all right now. Come on, who's up for it?'

Susan stared at him, stunned. James and Clare shook their heads. 'Not a chance, mate.' James stood up. 'Come on, I'll help you to the bedroom.'

Gordon's pathetic attempts at arguing were ignored, and James managed to manoeuvre him into Susan's one bedroom. Gordon fell backward onto the bed and was unconscious within seconds. James took off his shoes and left him.

James closed the bedroom door and slammed his fist into it. The night was ruined. He was wound up; he needed a release. He wondered if Clare would oblige him anyway? His question was answered as he walked into the lounge. Susan and Clare were both naked and lying on the sheepskin rug Gordon had recently bought. They knew he'd come in, but they ignored him as they kissed, their hands roaming each other's bodies. Breaking away, Susan bent her head and slowly licked her friend's erect nipple. Clare groaned with pleasure.

Clare turned her head and winked at him, beckoning him over. Susan turned her attentions away from Clare and slowly ran her hand down her body and between her legs. 'Can you take us both? Can you handle us?' Taking her fingers out, she licked them in a most erotic way that made him swallow hard and begin unbuttoning his shirt, his eyes never leaving the scene before him. Pictures of these women groaning in agony and pleasure filled his mind. He could hurt them both. He could be master of them both. His excitement almost became too much to bear.

The women laughed and slowly touched themselves as he took off his shirt and began undoing his trousers. He was so turned on, he wasn't sure if he could hold himself. He began peeling his trousers down his ankles. When Susan started giggling, he looked up.

'What's funny?'

Trying to suppress her mirth, she covered her mouth. 'Oh no, it's nothing, I've just got the giggles. By the way, love your undies! I haven't seen them in years!' The two women broke down and laughed uncontrollably. James glared at them as his erection quickly subsided and he pulled his trousers back up. Grabbing his shirt, he stormed out of the room, their howls of laughter following him as he found his shoes.

He looked at the knives that hung on the kitchen wall and his breath quickened. He reached out and took the biggest knife and held it; it felt good in his hand.

He could still hear the bitches laughing at him. How dare they. He was master of them. He smiled. Maybe it was time to use more force to get what he deserved? He purposely walked back toward the lounge and opened the door.

Two hours later, he stopped at the corner and looked back toward the flat. He'd turned the lights off after he was finished. The flat now silent except for the low snoring coming from Gordon, who still lay undisturbed by his hour or so of fun. And what fun he'd enjoyed.

The bitches' laughter soon changed into pathetic whimpering once he'd shown them both who was boss. Storming back into the room with the knife, he'd grabbed Clare by the hair, the knife to her throat, and quietly informed Susan that if she made a noise, he'd kill Clare in front of her and vice versa. Both became submissive very quickly and he'd pleasured himself to his full satisfaction.

Their deaths were quick and fairly painless, considering their humiliation of him. Poor Gordon. He'd left the knife in the bedroom, showered quickly and left, taking the bag of cold prawn crackers with him.

He wasn't aware of where he was going until he reached his car. He knew he was over the limit, but he didn't care, he knew where he wanted to be. He couldn't stop now. He would have all the bitches he had ever wanted and Bronwen Mortimer was first on his list.

Bronwen would be at that Kenward Ball. He seethed over the fact that he hadn't been invited; well, he would be waiting when she got back. Perhaps she'd be a little tipsy, easy to subdue. He could hardly contain himself as he pulled out of the small car park and headed toward Derwen.

***

Eira thanked Geoff for the dance and made her way back to her seat. Reaching for her gin and tonic, she tried to count how many she'd had already, and couldn't. Perhaps she should slow down? Then again, the pain was less when she was full of alcohol. It was always a choice, which was the worst of it. Have less pain but become a dribbling wreck, or put up with the pain and be respected in the community. Sometimes it felt such a hard choice.

She looked around the room. She knew Bronwen wouldn't be there, but she had to check. The surge of guilt she felt was quickly pushed away; it had to be done, for the better. The child needed her alone, to have time. She knew a dance with Adam would be humiliating and frightening for her and she'd hoped Bronwen would feel an urge to get away; it seemed to have worked. It would all work out all right in the end, if, the timing was right and, of course, if this was indeed the one.

Deciding to check the toilet, just in case, she slowly made her way into the hallway. An elderly woman called Olivia was waiting outside the bathroom. 'Is Bronwen in there?' Eira asked with a nod and a smile.

Olivia shook her head. 'No, it's Jonathan. I think he's fallen asleep!' She knocked loudly on the door and received a loud 'What?' from the other side. 'It's me, ya fool. Come on, I'm bursting!'

Eira grinned and turned away. Bronwen wasn't in the Great Hall. She glanced down the other end where the bar and the food table were; Bronwen wasn't there or in the bathroom. She looked up the stairs. She wouldn't go wandering up there, would she? She immediately decided against it. Bronwen had been terrified of coming. She'd relaxed a bit, but her forced dance with Adam had infuriated her as much as scared her; she wouldn't run upstairs. No, she'd need to feel free and go outside.

'Looking for someone?' Rosalyn leant against the banister, clutching a large glass of orange juice and no doubt a large quantity of vodka judging from her slurred words. 'It's not that Mortimer woman, is it?' she asked in answer to Eira's nod.

'Actually, it is, have you seen her?'

'Nope. Why is everyone so concerned for that woman? She's nothing important.' She had a drink and belched softly.

'My poor Rosalyn, don't you think you've had enough? You look as if you'll fall down, do you want to sit? I told you to go and eat something, and this'—Eira pointed to her drink—'is not food, is it?'

'So what? Who gives a shit about me? All I've heard tonight is "Bronwen this" and "Miss Mortimer that". It's sickening!'

Eira frowned and shook her head. 'Oh, you made your dislike of the woman perfectly obvious, it was pitiful. Are you going to tell me why you behaved so rudely?' Rosalyn shook her head and looked away. 'She's a nice woman, Rosalyn; if you gave her a chance you might see that. I know Adam is trying. Perhaps you could too. I know you're not here very often, but everyone needs friends and support and—'

'Support! Friendship! From that evil bitch!' She saw Eira's confused look, but couldn't stop herself. 'Oh, I know how she's conned you all into believing she's a frightened little bunny who wouldn't harm a flea, but all she did was change her last name thinking no-one would find out.'

Eira took a step toward her. 'Rosalyn, what?'

Shocked by Eira's tone of voice, Rosalyn looked down at her half-finished drink. 'It's nothing, really. I'm just uneasy about women… you know…after Catherine and all that.' She looked up. She could see Eira wasn't fooled and said defiantly, 'She's not what you all think, you know. She's not much of a guest, is she, sidling off like she has.'

'Have you seen her?' Eira's voice wavered slightly as she fought to control her emotions. She could see it had started to rain outside. Had it been long enough?

'Why? Leave her; she should be back at Adam's cottage by now.'

Eira scowled at her. 'Sometimes, you try my patience. Go and sleep it off.' She turned away and called over her shoulder, 'If you see Adam, tell him I'm looking for him.' Bronwen had been gone for at least twenty minutes. That should have been more than long enough. She had to find her now, to rescue her, bring her back. Too long and it could be fatal.

As it was, she found him first, in the kitchen, talking to an old school friend, Michael. He was John's son and they had practically grown up together. 'Michael, how wonderful to see you!' Eira gave him a brief hug and looked him up and down and then at the expensive bottle of malt whiskey they were sharing. Firmly, she picked up the bottle and replaced the cork.

'Boys, I need you both as sober as possible, I need your help.'

CHAPTER THIRTY-SIX

S HE COULDN'T SEE ANYTHING. THE darkness felt overwhelming and she shrank back from it, and then screamed as she touched something slimy. It was solid, and after a moment she registered that it was a wall. Moving away from it, she tried to take a deep breath and almost gagged as she took in the full force of the stench of the place. Urine, faeces, and general filth invaded her nostrils and she turned her head and spat on the hard floor.

In the far corner she could see a faint, blue light coming through a small circular window high up. It had bars crisscrossing it, but it was light nevertheless. She carefully shuffled her way toward it. She reached up tentatively and could just touch the cold metal, but she couldn't see where she was.

Suddenly, she froze; something moved in the darkness beside her. She turned her head toward it and stared. It looked at first like a large bundle of old rags, but as it moved, she realised, the rags were many blankets and sacks of some kind and it had hair, long hair that covered the face. She couldn't turn her face away as the person—she still wasn't sure if it was a man or a woman—moved and stretched and stopped when it became aware of her.

Something stirred deep within her. A memory that lingered just outside her thoughts, a knowledge she knew was important, but it wouldn't come. Her heart beat so fast, she thought it would burst, and there was some part of her that wished it would to take her away from this vision of hell. There was something that felt so familiar with all of this; it terrified her all the more.

The heap of rags fell back as the figure crawled toward her. Her eyes grew wide with horror, but none of her limbs would move. Her head screamed that she should be running, screaming to be let out, to escape this injustice, but all she could do was kneel there in the semidarkness and wait as the figure crawled slowly toward her.

As if a door had been flung open, it all came to her, and she choked back her sobs. She could now see that the pathetic figure was that of a woman, her grey hair lank and caked in filth, her dress torn and mostly shredded, and she could see the large, ugly bruises that littered the old woman's body. Her face was nothing more than a black, inflamed mess. Both of her eyes were so swollen, she could only open them a crack. Her lips were puffed out and covered in cuts. It looked like one of her cheekbones was fractured, as was her lower jaw. The woman could only whine and mumble something as dribble flowed from her battered mouth.

Bronwen recoiled as the woman tried to reach out to her. One arm was obviously broken; so were three of her fingers; they protruded in a terrible angle. Bronwen also knew that this woman had three broken ribs, a dislocated shoulder, and had been severely whipped. Even though she couldn't see the poor woman's back, she knew.

She couldn't breathe. She knew where she was and glanced around the small dark room: a cellar. She was beneath the ruins. This was where they kept their prisoners. Reluctantly, but knowing she must, she reached out and made herself touch the fingers of the broken woman. She jerked as if a bolt of lightning had struck her. Images flew through her head at breakneck speed, until finally she fell backward and fought for her breath. After what seemed like forever, she was able to say one word that sent shivers down her spine. 'Nia.'

***

'My lord, Sir Rhys has arrived.'

William gingerly lifted his head at the cry, but let it slump back onto the wet table and quickly fell back into his drunken stupor. He didn't care who came to his castle, especially Rhys. He never wanted to see him again. To see him was to remember and that went against everything he was doing. When he wasn't at Ludlow getting drunk and trying to focus on the restoration of the castle, he was at his castle getting drunk and forgetting the past. Rhys was a part of that past.

'It smells like an alehouse in here, and an old pigsty. You there.' He grabbed a passing pageboy. 'Go straight to the kitchens and fetch a large cauldron of hot water and scrub this room. It will also need fresh straw.' Going back out into the corridor, he watched Andrew run toward him. He nodded a greeting before they pulled William to his feet and half carried, half dragged him up to his bedchamber.

He wrinkled his nose at the smell of vomit on the bed, He yanked the old sheets off and let his friend fall backward onto it. Andrew shook his head while he pulled off William's boots. 'I'll fetch some food, my lord.'

Rhys noticed he made the sign of the cross as he left and frowned. He'd heard the rumours and the stories that usually circulated after a death of this nature, but seeing someone actually react to them was another matter, one he'd speak to William about when he was sober.

Sadly, that would have to wait until all the other serious business was dealt with. The King had given him the duty of warning William that his behaviour was not acceptable and changes needed to be made, or else. As a favour to Rhys, King Henry gave him a week to sort out William. Looking down on his friend, he could see how he had aged greatly since he'd last seen him only months before. He was only in his thirty-fifth year, yet he looked so much older.

Looking around at the neglected room, Rhys wondered briefly if the stories could be true. The servants had run away, refusing to stay in the cursed place. Rhys had found servants from farther afield who might not have heard the rumours to come and run the castle; they hadn't been doing a good job. No-one from the village came here any-more. They remained within the boundaries of the village, William's village, and refused to sell their crops to him. Rhys had been furious when he'd heard that William had not punished their insolence. Had the villagers truly placed a hex on William and his own?

He'd been there that day, standing beside his old friend and he'd watched and felt the fury and the anger of the crowd. He'd watched William and his bride stand together, side by side, yet a million miles apart. And he saw the shiver of revulsion run through William as the screaming finally stopped and he turned for the first time to look at his wife. It was the briefest glance, but one filled with such hatred, it would be burned into her soul for all eternity, he was sure of it.

He left the chamber, but he couldn't face the Great Hall and its stench, so he made his way up toward the guest quarters. As he reached his door, he thought he heard a child's giggle and looked around. 'Is anyone there?' No-one answered; he hardly expected it if it was the servants' children. He was reminded of how little Gwenllian had laughed and giggled, and he shut his eyes tight to hold back the tears. Such a beautiful girl, such a waste. His son had become betrothed to another three months ago. Margery, a nice girl, a good match. Politics was politics and sometimes he hated it.

When he'd sent a messenger with the news, William replied. 'Will she ever forgive me, Rhys? Will she ever forgive us?' Rhys sent another message: that he should grieve for his children. Grieve and rebuild, starting with his new home. After seeing everything today, he knew now William had never taken his advice, and his heart felt heavy for it.

***

The light drizzle had become a downpour by the time Eira found Adam and convinced him to look for Bronwen. Michael hadn't been convinced a woman in such a beautiful dress would go out in the rain, never mind walk home alone in the dark, and had run upstairs to double-check before meeting Adam at the front door. 'She's not up there, but are you seriously telling me this woman would go home with no coat and on her own?'

Adam shrugged on his waterproof and handed his father's to Michael. 'I've only met her twice, but yes, I think she is stubborn enough to do something like that.'

Eira punched him playfully. 'Oh stop it, you two. She'll have reached the cottage by the time the pair of you have your coats on.'

'So what's so wrong with that? She's a grown woman. She can walk home. It's not as if you get many weirdos around here, is it?'

Adam waited for her to respond; when she didn't he looked at her face, raised his eyebrows in a silent question. He couldn't read her expression. It was one he'd never seen from Eira before and it humbled him enough to quickly zip up his coat and open the door. 'All right, I'm going. I'll check the stables first. I doubt she'd have gone down there, but I'll check.'

Eira reached out and stopped him. 'No, you're right, she won't have gone there. Check the garden, the maze, around the house, before anywhere else.'

Michael shook his head. 'But, surely, she would have asked for a lift, wouldn't she? What kind of woman goes out in this?' They'd all stepped out into the porch and the rain hammered loudly on the slate roof.

'A nutter, I'm afraid, Mike.'

Eira rounded on Adam. 'What is wrong with the Kenwards these days? Has it gone out of fashion to be nice to a guest? If you had engaged her in conversation, perhaps before you pulled her onto the dance floor—'

Adam flinched from the hostile tone. 'All right, all right, Eira, I'm going.'

Eira's shoulders sagged; she knew she was being unfair, after all, she'd forced him to dance with her in the hope she'd need time alone. She was angry at herself. She shouldn't take it out on Adam. Bronwen had to be found. Now. She tentatively patted him on the arm and stepped back as a few guests staggered out into the rain. The three of them watched the small group lurch along the driveway, laughing and joking about getting soaked, before Adam looked across at his friend. 'Ready?'

With a nod, they both disappeared into the night.

'Where are they going, Eira?'

Richard staggered in the doorway. With a deep sigh, Eira looped her arm through his and slowly headed for the kitchen. 'I'll make us some hot tea and I'll explain everything.' The last thing she needed now was a large drunken crowd. She needed to get her thoughts together; soon it would be time.

***

The band was rounding up the night with some slow numbers. There were still a few couples shuffling around the dance floor, but they could tell that the night was coming to a close. Not many people were sober and some were worse off than others and were swaying unsteadily around the outside of the room, talking complete and utter nonsense, judging from the snatches of conversation audible between songs.

Martin, the lead guitarist, was admiring the young woman hanging onto a tall, muscular boy, her arms draped around his neck, her face buried in his chest. She had fantastic legs and he'd hoped to speak with her, but seeing the size of the young fella, he decided it would be a bad idea.

Finishing the last song, they bowed to the smattering of half-hearted applause and quickly began packing away. They'd been paid to play up to one o' clock, it was only quarter to, but it wasn't really worth it. Gary packed away his bass and grinned. 'I'm going for a quick snoop around while they're all pissed.' The others took little notice as he quickly disappeared out into the hallway. They all knew his love of anything old; he'd been very excited when they'd been booked to play at Kenward Hall.

'That's fantastic!' he'd cried when they'd told him. 'Parts of that Hall date back to the fifteenth century.' No-one had been in the least bit interested until he'd mentioned the haunting. He'd sat back, a triumphant look on his face knowing he had their attention. 'It's supposed to be haunted by a young girl and an old woman. The story goes that a girl was murdered in the fifteenth century and her body was hidden. The wrong person was accused and tortured, but the murderer was never brought to justice, and it's supposed to be her ghost who walks the building, looking for redemption.'

They hadn't really taken it seriously, but when they'd arrived to set up, none of them could shake off the strange feeling of unease. Martin didn't like the Hall. 'It gives me the willies! I'm not going to the loo by myself.' The others laughed at him, Gary had shaken his head. 'You big girl! As soon as I can, I'm going for a look around.'

Suddenly, Gary reappeared and picked up his guitar case and with a quick look behind him, headed out to the van; the others followed. They had already been paid, after all. Gary kept glancing nervously around him.

Martin leant close. 'What's up, mate? Seen a ghost!'

The others laughed, but stopped abruptly when they saw the look on Gary's face. He glanced again toward the Hall. The others looked too and suddenly felt uneasy. 'Come on, let's go.'

Martin started the van. 'What's wrong?'

Gary frowned. 'I'm not sure. They said there wouldn't be any children, right?'

Martin nodded. 'So?'

'So, who was the young girl standing on the stairs?'

'I didn't see anyone standing on the stairs, especially a child...'

Gary swallowed hard. 'You didn't see her?' The urgency in his voice made them look at him.

'No, mate, I didn't see any children, why?'

Gary said nothing as Martin reversed slightly before turning around and heading slowly away from the Hall. He was shaking and he thrust his hands deep into his jacket. Were they messing about when they said they hadn't seen her? Because he had definitely seen her, standing halfway up the stairs and she had seen him, and smiled.

***

William watched the building grow. Day after day, he made himself watch, and look over the plans, and nod, but he couldn't muster one ounce of enthusiasm for any of it. It had been over two years since that terrible day, but he still woke in the night hearing the screams and those cursed eyes, beseeching his mercy. Mercy that wouldn't come.

Sometimes, he would feel eyes upon him and he would turn, always in the hope that the stories were true and he would see his beloved daughter once again. It never was. It was always a man or woman of the village, their hatred for him evident, but kept to sly glances and whispered curses now. They had done what was needed; now he would pay for it.

'My lord, your home is coming quickly, the men are eager to finish it.'

William looked up as his ever-faithful steward approached. 'Aye, and I understand why they hasten to finish. I would most likely feel the same.'

Andrew bowed his head; what could he answer to that? He knew Sir William's pain, had witnessed it firsthand; the villagers in their fury had overlooked that. To come home from battle with honour to find his daughter murdered, his son dead, and his wife…he quickly looked away and forced her out of his head. No-one thought about her anymore.

He looked across at the smoke rising from the homes in Derwen and he followed the outline of the village. They were there, as promised. The trees were still young, but they grew, stronger and quicker than was natural. Andrew begged Sir William to allow him and a few soldiers to chop them down, but he had refused. 'No, they stay as a reminder.'

He turned back to the plans on the small table and compared the growing walls to the plan William was now staring at. 'My lord, when do you think you'll live in it?'

For a moment, he didn't answer, but remained quietly staring at the paper before him, the autumn breeze gently lifting the corners. 'I doubt that I will ever live in it.' He sighed loudly and rubbed his eyes. 'This home will not be finished by me, but by my nephew. I want the roof on by spring, though.'

'Spring? I cannot guarantee that, my lord, but I can—'

'No, Andrew, spring. I want to be able to hold a Ball here in May. It will be my only wish in this house. I will move away to a house in Ludlow and live out my cursed life there. I have left instruction to my brother.' Without a backward glance, William walked away.

Andrew watched him go and then looked back at the new Hall. *May, it would have been her birthday*, he thought, and with a heavy heart, began to see that his master's wishes were carried out.

***

She knew that she was lying on wet grass somewhere and that it was raining. A small corner of her brain felt utterly disgusted at herself for ruining such a beautiful dress. Why wasn't she getting up and going inside to dry off? Simple. Her body refused to listen to that small part of her brain and she could feel her fight slowly slipping away again. Then her body and the dress were forgotten as a fresh wave of fear gripped her, and she was back in the darkness and knew what was coming and could barely breathe.

They were coming. She could hear their approaching footsteps on the solid stone steps and she cringed away from the sound. They had told her what would happen to her at her trial. If it could be called a trial. It was nothing more than a sick and twisted meeting at which she'd been forced to confess to something everyone knew she was innocent of. No-one, not even Sir William, looked her in the eye. No-one, not even when they'd dragged her away, screaming for mercy. No-one.

She'd sat cowering in the corner, constantly waiting for the door to open, for him to come and renounce such an injustice; he never came. No-one ever came. No food, no water; she knew he hoped she would die quietly. She wished it too, but she didn't. The pain ripped through her every time she moved. She could feel the fever begin and wished it, held onto it so that it might dull the fear of what was to come; it didn't.

She closed her eyes when they finally came. She kept them closed as they dragged her out of the darkness and up the steps into the courtyard. She tried so hard to pray, to open her mouth and pray, to form words in her head, anything that might focus her mind elsewhere and find some peace; none came. Her lips, too puffed and swollen, refused to move, her mind, fevered and broken, refused to work.

At that moment, she hated God. She despised Him for allowing this monstrosity to happen to her. Why had He allowed it? Why wasn't He stopping it? She wasn't sure if she meant William too, at that point, but cursed both of them. She opened her eyes then and saw him. Only him, and her eyes never left his face.

Far away, in the midst of all the fear and the pain, the smoke and the noise, she could hear people talking. Their voices floated to her on the wind and she fought to hear. Gentle and insistent, they reached her in the darkest corner of her mind and she clung to them.

The noose suddenly tightened and the air was forced out of her body. She could feel the rope burning into her skin and she kicked out at thin air. She wanted to die now as the hot pain coursed through her broken body. She wanted those sweet, gentle voices, and stopped fighting. She stopped kicking and tried to open her eyes. Barely a crack, but it was enough to see them and remember.

***

'Bronwen! Shit! She's stopped breathing. Michael, do those chest compression things and I'll do mouth to mouth. I can't feel a pulse… come on, woman!' Adam pulled back her head and inhaled, his mouth inches from hers, but stopped. 'Hang on…Bronwen? She's breathing again…come on, I'll carry her…'

She could feel herself being lifted, and she let herself float in the darkness. Strangely, she felt safe and warm in the arms of this man she hated and feared with her last breath. She felt something being draped over her, something warm and comforting against the coldness and with it, the pain and fear went away as if by magic! She wanted to smile at her own joke, but couldn't make her face move, which felt weird. It was her face after all, wasn't it?

She heard voices floating around her and tried to focus on any one of them, but couldn't. They melted into one voice, then many voices all talking at once. Then she'd hear one or two words about hospitals and doctors, and she knew she would be safe. No-one would betray her now. She was safe. He hadn't let her die, after all.

CHAPTER THIRTY-SEVEN

CAROLYN KNOCKED CAUTIOUSLY ON THE bedroom door. Getting no answer, she knocked louder and called out. 'Debbie? Come on, you'll be late for the doctors…Debbie?'

Still getting no reply, she tried the door, it was unlocked and she eased it open a crack and slipped her head through the gap. 'Debbie?'

***

They arrived quite quickly. She heard the siren almost immediately, it seemed. A policewoman ushered her into another room and covered her with a blanket. 'For shock,' she heard someone say. Someone put a cup of tea in front of her, but she didn't touch it. They'd used one of Debbie's cups, but she didn't tell them that.

'No, I don't think she has a boyfriend, but I thought I heard someone with her a few times. No, I haven't seen anyone. Yes, I think she takes drugs for recreational purposes. No, I don't. I'm studying to be a nurse. Yes, we shared this flat; flats are so expensive these days. No, she was never late with her rent.'

The questions went on for a long time. She was dying for a cigarette, but she'd given up five months before. Debbie would have some in her room, but nobody would ever get her in that room again. She blew her nose and wiped her eyes with her sodden tissue and then closed them in her attempt to hide away from the multitude of people invading her home. The flat was full of photographers, police, people in white, all looking at her, talking, asking more questions, intruding, invading, wanting to know every last detail of their lives.

She put her head in her hands and began to cry uncontrollably. She doubted that she would ever be able to get the vision of Debbie, lying on her stomach, naked, her eyes wide open and her arms dangling down the side of the bed, out of her head. Poor Debbie. Her back ripped open by what looked like whip-lashes; she could see glints of bone. She knew she hadn't needed to check if Debbie was dead, that was evident, but, she thought later, it was her training, always check. Debbie had been stone cold. She'd been dead for hours.

All the while, as she was sitting with her head in her hands, the only thought that kept haunting her was that she had been down the hall, asleep. Untouched, safely asleep in her room, oblivious to her friend's torment. Would Debbie ever forgive her? Could she?

***

James showered slowly, enjoying the feel of the hot water over his body. He took his time, feeling his pleasure heighten as he moved his hand rhythmically along the shaft of his erect penis. Reliving last night, it was a small disappointment that he couldn't last and he sagged against the shower cubicle as he caught his breath. Feeling better, he washed himself and decided what to do next after last night's fiasco with Bronwen Mortimer.

He'd waited until almost two o'clock in the morning for her, but she'd never come home. He'd parked in the village at first, watching them walk home in the rain. He smiled as a group of men, very much the worse for wear, had collapsed, and laughed. He'd waited until they'd gone up past the pub before starting his car and heading toward the cottage.

Slowing down at the gates of Kenward Hall, he'd looked for her, but he'd only seen more people, some with umbrellas, others too drunk to care, staggering down the driveway. He'd driven on, slowly, half-expecting to see her hopefully staggering home alone. He'd parked opposite the cottage and thought about what he would do.

There weren't any lights on, but that could mean she'd come home early and already gone to bed. There was only one way of knowing and so he'd scrambled out of the car and dashed across the road and up the garden path. Peering into the downstairs windows, he couldn't see anything.

Going around to the back, he used his key, which he'd had cut, and let himself in. The cottage was very quiet. He moved silently into the lounge and up the stairs, all the while listening for either her return or her moving around in her bedroom; he heard neither. Instinct told him, even before he'd looked into her dark bedroom, that she wasn't there. Disappointed, he quickly walked back outside, locking the door behind him, and silently walked back to his car.

He shook the excess rain off himself, sat back, and waited. Pushing his soaking hair back every now and then, he'd begun to tremble with anticipation. The fury that she wasn't complying with his plans flared up almost to the point of becoming uncontrollable. He couldn't keep still, but constantly opened the car door and got out to look down the dark lane. Where the hell was the whore? As each minute passed, his anger and frustration edged higher. After an hour, he couldn't stand it anymore.

He resolutely refused to think about Susan and that other bitch who'd dared to laugh at him, their superior! And as their superior, he'd shown them what a man could do; they weren't laughing now. He smiled, and looked down at his hands; he could still smell the blood. Now that had been fun.

He couldn't go home; he'd wanted more fun. He had such an abundance of energy still battling to get out, he had to have someone. Starting the car, he'd skidded as he'd taken the corner; his urge to get to his drug-infested whore was overwhelming. He'd use her and then, in the morning, calm and collected, he'd come back and have more fun than he'd ever dared to hope for.

Now, drying himself, he looked in the long bathroom mirror and smiled. His eyes travelled down his lean body. Sunday should be a day of rest. He was glad Gordon had decided to close the office, not that Gordon would be in any state to deal with rich clients today! Neither was he. Today, he would not rest. Today, he would be spending it in Derwen, in Oak Cottage in the arms of Miss Mortimer. He would use her all day, he would make her scream and beg and plead.

He hadn't listened to Debbie's muffled begging and pleading. He'd ridden her for hours till she'd bled, whipping the skinny flesh of her drug-filled body until she'd stopped making any sounds. Once he'd checked that she was in fact dead, he'd found, much to his surprise, that he was aroused again and had claimed her as his own, one last time.

***

The sea of floating darkness suddenly broke away as a blinding light shone into her eyes. Pulling away from it, she turned her head and buried her face in something soft. The light was still there, though, she was aware of it now. Bronwen heard a whispered command and recognised the gentle voice of Eira. The light dimmed slightly, easing the crushing pain in her head.

She kept her eyes tightly shut as a wave of nausea threatened to make her retch again, but it quickly passed and she swallowed hard. Her throat felt raw, burning from the acidic vomit as much as anything else. She didn't want to remember the rope, choking the life from her, but, surely, it hadn't been her…she was so confused. She concentrated on not throwing up and after a few deep breaths, she felt slightly better.

She felt the weight of someone sitting down on the edge of the bed and hoped it was Eira; it was, and she squeezed her eyes tight to stop the flow of tears as Eira reached over and gently touched her shoulder.

'Oh, thank God, she's awake! Adam, fetch a glass of water, please.'

Bronwen allowed herself to be helped into a sitting position, and the cold glass was held to her dry lips. She kept her eyes firmly closed, aware of the room full of people and focused on the nectar that travelled down her burning throat. It eased her throat slightly and she fell back against what she now knew was a pile of pillows and licked her lips, moistening them with her tongue.

'Okay, everybody, there's too many people in here!'

She heard Eira clap her hands and the murmur of voices and felt their eyes on her, before the sound of shuffling of feet moving away. 'But what about the hospital? She did stop breathing…it might be a good idea if…'

She listened as Eira averted questions and soothed and reassured concerned people, until finally she heard the door close. 'You can open your eyes now, my dear.'

They felt heavy, but she forced them open and glanced around the room. She was in a large bedroom and she was lying on a double bed, with a blanket over her and two hot water bottles, one beneath her feet, the other lying heavily on her chest. Slowly reaching over, she dragged the blanket off.

Eira stood with her back against the door, watching her with an odd expression, as if she was waiting for something; she had no idea what that might be.

After a few minutes, Eira shook off her expectant look and walked quietly toward the bed. She sat on the edge and she hesitantly took one of Bronwen's hands. She felt very warm against Bronwen's own cold hands and she shivered.

'We thought we'd lost you.' The sadness in Eira's voice was quite a shock; no-one had ever sounded so sorry for her. She blinked back the burning tears, but said nothing.

'Adam and the others have retreated back to the kitchen; you can let it all out if you want to.' Eira squeezed her hand.

They came like a tidal wave, all at once and all-consuming. It hurt her throat, but she couldn't stop as fear and shock overwhelmed her.

She had nearly died. She had died, hadn't she? Her head hurt from the mixed pictures in her head. The other woman, Nia, she'd been there, with her, in that hellhole, but that was impossible. She'd been lying on the cold, wet grass; she knew that, she could remember that…

Being in the bed felt unreal, dreamlike and fuzzy. She wasn't sure which had felt more real, the noose or the grass, the cold, dark cell, or here, in this bed? She reached up and gently touched her throat. No noose, no torture, no broken bones. She was pretty sure her body was completely unblemished. Who was she? Where was she? When?

The niggling answers burrowed deeper into her mind and she shied away from them; she couldn't face any more strangeness. It couldn't possibly be true. Her mind wanted to shrink away and hide from what her thoughts told her. Memories of people, of a life, all long gone, all forgotten. She tried to focus on the one thing that felt safe: she was alive.

Eira sat patiently holding her hand until the tears slowed and she was able to control herself again. Passing her a wad of tissue, Eira waited until she'd finished before saying anything. 'Better?'

Bronwen nodded silently and attempted to smile; it was a pathetic attempt, but it seemed to reassure Eira enough and she reached for the tall glass of water and handed it to her. She drank thirstily and Eira got up and refilled it from a large jug of iced water next to the bed. 'Here, drink some more. You'll feel better. You're a little dehydrated.'

She took it gratefully, but sipped it this time, enjoying the coldness on her hot throat. 'What happened?' Her voice was no more than a croak, but she realised it didn't hurt as much as she'd expected.

Leaning a bit closer, Eira asked. 'Can you tell me?'

Bronwen couldn't answer for a moment. She couldn't think what to say. What could she say that was safe ground? To say what she thought out loud would make it too real, too true. Besides, surely Eira would think she was mad, because that's what it must be, a kind of madness. It couldn't possibly be real. It had to be some kind of psychotic episode brought on by the alcohol and stress. Maybe?

Could she be sure of anything? Gwenllian had been there. She'd grabbed her arm. She looked down at it, lying above the covers; no marks, but then, what did she expect? She knew Eira was watching her and she turned to her. 'I…can't really remember…'

'Not even Gwenllian?'

She stared frozen; her mouth moved slightly as she tried to voice her questions. 'You've said that name before to me. Do you know anything about her? Have you seen her?'

Eira looked down at Bronwen's hand and let go. She took a deep breath and let it out slowly. 'Yes, I…know her.'

Bronwen tried to put down the glass, Eira took it off her. Heaving herself into a sitting position, she waited. Eira refused to meet her eye and continued to look down at her hands, until finally; she seemed to make a decision and looked up. 'I've seen her, talked to her and…held her. You see, she was William's child, but, obviously, you knew that.'

'Yes, yes, I knew. She was murdered.'

Eira glanced away for a moment as if gathering her thoughts and then continued. 'She was spoilt, you see, having had his love for so long. She was his only child. Her mother, Jane, died giving birth to her. When she was five, her father, William, married…Anne.'

'Yes, yes, I know all that too. I went to the library like you suggested and I did some research on William and the battle of Bosworth and the murder of his daughter, poor girl.' She coughed to clear her throat and grimaced as it burned.

'Did you know that it was William who had slain King Richard? Henry Tudor was very pleased and gave him lands and titles and changed the spelling of his name. It was a great honour.' Eira stared toward the window. She seemed suddenly elsewhere.

'Erm, no, I didn't know that.' She searched Eira's face, trying to understand the way she was behaving.

'Honours meant nothing to William. He didn't care, you see, about anything when he found out…about little Gwenllian, his darling little girl.' Eira sounded bitter, but she stopped and turned back to Bronwen who was watching her closely. 'You see, Gwenllian and Anne didn't get along, you might say. Anne tried to love her, but…it was impossible. Gwenllian wouldn't share him. And Anne loved William so much. Gwenllian became a thorn in their marriage. If only she'd given him an heir, it would all have been different, you see, but, she couldn't.'

Bronwen sat up and leant forward. 'In my research, I found out Lady Anne had lost babies. Five, I think.'

Eira jerked round and glared at her. 'Six! She lost six!'

Bronwen flinched. 'I'm…sorry, I thought…'

'The last child had been a beautiful son. She'd waited so long for him. She was prepared to do anything to have him in her arms. Even dance with the Devil, but it all came to nothing.' She spat out the last word. 'She was betrayed and all hope died with him.'

'Hope? Eira, what are you talking about? And why are you behaving like this? Are you all right?' Eira was looking at her, but seemed elsewhere.

'Have you done research too? I haven't found any of this information, where did you get it?' Still getting no response, she reached out and touched her. Eira focused on her face. 'Eira, have you researched the family?'

'In a way, I suppose, I have.'

Bronwen could feel her fear rising, knowing what she wanted to say, but also suspecting how it might sound. She quickly licked her lips and began. 'Can you tell me who murdered Gwenllian? You see, this might sound a bit weird but I had some kind of vision when I first moved in, at those castle ruins and, it's become a bit strange. It's like I have some kind of connection with the girl. I keep seeing her. I'm sure she was there last night when I collapsed, and I see people dressed in old clothes from that era. I've seen and heard weird things and then, last night, I think—I think I had some kind of time-slip. Oh I don't know really, it all sounds so unreal, but it felt like I was in a cell with another woman, and I knew her, or I think I did. It freaked me out, whatever it was.'

Bronwen shook her head and roughly wiped her tears with the back of her hand. 'Eira, I'm scared, confused and my throat hurts and I think it's because I...I saw a woman being hanged and it's all so frightening and none of it makes sense and...' She knew she was babbling and she stopped. She was shaking even worse now that she'd said the words out loud. 'Eira, please, what's going on? Who killed her?'

Eira slowly nodded, her hands clasped tightly together. Their eyes locked and a tear escaped down Eira's cheek. 'I did.'

'What!' Bronwen pushed herself off the bed and clung onto the window seat as the room spun. Her head throbbed and she blinked quickly, trying to regain her focus on Eira, who hadn't moved from the bed.

'Stop being so fuckin' ridiculous! This isn't a joke. I'm serious! The woman I saw pushing Gwenllian over the wall of that tower was not you. And you probably know already that Gwenllian lived in the fifteenth century. You may be old, Eira, but that's pushing it!'

'My dear Bronwen, don't you recognise me, even now?' She slowly stood up and Bronwen felt a stab of fear. She had always known there was something familiar, but she couldn't place it. Something that had always been there.

'I know you've done research, I hoped you would. I left all the clues, the stories, the diaries. I hoped you'd find your way, but, it seemed one more push was necessary.'

'One more push?' Bronwen frowned, but took a step back. 'Eira, what the hell? Diaries? Stories? I don't...'

'In the library, you read my diaries, didn't you? The history of the Kenward family and their family tree, and did you find the names of all the people who worked for them? My memory isn't as good as it was. I think I remembered everyone. I know I remembered everyone of importance, anyway. And the death warrant, did you find that?'

Bronwen stared open-mouthed; she was trying frantically to make some sense of what Eira was saying. 'You're mad,' she managed feebly.

'Am I?'

'You must be. Those diaries and things were old, very old. You can't fake things like that. I don't think so anyway,' she continued, answering her own question. 'You could have forged them.'

Eira smiled. 'I didn't. The paper was brand new when I began writing.'

Bronwen clenched her fists. 'Stop it!' She swallowed and licked her dry lips. 'This isn't real! What you're saying is lies…you're delusional… why would you do this?'

Eira sighed loudly and shrugged. 'You know I wouldn't. You know, deep down, my dear, I'm not lying. You know me, as I know you. As Gwenllian knows you. You see, the villagers hated me for what I had done, and they broke the rules of God to punish me. They conjured up a spell to keep me locked in this body, cursing my pride, my anger, and my horrific acts. I had conjured up evil in my attempts to save my marriage, and my child, and they summoned evil to keep me here.' Eira leant forward. 'What those sad, pathetic simpletons didn't know was the proper way of doing such invocations and they trapped us both, the murderer and the murdered, locked together in our hatred. They bade me to live until she would return, and the curse would finally be lifted if she found it in her heart to forgive me.'

Bronwen stared open-mouthed, but finally managed to ask. 'Who?'

'You. The woman I blamed for murdering Gwenllian. The woman I was forced to watch being hanged for a crime that I committed.'

Seeing that Bronwen was too shocked to answer, she looked out of the window and continued in a quiet voice. 'They made this village my prison. Those damned oak trees my bars. Forever old, stuck in a body that's slowly rotting away, free but never free. To see those I've loved die, and be reborn, but for me, there was always this one body, no peace, no death, only pain and suffering, and five hundred years of memories…and regrets.'

Eira looked down at her hands clasped tightly on her lap. Bronwen didn't move. 'I killed an innocent child out of grief-stricken madness and the pain filling my heart for my lost son, for all my children, dead and gone. I felt such hatred for my body that would never again bear children, to know there was no hope left for me. I was a complete failure as a woman and a mother. I knew it was my own stupid fault. I tried to manipulate nature and God had His revenge. I despised everyone and everything for failing me, for betraying me. But the fact was, I hated myself.'

Silence fell on the room as Eira regained her composure, her gaze fixed on Bronwen. When she said nothing, Eira continued. 'The worst was yet to come for me. Henry Tudor granted William the title of Sheriff, but when he heard that in a fit of rage I had murdered Gwenllian, he decided that it would not be looked upon lightly and his enemies would hold it against him and William, so they hid the truth, and I let them. I hated you for pretending to care, for being a part of William's history, for helping to deliver my son and all my dead children. I thought you were bad luck in some way. I listened to your screams as they tortured you to confess…he made me. The people knew and William knew, and we…let it happen in the name of politics. I let it happen and they cursed me for it.'

Her voice was barely a whisper as Bronwen sat down heavily on the window seat, her legs giving way beneath her. 'Who…did you let them condemn to death?'

Eira's expression softened. 'It was Nia, the child's nurse. It was you.'

CHAPTER THIRTY-EIGHT

THE VILLAGE WAS QUIET. THE shop was shut, and as he quickly glanced around, he noticed most blinds and curtains were drawn. It was like a ghost town, so different from last night's frivolity. Perfect. He put the car into gear and sped away toward Bronwen's home, her haven, her safe place; at least, she thought it was. Parking a little farther around the bend, out of sight of the cottage, he switched off the engine and looked across at the silent cottage. It looked very much as it had earlier, only now the rain had stopped, leaving large puddles in the road. It had that same empty feel about it. Hadn't she come back then? Was she with someone? He clenched the steering wheel. *Bitch!* If she was being pleasured by another man, he would make her pay; she was for him, no-one else.

He tried to force the thoughts out of his head, but they wouldn't leave him. Her long hair splayed out around her head as she lay on her back, gasping with pleasure as some bastard fucked her slowly and lovingly and then hearing her begging for more, harder, deeper. He got out and paced. Damn her if she's somewhere else!

He glanced up at her bedroom window. If she was with someone, he'd have to be killed. He got back into his car and reached into the glove compartment. He pulled out his weapon and smiled. Women were easily frightened by a knife held to their eyes or their beautiful throats; he'd found that out only last night with Susan and Clare. But a man could be different. He pulled his own knife out of its covering and smirked; then again, it was a frightening thing to behold. A good ten inches of steel with a thick handle decorated with skulls, it looked the part. One thrust of this in the gut would be enough. He'd never had to use it, but kept it with him just in case. The first woman he'd killed by strangulation all those years ago for making too much noise, and he swore he'd try not to kill again, but it was inevitable now.

***

Nia hadn't been surprised to receive a message that Lady Anne wished to see her; she'd been expecting it for some time. What was strange was where she wanted to meet, at the East Tower. It had been almost a week since she'd finally allowed them into her bedchamber and let them take away her son. The stench of decay was overwhelming, but Nia persevered and gently cleaned the small body, with Lady Anne watching from the bed. She had wrapped him in a clean white blanket and carefully carried him to his small coffin where she laid him. A quick glance at her mistress confirmed that it was all right to place the lid, and he was taken away.

The next stage was to clean up Lady Anne. She had sat unmoving in a large bathing tub as her ladies poured in warm water. Rose petals helped make her skin smell fresh, but she acted as if she didn't notice, even when they stood before her with towels. It was as Nia was combing her long yellow hair that she noticed Anne watching her in the small hand mirror with a strange look on her face that disappeared almost immediately. Nia wasn't sure if she'd read it properly, but she became wary.

The bed had been destroyed, as were all the sheets, in a huge fire. Then they buried William's son, and for the first time, Lady Anne looked at peace. She knelt before the small altar and held onto her rosary beads, her head bowed. They knew she'd gone to the priest to ask for forgiveness, but what was said, and whether she was granted her request, no-one knew. Some had their own opinions about her behaviour. Nia was inclined to try to understand the woman's grief, but it didn't stop her worrying, though, and now, this message from her lady that she wanted to talk—in private. Was it regarding the birth? Did she want to find out what had gone wrong, find someone to blame? The chances of having more children? All three questions filled her with dread, as the answers were not favourable.

As she crossed the courtyard, Gwenllian ran up to her. 'Where are you going? Will you come and play?'

Nia slowed down, but carried on walking; she reached out and patted the child on the arm. 'Not now. I'm busy. Perhaps later.'

'Oh please. I'm bored and everyone is so unhappy about my brother and…'

Nia stopped and gently took hold of Gwenllian's arms. 'Darling, I said I'm busy, I'll see you later. Now off you go!' She spoke a little more harshly than she meant to, but if Lady Anne wished to speak privately, then so be it. Besides, it would be prudent to keep those two apart as long as possible.

She hurried away and didn't look back, knowing Gwen's mournful face would break her heart. She rushed up to the third floor chamber and knocked; receiving no reply, she gently pushed the door open. 'My lady?' The room was empty, but the small door leading to the battlements was open. Standing at the bottom of the narrow stairwell, she called up. 'My lady, are you up there?'

'Nia, come up.'

She climbed carefully until she reached the open roof. The warm breeze lifted her skirt slightly, and she fanned herself as sweat dripped down her chest. It was hot, too hot to be climbing three flights of stairs at her age.

Lady Anne had her back to her; holding onto the stone, looking out at the distant hills. *Looking for William, perhaps*, thought Nia and coughed. 'My lady, you—'

'Yes, I called for you. I demanded that you come here to me, and like a dog, you came.' She spat out the words but didn't turn around.

'I demanded the woman who had a hand in destroying my marriage. I demanded to see the woman who pulled my son's body from my own.' At this, her voice cracked, but she turned slowly and glared at the old woman who stood motionless, too shocked to speak. 'Yes, Nia, I wanted to look in your eyes, and I wanted you to look in mine, and see the pain you caused.'

Nia open her mouth, but she could only croak helplessly.

Lady Anne laughed cruelly. 'So, the woman who my husband relies on cannot speak. Can you not form words? Can you not beg for your life?'

Nia saw the glint of metal as her mistress lunged at her, but she ducked and stepped aside quickly enough so that the small knife whooshed past her neck. She grabbed onto the stone and pulled herself away as Anne turned and lunged again. This time, she felt the knife pierce the back of her shoulder and she cried out. She had to get the guards; it was all she could think of.

'Get off her, you foul woman!'

Both women whirled round to find Gwenllian standing at the top of the steps, scowling at Anne. 'You horrible bitch! You've gone mad! When my father hears of this, he'll turn you away, as he should have done years ago. You're useless! You can't even have children!'

For a moment, Lady Anne didn't move. Her breath came out fast and harsh. Nia tried to move, to get to the child. She could see the madness in her mistress's eyes and knew Gwenllian was in danger. Suddenly, it happened. Lady Anne moved so fast, Nia barely had time to register what she was doing. Anne's expression changed as she lunged at the child. Before Gwenllian could fight, Anne had her by the scruff of her dress and was pushing her backward. The child gasped once with the impact of the solid wall against her back, and then Anne bent down and lifted her.

Nia had time only to reach for the flailing hand of her charge as the child disappeared over the side. Gwenllian's eyes stared with horror at her oncoming death, and then she was gone.

Nia staggered against the wall as Lady Anne collapsed onto the floor. She could barely force herself to look over the edge.

Gwenllian was dead.

***

Bronwen's eyes flew open and she clutched her head in pain. She was lying on the window seat, one leg dangling, the other with knee bent. She sat up and winced as the throbbing increased. Eira moved toward her, but Bronwen quickly moved away and leant against the bedroom wall. 'What the hell happened? Have I been asleep or something? Damn, my head hurts.'

Eira sighed and sat down on the window seat. She rubbed her face briskly and wiped tears from her eyes. 'It will pass quickly. You haven't been asleep, as such. I showed you, that's all.'

'Showed me? Showed me what?' The pain was slowly subsiding and she became aware that her throat wasn't hurting as much.

Eira read her thoughts. 'I gave you some healing too. I thought it appropriate.' She looked a little embarrassed, but kept her gaze fixed on Bronwen.

'You gave me...healing?' She shook her head and covered her face with her hands, then slowly let them drop. 'You gave me healing and some freaky dream to do what, prove that you've gone mad or something? I liked you. I thought I had found a friend, someone I could talk to. I...I've never had a friend, a real one.'

She moved away from the wall and plucked at her damp dress. 'Oh, don't get me wrong, I always knew there was something weird about you and that's fine, I think. I've heard of women who can do things, heal and stuff, see into the future, talk to the dead, worshipping something while dancing naked on a full moon and all that. I figured you might have been into something like that, but a reincarnated murderer, now that's something else!'

467

Looking around the room, she saw her discarded boots and picked them up. She found her soggy shawl hanging over a chair and grabbed it. 'I'll be leaving now, thank you. Perhaps you could thank Sir Richard for me?'

Eira hadn't moved, but remained seated, her hands clasped tightly in her lap. 'Won't you listen? If you won't stay for me, stay for Gwenllian. She…we need you.'

Bronwen froze and stared at her in disbelief. 'Gwenllian! For God's sake, the child's a ghost. I see her everywhere. I'm sure she'll show up and yes, if I can, I'll try to help her, but this…' She flung her arms wide. 'This, is ridiculous. What the hell do you want from me? Forgiveness, wasn't it? Well, I forgive you for being crazy, all right?'

Eira ignored her ranting. 'You loved her once, tried to protect her.' Eira's voice was pleading, but she still didn't move. 'Please, you've lived through so much torment, so much pain and suffering and survived. You were always the strong one, even in this lifetime.'

'I don't know what you're talking about. Are you still in this delusional past or what? You don't know anything about me or my life. You're obviously having another one of your strange episodes, like the other week, maybe you're high on something, but I'm done here. I'm tired. My head feels mushy. I am going home.'

Before Eira could stop her, she flung open the door and was gone.

***

Eira listened as Bronwen ran down the stairs and heard the front door open. Slowly, she followed, but when she reached the door, she quietly closed it and leant against it, fighting back the tears. She was so tired.

Every bone, every muscle, ached, but more than anything, her heart was broken; she had failed. It wasn't going to end. Perhaps that was the last torture for her. The villagers had promised her a sentence. Had they messed it up so badly that even that wasn't true? Bronwen would never listen to her now. She had ruined it for herself and, perhaps, the child, and she listened quietly as the echoes of the past slowly faded away.

***

'What do you think is happening?' Lucy poured herself another cup of herbal tea and took out two paracetamol and knocked them back with a glass of water. Her mouth felt like moss and her head was splitting.

Adam glanced toward the kitchen door, waiting for it to open, but when it didn't, he shrugged. 'Who knows? I thought she'd still be groggy, but from their raised voices, I'd say she was feeling much better.' He bit into his piece of toast and sat back, cradling his mug of coffee on his stomach. 'I can't think why she and Eira would be arguing though…' He glanced around at the others, hoping they knew, but no-one said anything.

Sir Richard stood up and paced the kitchen. Michael watched him before resuming his eating. He could feel the tension in the kitchen and wondered just who this strange woman was? He tucked into his bacon and eggs and kept his mouth shut; it had been one hell of a night. Quickly glancing across at Rosalyn, he thought two things: Firstly, she was still as lovely as he remembered, but way too skinny, and secondly, she looked as if she was going to blow. He wondered when that would be.

'Do you think she's all right?' Sir Richard finally spoke. 'I mean, I personally think we should have taken her to the hospital, why Eira didn't—'

'Dad! Just shut up! Forget about the bitch, believe me, she's not worth it!'

Everyone jumped with Rosalyn's outburst and they all turned to her. Michael stopped eating and waited. Sir Richard frowned down at her. Judith clicked her tongue and shook her head at her rudeness.

'What the hell's got into you?' Adam asked suspiciously. 'You've never liked Bronwen, have you? Even before you met her you had something against the woman, so what is it?'

She fidgeted in her chair and clasped her cup of tea. Pushing her untouched plate of toast away, she licked her dry lips. 'I was going to tell you when we were alone.' She glanced across at Michael who was watching her, a slight smile on his face; she looked away. 'I hired a private detective to find out anything about her.' Seeing the shocked expressions, she quickly went on. 'Well, you never knew anything about her,' she said defensively. 'She could have been another gold digger, like that Catherine. I didn't want to risk anyone, being hurt again.'

'But, hiring a detective?' Sir Richard shook his head.

'It's a good job I did. She has a history, and, it's not pleasant.' Seeing she had everyone's attention, she sat back and took her time. She sipped her lukewarm tea and looked over the rim of the cup.

'I'm not sure I really want to know. I like Bronwen Mortimer. I spoke with her last night and she seems a decent sort of woman. A bit shy, perhaps, but decent. I think you were wrong to do this, Rosalyn Kenward.' Judith stood up and began collecting the dirty plates.

Setting down her empty cup, Rosalyn looked up at her. 'I wonder if you'd still think that, if you knew her name wasn't really Mortimer.'

Judith stopped collecting and looked at Rosalyn, waiting.

'Oh yes.' Rosalyn cocked an eyebrow, feeling very pleased with herself. 'That was her mother's maiden name. Her real name is Gillespie.'

Judith carefully put down the plates. 'Whatever her reason for changing her name is—'

'Her reason was murder.' Rosalyn interrupted. Her gaze fell on everyone in the room, but she stopped at her father who was staring at her with a mixture of disbelief and sorrow. She frowned and swallowed hard. Getting up, she found her big handbag on the sideboard and pulled out sheaves of paper and handed them to her father. 'Here, read it yourself.'

He slowly took the paper. He read the first one before moving to a chair, he sat down heavily and began to read the rest. When he'd finished, he slowly shook his head.

'What is it, Dad?' Adam sat forward but didn't attempt to take the paper.

It was Rosalyn who answered. 'Her name is Bronwen Gillespie. She lived with her father after her mother died when she was aged ten. Something about an accident, but my detective couldn't find out much. Anyway, a few years later, the police were called to her home and found her sitting in the corner of her kitchen, a huge kitchen knife in her hands, covered in blood. She'd killed her father, stabbing him repeatedly.'

She gazed around the room and felt a small glimmer of justification at telling. She'd still had doubts, but now that she'd begun, she couldn't stop. 'She was thirteen. In fact, it was a day after her birthday. Bronwen never spoke a word. The coroner's report showed that the father had been dead for about twenty-four hours, and Bronwen had done nothing. She was sent to some special hospital for minors with "problems", and she stayed there for a few months, until she finally spoke and told them her father had been abusing her for years. On her thirteenth birthday, he'd decided that she was old enough to take over his wife's role in his bed. He'd attempted to rape her and she'd killed him; she said it was an accident.'

'What happened to her then?' Lucy was sitting forward, her eyes wide.

'It is a bit hazy, but she went to stay in various foster homes until her father's stepsister took her on. Bronwen continued to have therapy, but it didn't seem to be a success. The aunt died not too long ago and she got everything.'

No one spoke for a long time. Adam reached across and read through the detective's report. Michael read it over his shoulder. Sir Richard stared at the floor and Judith and Lucy both stood up and carried on collecting and washing the dirty plates, but both looked stunned.

Finally, Lucy spoke, her voice no more than a whisper. 'You never know, do you? I liked the look of her too.'

Sir Richard's head jerked up. 'Now stop that! We don't know really, do we? She was a child, for Christ's sake. A child! An abused child! Who could blame her? I certainly couldn't.' He turned to look at Adam who was clutching the report but staring off into space. 'Adam, what do you think about it?'

Adam blinked, and looked at his father and sighed loudly; he glanced around at everyone as they waited expectantly. Abruptly, he pushed back his chair and threw the papers on the table. 'I couldn't care less! I have horses that need attention. I'll leave you to do the gossiping!' With that, he strode out of the kitchen and slammed the back door behind him.

'I think he was beginning to like her.' Richard turned to his daughter. 'I think you've burst his bubble.'

Rosalyn looked upset, but stuck out her chin defiantly. 'Then I've done the right thing. When will you get rid of her? Today, or do you have to give her notice?'

Richard looked surprised at the question. 'Get rid of her? I can't just throw her out over this.' He pointed at the discarded papers. 'She was a child, Rosalyn.'

Roslyn stood up and clenched her fists. She glared down at her father. 'Children kill, Dad, but had you forgotten that they can grow up and still be killers?' Storming out, she headed for the hallway. They heard her running upstairs and then a loud bang as her bedroom door slammed shut.

Everyone stared after her, too stunned to say anything for a moment. Judith finally spoke. 'And so, it would seem that she does remember.'

'After all these years. The poor lass.' Lucy slumped into a chair and looked across at Sir Richard who looked frightened, but he was trying to compose himself. He coughed and slicked his hair back. 'Sir, did you think she'd forgotten about…her?'

His eyes searched her face for a moment before his shoulders slumped and he visibly sagged in the chair. 'Yes, I really thought, no, hoped that she'd never remember that day. I hoped, that her mother's… accident would be something she'd grieve, but let go.' He glanced at the closed kitchen door and chewed his lower lip. 'Obviously, I was wrong.'

Judith nodded. 'Yes, I remember us speaking of it back then. We all hoped she was too young to understand. And when she never asked…' She shrugged and let the sentence fall away.

'What are you all talking about?'

They turned to Michael, who was still sitting quietly, watching the drama before him. He looked confused, but now he sat forward. 'Are you talking about those rumours I heard as a boy? The ones about the ghost that's supposed to haunt this place? Are they true? I've been dying to ask for years, but my father always said that I shouldn't because it might upset you, sir.' He directed his questions at Sir Richard. 'Is it true then that this ghost killed your wife?'

'Aye, it was.' Lucy answered instead, 'and the children saw it.'

'Bloody hell! Adam's never mentioned it.'

Sir Richard looked interested at this. 'Oh yes, well, perhaps he was never really sure if what he'd seen was real? No-one ever mentions the…the thing. We go about our lives, pretending it doesn't exist and somehow, we convince ourselves. Sometimes, it works, but then we lose someone and it's all brought back and we begin our pretence again.' He looked Michael firmly in the eye. 'It's fun being a Kenward. Being cursed because of something long forgotten is great. We husbands lose our wives, people we love get hurt, and our wealth slowly dwindles into nothing.' Every word dripped with sarcasm.

Michael looked embarrassed. 'I'm sorry, sir, I didn't mean anything.'

Richard attempted to smile reassuringly. 'It's all right. I just wish it would end. So many years of pain and bad luck and death in my family, I don't understand why.'

'I do.'

They all whirled round to find Geoff standing in the open door-way of the back door. Ignoring his muddy boots, he slowly entered the kitchen, closed the door behind him, and pulled out a chair. He sat at the head of the large table, and looked at every person watching him, before leaning forward and resting his arms on the table. 'It was something my grandfather told me as a boy. He died four days later and I often asked my dad if that was the reason. He would shake his head, but I was never convinced.'

'Geoff,' Richard barely managed to control himself. 'Frankly, after the morning of revelations, I'm in no mood to sit here and listen to ramblings. What do you know that we haven't already talked about?'

Geoff nodded. 'It goes back to the main ancestor we know about, William, who killed King Richard at the battle of Bosworth. He had a child, a daughter, Gwenllian. She was murdered. We know all this, I know, but my grandfather told me about the cover-up. Something to do with politics, and it was swept under the carpet, so to speak. Lady Anne was never brought to trial, and she was never charged. I don't know how or why, but the child's nurse was found guilty of it and was hanged for the crime. My grandfather said her body was buried somewhere on Kenward land.'

'What happened to this Anne woman?'

Geoff glanced at Lucy and shrugged. 'I'm afraid I don't really know. There were stories that she was bricked up in a room and left to die alone. Other people believe she killed herself. Apparently, William was never the same again and refused to acknowledge her. He spent much of his time away from home, doing King Henry's bidding. He oversaw the rebuilding of Ludlow Castle, for one, and, as we know, he was granted lots of land. He built a Hall on this site and died years later but he never lived in it'

Michael coughed. 'Erm, perhaps I'm a bit dumb, but, what has that story to do with your late wife being killed?'

'The villagers of Derwen were so disgusted at the injustice, they cursed the wife. Something about never being at peace until justice prevails. My grandfather told me of a piece of paper found by his father that confessed to the villagers' inability to perform the ritual correctly. The curse had gone wrong. It became obvious the murdered child was stuck too, kept away from Heaven until the one returns to forgive the crime. Well, something along those lines anyway. It said something about Masses and prayers being said for the release of the child's soul, but nothing worked.'

Geoff shook his head. 'The stories have become vague over the years, but Richard and I have both seen the child. She was there when Helen died and she has been blamed for many deaths in the Kenward family, mainly women, wives.'

Judith shivered. 'Yes, I've seen her too…and I heard her voice the other day.' Seeing Richard's reaction, she shook her head. 'I'm sorry, I didn't want to believe it at the time. I've tried very hard to ignore all the strange goings-on. But what I find so hard to understand is, she's a child. I've read bits about the first Kenwards, and if I'm right, she was barely eleven years old.'

Geoff nodded. 'And that's what I've considered all these years, why would a child be so evil? How could a child do such things? But, then I think, well, she's dead, what the hell do I know?'

Richard stood up. 'My head hurts from all this speculation and revelation, I can't take it all in.' Turning to Geoff, he nodded toward the others. 'They'll fill you in. I need to be alone for a while.'

Geoff watched him walk away before getting up and switching on the kettle. While he waited for it to boil, he leant back on the sideboard and crossed his ankles and arms. 'Okay, fill me in.'

***

William stared out of the window at the growing sun. He'd sat there since the first grey light chased away the black dark. Now streams of yellow and orange pierced the room and warmed his body. His hand curled around a flagon of mead, but it remained untouched.

From somewhere outside, he could hear cattle waking and the farmers who worked them calling to them to move along. He heard the shouts and the calls of the farmers and his villagers as they roused themselves to the day's work. Even after a long night of drinking and merrymaking, they still crawled out of their moth-ridden beds to tend the land and the animals.

He had watched them all night, drinking his best ale while feasting and dancing to the music of travelling musicians. They'd laughed and sung and a few disappeared outside to make love to their women. He'd watched silently from his chair at the top of the Hall, a tray of wine, meat, and bread by his side. Beyond a quick bow and curtsey as they'd entered his home, the villagers mostly ignored him, until finally, they'd taken their leave an hour before.

It had been three years since her death. Three long years since he'd stood and watched another die because of politics. Three years since they had cursed him and his own. Three years he waited to die. He hadn't, and he hated them for their incompetence, because for three years he had known he was a coward.

Easing himself up, he wandered over to the open window and breathed in the warm, sweet air, then froze. Outside in the meadow, he stared at the thousands of daisies that had sprung up over night, covering it in their pure white petals. He swallowed hard and banged the shutters closed. He then staggered back to the untouched flagon and raised it to his trembling lips and drank. He remembered the daisy chain, the last gift she had given him. Would he ever find peace? Would she ever forgive them?

***

She lay wrapped in the thick blanket and shivered. The fire had gone out, but she had no strength left to crawl over to the small fireplace and try to relight it. Besides, they'd only given her so much firewood; it would run out soon anyway.

476

She listened carefully to the sounds reaching her from outside. Just now and again she could work out what they were, a shout amongst his men or the cattle being moved from one meadow to another or the guards marching past far below. She'd cared at first, it was a connection of sorts to the outside world, but now, she'd lost all enthusiasm for life outside and pulled the blanket tighter around her head.

Her thoughts wandered back to better times, as they always did. Memories of her childhood with her beloved mother. She had been loved completely and the grief that came with it hurt. Many times, she dreamt of William, and in the early grey dawn, she could almost feel his arms wrapped around her, his lips caressing her body, demanding that she open to him, and she'd wake with a cry. Then, the realisation that it would never end would come flooding back with a vengeance, and she'd sob until she could sob no more.

He'd thought of a good way to kill her without touching her. Sometimes, she wished for the hangman's noose so that she would have peace. She didn't believe the villagers capable of magic. How dare they think they had any power over her? William and Henry had the power over her and this was it. This was her punishment for their decision. Even though she'd played along with it, it had been to their advantage that Nia be blamed. The order was to live and remember, to be always alone, to wallow in her guilt and remorse, but without the peace of a confessor. She glanced across at the small table near the door. The large knife lay across it. They always left it.

***

Bronwen half ran, half staggered down the driveway at first, expecting someone to chase after her and force her back into the Hall; no-one came. By the time she reached the gates, she collapsed against them, fighting for breath before pushing herself onward, to sanctuary, to her home.

She slowed her pace to a fast walk but she couldn't keep it up. Her head felt woozy, as if she were underwater or drunk. She knew she wasn't walking very straight at times, veering off to the left on occasions, but she didn't care what she looked like. She wasn't expecting to pass anyone and frankly, if Eira did come after her, she really didn't care what she thought, either.

What the hell had happened to her? The images that floated around her head brought many emotions and she had to wipe the tears out of her eyes as they blurred her vision. Had the child really shown her Nia? Tortured, frightened, and alone? She could feel her pain and felt ill with it as she remembered Eira's words. '*It is you.*' How could she be Nia? It just wasn't possible. In fact, it was ridiculous! It had to be.

And Eira. What a load of rubbish! Did she really believe it? Was she delusional? A schizophrenic, perhaps, who believed she was this Lady Anne from the past? Could she be possessed? Had this woman taken over her body after all the years of living in Derwen? She knew any of these were possible, but which one she preferred was asking too much at that moment. Her head and body felt absolutely wrecked.

She remembered Eira's lounge and the multitude of photographs covering every inch of the walls and sideboards. Many had been black and white. Many looked like Eira in different clothes and hair styles. Was it just that women in her family closely resembled each other? She knew she looked a little like her own mother, but there were differences. She tried to remember the photos and think of any particular differences; she couldn't and her stomach felt like it had dropped.

As she neared her cottage, she stopped and let her shoulders sag. She felt so tired, but she needed the fresh air on her skin and the breeze in her hair for just a moment. The last hour was unbelievable, but, in the scheme of things, since moving to Derwen, it was probably fairly believable.

If Eira was who she believed and *if* she was this Nia, was she in danger? After all, Lady Anne let her die. She was a murderer. Was she capable of harming her again in this lifetime? *If* she was Nia, it might explain why Gwenllian was drawn to her and why she had shown her the past.

It would also explain why she felt a connection with the girl. She wanted to protect her, wrap her in her arms and keep her safe. She stopped at the gate and felt the small crack as her heart broke with emotion. She thought of the lonely, little child, and she yearned to make it right, to save Gwenllian and, perhaps, herself. Then, she realised what she was admitting. Was she about to believe that Eira was right? Suddenly she felt very, very scared.

***

Eira sat in the large armchair and gazed around the study. She was lost, it was finished, that was all she could think about; saving her had not been enough. She vaguely heard doors slamming, people talking, and knew it was about Bronwen. Darling Bronwen, how was she going to make it right? How long would she have?

Sir Richard startled her as he strode in and slumped down in the opposite chair. He jerked back when he saw her and licked his lips nervously. 'We were wondering where you were.' He leant closer, then he suddenly knelt before her and took one of her hands. 'Eira, you look ill. Let me fetch someone?' Glancing around the room, he lowered his voice. 'Where's Bronwen Mortimer?'

She didn't bother to ask why he sounded scornful; he knew about her past, no doubt they all did. 'Bronwen has gone home. I'm worried about her.' She could hardly form the words; her face felt numb. 'I was hoping you might drive me over there.'

'I don't think so, at least, not until I've thought things through.' Richard looked embarrassed and looked down at Eira's cold hand, which he still held tightly. 'I think you should know that Rosalyn hired a detective and he found something about Bronwen; she killed her own father.'

He looked up then and searched her face. 'I know you like her, but…I just don't know what to do.'

She could tell he was trying to keep the pleading out of his voice, but she heard it anyway and tried to smile. 'It'll be all right. Richard. I knew about Bronwen, and I'll say this, listen to the whole story first before judging her.' She squeezed his hand as he stared open-mouthed at her confession. 'Secondly,' she carried on, 'I don't care that Bronwen is a killer. It was self-defence, because, let's be honest, aren't we all?'

CHAPTER THIRTY-NINE

ROSE AND DAVID SNEAKED AWAY from the open kitchen window and headed for the walled garden. They found a sheltered spot and slowly eased themselves onto the bench and shook their heads.

'What do you make of all that?'

Rose thought before answering. 'I can't believe it. I mean…she seemed so…so normal looking. She behaved as if she was shy, definitely, and apparently, people found her beautiful. I wonder what Adam is thinking?'

David rounded on her, the look on his face a mixture of hurt and anger. 'I couldn't give a damn what he thinks! If you still do, then this'—he flicked his hand between them—'this is never going to work. I won't be second to that sod!'

Rose stared back at him, secretly pleased that he felt such jealousy for her. She reached out and brushed away a strand of hair from his forehead. 'I don't care about him like that; not anymore.' She wondered if that were really true; after all, she'd only had the one night with David. Sneaking upstairs before anyone noticed had helped the passion, in the beginning, but after their first lustful encounter, he'd turned to her an hour later and slowly and thoroughly made love to her.

Sometime in the early hours, they'd woken to find themselves entwined in each other's arms and she'd felt something stirring inside her that completely took her by surprise.

Now, sitting here, his face inches from hers, his brown eyes penetrating her own, so intense, so full of emotion, she knew without a doubt she could love this man and know for certain, he could love her.

The sharing of such surprising news now proved what she'd first thought. This woman could cause problems for Adam. Perhaps he was more involved than he'd let on. He'd certainly stormed out quickly enough when challenged. If Adam had been seeing this woman, it didn't matter; at least, not to her. She realised, rather embarrassingly, that now she had the real thing, here, next to her, it had been nothing more than a crush.

David watched her for a moment, seeing the various thoughts show on her face. He reached for her and very gently squeezed her hand. 'I understand how you've felt over the last few months…I do, really,' he quickly added, seeing the doubt in her face. 'I've secretly been watching you for a long time. Hoping you'd look at me, notice how I felt, read my mind, but anyone watching could see you only had eyes for him.' He clenched his teeth and breathed heavily. 'He won't see you, ever, but I will.'

They sat in silence, her head on his shoulder, both lost in their own thoughts, until she broke it. 'Do you think they'll throw her out of the cottage?' She turned to look at him and continued shyly. 'I've…I've always fancied that cottage.'

David smiled and squeezed her hand again. 'I think that when, if, we're ready, you'll come and live with me, not in some cottage he's converted. I've bought an old barn off Dad that I've been slowly working on.'

She smiled back at him and kissed his cheek. 'I like the sound of that.' Changing the subject again, she sighed. 'I wonder what will happen now, though?'

David didn't answer; he didn't know or care. He was twenty-one, he had half a home built, and he had the girl he'd been in love with for almost a year. Adam could go and rot. He'd lost Rose, and now it would seem as if he'd lost this Bronwen woman. Sad, in a way; he'd liked her too.

***

James got out of the car for the third time and walked round the cottage; it was nearly dinnertime, where the hell was the woman? His patience had snapped hours ago, his constant niggling thoughts that she was with someone else increased over the morning, and now he just wanted to kill her, and he'd kill whoever she was with.

He wanted her to feel pain like nothing ever experienced. He wanted days with Bronwen Mortimer, not just hours, to break her completely before allowing her to die. He would torture the stink of another man off her before replacing it with his own, so that when she died, it would be his scent she remembered, not the other man's.

A noise alerted him to freeze. It was the sound of the small garden gate, he was sure of it. He stood, hidden round the side of the cottage. Now, he slowly edged his way to the front and peered round the corner. His heart raced at the sight of her holding onto the gate, pale and shaking, obviously distressed. He liked that. She suddenly let go and stumbled up the path, fumbling with the door key. He looked her up and down. She looked spectacular. She wore a green velvet dress that looked stained and wrinkled, and her hair was wild and loose, cascading down her back and gently blowing across her neck. He loathed and lusted for her even more.

He stood shaking with adrenalin and fury, his mind racing. Here she was, now was his chance. She was opening the door. There was no-one around to hear her scream. All he had to do was rush at her and he'd be in. A noise behind him made him spin round, his heart hammering in his chest. A small shed stood with its door half open. The door moved slightly in the breeze, and he sighed with relief. Turning back, he watched the front door shut firmly; she was inside. But opening his hand, he smiled. That didn't mean he couldn't get in, of course. The French door key glimmered in the sunshine, and he briskly returned to the back of the cottage.

***

Eira walked over to the bookshelves and ran her finger along the many binders. She wasn't seeing any of them, but they felt solid, while she felt as flimsy as toilet tissue. One more tear and she would break apart. Sadly, for her, it wouldn't end. She wouldn't find peace. Not her.

Richard silently watched her. She'd changed, yet she was still the same woman he'd known all his life, but she couldn't possibly be. It didn't make sense, any of it, and his head hurt from thinking. It was always there, always niggling away, but as quickly as he thought it, it was gone. The knowledge that she had always been an elderly woman was impossible. Perhaps that's why he'd never admitted it to himself, or others. They would have had to have seen it too. why hadn't anyone ever said anything?

As if reading his mind, Eira turned to him and came and sat down wearily. He wanted to reach out and hold her hand again, but he suddenly felt afraid.

'It's all right, Richard, I'm not going to hurt you. I never have, have I?'

He slowly shook his head and relaxed a little. It was true, she'd never hurt anyone, she'd always been there for advice, comfort, empathy; everyone turned to Eira. He attempted a smile. 'Sorry, I just… Eira, there's something I don't understand, well, I don't understand a lot of it, but…you…you…' He couldn't get the question out and he shook his head and leant back in his chair. How could he ask such a stupid question? *Are you real?*

He glanced across at her. She was staring at him, waiting. She knew what he was thinking. He could see it in her face; he looked away first. 'Yes, Richard, I am real. Should I be dead? Many times over. There are things about me that…perhaps it is time for people to know. If the spell has broken, then, perhaps it is time.'

'Spell? What spell?' His voice shook and he coughed nervously.

'You'll maybe have read about it amongst the papers I've left lying around in libraries over the years. I'm sure Geoff will fill you in, though I don't know what he thinks about it all. His great-grandfather was the one who started digging around; always did like to know everything… anyway, I'm digressing. I'm well over five hundred years old. Richard.' She raised her hand to stop his interrupting. 'Richard, I can tell you everything if you insist, and I will, it would actually be a pleasure after all these years of silence, but first, I need to talk to you about Bronwen. I'm worried about her.'

Richard sat too stunned to speak for a moment; he was trying very hard to comprehend what he was hearing. Mad or delusional sprang to mind, but that didn't explain his own thoughts, unless hypnosis was involved? That might explain everything, but he looked up and she was waiting impatiently. 'Bronwen? Do you know her then? I, mean, before she became my tenant?

Eira grunted. 'It would take too long. It's Bronwen I'm concerned about right now.' She seemed to drift off and stared beyond him, not seeing him, but someone else. 'I've cared for and loved you all your life, William, don't let us down now, please.'

'Let you down?' He frowned and quickly glanced behind him as the hairs on the back of his neck stood on end. He licked his dry lips. 'Hang on, you called me William. Eira, are you all right? You aren't making sense…' He hesitated, and after a moment she seemed to realise he was there and focused on him again.

'Bronwen, Richard, has been a part of our lives for a very long time. She is the key to saving us, but I might have ruined it by pushing her too hard. I need to know what you think of her, in case…well, in case something happens to me. I don't want her life spoilt in any way because of men, do you see?'

He sighed and ran his fingers through his hair; he was exhausted and he was having difficulty taking it all in. 'I won't condemn the woman before I've spoken with her. First, though, I'm taking you home and I'm fetching the doctor. You're worrying me with all this talk of something happening. We all need some rest.' He stood up abruptly.

She shook her head but otherwise didn't move.

Richard sighed loudly. 'Come on, I'll listen to everyone and we'll get to the bottom of all this and work something out.'

Mass hysteria, hallucinations, or mass hypnosis, he was going for one or all three theories for what he was hearing and feeling, but his body and mind were just too drained to think straight. Eira was worrying him, she had never looked so ill. 'Come on.' He reached down and pulled her up. 'You need some rest. You look very tired. It's been a long night.'

'Tired.' Her voice sounded strange, wistful, and she was looking beyond him again. 'Yes, I'm so tired.' Suddenly, her eyes flashed at him and her face contorted with scorn. 'Yes, I'm tired! Tired of living. Tired of seeing those I love die and find peace, but never me…never me! Oh, William, I'm tired of death that stalks me, but never finds me. I'm tired of the pain and misery, but more than anything, the absolute loneliness. I see those who have died come back in different skins and not know me, always having to start again.' She grasped his hand tighter and lifted it to her cheek. 'My darling William, haven't I paid the price a thousand times? Will you ever forgive me?'

He gently withdrew his hand and let out a long, shaky breath; she was losing it. 'Eira?' He spoke gently, but his voice quivered with fear. 'Eira, come on now, I'll take you home, to rest…'

She stared at him and it frightened him so much, he stepped back. She saw his movement and dropped his hand with a grunt of disgust. 'I am home, William. You built this home for me. You built a special room, don't you remember? When I didn't die, you brought me here and you left me in the dark. You left me to rot, William. You should have hanged me.'

The sudden anguish in her voice encouraged him to reach out and try to comfort her; this was Eira, wasn't it? But she backed away, her eyes wide and brimming with tears.

'Leave me alone.' She focused on him and then looked beyond him. She held her breath and then suddenly, she moved quickly. 'I need to go now.'

Before he could react, she'd forced her way past him and was opening the front door. She turned and looked at him once, then slammed the door behind her.

He stood frozen to the spot, his mind a whirl of questions trying to work out what had just happened. What was happening to Eira, the woman he'd known his whole life? The old woman, friend of his family for generations, she had always been a part of his life. He was sixty-three and if she'd always been old, then…God no! But that was impossible.

Something she'd said made him sit down suddenly. He'd told no-one about the small, secret room his grandfather found while renovating. There was no window, only a small, narrow bed, almost rotten, an old, wooden chair, and a rusted old chain still attached to the stone wall. 'In the dark,' she'd said. Did she know, or, could it really be possible? He reached for the brandy decanter and, with trembling hands, poured himself a large one.

***

Her legs barely made it to the couch where she collapsed. Her dress smelt of soil and rain and dirt and nothing could erase the image of Nia, sitting in the filth, knowing she was going to die by his hands. The man she helped bring into this world was going to take her out of it. She had felt the intense rage at being betrayed by William, but overriding it was the complete helplessness of her situation. No-one would listen to her. She was condemned.

She couldn't pretend anymore that it was some hallucination. The knowing she'd had in that dark cell refused to go away. She closed her eyes tightly and tried to remember every detail, every sight and sound. She tried to recall that strange afternoon when she'd had some kind of time-slip; the people, their clothes, their faces, but nothing solid would come.

She was shattered. Her head ached from the effort of thinking, her body ached from the effort of feeling, and the walk home had never felt so long, expecting someone at any moment. It didn't really matter anyway, she'd realised; they knew where she would be, where else could she go? She would have to face Eira at some time, but right now, her eyes were too heavy and her limbs felt like lead. She allowed her body to submit to the blackness and hoped Eira would give her enough time to recover.

*****

It was the dolls. Finding them hidden in Nia's small chest of herbs proved that she was guilty of witchcraft and murder; at least, that was what they had declared. Added to that was the fact that she'd been seen stumbling down the steps, whimpering and incoherent, as the guards raced up them. When she'd finally been encouraged to speak by the captain of the guard, she told him that Lady Anne had killed the child. Rushing up to the battlements, they found Lady Anne clasping a knife to her bosom, declaring she had tried to save Gwenllian and stabbed Nia in the shoulder in the hope that she would stop trying to push the child over the edge.

Being that the stab wound was from behind, they had to consider the possibility, and Lady Anne was obviously in shock, so the guards had carefully carried her down the steps. Nia, still whimpering, had been escorted to the Great Hall, where she was seated with two guards. The child's body was carefully wrapped in cloth and laid out in the small chapel. The steward had no idea what he should do, except someone had to pay for the crime. His heart ached with the loss. He'd loved the child, as had everyone. One of them was to blame; he would find out which one.

The search he ordered was nothing more than a need to find something, to do something, anything that might incriminate one of them. He'd never considered that Nia would have harmed the child. Anyone could see she worshipped her, but then, could Lady Anne? She'd looked so distraught and her ladies had taken her to her bed. Nia said nothing beyond that her lady murdered the girl.

When the blacksmith came forward and said he'd seen Nia speak sharply to Gwenllian only minutes before, he'd had no choice, though the men felt unhappy about it; they'd searched her things. Finding the dolls had been a great shock and they crossed themselves urgently. There was one that looked like King Richard, another that was the image of Gwenllian, and the third looked like Lady Anne. The steward had not stopped to think or to attempt to make sense of it. All he knew was anger and sorrow for the child. Heading back downstairs, he was at the front of the group of men as they'd surged into the Great Hall and descended on the old woman.

**

Her eyes flew open as her senses told her she wasn't alone. The room was bright as the setting sun shone in and warmed her face, but her stomach clenched with fear and her throat constricted as she looked up into the face of the estate agent.

She froze for an instant, and then rolled off the couch and jumped up, keeping it between them. She backed away a little, but stopped when she felt the cool wall behind her.

Neither one looked away.

Now, he slowly moved his gaze down her body and back to her face. The shadow of a smile played around his mouth and he raised an eyebrow. 'You do look lovely when you sleep. Had a hard night?'

She heard the unkind tone with the question and briefly wondered what he meant.

'What are you doing?' It was all her voice could manage and that was nothing more than a croak. Her hand went automatically to her throat and she swallowed, but she had no saliva.

He stood watching her closely. His hands behind his back, he looked perfectly relaxed and calm. Now, he brought his hands around to rest on his stomach. In one he held a large knife. She felt dizzy with fear but kept her eyes locked on his. A slow smile spread over his face as he watched her reaction. 'So, how are we going to do this?'

Bronwen desperately looked around for anything she could use as a weapon. He watched her and laughed; he was enjoying himself. Perhaps the small coffee table, if she could reach it in time, pick it up, and throw it? Use it as a shield, perhaps? She glanced toward the front door. Had she locked it? Could she get to it and make a run for it? The French doors? Were they locked? How had he got in?

Reading her mind, he took a step forward. 'You should never leave the doors unlocked, strange men could get in, but if they already have a key, you're fucked. Men like me, for instance.' He stepped closer; he was determined to take his time. She looked like a frightened rabbit again and he loved it. He hoped she'd try to fight.

'I don't know what you think you're doing, but...'

Her voice quivered and he grinned maliciously. 'My darling Bronwen, I know exactly what I'm going to do with you, so there's no need for you to worry about that.'

He stepped closer. There was, perhaps, seven feet between them and the couch. She could feel the adrenalin pumping around her body and felt her chest constrict as he took another step. There was nowhere for her to run, she had to be ready when he attacked. She unconsciously flicked at her nails to test how long they were. Not too bad. Perhaps she could claw him to death before he used his knife?

The absurd idea almost made her cry, but she sniffed the tears back. She had won once. She'd been a skinny thirteen-year-old against an overweight man; she'd succeeded then. Okay, he hadn't a huge knife, she'd had that, and had the element of surprise, but, surely, she had a chance? She had to believe that. He expected her to be compliant—they always did. Could that be her element of surprise? She would fight him with every last breath. She would die before—

Out of the corner of her eye, she was sure she'd seen movement. She dared not hope someone would come now. Her legs almost gave way completely as the head quickly popped around the front door and withdrew. Adam! She had to keep that agent talking, looking at her. 'You don't scare me, you know, I've killed a man before, for… for trying it on with me. I can do it again. My dad never knew I had fight in me until I struck out.'

James found this amusing and laughed out loud, but stepping closer as he did. 'Darling, I'm not trying—'

'I killed him…with a knife. He liked young girls…do you?' Her voice sounded weak, but she kept going. 'He wanted me to do things… why are there sick men in this world?' She could see Adam slowly creeping into the hallway, his eyes fixed on James. 'What made you sick and twisted?'

James ignored the questions and edged closer. 'I don't like girls. I like my women mature, full breasted, and ripe, like you.' His eyes travelled over her body and he licked his lips. 'I have the knife today, you naughty girl. You should be punished for killing Daddy. So, can I undress you, or would you prefer to give me a striptease, instead? I'll give you ten seconds to decide.'

She cringed, feeling the solid wall behind. There wasn't anywhere for her to run, no escape, she would have to stand and fight and hope. Adam was, perhaps, ten feet away. James was slowly counting down. She could see a faint sheen of sweat on his brow and he looked over-excited. Could she use it to her advantage?

He reached the number three when Adam suddenly dived forward and sent him crashing to the floor. She hadn't seen him make the leap or had time to warn him about the knife. James turned in that fraction of a second as Adam flew across the lounge. She watched as they wrestled on the floor, gasping for breath as each man fought for the knife. She saw a flash of metal and gasped with horror, but she couldn't look away, or move. She was frozen to the floor, knowing her life and Adam's were forfeit if James succeeded. She heard a grunt and a strangled cry. It broke the spell. She tore away from the wall and fled toward the kitchen. She had to get herself a weapon.

She knew someone was behind her almost instantly. She knew it was James. She cried out in fear, even before she felt his hot breath on her neck and his arm around her waist. He threw her back toward the lounge and stood glaring down at her as she lost her balance and fell face down, the wind knocked out of her. She had time to glance behind her, saw the blood smeared on his shirt and looked toward the motionless body of Adam. His face was turned away from her, but she could see the red stain slowly spreading over his blue T-shirt.

It was all she had time to see before James was on top of her, his weight pinning her down; she fought for breath. He flipped her over easily. She had no strength to fight at that moment; she felt utterly defeated. Was Adam dead? If he was, so was she. No-one else would come.

She looked up into James' smug face and felt physically sick. He knelt over her and slowly began to massage his erection, all the time watching her face, smiling at her reaction. She turned her head away and he yanked it back. 'Now, now, that was naughty, wasn't it?' He licked her lips, and then licked his own. 'You will watch how I like it. You're mine now, Bronwen darling, for as long as I desire you, and you will do as I say.'

'Never!' It was all she managed before his hand closed over her throat. Her own hands were pinned beneath his legs. She struggled to free them, to fight back as she fought for air and consciousness. She had to stay awake to have a chance. Her chest heaved and she saw dark patches before her eyes, but at that moment, he let her go and lay on top of her. She coughed and gasped for breath as he kissed and bit her neck violently.

She couldn't focus on anything beyond staying awake and fighting for breath, while at the same time her skin wanted to retreat anywhere as long as it was away from his violating lips. The fury she felt was overwhelming and it gave her the strength to begin squirming enough to free her hands and pull his hair. He gasped and fought back, slapping her cheek hard enough that she tasted blood.

'Now, now, darling, is that anger you're feeling? I always knew you were a wildcat. I saw that in Shrewsbury, didn't I, you bad girl. You'll have to pay for that, you know.' His mocking tone infuriated her and she tried to fight again, but he held onto her wrists and pinned them above her head. 'Oh yes, please, fight again, I love it.'

She could see and feel just how much it did excite him and she stopped and lay unmoving. 'I'll never do what you want.'

He moved his face closer to hers so that his lips brushed the tops of her own. 'Oh, but you will, Bronwen darling.'

'Don't use my name.' She spat the words at him and turned her face away. She could see Adam, still lying motionless, his arms spread-eagle, his face turned away. There seemed to be so much blood, he couldn't possibly be alive.

James followed her gaze and rested his cheek on hers. 'Oh, don't worry about your boyfriend. He's gone to a happier place. I'll let you join him when I've finished.'

Fear gripped her and she felt the tears welling up. James raised his face off hers and slowly lifted himself and knelt over her waist again, the knife still in his hand. 'Don't cry for him, darling. He wanted you as much as I do. Haven't you learnt yet? All men are animals when it comes to women. Was he all romance, flowers, chocolates, and chivalry? He wanted the same thing as I'm going to get. Only, now, he's dead!'

She flinched at his words. 'He's nothing to do with me.'

Momentarily off guard as he laughed at her, she conjured all her energy and twisted, sending him sideways. His shock gave her enough time to roll away and get to her feet just before he lunged at her. He grabbed both her arms and she kicked out, wishing she still had her boots on; her bare feet did minimal damage. He grunted with the impact and dodged as she used her knee. Her aim hit his hip, and he threw her over the couch and dived on top of her.

She managed to claw his neck before he had her wrists in a tight grip. They were both breathing hard as he fastened his mouth on her lips, bruising them as he forced them open, his tongue thrust into her mouth. She gagged and turned her face away as he began his descent. Her neck, her shoulder, transferring both wrists into his one hand, he used the other to grope at her breasts before grabbing the seam and tearing. She gasped as her breast was exposed. He grunted with the effort. 'Very nice!'

He glanced up at her. His taunting smirk made her feel ill and she looked away, squirming to be free. He tightened his grip before bending his head to her exposed breast.

She stopped fighting and lay still, trying to detach herself and going to her special place. She had done that once before, when they'd found her. She couldn't remember the two policemen, the ambulance, or the hospital. She had gone somewhere else, where she could float above a beautiful garden on her own. No-one ever went there; she was always safe and loved. She tried desperately to go there now as she felt his probing hand pulling on the hem of her dress, inching it higher, exposing her legs, grasping her knickers and yanking them down.

He began fumbling with his trousers, then, he abruptly stopped and froze. She didn't comprehend why at first, until she saw the sword, its tip resting just behind his ear.

'Get off her, you filthy, rutting creature!' Eira prodded him with the sword. He drew in his breath as the point drew blood.

Very slowly, he let go of her wrists and eased himself off Bronwen. Kneeling, he looked up at Eira, the sword inches from his neck. 'Well, well, what have we here? Granny Smith to rescue the day!'

'You shut up! Dirty little vermin!' Eira glanced quickly toward Bronwen, who hadn't moved, but lay frozen, unable to understand the reprieve. 'Come on, Nia. Get up now.'

James glanced quickly between the two. 'Nia? You've rescued the wrong woman, you stupid cow!'

Eira jerked the sword, leaving a long scratch down his neck and grinned when he yelped. Her grin disappeared as he suddenly lunged toward her, dodging the heavy sword and knocked her backward. Losing her balance, she let go of her weapon and flung out her hands to grab onto something. The kitchen door broke her fall, but he quickly bent, picked up the discarded sword and thrust it into her stomach in one swift movement. She cried out with the impact, her eyes wide with pain and horror, before he yanked it out and threw it into the far corner of the room.

He stood over her as she slowly slid to the floor, her blood leaving a stain on the wood. He bent down and grinned maliciously. 'Don't you know that it's bad for a man's health to be stopped in mid-flow? Do you, old woman? Now, the last sounds you'll hear will be the groans of pleasure as I finish fucking your friend.'

***

She'd barely had time to pull herself up when James thrust the sword into Eira's body. As Bronwen watched, a strangled sob escaped her lips. The disbelief of what was happening was too much to take in. But seeing the blood and hearing his voice, she felt the rise of pure fury. His knife lay on the floor; she grabbed it and thrust upward as he turned to attack her again.

He saw the movement but didn't react fast enough and the blade took him in his neck. She left it there as the contact vibrated up her arm and she let go. Her legs gave way beneath her and she collapsed onto her knees, watching as he fought for breath, blood spurting from the wound and dripping from his mouth. He made a strange gurgling, croaking sound before collapsing face down. He twitched once, twice, and lay still.

She was shaking so badly, it took a while to reach Eira, who sat propped up against the wall. 'Eira! Oh, God, Eira!' Her teeth chattered so much, she could hardly speak. Eira was pale, but conscious. She grasped Bronwen's hand as she knelt before her and managed a thin smile. 'Eira, what do I do?' Bronwen looked at the blood and cried. 'An ambulance? Yes, I'll run to the village and find a phone and…'

Eira squeezed her hand. 'It's all right, I don't need an ambulance. I've saved you…Nia, I've done it…haven't I? I can die now.'

Bronwen shook off Eira's hand and began applying pressure to the wound. 'Fuck that! You will live and be okay—'

A loud groan from behind her made her whirl round and reach for the sword, but she stopped and frowned. It wasn't coming from James. She edged around the couch and her heart leapt.

Adam was on his stomach, trying to crawl toward her. He looked up and saw her. 'Fuck! This hurts! Is Eira all right? I have a mobile in my pocket. Can you reach it?'

Bronwen ran forward and fell to her knees beside him. She could see that his wound wasn't as bad as she'd thought, but bad enough. A large bump on his head showed why he'd been unconscious; she let out her breath, relieved. Reaching round, she found the mobile in his pocket and handed it to him. 'I don't know how to switch the thing on!' She shrugged and ran back to Eira.

She heard him chuckle and looked back at him questioningly.

He grinned sheepishly. 'Well, it's only that I was going to say that old phrase about a mobile in my pocket, or are you pleased to see me!' He groaned and licked his lips. 'Another time, eh?'

Her eyes met his for a moment before he looked away and began dialling. She turned her attentions to Eira who was getting weaker every minute. She knew she couldn't be saved, but a small part of her refused to give up. She ran into the kitchen and grabbed a load of dishcloths and pressed them to Eira's stomach. 'Come on, Eira, please don't give up!'

'Oh, darling Nia, this isn't giving up. This is finding peace.'

'Eira, I'm…' She'd been about to say that she was Bronwen, but she knew Eira was right. There was no use fighting it anymore. Eira recognised her for who she had once been. Then, without warning, all the memories and feelings toward her mistress came flooding back. An agonised sob escaped her lips and the tears flowed down her face. 'Oh, my lady!' It was all she could manage for a moment as the wave of emotion swept over them both.

Eira was crying freely too. 'I…don't know…what to say…to make it right with you…Nia?'

Shifting her position, Bronwen gently lowered Eira so that her head was resting on her lap. She grasped her hand and with her other, slowly stroked Eira's hair. 'Tell me, then.'

She heard Eira sigh before she began. 'I let them kill you because I needed someone to blame. You had…been there for every birth of…our children. You were a connection to my failure as a wife and a mother. I…I…hated you.'

Bronwen took a deep breath, held it for a moment, trying to calm down and finally let it out. 'Go on, my lady.'

'They cursed me for it…and I deserved it, but, perhaps, so did William. He knew, you see. He knew I had killed Gwenllian, but…but the King would not allow him to make it public. William was a hero. He killed King Richard and put Henry on the throne. How would it look if the great hero's wife be found guilty of murder? Henry's claim on the throne was weak, he had many enemies, he couldn't take the chance and…he wasn't sure of William's loyalty completely; this would ensure it.'

Though her voice was weak, Bronwen could hear the tone of scorn with each word. She felt like her heart would burst. She had been tortured, hanged, and dumped in unhallowed ground because of politics. She understood now why she hated and distrusted men.

'You were made the obvious scapegoat,' Eira continued, more to herself now. 'You were there, you see. You tried to save the child. It was easy slipping those dolls I'd made…into your chest of herbs.

After I'd killed you in self-defence, they would have found them and believed my story, that you were a witch and that I had found out that you cursed my babies and…it didn't matter in the end, they became useful another way, didn't they?'

Bronwen swallowed back her answer; she knew Eira wasn't really expecting any. The hand that held hers was cold and weak; the pulse, barely a whisper. 'Try to rest now…'

Eira carried on regardless, her voice weak. 'The King ordered justice though, especially after he heard how the villagers responded to…to your…death. He had me locked in my bedchamber…alone. William was forbidden to see me, not that he would have. He despised me. He looked at me once…and never looked at me again.' Her voice broke with emotion and Bronwen felt the warmth of the tears on her knees.

'Calm now, it's over…I can hear sirens. Help is coming…my lady.'

'I…don't want help now. The villagers tried to meddle in powers they couldn't control. Trapping me, they trapped her too. As long as I had no peace, Gwenllian was left wandering the earth. Soon, her own pain and anger took hold and she began tormenting the descendants of the villagers and the Kenwards. It was never her fault, she was innocent, she had no choice how they saw her. My torment was living, hers was death. I have lived…in this body, trapped in this village, never having peace from it. Until…I saved you. Nia, oh, Nia, I've done it, haven't I? You do forgive me. You are safe now?'

Bronwen swallowed hard. 'Yes, my lady, I forgive you. I am safe.'

***

She watched through a haze of tears as they tried to resuscitate Eira, but she knew it was pointless. She watched the ambulance crew with Adam, who was barely conscious. She allowed a policewoman to walk her slowly to an armchair—the farthest one from James's body—and place a blanket gently over her shoulders and across her exposed breasts. It was at that point she realised that Adam must have seen her, but he'd kept his eyes fixed only on her face. She felt, amongst many other emotions, a rush of gratitude toward him.

She sat alone for a moment, watching the goings-on in a strangely detached way. Her attention was caught by a small movement outside the French doors, and she slowly turned her head. The child stood motionless, staring back at her with so much love in her eyes that a fresh wave of tears spilled over her glistening cheeks. She could barely get the words out, but she managed a whisper. 'Gwenllian.' She swallowed the giant lump in her throat and tried again. 'My darling Gwenllian. It is over. You can go now.'

The child slowly raised her small hand and pressed it against the glass. Bronwen tentatively reached out and did the same.

'Thank you…Nia.' The child smiled lovingly before slowly melting away.

'Come along, love. Let's get you out of here.' The paramedic woman gently lifted her to her feet and held onto her elbow as she walked her toward the door. Bronwen stopped once and turned round to look back at the glass. For just a brief moment, she saw the small handprint of a child, before it slowly faded away.

EPILOGUE

'I THOUGHT I'D FIND YOU here.'

Bronwen didn't turn round. Adam climbed down from his horse, and he let it munch at the grass. 'Are you avoiding me then?' He asked the question as lightly as he could, but she heard his insecurity.

He sat down next to her on the large slab of stone and peered at the pencil drawing on her lap. He glanced up at the ruins and grinned. 'You've got it just right. Have you always been a good artist?'

She let the pencil rest on the pad and shrugged, her eyes never leaving the ivy-covered stones. 'No, I've never even tried before, I guess…' She blushed deeply and looked down at her drawing. 'I guess I'm finding a lot of things I'm good at, these days.'

The early September sun warmed the top of his head. He glanced up at her large brimmed hat and wished he'd worn his own cap. He shifted his position and stared up at the ruins. They were silent for a long time. Both could sense the other wanted to ask questions, but it still felt too raw, too uncomfortable. They'd shared something terrible; how were they to get past that?

Finally, Adam couldn't stand it any longer. 'It's been four weeks since the inquiry. How are you? We've all been worried.'

She noticed he emphasised the word 'all' and bit her lower lip. 'Getting my life in order slowly, you know. It's…been hard.'

He heard the tremor in her voice. 'I'm sorry. The last thing I wanted to do was to come and upset you. We...I just wanted to make sure you're okay.'

When she didn't answer, he stood up and walked round the large ruined gatehouse. It felt strange being there after so many years of fearing the place, but then everything had changed in the four months since Eira died. He impulsively touched his own scar, and thanked the gods again for his own miraculous escape from death.

He had so many questions running around his head and he knew Bronwen had the answers, or at least, she knew what Eira's answers would have been, about all that stuff about Lady Anne, and murdering a child and Nia. They'd found an old diary when they'd cleared out Eira's cottage. An antique dealer whose speciality was old books had confirmed that it was indeed fifteenth century. Had Eira found it, read it and begun to believe the terrible story written within its pages? Or had she truly been some kind of reincarnation of a murderess?

While he'd been in hospital, his father told him about the police, digging up the cottage's garden, under the old shed. The bones they found were hundreds of years old. He knew Bronwen had been questioned—after all, she was the one who told the police that they were there. How had she known that?

Abruptly he turned to her. She was watching him closely. 'Do you believe those old bones were once you?'

She sighed heavily and nodded. 'I think so. I have all of these memories, which aren't mine, but they are there.' She stared down at her drawing. 'There wasn't much left. I feel strangely grateful to the vicar for allowing those bones to be given a proper burial. Am I grateful for myself, or because I'd grown close to the people?'

'You mean, the child?'

'Yes. I feel such grief for her, yet she died hundreds of years ago, but for me, sometimes, it feels like yesterday. It feels normal to grieve for someone I loved.' She sniffed. 'She's in the chapel, behind the ruins. There's not much left, but the vicar came up and blessed it.'

Adam came and sat down next to her. 'Yeah, I heard about that. Sorry I couldn't be there.'

'It's okay. Your dad came, so did Judith and Lucy, and they told me you were busy. I heard you had taken Mathew up to Ludlow to see some horses.' Too late, she realised she'd let it slip she knew about his movements. 'Erm…how is he? Seeing Gwenllian and feeling all the negative energy terrified me the first time. So much so, I sat with a knife for hours. I feel for Mathew…'

He smiled warmly. 'He's on the mend. They allow him out for a few days every week now, and his father told me they are hoping he will be recovered enough to come out of hospital permanently by the end of September, so that's good.'

She nodded, but said nothing, so he quickly added, 'Talking of horses, Scarlet is finally pregnant. Hopefully, with Eira's kind gesture in her will and my business, we may be able to save the Hall, and perhaps it's time we thought about rebuilding this.'

She shook her head. 'No, don't!' She blushed. 'I mean…it's special, the way it is. Let nature have it now.'

They fell into silence again and after a while, she stood and packed away her pencils. Adam stood and gently reached out and touched her hand. 'Listen, how do you feel about speaking with a counsellor? I know a good one. I've been seeing her.' He looked uncomfortable when she met his gaze and smiled. 'Well, it's not every day you get stabbed trying to save someone.' He spoke the last word softly.

She looked away first and licked her lips. 'Thanks for the offer, but I'm done with counsellors. I came here to start a new life. I survived James Hawthorn, and I survived fifteenth-century men, in a strange roundabout way…so I can survive this.'

He felt nervous and unsure, but he had to try. 'On that note of surviving, perhaps you might join me for a coffee or a whiskey? I know of a lovely little pub not too far away.'

He thought she wasn't going to answer as she stared straight ahead at the tower. He could almost see the thoughts racing through her head as she frowned before she smiled slowly. She turned to look at him and nodded. 'Perhaps, Adam Kenward, perhaps.'

'Live so that thou mayest desire to live again—that is thy duty—for in any case thou wilt live again!'

~Freidrich Nietzsche

NOTES FROM THE AUTHOR

Although I have used historical people and events, the story is completely fictitious and no character is based on any person in my life, past or present. There are a few theories as to who actually killed King Richard at the battle of Bosworth, and of course, none can be proved one way or the other, without having to actually go back in time and witness the event ourselves! So I created my own character to live alongside the factual ones.

The village is fictitious, but the castle and library in Shrewsbury are real and I would like to thank the librarian who helped me with all my research. I would also like to thank the librarians who allow me to hold book signings occasionally in their beautiful, historic building. It is well worth a visit.

I would like to thank the people who have supported me throughout the years while this story has slowly grown: my husband, Martin, our daughter Megan, and my dad for believing in me.

www.pjroscoe.co.uk

Enjoy Other Books By

Doce Blant Publishing
www.DoceBlant.com

Alys
by Kiri Callaghan

Hardbound ISBN: 978-0-9978913-8-6
Paperback ISBN: 978-0-9978913-9-3
ePub ISBN: 978-0-9984294-0-3

The Déjà vu Chronicles
by Marti Melville

Midnight Omen (book 1)

Hardbound ISBN: 978-0-9971023-3-8
Paperback ISBN: 978-0-9971023-4-5
ePub ISBN: 978-0-9971023-5-2
Library of Congress Control Number:
2016906558

The Tales of Barnacle Bill: Skeleton Krewe
by Barnacle Bill Bedlam

Hardbound ISBN: 978-0-9967622-3-6
Paperback ISBN: 978-0-9967622-2-9
ePub ISBN: 978-0-9967622-4-3

The Next Victim
by Cutter Slagle

Hardbound ISBN: 978-0-9967622-6-7
Paperback ISBN: 978-0-9967622-5-0
ePub ISBN: 978-0-9967622-7-4

'Til Death
by Cutter Slagle

Hardbound ISBN: 978-0-9978913-0-0
Paperback ISBN: 978-0-9978913-1-7
ePub ISBN: 978-0-9978913-2-4
Library of Congress Control Number:
2016949335

Never Surrender
by Deanna Jewel

Hardbound ISBN: 978-0-9971023-0-7
Paperback ISBN: 978-0-9971023-1-4
ePub ISBN: 978-0-9971023-2-1

Lightning Source UK Ltd.
Milton Keynes UK
UKOW06f2235180817

307545UK00002B/231/P